Please return/renew this item by the last date shown on this label, or on your self-service receipt.

To renew this item, visit **www.librarieswest.org.uk** or contact your library.

Your Borrower Number and PIN are required.

About the author

A British-American citizen of Italian heritage, Alexia is an editor, teacher and writing consultant. After studying psychology then educational technology at Cambridge, she moved to New York to work on a Tony award-winning Broadway show before completing a PhD and teaching qualification. In between, she worked as a West End script-critic, box-office manager for a music festival and executive editor of a human rights journal.

Also by Alexia Casale
The Bone Dragon

ALEXIA CASALE

HOUSE OF WINDOWS

FABER & FABER

First published in the UK in 2015
by Faber & Faber Limited
Bloomsbury House, 74–77 Great Russell Street
London, WC1B 3DA

Typeset in Garamond by M Rules
Printed and bound by CPI Group (UK) Ltd, Croydon, CR0 4YY

Text © Alexia Casale, 2015
Maps illustration on vi and vii © Nathalie Guinamard, 2015
Epigraph taken from *Time to Be In Earnest* © PD James, 2010 and reproduced by
permission of Greene & Heaton Ltd

A CIP record for this book is available from the British Library

978-0-571-32153-7

4 6 8 10 9 7 5

For my mother, who has believed in this story since
its first (very different) incarnation,

for my Fiercely Wonderful Aunty Pat,
always my First Reader, and

for Kate and Luna, who gave me Dragon Treasures
just when I needed something to hold on to.

Cambridge

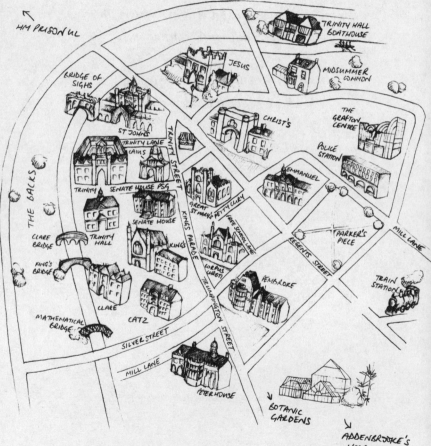

Trinity Hall

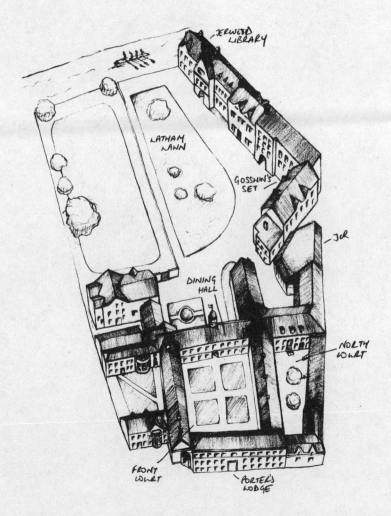

The body is a house of many windows: there we all sit, showing ourselves and crying on the passers-by to come and love us.

Robert Louis Stevenson, 'Truth of Intercourse',
Essays: English & American

What a child doesn't receive, he can seldom later give.

P. D. James, *Time to Be In Earnest:
A Fragment of Autobiography*

Chapter[1]

(28 × August)

Happy fifteenth birthday, genius! Just think: this time next year you'll have a first-year Cambridge First and a bunch of mates who might just keep up with you.

Love, Gerry

Nick let his fingers linger on the overprinted surface of the card, cold and slick as water.

A glance up at the clock: time to go.

He slipped the card between the pages of his book. 'Dad!' he called as he tucked the book into his rucksack. He hitched the strap over his shoulder as his father emerged from his study, shoulders hunched, a fretful look on his face.

Nick glanced back at the apartment as they crossed to the door. He'd been expecting the phone to go all morning, stomach tying itself into progressively more intricate knots as the clock ticked on. Now, standing with his hand on the front-door latch, disappointment was almost swallowed by relief at the ring. Almost.

It wasn't even the phone call. It was his father's soft sigh of relief: the way all the tension in his shoulders suddenly vanished.

Don't bother! The words shouted themselves so loud across the inside of his mind that it was precious seconds before he realised he hadn't even whispered them aloud; if he spoke them now, it would sound rehearsed, like a character playing a part. Like his father, pantomiming dismay as he drew his mobile out of his pocket.

What's the point anyway? he muttered. *Shouting isn't going to change anything. It's not going to make you want to go with me.*

'What?' his dad asked, covering the phone with his hand. 'Did you say something?'

Nick shook his head. Words stuck in his throat like water breathed down the wrong way.

'What? Now?' his father asked the phone. 'I'm meant to be in the car with my son. I've told you a dozen times it's his birthday today and we're celebrating by moving into the new Cambridge house. We've got furniture arriving in a few hours.'

Nick flinched as the study door snicked shut.

He slouched, reading, against the kitchen counter, until Michael reappeared. The words on the page broke apart, refused to coalesce as he tried to ignore his father's worn-out placations: 'Terribly urgent . . . so sorry, Nick . . . get the train down as soon as I can . . . I wish . . .'

No, you don't, he told the book, trapping the words against the pages. The pain in his chest tightened to a white-hot pulse of grief and anger and frustration. *I wish. I'm the one who's sorry.*

A sigh from Michael. 'Nick, please stop mumbling into that book.'

'Is the Replacement insured for the car?'

'I wish you'd stop calling my assistants "Replacements" just because you don't like them as much as Gerry. Gerry may have been head and shoulders above everyone who's come since, but it's still rude.'

Nick met his eyes. 'And calling them the wrong name like you do isn't?'

'The car insurance's set up so it covers all additional drivers now, so tell . . .' The current Replacement's name was clearly just on the tip of his father's tongue. 'If you keep above eighty on the motorway, you should be there in time for the delivery men. I'll pay the fine if you get one.'

When Michael turned back to his phone, Nick retreated to his bedroom. It looked strange without his things, like the guest room it had been before he'd moved in four years ago. The single crumpled ball of paper in the bin looked forlorn and abandoned. He shivered, as if there were a window open, though he was the one who'd gone round checking that everything was shut before their abortive attempt to leave.

He took his book out to the living room, curling himself up into someone else's troubles.

Twenty minutes later the sound of the doorbell jolted him

back from a life where every question had an answer, every problem a solution.

'Bye, Dad!' he called as he buzzed the Replacement into the building. He bookmarked his page with Gerry's card again, wondering if the current Replacement would even bother to comment on the day.

Michael appeared for a moment at his study door, phone to his ear, and pulled an expression like a Greek tragedy mask.

'Ready to go?' Nick asked the Replacement when the lift doors pinged open in the hall.

The Replacement's look went from friendly to surly. 'Shouldn't I check in with Michael first?' He slipped into the apartment for a spot of hasty ingratiation.

'Never gets out from under it, does he, your old man?' asked the Replacement as he flicked the apartment door shut behind him a few minutes later.

In the glaring light of the basement, the car looked murderous, polished to a vicious shine. The Replacement sank into the driver's seat with a moan of delight that made Nick shudder. He tapped the SatNav into life, checking the traffic reports to forestall further conversation, though the Replacement seemed temporarily content, stroking the steering wheel, wriggling unpleasantly in his seat, playing with the controls on the dashboard.

'So, excited about the move then?' the Replacement asked. 'Know if there are any other pint-sized geniuses heading to Cambridge?'

'Not this year. And I'm not actually a genius.'

A snort from the Replacement: the type that said 'pull the other one' and 'your false modesty sucks' and 'looking for compliments?' all in one neat little package of spite.

'I started school a year early, when I was four, because I was already reading. Then I went up two years when I was eleven. That was when I moved in with my dad, so I was changing schools anyway. He persuaded the new school to let me join the year ahead 'cos I'd been finding the work at the old place too easy.'

'So it's not just me that your dad pushes, then? You must have loved all that extra pressure at school on top of moving and having to make new friends.'

'Actually, that was the best bit. It gave me something to do, seeing as how no one was all that keen on making friends with the new kid – especially when they found out I wasn't just short but two years younger. But I was still bored because even then the work wasn't that hard, so after a month I got Dad to talk them into moving me up another year so I could start the GCSE syllabus. That meant I did my A levels three years early. That's the only reason I'm going to uni so young: it's not like I proved the Riemann Hypothesis or anything.'

'I thought you were one of those maths prodigies?'

'My dad's good at making it sound that way, but I'm not that special.' He bit his lip over the automatic rush of defensiveness. 'I did well enough in my Cambridge interview and STEP maths admission tests to get a place fair and square with my predicted A levels. Then I said the right things about why I wanted to study there straight after sixth form rather than take a gap year ... let alone three.'

That wrung a bark of laughter out of the Replacement.

'Anyway, they don't like Maths students having a pause before uni so ...' He shrugged.

'You're not so bad, kid. For a genius and all.'

'You know my dad'll expect you to get all the flat-pack furniture made up before he arrives, right?'

The Replacement's look of horror sustained Nick for a further forty-five minutes.

'You nervous about it yet?' the Replacement asked as they finally merged on to the M11.

Nick shrugged. 'Not really. I've still got a month to go before Induction, since Cambridge Term doesn't start until October. Besides, it's got to be better than school. If nothing else, the work will be interesting.'

'I like the confidence, kid.'

No, you don't. You don't like it or me at all, Nick whispered to the side mirror.

'Don't like this station?' the Replacement said, fiddling with the radio. 'You maths geniuses like classical, right?'

∞

'I thought you said I had to set up the flat-pack stuff?' the Replacement grumbled, following Nick puppy-like into the kitchen to set about unpacking the 'emergency caffeine rations' box.

A crash sounded in the hall.

The Replacement hurried away, already yelling at the delivery crew. 'You might want to take some care on this one, boys! My boss makes a living out of suing people.'

And people think I am socially awkward, Nick told the coffee tin. He left the kettle to boil only to find the Replacement in the hall, squaring up to one of the delivery men with his hands on hips, chest puffed out, his accent getting posher by the second.

'Why don't we bring in the rest of the stuff from the car?' Nick suggested.

The Replacement made a noise like a poodle trying to growl and stalked out of the front door. Nick grimaced at the delivery man as he lifted his shoulders in a 'what can you do?' shrug.

With the unloading done, Nick left them arguing about where to drill the holes for the TV wall-bracket – 'I'm calling my boss,' whined the Replacement – and slipped away upstairs: one flight, turn, another. When they'd bought the house, Michael had sent in the builders to gut it and replace the plumbing and electrics, then put in an attic conversion for Nick, complete with en suite.

He could barely get in the door of his new room for all the boxes. The delivery men had left the packaging on the mattress but at least it was already sitting on the bedframe, tucked neatly under the window overlooking the back garden. Past sagging fences, tangled gardens stretched away to left and right: a rusting mini-trampoline; a slide spattered with startlingly purple bird-muck; a rotting wooden patio with a crumpled bamboo summer shelter; a path of warm brown stones, sunk into the grass; a cat flopped on its side in a patch of sunlight. He rotated the window catch and shoved the bottom pane up under the top one, closing his eyes as the hot summer wind moved across his face.

Sprawling across the bed, he reached for the closest box and ripped the tape off, dragging out the books inside and piling them on the bed, then shuffling to the end and leaning over to slot them into the bookcase against the side wall. The photo frame was waiting for him at the bottom of the third box. He'd forgotten it was there, but when he lifted out the last of his Harry Potter books, there she was, looking up at him with that funny expression he could never pin down. A frown? The start of a smile? Her eyes looked grey and uncertain, though they'd been blue: a strange colour, like bonfire smoke curling up into a night sky. Just like his. Sometimes he caught the same expression on his own face in the mirror, but even then he wasn't sure what emotion lay behind it.

Biting his lip, he tried to nod at the picture, but couldn't, found himself camouflaging the movement as an attempt to see where on the shelf to set the frame, though there was no one to pretend for: no one to trick but himself. Snapping the stand closed, he slid the picture between two oversized books, pushing it to the back of the shelf so it was all but hidden. He watched his hand hover mid-air as if unable to leave the photo there.

'Hello?' someone called up the stairs. 'Not sure where the last stuff goes,' the delivery man said, as Nick slouched reluctantly down, 'and I'm done asking Upper Class Twit of the Year. How'd you get stuck with him anyway?'

'It's more "How did he get stuck with me?" It's not really his job to . . .' He gestured around at the packing crates.

'Must be weird, doing the move and all that without your dad.'

Nick shrugged. 'He'll be here later. To be honest, if he were here now he'd just be wandering around down the bottom of the garden, yelling into his phone, driving the neighbours up the wall.'

The delivery man laughed. 'Got to look on the bright side. Though I'm not sure there's a bright side to that lump downstairs. You have to deal with him a lot?'

'He's new. Last time I had to move somewhere by myself it was . . .' He swallowed down the rest of the words about how the first move had been different because of Gerry: Michael's original articled clerk. The one all the Replacements failed to measure up to.

To be fair, Gerry had set a high bar. When Nick had opened Roger's front door for the last time, hoping against hope his dad was on the other side and finding Gerry instead, Gerry's first words had been, 'So your stepfather's a bit of a dick, then. I'm afraid your dad's caught up at work – we're meeting him at the flat later – but he's given me the expenses credit card and *carte blanche* to buy anything that will make the move easier to bear.' There had been more sympathy than

9

pity in Gerry's face. Best of all, he'd said nothing about Nick's mum, why Roger had responded by throwing him out, or what his father thought about Nick moving in without even a day's notice.

Unlike the current Replacement, Gerry had made himself useful without fuss, staying to help Nick unpack his old life and rearrange it into something new.

At least he was sure that the current 'something new' was also 'something better'.

It was easy enough to persuade the Replacement to leave almost as soon as the delivery men had finished: people tended to listen when you told them what they wanted to hear. Gerry was the only one who'd risked treading on Michael's toes to do the decent thing, whether that was making sure Nick didn't have to come home from school to an empty flat every night while Michael was away on a business trip, or just keeping him company when he had to go to the dentist. Gerry's birthday card brightened the new mantelpiece next to the ones from 'Your fond Godfather Bill' and Secretary Sandy.

Michael's phone was endlessly engaged or off when Nick tried it at five past each hour. At nine, he gave up and settled down with a packet of biscuits by way of dinner, stacking them into a tower and forcing a birthday candle into the top one until it split. He propped the candle between the pieces and lit it, sighing as it promptly listed to the side, dripping wax down the edge of the stack.

I wish that this time next year I'll have a First in my Part

IA exams and some friends. The puff of breath sent the candle tumbling across the table, painting a streak of wax after it. *Birthday candles are not meant to be bad omens*, he told it, tossing it into the bin. The attempt at humour felt pathetic, worse than the silence.

Sighing, he curled into one of the new kitchen chairs and opened his notebook to the page where he'd been working out a series of formulae for integrating trigonometric functions involving powers. He'd been playing around with the formulae since he'd printed out the first term's example sheets from the Maths Faculty website, hoping to find some shortcuts for his Differential Equations course. So far he'd been guessing at the formulae, working from simple examples to see if he could spot a pattern.

Tapping his pen against his cheek, he glared at the page. There had to be a reason that $sin^n a cos^m a$ seemed to follow different rules when n and m were both odd or even, versus when one was odd and the other even. That couldn't be right, unless there was some principle at work like two negatives make a positive, while a positive and a negative make a negative. Or maybe the whole thing was wrong: some random quirk of only using examples with n and m less than ten.

'If I were a maths genius, I'd understand how it all worked,' Nick told his Caffeine Addict mug. 'Though I'd probably still be talking to myself.'

With a sigh, he crossed his arms on the table and lowered his head on to them. While some of his university materials looked horrifying, he had to believe the lectures would explain everything. After all, the Faculty was too big to be comprised entirely of geniuses. Most of the others had to be like him: clever enough to use logic to plod their way to the correct answer, rather than having it appear, miraculous and fully formed, in their heads.

Chin propped on the heel of his hand, he let his eyes blur on the chart of formulae. He jumped when his phone beeped.

Dad:
> Heading out soon. Catch you before bed? Sorry later than expected. Is router set up?

Nick pushed himself to his feet and scowled his way into the sitting room. 'So much for the birthday pizza,' he told the mess of boxes, or maybe he only thought the words: he was so used to no one being there to hear that sometimes he wasn't sure what he said aloud and what stayed in his head.

The road outside grew dark, then orange with the glow of the streetlights. The overgrown shrubs in the tiny front garden became alien: leathery and shiny, highlighted with poisonous stripes of reflected colour. Even though it felt like conceding defeat to admit that it was dark – that his birthday was almost over, no chance of rescuing it now – he put on the kitchen light, then both of the living-room lights, then the hall light, and the light over the front door, and still the house felt huge and strange and empty; even with the stereo blasting out cheery cheesy pop music, it was full of echoes and shadows.

He trudged upstairs for a jumper, took out the brand-new blue cashmere. Then he remembered Michael's look of puzzled surprise as he'd watched Nick unwrap it that morning, forgetting for a moment to pretend that he was the one who'd picked it out, rather than Secretary Sandy.

His favourite jumper was at the bottom of his box of A-level textbooks. Worn and disreputable, with holes under the arms, it no longer smelled of his grandmother, but there was something in the texture of the weave that *felt* happy: the echo of a memory so far down in his soul it was all emotion, a burst of colour and warmth, adrift from time and place. The smell of fresh lemon cake and jam pastries. Flour on his nose, batter smeared into his clothes. Laughter, and games, and walks in the woods. Great Adventures to the nearest town to buy books. Soft warm *enormous* towels after a bath. Story after story before sleep.

Her photo smiled from his bedside table. He turned the frame so that the glass reflected the light, hiding the picture.

By the time he'd taken the brand-new duvets, pillows and bed linen out of their packaging and made his bed, then Michael's, the house was starting to feel more familiar: there was something homey about the way he hadn't stretched the fitted bottom sheets enough, so the mattresses showed where the fabric wouldn't pull down to the bedframe. He already remembered which part of the floor in his new room squeaked, and which step made the most noise on each staircase. His books were on the bookcase. His clothes in the chest of drawers.

And it's not like I had any real friends back in London to miss, he was telling his desk lamp when there was a scratching at the front door.

His father blinked in surprise when he pulled it open. 'I didn't think you'd still be awake.' Michael pasted on a smile a moment too late to render the words glad.

'Coffee?' Nick called over his shoulder as he led the way to the kitchen. *Birthday cake, if you've remembered one?* he mumbled into the cupboard. 'Are you off early tomorrow?'

'No, I'm good to go down to College with you, like we said. Anyway, how's everything here? You should use the household card if we need any pots and pans, stuff like that.'

Nick sighed. 'I guess I should learn how to cook spaghetti at least.'

'Well, we've made boiled eggs before,' his father said. 'I seem to remember your mother saying that roasting a chicken and potatoes was just putting everything in the oven until it was brown but not black. Think we could manage that.' The words puffed out in jolly staccato bursts: a 'ho ho ho' of overwrought cheer.

'I don't remember her cooking. Not with Roger,' Nick said softly.

Michael's face fell. 'She had a fad of it the year before we separated. Bought a whole shelf of recipe books and half a ton of ingredients. Lasted a few months. She was just getting the hang of baking when . . .' He stopped to rub at the bridge of his nose. 'Anyway, she lost interest. You know how it was.' He picked up his phone again. 'Better just reply to this email.'

Twenty minutes later, Michael was still sighing over his phone.

'Think I'll get to bed then.'

His father glanced up with a smile. 'Night, Nick. Thanks for holding the fort.'

Michael was fully focused on his mobile when Nick paused to dither in the doorway before turning himself around again. His steps sounded heavy on the stairs, but his father didn't call after him.

'It'll be tough for a while, but we'll get there, right?' Michael had said the night Nick first installed himself in the guest bedroom of his London flat.

If we're not there after four years, I'm not sure it's happening, Nick told the face looking out at him from the window behind his bed. He shuddered at the expression that met these words, slammed off the light. His reflection vanished, leaving the window clear. Below, in the garden, a cat leapt on to a fence post. It stalked towards the house then settled, looking up at the sky, its eyes silver in a shadowed face.

∞

The dream, when it came, wasn't a surprise. He was back in his STEP admissions test, only he didn't seem to understand any of the questions because they had apparently been written in the Cyrillic alphabet. He was telling himself not to panic, that he just had to put up his hand and point out that he'd been given the wrong paper, when someone knocked a metal pencil case off a desk somewhere behind him.

There was a dull clang as it hit the ground: a rattle as pens spilt out and across the floor. But the sound didn't fade as it should have. Instead it echoed back and forth across the room, building until it rolled like thunder.

A soft tinkling started to chime below the roar just as a pen came to rest against his toe, under the exam desk.

And suddenly his feet were bare and the pen was wet, slippery. And then it started flapping, flicking frantically against his foot. The floor of the classroom was slick with water. The dying echo of the dropped pencil case faded into a faint clapping of fins beating against the ground.

He woke with his heart rushing, the blood loud and tight in his ears.

Moonlight was falling through the open window, shining through a cobweb on the other side of the glass. As it billowed in the breeze, the walls seemed to ripple in the darkness as if seen through water. Shuddering, he wrenched himself to his knees and swung his arm out under the window pane. The cobweb felt like a shadow on his skin.

Chapter²

(29 × August)

Walking down to College the next morning, they could have been in almost any town where the homes were primarily narrow three-storey Victorian townhouses of grey or red brick, with white-painted eaves and shallow front gardens: a low wall, an overgrown shrub, a paved path to a tiny porch with a gloss-painted front door. A little triangle of park provided a landmark as they turned down another street and suddenly Parker's Piece opened before them.

House-hunting with his father had only involved driving the streets immediately around the station rather than exploring further, while Nick's trip to Cambridge for his admissions interview (the Replacement was drafted in to accompany him when Michael got caught up with a work 'emergency') had taken in the centre of town and little more. Nick had yet to walk the route from the new house to College, so though he'd spent the last few months studying maps of Cambridge and Google StreetView, it was bewildering trying to make it match up with reality. Parker's Piece was a little green rectangle on the map, a blurry stretch of browny-green on StreetView, not an immense expanse of torn-up grass that dwarfed the surrounding buildings – a school, the police station – turning them squat and ungainly.

They passed two football games going on side by side, then cut across on the diagonal path, past an ornate green and red lamp post with 'Reality Checkpoint' scribed into the paint: the Cambridge version of entering Narnia. It might as well have read 'This is where it all gets weird. From here on, it's another world.'

'That's Downing College,' said Michael as they emerged on to Regent Street opposite the gates. 'And ahead is Emmanuel – Emma to you, now you're a student.'

They passed from plastic shop-window displays to the long grey frontage of Christ's College on the right, all crenellations and regimented windows stretching to a huge carved-stone doorway. Michael led them to the left, into the pedestrian zone, turning down what Nick remembered from his maps as Petty Cury. A series of ugly 1960s concrete blocks, with shops in the bottom floors and offices above, gave way to the market: a cramped square of tiny temporary stalls, all pipework and striped awnings, with Great St Mary's Church towering above. In a way it was ordinary enough, but not quite: like the world was slowly starting to change shape, strangeness drifting in, gradually taking over.

'Residency rules are that students have to live within three miles of GSM during term-time,' Michael said, gesturing at the church tower. 'For three miles in every direction you're officially within the "precincts" of the University. Odd, really, since Senate House is just there.' He pointed past the tall spiked railings around the churchyard to the building opposite. 'Senate House is where you'll come for your exam results. And Graduation, of course.'

Nick had seen it before, but couldn't help thinking it uninspiring next to the grandeur of King's College. It was too white, too stark: all clean straight lines, like a Regency stately home. Even the colonnade was disappointing, too few arches, too much heavy white stone between them. Squatting next to the soaring majesty of King's Chapel, Senate House's too-green, too-stripy lawn seemed staid and ordinary. A stone plinth in the middle of the grass bore a hideous urn, the copper stained turquoise with verdigris. Maybe in a different light King's would look smudged and dirty, but in the sunshine it glowed cream and gold, all gorgeous stone tracery and tiny jutting spires, too beautiful and delicate to be real.

Here it was: the Cambridge of photos. The Cambridge that didn't seem part of the real world, as if time existed differently here. As if the past *was* the present, overlapping, interlocking, not one or the other but both.

Nick tried to keep his gaze roving, taking in everything, but it kept returning to the folly of the King's frontage: a long thin wall pierced at intervals with open lancet windows and topped with a stone trellis, complete with purposeless little spires. Everything about it was pure excess. An extravagance of beauty.

I can't imagine ever being truly miserable here.

'Why would you be miserable at all?' Michael asked.

Nick started, not used to his father paying enough attention to hear him when he mumbled. He was still trying to think what to say when they plunged into the gloom of narrow, cobbled Senate House Passage and the moment was gone.

'So we've got Gonville and Caius on our right, but that's pronounced "keys",' said Michael. 'Oh, and remember Magdalene is "maudlin". That's Old Schools, behind Senate House on the left, and Clare College opposite. The gate at the end of the path goes to King's Chapel, but it isn't open all day: mostly you can count on it around Evensong, which you're entitled to go to whenever you want. And here we are: Trinity Hall.' They stepped into the Porter's Lodge, Michael nodding to the porters at the desk as he led the way past the fireplace. 'Now, all these little shelves are called pigeonholes.'

'For post,' Nick said, moving to his father's side to peer at the names. His pulse kicked oddly as he looked for his own.

'Remember to check every time you come through,' Michael said. 'Here we go.'

Derran, N.

Nick found himself smiling, reaching out to touch the name tag as if it were something extraordinary. 'Is there always someone on duty in the pee-lodge?'

His father laughed. 'It's pronounced "plodge". And, yes,

any time you're likely to be here there'll be someone on duty. Just remember that most of the porters are ex-military at TitHall and act accordingly.'

Nick couldn't help the snort.

Michael rolled his eyes. 'There's no point sniggering every time someone says it.'

'They seriously couldn't think of something better to shorten it to? Like T-Hall? Or you could say you were "in THrall". It's a cheat but it would be funnier.'

Michael sank on to one of the wooden window seats looking out into Front Court and took off his shoe, tipped a shard of pebble out of it. 'You have to remember it's pretty recently that the University opened up to more than a token number of students *not* from public schools, let alone *girls*, so you get what you'd expect from a language invented by Etonians.'

'No wonder the locals mock the students.'

Michael pushed himself back to his feet. 'Townies, Nick. Students are gownies and locals are townies.'

'I know. There was a "basic Cambridge vocab" list in my Induction pack.'

'That's practically cheating. You're meant to spend at least the first term never quite sure what anyone's saying.' Michael turned from the window with a grin only to start when he realised that Nick was standing at his shoulder, beaming up at him expectantly.

Nick's smile faded with his father's. 'What's wrong?' His eyes darted away from his father's sudden worried frown. 'Did you remember something about work?'

Michael coughed, dug his hands into his pockets. 'No, no. Just thinking I'm … Well, I'm really proud to be here with you today. Pretty cool to be introducing my fifteen-year-old to College. Wonder if I'll bump into anyone I know.'

Nick moved his face into what should have been a smile, but somehow wasn't.

Michael ducked his head and pushed through the wood and glass p'lodge door into Front Court, hurrying down the central flagstone path while Nick dawdled behind, staring up at the stone buildings all around. To the left and right were two storeys of tall windows under grey slate roofs set with a third storey of matched garret windows. The stone blocks of the walls, a strange creamy golden-brown, seemed almost to glow. To the left and right, the courtyard buildings were broken on the ground floor by an arch: on the left side was the chapel, marked out by a pair of two-storey stained-glass arch windows, a third smaller one perched up in the far corner. On the far side of the courtyard, opposite the main gate, was a double set of dark wood doors; above, the walls rose up to a triangular apex, decorated by moulded scrollwork and a crest below a grey-painted hexagonal plinth bearing a little cupola: thin white pillars supported a tiny silver-blue dome surmounted by a finial spike emerging through a golden ball.

The courtyard itself was quartered into neat little squares of lawn by a flagstone path edged in cobbles. Along the walls, narrow flowerbeds and window-boxes spilled over with geranium and lobelia and wallflowers. The girl in tiny pink hotpants standing in the centre of the courtyard, tapping a message into her mobile, was jarringly alien.

Nick had memorised the map of the College, but like everything else in Cambridge it was far more higgledy-piggledy than any plan allowed for. Michael cut right in the centre of the courtyard and through the low, narrow arched tunnel into North Court, all brown brick and black bike racks. He led the way up the steps to the left, past the bar, to the JCR.

'Junior *Combination* Room,' he reminded Nick, '*not* Common Room.'

Nick gave a hum of assent as he stepped up to the huge plate-glass windows that fronted the tattered room, turning his back on the stained carpet and filthy cushions upholstered in vomit-coloured fabrics.

'Mumbling again?' his father asked. 'You'll have to learn to speak up in supervisions, you know.'

In the glass, his face tightened with irritation: his mother's face, pale and pointed; her eyes, sullen and difficult and far too intent for anyone's comfort. 'I always speak up in class. You're the one who said I shouldn't talk so much if I don't want people to think I'm showing off.'

'Well, that's what's so great about Cambridge: it's *all* about showing off whenever you can,' someone said.

Nick and Michael turned as one to find a tall, dark-haired young man standing behind them.

'Ah, sorry for interrupting. I'm Tim. Professor Gosswin said I'd find you here around now-ish. She's um . . .'

'In one of her moods?' Michael asked, with a grimace.

'Yeah, something like that. We might want to take our time heading down there.'

'Can't be anything I haven't seen before,' Michael said. He stepped closer to the windows. 'Is one of these a door?'

'Here,' Tim said, sliding a panel to the side. 'She mentioned you did a summer as her research assistant too.'

'Give or take quarter of a century ago, but I doubt much has changed,' Michael replied as he stepped out on to the flagstone patio, while Tim saw Nick through the door then slid it to behind them. 'She still wind up to a tantrum with the whole gnashing of teeth thing?'

'Yup. Did she *really* throw a hedgehog at the Bursar once?'

'Neither of them was very happy about it. To be fair, Gosswin meant to grab the budget, not the hedgehog – and don't ask me why there was a hedgehog on her desk – but she didn't actually throw it. Mostly because they became … rather attached at that point. I hear it's still an Addenbrooke's A & E record for Most Erudite Swearing.'

Tim glanced over his shoulder to grin at Nick, quickly losing his smile when all he got in response was a look of bored disdain. 'Sorry. Should have introduced myself properly,' he said, stopping to hold out his hand.

'You did. You're Tim.'

'And you're Nick and your proud dad's Michael Derran. Gosswin filled me in. Ready to dare the lion's den?'

Nick's look darkened into a glare. 'Yeah, tea with my Cambridge Tutor is going to be *so* much more intimidating than my first week in the Sixth Form Common Room aged thirteen.'

Tim laughed. 'I cannot wait to see you and the Prof face off in a glaring competition. Do you play chess?'

'No.'

'Pity. Gosswin does her best glaring over chess.'

'She didn't say it was a requirement at my admissions interview.'

Tim beckoned them to follow as he set off towards the stretch of Latham Lawn just visible past the buildings to either side of the steps down from the JCR. They turned to the right, following a curving building of deep red brick and grey stone tracery. Nick frowned up at it, trying to work out when it had been built. Some of the elements looked gothic, but surely the bricks weren't quite the right colour and the doorways weren't the right shape . . .

His father's hand, tugging at his elbow, startled him.

'Try to be friendly, Nick,' Michael whispered. 'This Tim's a nice kid. He's not patronising you, so relax a little. Try a smile. You're not going to make any friends frowning.'

Nick dropped his gaze to his feet. *Yeah, he's so eager to make friends with me he spent most of the time buttering you up. And he looks like he's good at sports.*

Michael heaved a sigh. 'And stop *mumbling*, Nick. I know you don't mean anything bad by it, but it's really very off-putting.'

Tim was holding open a thick, age-blackened oak door under a high arched gateway.

'Did you take them via Ely Cathedral?' The voice echoing from above was lemon juice and smoke, like a growl poured over cracked ice.

'Wanted to give you time for a constitutional in case all that shouting earlier had tired you out,' Tim called back, bounding up the wood-panelled staircase. He gestured them through a doorway to the left as he stepped into a kitchenette on the right.

Nick stopped at the threshold in surprise. The room was full of light, streaming through a grand bay window taking up almost an entire wall of the spacious study. The floor was uneven burnished wood, the walls entirely books, floor to ceiling.

'Note that young man there.' Professor Gosswin gestured to where they could hear Tim thumping about in the next room. 'He is a rude and reckless boy. Your father and godfather always conveyed a very healthy level of terror in my presence. See that you do the same.'

Nick squinted into the darkness of the corner where the Professor was sorting books on to her shelves. 'Tim said we had to have a glaring match. You may not have realised this from my interview, but I'll win.'

The Professor turned. 'Indeed,' she said coldly, looking him up and down.

Nick met her sharp gaze. 'Indeed,' he said.

'I think this might be the beginning of a beautiful friendship,' drawled Tim, shouldering the door open and carrying a laden coffee tray over to the desk, where he had to balance it precariously on a corner while he moved a stack of papers to create a level space.

'You're disordering my research, you vandal!' hissed the Professor, breaking eye contact with Nick to snatch her papers away protectively. 'How am I expected to work with all these careless children underfoot, creating havoc in my very own set?'

'Sett as in badger?' Nick whispered to Michael.

'Set as in set of rooms, but badger sett might be more appropriate,' his father whispered back.

'Did you just refer to me as a badger, Mr Derran?'

'I was asking a question about etymology,' Nick replied.

'Do you realise that badgers are related to the weasel family? Are you suggesting I am weasel-like?'

Nick frowned at her thoughtfully. 'You're more like a polecat. Those are related to badgers too.'

'Indeed,' snapped the Professor.

'Indeed,' replied Nick.

'On which note, I'll have to excuse myself.' Michael slid his phone from his pocket, pulled a face at it. 'Got a text. I'm needed at the office. Knew I had to get off soon.'

'It's much better that you go now so we can move the conversation on to more civilised matters.' The Professor turned her back on him in clear dismissal. 'We'll see you again far too soon, I dare say, now that you are once again resident.'

'Bye, Dad,' said Nick.

'And you,' she said to Tim, the moment the door had closed behind Michael. 'Off you go, Mr Brethan.'

'Um . . .'

'Did you just "um" at me? Go away, I said. At once. *Instantly*.'

'She's dead fond of me really,' Tim stage-whispered to Nick.

'You are an *odious* creature, Mr Brethan. You are always *smiling*. I have endured quite enough of your buffooning about for one day.'

'See ya, Nick! Bye, Prof.'

'Odious boy!' shouted Professor Gosswin, turning quite purple with the effort, as Tim slammed the door behind himself. 'What are you looking at?' she snapped at Nick.

'Are you imperial purple, do you think?'

Professor Gosswin stepped back to look at herself in the mirrored surface of a brass plate on the wall. 'Certainly. Imperial from *imperator*. You should think of me as such in relation to your chances of success at Cambridge.'

'I thought you were a Law professor?'

'Mr Derran, I am the College's only current Life Fellow, in residence in these rooms since before your father trod these halls. I am considered one of the great minds of *several* Cambridge generations. The execrable Mr Brethan aside, I am generally accorded the respect and fear that are my due. Now, I recall you telling me quite frankly, on our brief first meeting at your interview, that you were of exceptional intelligence, without being a genius. On that basis, while you may be advanced for your age, I am advanced for *mine*.'

'So advanced squared.'

'I think you will find it is an exponential function. Now, sit down . . . No, not *there*, you foolish child, *there*! In front of the chess board.'

'I don't play chess,' Nick said.

'Then you have even more to learn than I thought. It is quite ridiculous how ill-prepared students are becoming. No more excuses. Make your move.'

Nick stared into Professor Gosswin's cold, dark eyes and tried not to think how very much like a polecat she looked at that moment: a polecat in its den, getting ready to show its teeth. There wasn't a hint of a smile around the thin lips, the lined eyes, just the sharp intelligence of a predator.

A year ago, at his Cambridge admissions interview, the Professor had greeted him with the disconcerting statement 'Three years of your father and godfather for my pains and now they send me *you* to look at.'

'I think I'm meant to be looking at you too,' Nick had replied and, against the odds, Professor Gosswin had smiled.

'You may have all day, Mr Derran,' she snapped now, 'but if I have to endure your company then it shall be in the service of equipping you with at least a little skill. Now *make your move.*'

∞

'Hey, Nick!'

He looked up to see Tim hurrying his way from a small courtyard by the chapel. A very pretty girl was staring after him. Nick watched her hands rise into the air, clenching into fists, her face distorted with fury, before she turned in a whirl of glorious dark hair and stalked away.

'So you survived the Dragon's Lair,' Tim said.

Nick gave him a flat stare.

'Right. Sorry. Forgot you're not convinced by my startling wit. You're missing out, you know.'

'No one's watching, Tim. You don't have to be nice to me now.'

Tim was either a much better actor than Michael or he was genuinely puzzled by this response, his face twisting into a bewildered frown before Nick had even finished speaking. 'Why would anyone be watching?' he asked. 'You don't have some weird paranoid ... Um, I mean, you're not Asperger's or schizophrenic or anything, are you? Not that that's a problem, but—'

'I'm not an idiot savant,' Nick interrupted.

'Right. Good to know.'

'And I'm not a genius either, in case you were wondering.'

Tim grinned. 'I wasn't actually, but I suppose that's good to know too. Grist for the rumour mill and all that. Our porters are gossips but they're nothing to our manciple.'

'Your *what*?'

'Manciple. Like the butler of the dining hall.'

'Manciple. Got it. Anything else?'

Tim sighed. 'Nope. I get the message loud and clear. I'll get out of your hair. But maybe you could have a go at losing the chip on your shoulder, Nick. Sometimes people really are just trying to be nice.'

Nick watched him set off across Front Court, suddenly cold in the bright sunshine as he tried to think of something to say, even though it was already too late to do more than make a fool of himself by shouting. Tim ducked instinctively as he reached the low, narrow passage into North Court and glanced back over his shoulder. He grinned, raised his hand in a brief wave when he saw Nick looking, and Nick had time to answer both the smile and the wave before Tim was on his way again.

Don't screw it up before you've even started, he told himself as he set off out of College.

He turned left, thinking to go down by the river, but quickly changed his mind when he saw a horde of ravening French tourists swarming up narrow Garret Hostel Lane. Just as he was about to turn the corner to follow Trinity Lane up to the centre of town, a small door opened within the great doors of an elaborate gateway and a man stepped over the lintel. Nick caught the door before it swung to. On the other side was an open-air space hemmed in by grey buildings. A dark passage led through the building on the right, plunging Nick into cool damp gloom. He emerged into the dazzling sunshine of an immense quadrangle.

'Courtyard,' Nick corrected himself, remembering his father telling him that it was 'The Other Place' (aka Oxford) that had quads.

Squinting into the glare, Nick saw a fountain topped with an ornate crown of carved stone. Trinity. This was the Great Court in Trinity. Ahead was the chapel, all creamy-grey stone and, to the right, the Great Gate, looking like it should be part of a Tudor castle. Beside it, running along the rest of the college frontage and then down the side behind him, were lower buildings of golden-brown stone with gabled windows.

I get to come here every day, he told the air, finding a smile breaking across his face.

He wandered the College for an hour, eventually finding his way to a quiet courtyard with a circular lawn around an enormous tree that towered above the surrounding roofs. An arched gateway let out on to the Backs, falling away to a stone bridge over the river and, beyond, an avenue of lime trees, all green and gold, ablaze with sunlight. Somewhere to explore another day.

He turned with a sigh and headed back into town to buy some more kitchen and bathroom essentials. They'd forgotten everything from bins to toilet brushes on the 'keeping the house clean' front.

When Nick staggered out of the department store an hour later, laden with bags, he hailed a taxi to take everything home, then set out again for food. A short walk led him to Mill Lane, where he'd seen a bunch of shops as the Replacement drove them past the day before. One of the small family-run supermarkets was halal and the other stocked mostly with Asian ingredients, labelled in characters he couldn't even begin to decipher. In place of the hotdogs and garlic dough balls he'd planned to buy, he gathered up the weirdest-looking fruit he could find (including something leathery purple-brown that a handwritten sign identified as 'mangosteen'), some chilli-flavoured crisps and a box of eggs, then took it all home.

The fridge looked less clinical with things on the shelves, and the kitchen brightened with a bowl of apples and bananas on the counter. Or maybe it was the sunshine, spilling in the huge bay front window and reaching every corner of the living room. There were no curtains yet, but Nick had fallen in love with the wide wooden window seat the first time he had seen the house. Soon he was curled up with a mug of coffee and a book, the dust motes dancing above the pages, bathed in light and warmth.

In the street beyond, a child laughed and Nick looked up to watch the family pass: a father and two toddlers, chasing their way down the street. A beep from his mobile startled his eyes away from the road.

Dad:
Might be home late. Sorry.

By the time he looked up again, the street was empty.

Chapter³

(1 × October)

'You've really improved the place this month, Nick,' said Bill as he made himself comfortable in an armchair.

'Hey, how do you know some of it wasn't me?' Michael asked.

'That is not an appropriate question to ask a man you shared a set with for two years in College, and then a flat for five years in London.'

'You never know, I might have—'

'No, Mike. You mightn't. Anyway, Induction tomorrow, Nick. You ready to meet your new classmates?'

'If I say no, will you find a way to pause time so I can get used to the idea?'

Bill laughed. 'They'll be nervous too, Nick. Maybe more than you, because they won't know the town yet. You could offer to show people about.'

Nick shrugged, leaning forward to tidy the mess of papers

from his Induction folder that had been spread across the coffee table. 'I guess I can try that.'

'Maybe a good start would be to try being a bit more positive,' Michael said.

'Talking of positives,' Bill cut in, 'any news about your place on the law firm letterhead, Mike?'

Michael pulled a face. 'Nothing concrete.'

'Which probably means you're working even more hours than God sends. Exactly how late are you getting back?' Bill asked.

Nick watched his godfather's eyes flick in his direction.

Michael sighed. 'It's a bit hit and miss, but I'm doing the best I can, right, Nick? You're going to be too busy to even notice soon. Whatever the ups and downs of Cambridge, it's bound to be better having a tough time trying to fit in with the smartest kids in the country than getting bullied by halfwit schoolboys.'

'I'm not sure that's the most appetising way to sell the concept,' said Bill.

Nick looked down, picking at a spot of mud on his jeans. 'I wasn't going to have a social life at school and maybe I will here. If not, at least I'll be achieving something. That's got to be a step up from where I was,' he said quietly. He saw Bill lean forward, frowning at his tone.

'Exactly!' his father said. 'And if it doesn't go to plan, you can always degrade and have another go next year.'

'I haven't even started yet,' Nick bit out. 'Could we not assume I'm going to fail from the outset?'

Michael rolled his eyes. 'I never said that. I'm just trying to point out that even if that were the case – which it isn't, since you've never failed at anything academic – it wouldn't matter.'

Bill cleared his throat awkwardly. 'Isn't it time to order some food, Mike? Why don't you take care of that while Nick shows me what else he's done to the house and I put my bags in one of the guest rooms?'

They each took a bag, trudging up the stairs in uncomfortable silence.

'Bet it's nice to have your own self-contained space if you can't be in halls, right? Not too bad as student digs go,' Bill said, as he put his bag down in the corner of the room next to Michael's.

The whole house's my own self-contained space most of the time.

'What?' Bill asked, turning from peering into the bathroom.

'I finally bought bins, like you said.'

There were also bedside lamps and curtains. Bill stepped out into the corridor, put his head around the door into Michael's room.

'I was going for smart hotel,' Nick said, the words coming out sharp, turning humour into bitterness.

'It's a little . . . impersonal,' Bill agreed. 'Why doesn't he get a picture or two? An ornament?'

Nick shrugged. 'I asked if he wanted anything. He told me not to bother.' He jumped when Bill put a hand on his shoulder.

'Sorry. Nick, I just wanted to say ... Well, I wanted you to know that you can call me if ... Well, if Mike's not here and you need help with anything.'

Nick looked up at him, knew from Bill's reaction that his expression must be that cool intense one that always unnerved people: the look that made him the picture of his mother – waifish and delicate, all high cheekbones, over-long lashes and huge blue-grey eyes, like a storm caught in blown glass.

'I thought now you've got the guest rooms set up you might not mind the odd visit too,' Bill said, the words awkward and tentative. 'I know you'll have all your new friends but we've had some fun times too, haven't we? That time your dad went off to New York and you stayed with me?'

Nick looked away when he realised that Bill was waiting for a response. 'It was nice.'

'Well. Good. Anyway, I didn't want to invite myself out of the blue, but just so you know I'm there if you need a hand. So, anyway ... I guess we'd better catch Mike before he orders anchovies on the pizza.'

Nick flinched when Bill put his arm about his shoulders to lead him downstairs. 'Sorry,' he said. 'Jumpy about tomorrow.' But somehow he couldn't get his muscles to relax, couldn't stop his movements reading tense and awkward, even though it wasn't as if he minded Bill touching him.

I'm just not sure what to do with my body, he wanted to say but couldn't because it would have made him sound like an idiot. *I just don't get a lot of practice. I don't know what to do.*

Chapter[4]

(Induction Week
[≈ first week of October])

The gym hall at Kelsey Kerridge was packed with rows of Freshers' Fair stalls, second and third years hawking the various University clubs and societies from behind rickety laminate desks and trying to stop home-printed posters falling off unstable head-height partitions. Squinting at the diagram in his hand, Nick squeezed into the tight-packed column of students squirming clockwise down the middle aisle. He stumbled out of line at the Fantasy Book Club stall, accepting the leaflet that Gandalf thrust brusquely into his hands.

'Fridays at six during Term.'

'As opposed to what? The holidays?' Nick asked.

Gandalf heaved a weary sigh. 'Full Term's an extra week before and after Term. We only meet in Term.' Another sigh as Nick's face went even blanker. 'Term is Weeks 1 to 8 when there's teaching. You do at least know weeks start on a Thursday, right?'

'Oh yeah,' Nick drawled. '*Everyone* knows that Cambridge is in a time-warp where different temporal rules apply.'

Gandalf pointedly turned his back to greet a new student.

'We take it in turns to host in our rooms,' Spock said, taking pity on him. 'All we ask is that you nominate your chosen linguistic speciality by Week Three so we can assign a tutor.'

Nick tried but failed to stop himself staring as Spock set to stroking the point of his left ear lovingly. 'Linguistic speciality?' he parroted.

'We recommend one of the Elvish languages, or Klingon. But we will accept Vulcan as well as the language of the dwarves or that of the gnomes,' Spock said, yawning as he passed over a clipboard.

Nick stared at it.

'You put your name, College and email address.'

'In Elvish?' Nick asked, and handed the clipboard back.

Contemplating the heaving mass of students, he stared dismally at the desk to his right and wondered about the feasibility of getting down on his hands and knees and trying to crawl under the tables to reach the end of the aisle.

A girl stepped into his path. 'Ready to start thinking about how you can get a University Blue?'

'A blue what?' he asked.

'A sporting Blue,' she said, rolling her eyes.

'Oh. Like Cricket Blues,' he said, thinking of Bill and Michael.

'You can get Cambridge Blues for all sorts of things nowadays. You just have to represent the Uni at a Varsity match or national competition.'

'Sounds great,' said Nick. 'Only I hate every sport ever invented. But thanks for thinking of me.'

'Yeah, really glad you appreciate me being nice and inclusive, seeing as how you're the puniest excuse for a Fresher I've seen yet,' she sneered. 'Ta now. Enjoy being a pathetic loser.'

And this is why I hate all sports. Nick squeezed back into the crowd and let it carry him away.

By the time he emerged into the light and fled across Gonville Place into the expanse of Parker's Piece, he felt battered and sweaty. A young man in a military uniform stepped into his path. 'Cambridge University Officers' Training Corps? We get to do parachuting and actual shooting.'

'My favourite things!' There was a vicious delight in letting sarcasm drip from the words.

The officer in training gave him an unapproved middle-finger salute.

This bodes so well for what College Induction has in store, Nick muttered as he set off across the grass.

By the time he reached the pedestrian zone, he'd been shouldered into two walls. It took him five minutes to push through the crowd blocking the width of Petty Cury. When he finally wriggled out into Market Square, Nick found the perimeter gridlocked with cars. Many of the drivers had their doors open, peering about: others were leaning on their horns.

Suddenly one car moved by the frontage of Paperchase, and then another. Very slowly the line of cars started disappearing up past Holy Trinity Church. People dispersed, melting back into shops or between the stalls. Nick had just wound his way to the corner by the Cambridge University Press bookshop when a flash of electric blue caught his eye.

A very short thin girl with wild white-blonde hair, wearing an enormous pair of blue fairy wings that rose up above her head and trailed down nearly to the ground, was skipping her way down the line of cars, pausing at each to whisper in at the driver's window.

'Hey, Ange!' A girl hurried across the street to the fairy, who squealed with joy and threw her arms about the newcomer.

'I'm on a rescue mission. Halt!' the fairy yelled, holding out her hand to a car that was about to pull past them. She leaned down to speak to the driver, then straightened up again, gesturing the car on. 'Some idiots from Magdalene dressed up with police hats have put cones across the turn on to Jesus Lane. They seem to think it's amazingly funny to send people round and round the one-way system. Don't they know the proud history of University pranks? Where is the equivalent of the Austin Seven van on the roof of Senate-House? Hang on a sec.' She bent to talk to the next driver in line as Nick turned away to Senate House Passage.

He found that Trinity Lane had become a car park. Cars lined the length of the street, boots and doors open. Parents and students were carrying suitcases and boxes and bags and plants and tennis rackets, and even a life-size cardboard cut-out of a film star, through the College gateway.

'You're practically living in a museum!' a little girl was saying to her sister, staring wide-eyed around at the courtyard. 'It's like one of those stately homes.'

'Off! The! Grass!' bellowed a passing fellow at a family cutting across the courtyard on the diagonal. They jumped as one and scuttled back to the nearest path.

Nick kept to the cobbles that edged the grass, squeezing past a group poring over a College map, oblivious to the angry shoving beginning around them. A cluster of students were waiting in the lee of the chapel, where they'd been told to meet for the Freshers' College Tour.

Tim was with them. 'Hey, Nick.'

'This your little brother?' one of the girls standing beside Tim asked.

Nick tried not to make a 'going to be sick' sign when she dimpled her cheeks at Tim, winding a ringlet about her fingers.

'Nope,' Tim said, grinning down at the girl. 'This here is TitHall's own *bona fide*—'

'I'm not a genius,' interrupted Nick acidly. 'I just work hard.'

'As I was *about* to say,' Tim said, 'this is TitHall's shortest smart-alec pain in the arse. Let's just agree that most people here are advanced in the brain department and somewhat stunted in the social one. If you don't fit that profile, you probably don't belong. Now, if you'll all follow me, I will begin the Grand Tour.'

'So what're you studying?' the girl asked, falling into step beside Nick. 'I'm doing Natural Sciences.'

'In Cambridge, we don't study subjects, we *read* them,' Tim cut in. 'In any case, the correct response is "I'm a NatSci" – spelt "s-c-i", pronounced "ski". Nick here is a Mathmo. Any other Mathmos?' There was a desultory show of hands as they moved under the nearest arch and into a rectangular courtyard, divided on the diagonal by a flagstone path edged with triangular flowerbeds enclosed by low box hedges. The huge arched windows of Clare College Chapel loomed up on the far side.

'That door is the office of the JCR President: bottom of F staircase,' Tim said, gesturing at a little arched opening on their left. 'Everything works by staircases in Cambridge. Off there is the stately F-staircase gyp room: that's a mini-kitchen, for the uninitiated.'

Despite the bustle of students and families filing past, the courtyard felt hushed, calm. The whitewashed building on the right, half hidden by the tall plants in the beds on either side of the path, had the feel of an overgrown cottage. The grey-brown of the towering Clare Chapel wall seemed like a misplaced film backdrop. As if two different places and times had been stuck together with no effort to join them. Ten steps in any direction was a transition into a different world: the damp cold of the stone staircase, the mayhem of Front Court, the reverence of the tiny panes of the chapel windows.

'Now, the lovely people who will come to rouse you out of

bed at a reasonable hour once a week so they can douse your room in bleach are called "bedders". They are not actually for bedding. On which note, watch out for Predatory Third Years – and, yes, that's an official title. You may end up bedding one of those, but I'd generally recommend against.' Tim beckoned them back towards the chapel and along the path, then through the double doors under the cupola, which were standing open to ease the flood of people. 'On the right we have the buttery, where you buy food. And on our left, Hall, where you eat it. When you see a charge for "KFC" on your end-of-term bill be aware that in Cambridge it stands for Kitchen Fixed Charge, which you have to pay, whether you ever eat in Hall or not.'

They passed out under the far arch, under a Victorian-style lantern. To the right was the Old Library, two scant storeys of brickwork the colour of long-dried blood, overgrown with roses and fronted by a deep herbaceous border, the fading summer flowers tilting drunkenly into each other.

'To the left we have the Master's Lodge.'

It was an ugly mess of too-yellow stone, squatting behind a circular patch of lawn. But ahead was a little copse of trees and beyond Latham Lawn, with its glorious copper beech.

'The Fellows' Garden is behind that big wall on the left. The Master has a garden party there in the summer and for one day only we all get to go and be envious, but generally, like most pieces of grass in Cambridge, it's Strictly Off Limits to students.'

'What's the thingie?' someone asked, pointing to where

a series of stepped platforms were being built on the edge of Latham Lawn.

'*That* is for your Matriculation photo tomorrow. Do *not* forget your gowns. Feasts – like Matric Feast tomorrow evening – and Friday Formal Halls are basically the only times you need your gown, but, trust me, there is no leeway. And so to the local fauna: the short, grey dude who just passed us is the Master. You probably won't have much to do with him. You get to shake his hand sometimes on special days and he'll mumble something generically complimentary to you. You can mumble whatever you like back: he's kinda hard of hearing. Any questions?'

'It's not about the Master, but why do I have a Tutor who's an English professor when I'm doing Maths?' asked a girl with a tumble of dark curls.

'You're getting confused about the Senior Tutor: she's head College honcho when it comes to all things academic. *Personal* Tutors are responsible solely for your pastoral care. They're usually from a completely different subject area just to make the point that they're there to check up on you at the start and end of each term, largely for liability purposes: basically, so College can sign off on the fact that you're still breathing and at least passing for sane. The important thing is to stay on the right side of your Director of Studies – in other words, your big-D little-o big-S – who is responsible for – you got it! – your academic progress. Or lack thereof. So remember that your "doss" will not appreciate jokes about his or her role in helping you learn how to doss about. And if you think that acronym is unfortunate, consider what the Board of Graduate Studies abbreviates to. Now, let's do some "getting to know you huddles". Mathmos, you take that bench down by the river. Natscis, you have the bench by the Fellows' Garden . . .'

The group drifted apart. Nick found himself perching on the wall beside the girl who'd asked about tutors. She offered her hand with a grin. 'I'm Susie and I'm fully intending to wipe the floor with everyone here, even you. But, seriously, you've *got* to be a genius to be at Cambridge when you're, what, thirteen?'

'I've just turned fifteen, thanks,' snapped Nick.

'Oh,' said Susie. 'Sorry. It's just—'

'I'm short for my age? Thanks for that.'

'Making friends?' Tim said, appearing next to them.

Nick cast him a glare.

'Right, making enemies then. That can work too, you know, as a starting point. Not necessarily the way I'd go but . . . I'll leave you to it.' He wandered away towards the Natscis.

'Hey, sorry about that,' said Susie, jostling her shoulder against his and making him jump. She heaved an exaggerated huff of a sigh. 'I wasn't trying to be mean, all right, so don't get in a pet. Looks like it's down to me to be organiser.' She pushed herself to her feet and blew a sharp whistle that made the loosely clustered group wince. 'OK, we've been told to introduce ourselves, so how about we get in a circle and go around and say our name and something about ourselves?'

Several people rolled their eyes or muttered under their breath, but they did so while shuffling obediently.

'I'll kick off, shall I?' asked a tall boy with a grin that suggested he was used to being admired. 'I'm Frank – by name if not always by nature. If it's got something to do with polo, yachting or clubbing, I'm your man.'

When it got to Nick's turn, he managed to force out his name, and the fact that he liked reading, without looking anyone in the eye. He let his breath out in relief a moment too soon.

'Hey, you can be like our class mascot, Nick,' said Frank.

Susie's mouth fell open in a little O of distress.

'I'm not hearing much talking over there!' called Tim.

'We were just ...' Susie trailed off, casting a look of reproach at Frank.

'OK, enough with the huddling. Regroup! There'll be plenty of time for further introductions tomorrow, while you're knocking each other off the Matric scaffolding by standing on each other's robes,' Tim said, as they gathered around again. 'Now, if you haven't got yourself a copy of the Reporter to check your timetable, you'd better go look it up online 'cos, unlike at school, no one is going to know or care if you don't make it to lectures. Though you will be charged if you miss supervisions without giving notice. And here ends the Tour. Fare thee well and may the rest of Freshers' Week be filled with joy, merriment and far too much alcohol.'

'Who's for the pub then?' asked Frank.

They set off en masse before Susie realised Nick wasn't

following. 'Aren't you ... Oh, the *pub*. Look, I'll smile sweetly at the barman and I bet it won't be a problem—'

'I've got a meeting anyway,' Nick interrupted. 'See you later.'

'See you, Nick.' She tossed a smile over her shoulder as she marched away to where the others were waiting for her in a little cluster by the Old Library. Nick watched her sail into the lead, the rest trailing after her like ducklings as she led them through the doors by the dining hall. He waited until they were out of sight before making his way back around Latham Lawn, only to collide with Tim as he stepped backwards out of a doorway followed by a very pretty brunette.

'You may look like butter wouldn't melt in your mouth, but you're a skunk, Timothy Brethan,' the girl said, poking him in the shoulder.

'That's not really fair,' protested Tim, reaching for her arm. He sighed, letting his hand fall, when she marched off towards the river, looking like she was either going to cry or savage someone with her teeth. Tim flinched when he turned to find Nick watching. 'Oops?' he said, raising his hands in a 'who, me?' gesture.

'Why have I already seen two women angry with you when you make this big deal of being an "everyone's best pal" sort of person?' Nick asked.

Tim ignored the question. 'What happened to the other newbie Mathmos?'

'Pub.'

'Why didn't you suggest a coffee shop instead?'

'Because I don't need to start term with them all resenting me.'

'For making them go for a coffee instead of a pint at ...' Tim slipped his phone from his pocket, checked the time. 'It's only noon. That's early even for Freshers.'

'I want people to get coffee because they want me to be there too, not out of pity, OK?' Nick snapped.

'They don't even *know* you yet,' Tim said. 'If they start choosing to go to the pub when they *do* know you better, *then* you can take it personally.'

'You really think reminding them that I'm too young to drink is going to help me make friends?'

'It's the truth. And maybe one of the others doesn't drink anyway.'

Nick snorted.

'Yeah, OK, it's unlikely, but honestly, Nick, if you go about expecting the worst of everyone so you never give them a chance to like you fair and square, don't you think that's kind of a self-fulfilling prophecy? Maybe they simply didn't think. Sometimes people are just straight inconsiderate – or outright thick. It's more common at Cambridge than you'd imagine: heads in the clouds, feet in our mouths. Hey, was that almost a smile?'

Nick bit his lip, but his mouth pulled up into a grin anyway.

'Come on. If you're heading home, you can tag along with me to Trinity Street while I continue to dispense sage advice. Like, next time you should get in there first with a suggestion of coffee – or better yet, tell everyone you want to go get currant buns at Fitzbillies for the sake of tradition. If they still insist on going to the pub, I give you permission to sulk to your little heart's content.'

They pushed into the p'lodge, Tim detouring past his pigeonhole.

'Here,' he said, grabbing a couple of student newspapers off one of the window seats and thrusting them into Nick's arms. 'A copy of the first *Varsity* and *TCS* of your Cambridge career.'

'So why were you giving the tour anyway?' Nick asked, falling into step beside Tim as they let the street-side door of the p'lodge swing shut behind them.

'Gosswin arranged for me to do some work for College over long vac to pay for my rent, 'cos I've been a bit short of blunt. Part of the deal was helping out with Induction.'

'Didn't you go home at all then? Is that usual for ... What are you? MPhil? PhD?'

'MPhil, converting to a PhD. At least that's the plan. You can't go directly to PhD any more from a BA.'

'Well?' asked Nick, when Tim didn't go on.

'Well what?'

'Why were you here all summer?'

Tim shrugged. 'I like it here.'

'But how about your family?'

'Look, Nick, the invitation to walk together doesn't mean it's open season on my private life, OK?'

Nick stopped. 'Right. So you get to criticise everything I

do without even knowing me, but I don't get to ask you why you're messing around with first years? Good to clear that up. See you around.'

Tim watched him hurry back into College. 'Nice, Brethan. Exactly what Gosswin meant when she asked you to be friendly.'

Chapter[5]

(Induction Week × Matriculation Day [≈ first week of October])

So much for being a font of local knowledge. Nick trudged after the rest of the Freshers, following the JCR Welfare Officer leading the 'Beyond College' Tour. They'd started with the New Museums Site, where Nick would be having most of his lectures, and then headed over the road and through one of four huge arches into a courtyard filled with balustraded stone staircases, gothic towers, copper-plated cupolas, grand oriel windows and even a stretch of lawn.

'Just remember that the Downing Site, where we've just been, is not actually part of Downing College, but home to various lecture theatres and departments,' said the Welfare Officer, leading them back out to Tennis Court Road.

A right took them down Trumpington Street; where it met King's Parade, they turned left on to Silver Street. On the bridge, the Welfare Officer pointed downriver to the wooden

Queen's College Mathematical Bridge. 'When Isaac Newton first constructed the bridge, he built it without a single nail. Then students took it apart to figure out how it worked, but they couldn't solve the riddle so it had to be bolted back together. There's a reward for anyone who can return it to its original form.'

'How big a reward?' one of the Freshers asked.

Nick turned away, grinning, wondering if he should tell the others that it was all a fib: a prank played on tourists.

Coe Fen stretched out on their left and, beyond, the start of Granchester Meadows, with the river winding through the waving beds of reeds and marsh grasses.

Nick let the paths of the Sidgwick Site wash over him, barely listening as the Welfare Officer listed the faculties and departments that made their home there. On West Road they turned right, back towards town.

Nick hooked a finger into his shirt collar, pulling against the stiff fabric, then tugged wearily at his tie. All the others were in normal clothes, but there wouldn't be time between the tour and the Matriculation photo for Nick to get home to change, so he was already in his suit, gown bundled awkwardly under his arm.

'What's that?' someone asked, pointing towards an ugly tower of iron-grey brick rising above a line of trees on their left.

'That, my friends, is HM Prison UL,' said the Welfare Officer.

'A prison? Right in the middle of the town? Is that safe?' one of the other Freshers squeaked.

Nick rolled his eyes. 'UL stands for University Library.'

The Welfare Officer made a face at him. 'It's a prison for books, not people: only third years and graduate students are allowed to borrow the books, you see.'

The others turned to Nick for confirmation.

'Seriously,' said the Welfare Officer. 'Scout's Honour and all that.'

They crossed Queen's Road at the traffic lights by King's, then followed the Backs to the left. A right into Clare let them on to a long straight path bordered by gardens on the left and King's Meadows on the right. At the end of the path, a beautiful black-painted filigree gate of wrought iron curtained the path from the grey stone bridge beyond.

They walked under an arch of grey-white stone, emerging into Old Court, then out another arch and finally through the front gate into Trinity Lane. A few dozen paces and they were back at Trinity Hall. The others hurried away to throw on their suits and gowns, while Nick wandered slowly towards Latham Lawn, where they'd been told to gather at eleven on the dot.

The day before, the College had looked enchanted in the sunshine: the warmth of the golden brick of Front Court, the autumnal glow of the buildings around Latham Lawn, the purple of the copper beech leaves, the riot of late-blooming flowers in the beds. Now, it was all shades of brown and grey. Instead of smiles, people's faces were pinched and reddened by the icy wind.

'How long's this going to take?' whined a girl to Nick's right.

A group of begowned fellows were signalling for attention from the path in front of the Jerwood building. Slowly the crowd turned to face them. There followed a few brief speeches that were largely torn away by the wind: stuff about 'welcome' and 'privilege' and 'opportunities' and 'make the most of' and, bafflingly, 'penguins'. At one stage, the wind dropped and he caught 'Matriculation marks the time you officially become part of the University. Even when you graduate, as alumni you'll still be part of this great institution. So look around at the class you're matriculating into. These will be your peers for the rest of your life. The Matriculation photo we're about to take is part of our formal record of matriculating students, which makes it important enough that we will be dispatching porters to find anyone missing when we take the Matriculation register. If you know any of your friends to be absent, we suggest you consider phoning them now or even slipping very briefly away to roust them from their beds before we do so. On a more serious note, we urge—' The rest was lost to the wind.

Finally, they were herded in alphabetical order on to the scaffolding, a process complicated by the fact that in a crowd of over 120 students it was almost impossible to hear whose name was being called.

Nick smiled hopefully at the girl standing in front of him in the queue. She smiled back, but quickly, turning away. Nick sighed, fixing his eyes instead on Latham Building: trying to remember that even being here was an opportunity and privilege that should be enjoyed and cherished. But it was hard when his face and fingers were numb with cold. When no one had spoken to him all day.

An opportunity to perfect being lonely in a crowd.

He started, not sure for a moment if he'd spoken aloud. If so, no one had heard.

'Oh finally,' said the girl in front as they were hustled up on to the stand. They shuffled to the middle of the second tier from the top then turned to face the river. Past the Fellows' Garden on the left were the roofs of Clare and, beyond, King's, cold and beautiful and close: so close that the chill misery of feeling so alone didn't seem possible among the gardens and spires around him.

'Everyone looking at the camera,' shouted the photographer.

Nick blinked, tried a smile that felt like it was mostly teeth.

There were some changes to the front row. Special people in. Special people out. New special people in. And then they were all climbing back down to the lawn. Nick looked around for Susie, Frank, any of the other Mathmos, but they were all gone. He looked in at the JCR, but there was no one he knew: no one who looked interested in talking to him.

He was wandering down the path around Latham Lawn, heading towards the Jerwood Library, when a window opened above him.

'Mr Derran,' an imperious voice hailed him, 'it is time for tea.'

He squinted up into the sharp white light breaking through the cloud behind the building. Professor Gosswin was glaring down at him.

∞

By the time he left Professor Gosswin's set, it was fully dark, the air burning cold. Around him, the many windows of the College, and Clare next door, were alight: yellow and orange against the black and blue of the night, somehow near and far. As he walked around Latham Lawn towards the corridor between the dining hall and the buttery, the tracery of the delicate stonework around the windows seemed to glide through the air, the shining glass letting on to a different world, somehow more real than the one he was walking through, all dim and vague with shadows.

Over tea the Professor had ordered him to bring a box of chocolate biscuits through from the kitchen with the advice that 'In Cambridge the word "feast" has come to be used to indicate that a meal will be more than usually inedible, so you need have no qualms about spoiling your appetite before tonight's Matriculation Feast: better now with chocolate than later with slivers of dead swan.'

The smells, as he passed the buttery, supported the Professor's scepticism.

Front Court was crowded, the air fizzy as in the moment after lightning. Skin was orange and yellow in the glow of the lights, faces masklike from the shadows. Bodies seemed to merge strangely as people flapped their gowns, put them on, took them off again, trying and failing to help one another settle them elegantly. As Nick looked, one short girl simply bundled the trailing lower half into her arms and stood cradling it like a baby.

'Alphabetical order!' shouted a dashing man in an extremely smart suit. 'Matriculating students into alphabetical order.'

There was much pushing and shoving and odd bits of standing on the grass as the crowd slowly resolved into a line running down from the double doors to the dining hall, along the chapel wall, then into the middle of the courtyard. The whole crowd was shuffling from foot to foot in an awkward dance to combat the cold.

'Gown!' the man in the suit shouted, pointing. Nick and everyone around him turned to watch a tall boy with startlingly orange hair quail like a cartoon character. A moment later, he scuttled off towards North Court.

'No one in Hall without a gown! And quiet!'

A hush fell. Nick squeezed to the edge of the cluster of students around him to peer out across the courtyard. The scene didn't look real, didn't feel real. All these people towering above him, boys in suits, girls in evening wear, everyone begowned. Even the taller students didn't seem to fit the gowns: strange things with great batwing sleeves and so much pleating of the voluminous fabric around the shoulders that they looked to have eighties shoulder pads. There was a stiff scratchy semicircle of a collar that was clearly meant to fit around the neck but gaped on almost everyone so that the heavy fabric pulled the gowns awkwardly backwards. Nick had assumed that gowns would be like Hogwarts robes: black hooded dressing gowns, not round tablecloths folded in half and pinched together at the sides for sleeves.

'God, I feel like a prat,' someone muttered, flapping his gown sleeves. 'It's like a poncy version of super-hero dress-up. So much for the solemn occasion.'

A wash of laughter ebbed through the crowd.

'Matriculating students, quiet!' shouted the man in the suit.

'Cold. Bored. Cold,' mumbled a girl to Nick's left, blowing miserably on her hands.

Then finally they were moving. Waiters stood at the front of the dining hall, directing them along the benches to the left. Three long tables marched down the length of the room, each set on either side with long benches of wood so dark it looked black. At the far end, on a low wooden platform, a further table sat across the width of the hall, this one set with chairs.

Filing along the line of benches without treading on your own or someone else's gown was clearly an art. Several people ended up in impromptu embraces as they fell on to each other. When the shuffling in Nick's line stopped, they all collapsed gratefully on to the benches. The table was set with enough silverware and crystal for a week.

'Bollocks,' said the boy to Nick's right. 'We're not meant to know which fork to use, are we?'

'Was it in the Induction pack?' asked the girl who'd flirted with Tim on the College Tour.

'Start from the outside and move inwards,' said Frank, his tone adding an unspoken *you uncultured morons*.

The walls were gleamingly white, decorated in intricate plasterwork shaped into faux Corinthian columns, the capitals tipped in gold.

'Oh, look,' said Frank, pointing at the portraits hanging above them. 'I think I see dead people.'

Chapter[6]

(Michaelmas Term × Week 2
[≈ third week of October])

Pushing through the glass-and-wood-slatted door into the corridor that led to the music room, Nick found Susie sitting on one of the padded benches on the right. She looked up with a smile that faltered when she realised who it was. 'Oh. Hi, Nick.'

Her face brightened when the door opened behind him, knocking into his backpack, and Frank stepped through.

'Hello, hello, are those my students I hear?' A door had opened halfway down on the left. 'I'm Dr Davis. Come in, come in.'

The room was small, cramped, bare: a meeting room rather than an office.

'Been getting to your lectures OK, then?' Dr Davis asked.

'Right at the front,' said Susie brightly, taking out a smart new notebook and a fountain pen.

Frank coughed and bent to fish in his bag.

'Well, let's get started, shall we? Now, obviously we didn't have a supervision in Week 1 so you'd have time to settle in: get to grips with things, work on that first set of problems I sent over by email. But from now on we'll meet here at this time every week. We'll be covering two courses together each term: you'll have another supervisor, or supervisors, for the other two. Our Michaelmas Term courses will be Differential Equations and Vectors & Matrices; then we've got Vector Calculus and Dynamics & Relativity in Lent. Easter Term only has three teaching weeks and they're dedicated to revision.'

He paused to smile around at them, his face falling when he found Frank playing with his phone, though he perked up when he realised Susie was sitting on the very edge of her seat.

'Onwards and upwards,' Dr Davis said. 'Supervisions in Maths are usually in pairs, but we've got an uneven number this year, so the three of you it is. We try to persuade students not to spend supervisions taking notes: most people find they get more out of focusing on understanding instead, though it *is* a good idea to write up some notes directly afterwards. Each supervision I'll be writing out some proofs and solutions and then giving my notes to one of you to take away and share with the others. So without more ado, let's start by taking a look at your first piece of marked work.' He opened a file and passed over their corrected assignments.

'What does this mean?' Nick asked, pointing to a Greek letter at the top of his paper.

'We don't give grades for supervision homework, just alphas and betas.'

'So what's an alpha?'

'About three-quarters correct, and a beta is the equivalent of half correct.'

'But how will we know what Tripos grade we're likely to get from this?'

Frank slumped back in his chair, half-turning to look out of the window.

Dr Davis's smile became fixed. 'Let's not get too caught up in all that right at the start, Nick.'

Nick frowned down at his page. 'But—'

'Just try this for a while and if you don't feel it's enough information, we can think again, OK?'

Nick blew out a frustrated breath. 'So how many people in our year got alphas this time?'

Frank shifted in his chair, huffing an irritated sigh and pointedly rolling his eyes, while Susie started popping the top on and off her fountain pen.

Dr Davis darted a quick look at them and smiled even more widely, clearly not realising that this made him look more like a Halloween pumpkin than the picture of reassurance he was obviously striving for. 'Supervisions are more about learning, Nick, than competing with each other, but I can tell you that you're doing really well. One of the best answers out of everyone I supervise on this course, so you don't need to worry: you're more than showing you deserve to be here. Now, Susie, why don't we start with you since your solution was the most ... interesting in terms of recapping the key principles.'

By the time they were finally organised around a tiny table barely big enough to fit Susie's paper and the supervisor's notebook side by side, Frank had stopped shooting slit-eyed glares in Nick's direction.

'I'll do better next time, I swear I will,' Susie was saying, almost furiously, her eyes suspiciously bright. 'Now that I know what to do it'll be *fine*. I mean, I'm usually so *organised*. I don't know what's *wrong* with me. I don't think I've been managing my time very well,' she mumbled, fixing her eyes on their supervisor's pen. 'It's not like me. It's really not.'

Dr Davis smiled kindly. 'It is always an adjustment from school to university: having to plan everything for yourself, with no one to tell you what to do or when.'

'I just wasn't expecting it to be so ...' Susie spread her hands wide. 'There's just so much *stuff* going on all the time. People always inviting you somewhere.'

Nick bent to tie his shoelace. *It's OK for some.*

'That's absolutely as it should be,' Dr Davis was enthusing to Susie with a look of quite horrifying avuncular fondness given that they'd only met him ten minutes ago, 'but of course you need to leave time for your academic studies too.'

'I think it was just 'cos I got a bit behind in Freshers' Week. I meant to read all the course notes and stuff then. But I'll get on top of it,' she said, brushing her skirt down over her knees so the seams fell straight. 'So, what's next?' She leaned forwards, lip caught between her teeth and hands curled into fists in her lap as she watched Dr Davis work through the model answer.

'We're not meant to be taking our own notes,' Frank hissed as Nick bent over his knees to scribble in the margins of his assignment.

Nick held the page up to show him. 'That's five pencil strokes in total, OK? I'm not writing an essay.'

By the end of the supervision, Frank was looking positively thunderous, Susie strained and unhappy. Both scuttled off in different directions the minute they stepped out into the corridor.

So much for suggesting coffee instead of the pub.

'Oh, sorry, Nick,' said Dr Davis, bumping his shoulder as he stepped out into the corridor behind him. 'Didn't mean to mow you down. Actually, do you have a minute to walk with me? Now, don't take this as a criticism,' he said, as they started down the stairs, 'just a piece of friendly advice, but, while Cambridge is obviously all about being the best and brightest, sometimes it can be rather ... counterproductive to get too caught up in competitiveness. I'm not saying you shouldn't *feel* competitive inside, because that's partly what pushes us to do our best, but maybe it'd be better to keep it under wraps a bit more in supervisions. Some people find it a bit, well, intimidating.'

'I don't see why,' Nick replied, trying to keep the temper from his voice.

Dr Davis sighed. 'You have to remember, Nick, that while everyone here really is superbly intelligent, some people are ...

Well, different people have different strengths. There might be a course that's a bit tougher for you and then maybe you won't want—'

'If I don't know how I measure up, how do I know how much harder I need to work?'

'It doesn't always have to be about other people, Nick. If you just do your best—'

'Well, *obviously*. But it's *always* possible to do better. At least if I'm at the top of the pack that's a good place to start from.'

Dr Davis rubbed at his eyes. 'I don't want to be discouraging, Nick, but no one's the best all the time.'

Nick shrugged. 'But that's exactly when I need to know, so I can just keep working until I get there. Or as close as I'm capable of getting.'

Dr Davis shook his head. 'Well, I can't knock your work ethic. Just try to enjoy it too, OK? It's about learning, not just marks.'

Nick frowned. 'Yeah, but it *can* be about both. How do you know you've learnt anything otherwise?'

'Let's revisit that question at the end of term,' said Dr Davis. 'See you next time.'

Nick wandered away, kicking irritably at a loose stone. He stood for a while in Front Court, looking about for inspiration. He peered into the buttery, then the dining hall, but didn't see anyone he recognised. There were a few faces that seemed familiar, but he couldn't think of anything to start a conversation.

Just like school, only with more interesting work.

He set off home before he could dwell on it. No point walking endlessly around College, hoping for someone to catch his eye and make an overture of friendship.

As he walked up Senate House Passage, he tried calling Michael, only to get his voicemail. He didn't bother to leave a message: his father was due home in a few hours anyway to oversee a tree surgeon coming to sort out a dying ash that was threatening the neighbour's conservatory. But when he let himself in the front door, it was to find the Replacement sprawled across the sofa with his feet up on the coffee table.

'Did my dad say when he might make it back?' Nick asked by way of a greeting.

The Replacement pulled a face, turning the TV off and tossing the controls aside. 'He's kinda . . . in New York.'

Nick felt his eyes go wide in horror. 'How long are you staying?'

The Replacement laughed. 'Don't freak out, kid. Your dad's calling your godfather to stay this weekend. I'll hang out until after they're done with the tree, but I'm afraid I can't stay the night. You'll be OK, though, right? Got some local friends now to call if you need anything?'

The arrival of the tree surgeon saved them from having to find something to talk about. It was sorted within a few hours and half an hour after that the Replacement made his excuses. As soon as the door closed behind him, Nick started turning on the lights, even though the sun was still gilding the top of the fence. He added the sound of the TV to the mix before retreating to the window seat to read, curled up on the oversized cushions he'd bought in the market. For a while, he was content, warm in the low-slanting sun.

The landline rang promptly at eleven. 'Hey, Dad.'

'I could have been Bill,' said Michael.

'It's eleven here. Bill would expect me to be in bed.'

Michael snorted. 'That man would have made someone an excellent mother.'

'Sexist, Dad.'

'Really? Why is that sexist?'

Nick sighed. So did Michael. 'I had my first supervision today.'

'Oh? Already? So what grade did you get for that first assignment?'

'An alpha.'

'What the hell is an alpha? When did Cambridge start marking in Greek? We're usually more about badly conjugated Latin. Don't they do normal classifications any more?'

'I think it's sort of like an A. It's like seventy-five and a beta is fifty.'

Michael made a noise of disgust. 'But then everyone's got one of two grades. How on earth can you tell where you are in the class?'

'Well, the other two in my supervision got betas so—'

'Good for you, Nick! See, I told Bill that you'd be fine with the work.'

Nick drew his feet up to poke at a hole in his sock,

rearranging the fraying fabric over his toes. 'It's harder than school, but in a fun sort of way – so far, at least. Mostly you just chip away at it: if one approach doesn't work, you try another. There's a bit about the underlying theory and that's pretty tough, but mostly I just need to be able to get the right answer out of an equation.'

'Well, that sounds promising: exactly what we were hoping for, isn't it, a bit of complexity? But this alpha/beta stuff is ridiculous. Did you ask what exam grade you would have got?'

'I tried to, Dad, but my supervisor says I shouldn't be so competitive.' He gave up on the sock, tore it off and threw it towards the bin in the corner, watching it crumple to the carpet only a few feet away.

'More of that touchy-feely mustn't-let-the-cretins-feel-inadequate bollocks, huh? That attitude won't get anyone far in the real world. Anyway, have to dash. Just wanted to check in. Bill's coming down tomorrow.' A pause. 'I sort of suggested that I wasn't flying out until the morning. You know how he worries, so . . .'

'Got it, Dad,' Nick said. 'Hope the trip goes well.'

'Just don't throw any of those rave parties advertised on the internet, OK?'

'Chance would be a fine thing, right, Dad?' Nick told the phone as the dial tone blared from the receiver. He sighed. *Why is it never easy for us?*

∞

There seemed to be a lot of giggling happening on the other side of the door. Nick took a deep breath, let it out, then knocked. This prompted a fresh wave of giggles from the room beyond. The door opened.

'Is this the Children's Book Club Squash?' he asked before he realised what he was seeing.

The girl who had answered the door was wearing very pink pyjamas, her hair sticking up in a series of little bunches. She had a large sparkly pink teddy bear under one arm.

'A boy!' the girl squeaked.

'A boy!' came an echo from behind her. The room was full of girls in pyjamas, each with a stuffed animal in her lap.

The girl opened the door wide. 'Welcome, Boy!'

Nick reached forward and slowly tugged the door closed. He walked quickly to the end of the corridor, aware that the door was opening again behind him, and then pelted down the staircase, not stopping when he reached the bottom. He raced across the grass of the courtyard outside (to much shouting from various porters and fellows) and out through the Corpus p'lodge into the street beyond.

'Hey, Nick, you OK?'

Susie was reclining elegantly against a lamp post, looking at him with amusement.

He raised his hands to smooth his hair down, trying to calm his breathing. 'Fi-ne,' he panted. 'Just came from . . . one of these "welcome to our club" squashes, only it was . . .' He shuddered.

Susie grinned. 'Yeah, I went to a few of those as well. I've also managed to get chucked out of a society.'

'It's still only Week 2.'

Susie shrugged. 'Yes, aren't I efficient?' She sighed, turning to lean her back against the lamp post so she didn't have to crane sideways to look at him. 'I overheard some of the society officers talking about their accounts, so of course I went over to have a little look, and then I spent a little while explaining the many things they were doing wrong and why they should appoint me secretary on the spot ... and then they asked me to leave. So, really, their loss. If they hadn't made me secretary I wouldn't have stayed anyway.'

Nick opened his mouth, closed it.

'Well?' Susie demanded, crossing her arms. 'What were you going to say?'

'I'm not going to say anything. At least about you being secretary. I am trying to be more easy-going.'

Susie snorted. 'Not to be discouraging, Nick, but I don't think that's likely to work out for you. You might as well start as you mean to go on.'

'So you love my charming personality?'

Susie grinned. 'Touché. To be fair, until you stop being the best in every supervision you're kind of on my blacklist. I'm not much enjoying my fall from being top of the class at school. But give me a few weeks and we'll see.'

With over an hour left before dinner with his 'College Parents', there was just time to try the other literary society squash of the day. By the time he arrived at Pembroke and found the right room, the meeting had already kicked off, but the door was ajar so he slipped in almost unnoticed.

Someone offered him a wine glass filled with something surely too yellow to be wine and a plastic cup of something surely too orange to be potable. He accepted the orange drink, grimaced a smile of thanks and slid into a seat at the back of the room.

'But the problem, of course, is that this essentialises the Other as atavistic and unchanging without a concurrent appreciation of the socially constructed nature of this framing device. It also implies that patriarchy belongs to the Global South, failing to address its primacy in all forms of hegemonic masculinity,' said the person standing at the front of the room, waving a book bristling with page-markers.

'But don't you think that the carnivalesque mode of the intertextual references problematises the binary oppositions implied by the Orientalist discourses the author appears to be prioritising?' someone else called out.

'Yes, but doesn't Derran's notion of Zylonation explain both those objections?' Nick interrupted.

For a moment the room was silent. Several people nodded. A few murmured in assent.

'Good point,' said the man at the front of the room. 'Would you care to expand further for us?'

'Not particularly. I'm not sure I'm up for weekly meetings of talking rubbish, just with really clever-sounding words. I think I'll go and Zylonate elsewhere,' he said, getting to his feet.

A heated debate broke out behind him as he slipped away. Nick arrived back in College in time to find Tim hurrying across Front Court, a redhead in pursuit, screaming incoherently at his back.

'Oi! 'Nuff of that!' shouted a porter, leaning out of the p'lodge. 'Ange,' he called, gesturing to someone passing through the gateway behind Nick. 'You'll go sort that for me, won't you, love?'

'Sort what?' asked a short figure so muffled between a huge trenchcoat and a furry black Russian hat that almost nothing of her face was visible. She tilted the hat back and peered ahead. 'Oh, that,' she said, and heaved a sigh. 'You'll owe me a hug,' she told the porter. 'A really big one.'

Nick saw Tim's face do something very odd when he spotted the small figure in his path, his expression half relief and half guilt. He darted around her and sprinted out through the gateway while the redhead gave one last scream of fury and frustration as she slowed to a stop. The girl in the Russian hat stepped forwards and put an arm about her. The porter ducked quickly back into the p'lodge while Nick hurried on, eyes averted from the crying and shushing.

Susie was leaning against the wall in the narrow tunnel into North Court, waiting outside the Senior Tutor's office with a form. 'You look like your day's not improving,' she told him.

'I obviously followed a white rabbit with a pocket watch this morning and have since suffered traumatic amnesia about that fact.'

She shook her head. 'Cambridge is mostly like this. Trust me. I grew up here.'

'Explains some things,' Nick said. With a sigh, he headed past into North Court and then up to the A staircase set where his College Parents had asked their 'children' to gather.

His College Parents turned out to be a Laurel and Hardy couple who had decorated their sitting room with photos of Harrow-on-the-Hill and class portraits of boys in a variety of startlingly coloured blazers.

'Perfect,' said the tall one, when Nick sank on to the corner of the sofa. 'Our little family is complete. Now, you should just think of us as your gay Cambridge dads.'

'Only we're not actually gay and, like, incest with your College Parents is totally the done thing, so don't be shy, girl-children,' said the short one.

The tall one laughed into the stricken silence. 'So this is just a little "get to know you" gathering, but of course our role in your lives is to provide support and info and the low-down on all things Cambridge, like where to get the cheapest booze and how to get the best grades with the least work. Lots of fun ahead. First up, Pot Noodles for all. Tallest Child,' he said, pointing to a boy folded uncomfortably into a low armchair, 'can you bring cutlery while we dish up? Oh, before I forget, I've got a present for the baby of our family.'

The short one reached into a drawer, scuffled around in it and then raised his hand aloft in triumph, brandishing a dummy and a bib. 'Haha!' he said.

On his way down A staircase a minute later, Nick stopped to glare at a poster advertising 'Linkline: Listening and support for students by students'. *At the moment, I shudder to think.*

He turned away from the sound of laughter echoing from the JCR and hunched into his jacket. In the p'lodge, he pulled the Friday SuperHall sign-up list towards him, only for a porter to pull it away. 'Why can't I put my name down?' he snapped.

'Sorry, Nick. You're fine at regular Formal Hall next Thursday if you've got an adult with you, but there's no visitors at SuperHall so it's a non-starter, that.'

'What if I got one of my friends to be my responsible adult?'

The porter shook his head. 'The day they make a responsible Fresher is the day I grow my hair out and dye it green. Don't take on, OK? SuperHall's no great shakes. It's a dinner of rubbish foreign-themed food and a load of rowdy drinking games—'

Nick shoved away from the counter and stormed out of the street door while the man was still speaking.

Senate House Passage was damp and grey, a fine mizzle turning the world distant and untrustworthy.

So much for never being miserable here.

∞

At nine o'clock, with no message from Michael that he'd get home at all, Nick set off, head down into the blustering rain, for the post-SuperHall 'Viva' disco. The sound of the cars on the wet roads, the water cast over his feet by their tyres, turned the pavement into a storm-soaked sea promenade. He barely looked up until he reached the p'lodge. In Front Court, the buildings glowed eerily through the rain, the stone a fleshy white-gold. The glass in the windows throbbed dully with the bass beat of music from the JCR, humming in his bones and making his fingertips tingle.

Up the stairs between Latham Building and the Old Library, he found students sitting in listing clusters, eyes blindly reflecting the light. Over-bright liquids shone poisonously through the flimsy white plastic of disposable cups. One had spilled, a tiny aquamarine cataract flowing down the steps. A boy puked into the stone birdbath in the corner. The flashing lights, strobing like emergency vehicles, made the scene look like the aftermath of a disaster.

Nick wound his way up the steps, unable to shake the sense that the laughter was shrieks, the shouts horror rather than delight. He slipped into the line of people waiting to enter the JCR behind a girl wearing little more than gold straps, her lips purple-blue, perhaps from make-up, perhaps from the cold.

'Students only,' said a porter, holding a hand across the door when Nick tried to step through.

'I'm Nick Derran. I matriculated this year.' He fished his ID out of his pocket.

The porter glared down at it. 'Oh, the genius kid,' he said.

'I'm not . . .' He broke off with a sigh, taking his ID back. 'Can I go in now?'

The porter shook his head. 'Sorry. Over-eighteens only.'

'Some of the others are definitely seventeen still.'

'Maybe. You're definitely not.'

'But—'

'What's the hold-up?' someone shouted behind them.

'Let's not argue, Nick,' said the porter. 'It's not going to happen. Your parents can talk to the College if they want, but I'm pretty sure the word'll stay the same. Either way, it's a no for tonight. Off you go now.' He gently tugged Nick to the side to clear the doorway.

Nick flung the porter's hand off and shoved his way back down the steps, nearly toppling over the shoulder of a girl who suddenly leaned sideways into his path, vomiting on to the stone. At the bottom of the stairs, he turned and glared up at the party above.

'About the only fun you'll have watching from here is seeing who ends up bundering in the bushes,' someone said.

Nick spun to find Tim standing behind him.

'You might want to turn that frown upside down before you head up to the bop,' Tim said. 'But, hey, you get points for turning up to be sociable.'

Nick heaved a sigh and looked away to the river.

'You haven't been hovering out here all evening, have you?'

'I thought we weren't doing the whole "asking questions, getting to know each other" thing?' Nick snapped.

'Just go on up, Nick. It won't be so bad. You do a bit of the Amazing Pointy Dance,' Tim stuck a finger in the air then pointed it downwards to his opposite knee, 'and you sway a bit from side to side, and there you have every step you ever need to know for College bops.'

'How drunk do you have to be to want to do that for five hours at a stretch?'

'Pretty drunk, but just go with the flow. Trust me, no one will think you look stupid: for a start, no one can even see straight by this point.'

'So why are you standing around talking to me? Why don't you go and get pointy dancing already?'

'Seriously?' Tim shuddered. 'Do I *look* like I want to hang out with a bunch of lacquered undergrads?'

'Then why are you so dead set on sending me up there?'

'Because this is *your* first Trinity Hall Viva! It's a rite of passage. Go thou forth, little Fresher, and … OK, so no drinking till you puke for you … but you could go and snog a bunch of inappropriate people.'

'Oh yeah, because eighteen-year-olds love snogging short fifteen-year-olds. And then there's the whole possibility of going to jail—'

'I said go and get your snog on, not go and sleep with anyone. There will be plenty of people up there so drunk they'd snog the Master if he gave them half a chance. And, OK, you're a bit on the short side, but you're taller than *some* of the girls … and I'm sure there are plenty of boys who like short guys if you're more that way inclined.'

'Just when I thought my evening couldn't get worse, there's you and this conversation.'

Tim frowned at him. 'It must be bad: you forgot to mutter. What's got your knickers in a twist now? I mean, you can't have been expecting SuperHall food to taste like, well, food. I mean, you were at the Matriculation Feast: you had to have guessed that SuperHall was just going to be all the bad bits squared and a tenner for your stomach pains.'

'Don't you have somewhere else to be?'

Tim grinned broadly. 'Definitely, but since I'm having so much fun basking in the warmth of your charming company—'

'Mr Brethan, I can hear you trying and failing to be humorous from my room,' cut in a sharp voice. Nick looked around to find Professor Gosswin glaring up the stairs to the JCR. 'Why must these dreadful sounds be amplified past all reasonable limits? Surely there is some health and safety regulation against it.'

'Nope,' Tim replied, rocking backwards and forwards on his heels. 'They'll shut it off just after midnight like they do every bop. But we can stand here and listen to you whinge till then if that'll brighten your evening.'

Professor Gosswin gave him a withering look. 'Good night, Mr Brethan.'

'Oh, but Nick and I were—'

'Go away, Mr Brethan.'

Tim grinned, but sauntered off obligingly.

'If you are going to go and permanently damage your hearing, you should get on with it, Mr Derran.'

'The porters threw me out,' Nick snarled. 'They wouldn't

even let me go to SuperHall. I promised I wouldn't drink but—'

'That is understandably naïve of you, Mr Derran, but it has been my long experience that it is nigh-on impossible to attend College functions without being practically *doused* in alcohol. You might be *willing* to abstain but I'm sure that one of your drunker and stupider compatriots would take great pride in finding a way to ensure that you imbibed.'

'Why can't my dad just sign some legal disclaimer that he won't sue the College no matter—'

'I imagine that the College's legal position is more complex than that. Regrettable as it may be, Mr Derran, your situation in this regard is a lost cause. In any case, I do not think you are missing much. By the morning the College will have been bathed in regurgitated alcopops and most of the undergraduates will be suffering from temporary memory loss induced by alcohol poisoning. You will be quite safe in pretending you were there if you feel that your absence will somehow hamper your social standing. No one will be any the wiser. Now, while this racket continues to prevent me from retiring at a reasonable hour, we shall continue your chess education. You may put the kettle on.'

By the time Professor Gosswin had barked a thousand orders from the Keeping Room – as she tartly instructed him was the proper name for any room in a college set that was not a bedroom – regarding the precise way her tea should be prepared, Nick no longer felt the bass beat of the music from the JCR as a throb of anger in his temples.

Tonight, there was a space beside the chessboard for the tea tray and a second chair drawn up in invitation by the white pieces.

'You know, you don't have to feel obliged to invite me for tea just because—'

'*Mr* Derran,' snapped Professor Gosswin, 'when has it struck you, in our admittedly brief acquaintance, that I *ever* feel compelled to do that which I would rather not? Now *sit* down this instant and get on with it. While you do, indulge me by expanding on how you are faring at College thus far.'

'Well, the city's beautiful. And I'm enjoying the work. Everyone says Maths gets hard about Week 3 or 4, though, so I guess I'll just have to wait and see.'

'And the people?'

Nick fumbled a knight into position.

Gosswin sighed. 'Send me patience,' she begged the ceiling.

'The people are OK,' Nick said.

'That was not a rousing endorsement, Mr Derran.'

Nick shrugged.

'And a shrug is not an acceptable elaboration any more than that move is worthy of your intellect. No, not the *bishop*!'

Nick moved his knight again.

Professor Gosswin grunted. She let her hand hover over a castle, then her queen.

'I guess I get on OK with the people I have lectures with.'

'And your supervision partners?'

'I make Susie condescending or tearful, and Frank doesn't like that I keep doing better than he does.'

'A fact that you take no trouble to hide.'

Nick threw up his hands, slumping back into his chair. 'Why should I always have to pretend I'm not as clever as I am? If I can't be smart at Cambridge—'

'You are quite well aware, Mr Derran, that there is something of a difference between being smart and being a smart arse. You need to decide what matters more to you: forming friendships or challenging yourself with the work in the way you most enjoy. Try something with that rook.'

'I want to enjoy the work,' he said, eyes fixed on the board. 'Susie and Frank are OK and I could probably get on better with them if I kept my mouth shut, but I'm never going to have a proper friendship with either of them. They're just not ...' He shrugged.

'*Words*, Mr Derran.'

'Susie seems really confident outside supervisions, but she just keeps going to pieces over the work. I think she's embarrassed that I'm there to see that. Frank slacks off and then gets cross when I want to know how well I'm doing: I'm working twice as hard as he is and he knows it, so why should I worry about him feeling inadequate when I get better marks? If he cares, why doesn't he try harder? And if he doesn't care enough to work more, then what's the problem?'

'That is a rational and logical argument, Mr Derran. However, as you will concede, people, even mathematicians, are usually no more logical or rational than anyone else when it comes to life … and their ego.'

'But this is work!'

'For some people it is the same thing.'

'For people like me. Frank doesn't give a toss. He had a hangover last supervision. *And* he was late.' Nick slammed a pawn off the chessboard with a swipe that sent it rolling on to the rug. 'Sorry,' he said quietly, reaching for it and setting it carefully to the side.

'Your work may take up more of your time, and be more integral to your sense of self, than is the case with your supervision partner, but it does not follow that he is necessarily the type to appreciate the distinction. Or your willingness to make a point of it.'

'But I'm *not* making a point of it,' Nick said, then winced at how loudly the words had come out. 'I'm not trying to make a point of it to *him*.'

'Indeed,' said Professor Gosswin. 'I am not criticising your choices, Mr Derran, but I *am* suggesting that they have consequences, which means you must look further afield for friendship. Because that *should* form a part of your time here. Look at your father. He and Mr Morrison have always made something of an odd couple, but while they were friends before they came up to Cambridge, I dare say it was their college days that enabled them to stay *great* friends even after they went down.'

'Dad and Bill had cricket. What do you want me to do? Join a sports team? Oh, they'll love me in the rugby squad.'

Nick snorted a bitter laugh. 'I'm no good at tennis. I can't sing. I can't act—'

'But you have one natural advantage for a key Cambridge activity.'

'I do?'

Professor Gosswin gave him a look of deep disdain. 'You have an excellent mind, Mr Derran. You must learn to use it in *all* areas of your life. Consider this: you are shorter than most students and very slender.' When Nick's face remained blank, she rolled her eyes. 'You would make an ideal rowing cox. I understand from a colleague that they are trying to establish a Men's Third boat and are missing a cox.'

'Rowing?'

'Use your *mind*, Mr Derran, not your vocal cords, at least not *sans* cogitation: you are not a parrot.' Snatching a bishop from the board, she punched it down by his queen. 'The other natural advantage that suits you to this endeavour is your capacity for insult. Some coxes strive to encourage their crew, but most focus on "tough love". You should have no problem administering some of *that*. If you show some initiative and learn to tip yourself out of bed at ungodly hours of the morning, you may find yourself with a team of fellow students who are instantly well disposed towards you.'

'I thought you were going to suggest something like the chess club.'

Professor Gosswin gave a long-suffering sigh. 'No, Mr Derran. At present, that would be *most* unsuitable indeed.'

Chapter[7]

(Michaelmas Term × Week 3
[≈ end of October])

Four mornings later, seven o'clock found Nick walking downriver along the towpath, watching the sky blush to the blinding line of the yellow-white horizon. Mist curled dispiritedly over the water, stagnating about the reeds. The moisture hanging in the air made the discarded sweet and crisp packets bobbing at the waterline glow with sudden colour against the brown- and grey-green of the water, of the land.

A tall man in a waterproof jacket was standing in front of the Trinity Hall boathouse doors, along with a group of yawning students.

'Nick?' the man called, beckoning him over. 'I'm your coach. And this sorry lot's your crew.' He gestured at the students standing in an uneven crescent around him.

As Nick raised his hand to wave, one of the students

mirrored him, wiggling his fingers tauntingly. Nick quickly dropped his hand.

'Since this boat was so pathetic on their mandatory initial session with an experienced cox, they had to have a second session,' said the coach, 'so no harm done that you're joining us a few weeks late, though it's a pity you've missed the official Combined Boating Clubs induction.' The coach shook his head as he looked Nick up and down. 'At least you're small,' he said, to sniggering from the crew. 'Button it.' He made it a command without even raising his voice.

The crew went quiet, eyes on their shoes. Nick looked from one to the next, hoping for a friendly smile. Two of the students were clearly twins, dressed near-identically, standing in exactly the same way, with exactly the same smarmy grins.

'Time to look lively. What's the first thing you do, Nick?' asked the coach.

'I check the app on my phone for the lighting-down time, which is actually when the sun comes *up*,' Nick said.

'Don't tell me: show me.'

Nick resisted the urge to roll his eyes as he brought the app up. 'Lighting down was one minute ago. So in fifteen minutes we can go on the water without static lights, right?'

'*But . . .*' prompted the coach.

'But Third Boats aren't important enough to be on the water before seven-thirty, so we can't even go on the river *with* lights for fifteen minutes anyway.'

'And what else do you need to check?'

Nick tried to envisage the Handbook, tried to see the page about lighting up and preparing for an outing.

'Before you go on the river,' said the coach, with a long-suffering sigh, 'you check the flag. Which flag do I mean?'

'It's on one of the boathouses, but I can just check it on the website.' He looked up to find the coach standing with his hands raised as if in supplication. 'Right.' He brought the page up on his phone. 'It *was* yellow, which is only for the really good boats, but now it's green, which is for everyone.'

'Now, what is it that you, personally, are missing?' The coach heaved a dismal sigh at Nick's blank look. 'What goes on to the river with you and not your eight?' At Nick's even blanker stare, he fixed his eyes on the sky as if Nick were too stupid to look at. 'Your eight: your eight rowers. Why do you think your boat is called the Men's Third VIII? Didn't you even skim the Handbook?'

'There's just a lot to remember—' He looked away, took a deep breath, then a second. 'I need to get a life jacket.'

'Am I stopping you?' The coach made a shooing gesture.

Such a great start to my rowing career.

Nick walked into the boathouse and set about looking for the life jackets. When he finally found and fought his way into one, he turned to find the coach and crew waiting behind him. They gave a little cheer as he stepped towards them.

Nick bit down on the inside of his cheek. By the time he'd supressed the rudest retorts in his head, trying to think serene thoughts about the gentle ripples of the water visible through the open boathouse doors, the time for saying anything witty and confident was gone.

'Now,' said the coach, beckoning Nick over to stand beside him, 'the key is to give commands as early as possible. On the river, you need to plan three boat-lengths ahead. It's safety first, so the only priority for today is to have an outing with no accidents. I don't care how slow and messy it is provided you respect the rules of the river. I'll be with you the whole way on the bank to prompt you if need be.'

'How come I'm the only one in a life jacket?' Nick asked.

'The crew are lower in the boat than you and better anchored with their blades and their feet. Coxes aren't allowed to fix themselves in, so they're the most likely to fall in the drink.'

'Or be tossed in!' came a call.

'It's traditional after a win at the Lent and June bumps – the races next term and after the exams – for the cox to get dunked in the river,' explained the coach. 'It's not likely to be an issue for you with this lot. Let's get this disaster waiting to happen over and done with, shall we?'

'River! Five minutes!' Nick ordered. 'Get the ... stuff ready!' His shout seemed to bounce off the wet air and back into his face. A few members of the crew giggled.

'On the river!' bellowed the coach, giving Nick a haughty look when all eight of the crew scrambled towards the boat. 'Stroke side opposite your riggers! Prepare to lift! Nick, give the order.'

'Hands on!' he said, wincing when it came out more squeak than shout.

The twins sniggered.

'Oh shut up,' Nick growled, and got a look of approval from the coach. 'Prepare to lift one inch only! Lifting on three, two, one, lift!' It was close enough to word-for-word from the Handbook that the coach just raised an eyebrow. 'Walk it out!'

Nick and the coach led the way on to the wide concrete path between the boathouse and the river.

'No, you idiots! Stern goes upriver! Stern!' shouted the coach. 'The back bit goes to the left! Nick, you command the turn.'

Eventually the boat was the right way up and facing in the right direction. The crew slowly lowered it to the surface of the water. Nick crouched on the edge, holding the rudder steady so that it didn't smack into the bank as the crew scrambled awkwardly into the boat, making it pitch dangerously to one side then the other. People passing on bikes and in jogging gear didn't even turn to look. A dog stopped thoughtfully by the open boathouse doors, then peed against the jamb.

A heron landed on the far side of the river. Nick watched it stalk into the reeds, digging at the bank. Upriver, the St Catz boathouse was sodden and grim in the fine rain. The dark blue paintwork of the bay doors along the front ran with moisture.

Finally, the crew were settled, shoes off and feet fixed into place. They called off their positions one by one. With one last look over his shoulder at the river, Nick took a breath and carefully slid from the bank to the stern.

'Push off when you're ready!' called the coach.

The boat wobbled, pitched, made a jerky sideways motion. Nick flinched as the stroke slid towards him. He hadn't realised how intimidating it would be to have someone pulling forward so close, and the rest of the crew behind, all rushing at him while he had to sit still at the stern, focusing on the river. When he had imagined his first outing, there had been versions where they all fell in the river; versions where they ran aground; versions where the coach ordered him out of the boat never to return; and versions where everyone simply fell into pace with each other, as if it were the most natural thing in the world.

Reality involved getting soaked to the skin by the mizzle as they fought their way upriver in fits and starts, almost colliding with the bank when they had to cross over after the first ninety-degree bend, which the coach named as Ditton Corner, and then back again after Grassy Corner, the second sharp bend. Their attempt to 'spin' by Baitsbite Lock, which marked the end of the stretch of water given over to rowing, collected a crowd of dog-walkers and parents with pushchairs, all delighted by the farce being enacted for their viewing pleasure as the Trinity Hall Men's Third VIII tried and failed and tried again to turn their boat towards home. Nick let the coach's voice fade into the background as the orders became progressively shorter, sharper and ruder. Slowly, waveringly, the boat started to turn.

There were bulrushes beside the bank upstream, away from the lock. A clump of wild geranium tumbled orange and scarlet over and between the filigree of a fallen tree branch. The brambles were wine-dark, the leaves the purple-black of an aubergine, catching the odd slant of light through the cloud.

Then suddenly the trees were blazing yellow and amber and green as columns of sunlight streamed down the bank, on to the water, and just as suddenly were gone. A sharp tug of wind shunted the boat sideways. The crew hunched stinging cheeks into their shoulders.

'Stop admiring the wildlife, Nick!' shouted the coach.

Nick started. He corrected the rudder to move away from the bank then had to re-correct back the other way.

'May we come past?' came an amplified shout from behind.

'Easy the boat! Bow side, I mean stroke side ... Passing side, watch your blades!' Nick shouted, heart thumping as the boat overtaking them burst into jeers and catcalls, while his own crew glared mutinously.

The other boat pulled level, the cox grinning maliciously.

'Watch your own bow, you onion-eyed foot-licking measle,' Nick told him.

Silence descended over the river. The other boat pulled past, their cox turning to stare back. Nick watched with satisfaction at they steered into the bank.

When he turned back to his crew, the stroke was grinning at him.

There was no time to admire the fields and woods, the willow trees feathering into the water. The coach talked him through a series of simple commands about 'backstops' and 'half slides', while Nick fluffed the steering and the crew failed to pull in unison, let alone with equal power. The boat weaved and jerked its way back downstream.

Nick tried to keep his eyes on the river but they kept drifting back to the boathouses that periodically dotted the final stretch of their journey. Picked out in the appropriate College colours, each displayed a plasterwork crest but no other signpost to distinguish one from another. Somehow he couldn't stop thinking of them as posh garages, lined as their fronts were on the ground floor with high double doors. He supposed the height was to give ample clearance for the expert crews, who carried their boats out above their heads.

Ahead, he spotted the Trinity Hall boathouse. Triple lead-light windows jutted out on thick oak-beams over the forecourt at either end; matching gables rose into fancy swirling plasterwork below sharp-pointed brown-tiled roofs.

They managed to 'park' in front of the boathouse without falling in or losing any oars, but it was a near thing. Then they nearly dropped the boat as they turned it upside-down to rack it again. By the time it was safely stored, the crew looked hollow with humiliation and exhaustion.

'Any words, Nick?' the coach asked.

Nick looked at his fingers, purple and white with cold. 'I

need to invest in better gloves.' He shrugged. 'I thought we should end on a positive note, but that was all I could think of.'

The stroke laughed.

'Same time Friday, boys!' said the coach to a general groaning and grumbling as the crew trudged away up the towpath towards the footbridge to Midsummer Common.

The stroke, arm over the shoulders of one of the twins, looked back suddenly. 'You waiting to be carried, Nick?' He made a 'come on then' gesture.

It meant going back to College in his wet things, where everyone else separated to shower and get ready for lectures, leaving him to double-back on himself to head home, but it was worth it to spend twenty minutes as part of one of the loud boisterous groups jostling across Midsummer Common. Even though no one spoke to him specifically, and he added nothing to the conversation, it was nice to belong there: to be part of something.

Chapter[8]

(Michaelmas Term × Week 4
[≈ start of November])

He pulled the front door open with his eyes fixed on the mat, looking among the junk mail for the DVD he'd ordered. A noise that sounded incomprehensibly like it had come from the kitchen made him look up.

'Dad?' he called as he bent to pick up the post.

A shout from the kitchen. A flurry of noise.

The living room was a mess.

Understanding hit with a feeling like walking through glass: a time-stopping crunch, cutting cold and deep. His fingers fluttered against the doorframe, the emptiness of the hall hollow and loud with silence.

Then a clack and clatter from the kitchen. A muffled shout. The sound of someone throwing themselves over the back fence.

His heart stuttered against the inside of his ribs. Like

waking from a nightmare, the need to breathe made his head swim. The air felt thick as oil, choking him. The sound of his own cough sent him cowering to his knees, ears straining for the faintest sound over the noise of his own body betraying him. But the coughing eased with no pad of footsteps above or in the kitchen.

He fumbled his phone from his pocket, considered backing out of the front door, then took a deep breath and eased to his feet.

They're gone. They heard you and they ran.

His phone showing 999, his finger over the dial button, he shifted his weight forward. Stepped forward. Another slow, sliding step. Another.

The TV was at an odd angle. The stereo and Sky Plus box were gone, the wires trailing dismally across the floor. The cupboard spaces at the bottom of the bookshelves were open, things landsliding from them on to the carpet. A trail of Monopoly money petered out under the coffee table.

He padded slowly into the middle of the room and peered through to the kitchen. Almost all the cupboards were open. There was a space where the microwave had been.

He hit dial and brought the phone to his ear. The police told him to go and wait with a neighbour until they could check that the burglars were gone.

Once he'd hung up, he crept slowly upstairs.

Don't be a wimp, he told himself. *There's no one here.*

Michael's room looked like it had rained boxer shorts and socks. The electric razor was gone from the en suite.

Climbing the stairs to his floor made sour spit rise in his mouth, but his room looked untouched: everything as he'd left it, from the messy desk to the piles of books and box files, the scattering of pens and overflowing laundry basket tucked behind the door. He'd left at eight-thirty for a nine o'clock lecture, then headed straight home. It wasn't even eleven yet: it felt too early for burglars to be starting their rounds, but at least he'd disturbed them before they'd reached his attic.

He pulled on his grandmother's jumper, shivering into the folds and pressing the cuffs over his nose, breathing through the scratchiness of the wool until his pulse had slowed. Sound was starting to return to normal, his ears no longer straining after every real and imagined creak in the house, every whoosh of a car passing on the street.

He waited for the police outside, sitting on the low front wall. He called Michael as he waited, left three messages apiece on his mobile, landline at the office and landline at the flat. Then he stared at his contacts list for a while before calling Michael's mobile again.

When the police arrived, the officers checked the house together, then one set about taking photos and presumably checking for fingerprints while the other insisted that Nick find his father. He called Secretary Sandy only to get a recorded message that she was on leave but would be back tomorrow. He called the main switchboard at the law firm. They reported that Michael was out of the office. He called all of Michael's numbers again and left new messages on each.

'Look, Nick, we really need to talk to a responsible adult.

Surely there's *someone* else you can call. An aunt, uncle, older brother, family friend . . .'

Nick stared down at his contacts list. 'My godfather's in London.'

'Why don't you give him a bell while you're waiting for your dad to call back?'

Bill's phone went straight to voicemail. Nick hung up. 'If he's not there, what's the point worrying him?' he asked when the policewoman frowned.

'I'm sure he wouldn't mind,' she said, putting a hand on his shoulder.

He flinched without meaning to, hunching away from the mingled pity and irritation on her face.

'I'm afraid we really do need to call *someone* for you. How about a teacher? A friend whose parents could come over?'

'I told you: I'm at the University, not school.'

'Then surely there's someone at College who's over eighteen who could pop down.' The policewoman was grinding her back teeth, her cheek ugly with the bulging and tightening of the muscles.

'Professor Gosswin's my tutor,' Nick told the dandelion drooping between the bottom of the wall and the pavement.

He averted his eyes as the policewoman looked up the number for Trinity Hall on her phone, called the p'lodge and got put through to the Professor. Twelve words in, she went silent. When she spoke again, her tone was quiet, deferential. Apparently the Professor could intimidate even at a distance.

The policewomen were standing ready to receive Gosswin

when she emerged majestically from the back seat of a taxi fifteen minutes later. She barely spared them a glance before fixing her eyes on Nick. 'Mr Derran, you should be inviting me into the kitchen and offering me a cup of tea,' she told him.

She took in the mess in the living room with a curl of her lip, but followed him into the kitchen without comment. 'Now,' she said, as she seated herself at the table, 'I require you to explain why it was the police and not you who called me.'

Nick turned away to fiddle with the kettle. 'I couldn't get hold of my dad. I'll keep trying.' He took out his phone and demonstrated his efforts, setting it on the counter when he'd dialled all three numbers to no effect. 'I even tried Bill.'

A flicker passed over Professor Gosswin's face. 'But he was also not available? That is a pity. Should there be a further occurrence of this or a related sort, you will call me first, except in the unlikely instance of your father being home.'

Nick shook his head. 'I'm sorry the police bothered you. I tried to tell them it wasn't your problem—'

'Mr Derran, you are frequently problematic, but this is not one of those occasions.'

Nick turned away to fetch the milk, absently tracing patterns into the condensation on the bottle. 'It's not your job to take care of stuff like this.'

'It is my job as Tutor to see to the needs of my tutees. I have dealt with far more unusual problems than being called to stand as responsible adult in the case of a burglary.' She caught Nick's interested look and her gaze darkened. 'That was not an invitation to ask impertinent questions so you can gossip about confidential matters. Now, when might we expect your father to grace us with his presence if he does not check his messages until the end of his work day?'

Nick fixed his eyes on the floor. There was a scuff in the paintwork of the skirting board that looked almost like a face. It was sneering at him.

'From this dismal silence, I take it that perhaps we are not to expect your father at all.'

Nick met Professor Gosswin's eyes. He shrugged.

'And how often do Michael's peregrinations see him away from home not just during the day but throughout the night?'

Nick shrugged again and looked back at the disdainful face in the skirting board.

'I take it no one else is aware of this situation? Neither you nor your irresponsible parent has thought to make an arrangement with a relative or family friend – Mr Morrison, for example?'

'Yeah, Bill's always had a driving ambition to babysit a teenager six nights a week. I don't have a bunch of aunts and uncles and cousins and grandparents to keep me company, but I'm fifteen, not five. I don't need anyone to tuck me in at night.'

Professor Gosswin raised an eyebrow. 'It is irrelevant whether or not you have a large network of people related to you by blood. The issue is that the family you *do* have is not *here*, in the home you should be sharing.'

'It's not always like this: it just goes in fits and starts.

Induction week, Dad was home almost every night: a few days he was even in time for a late dinner. That's how it's always been with him. No one worried when I was ten, so I don't know why it's a problem now.'

'When you were living together in London, your father was not only in the same city – a relatively short distance away – but likely to turn up at some point during the night,' Professor Gosswin said. 'You have to know that *this* situation is not equivalent – or remotely acceptable. You cannot live almost entirely alone aged fifteen.'

'I don't mind—'

'I was not talking about it being acceptable to you. It is not only illegal, it is unacceptable to *me*, and that is a problem of a different order because I, Mr Derran, am not irresponsible or derelict in my duty. Nor shall you persuade me to be,' she said loudly over Nick's attempt to interrupt, 'since it would be unkind to dismiss legitimate concern from someone who has a care for your happiness and well-being.'

Nick darted a glance at her, then away, flushing.

'Now, we don't want to start getting sentimental, so let us move on to the practical step we shall take to resolve this situation. Since you already know Mr Brethan, it should all be simple. He will move in here as a lodger.' She smiled as the look of horror on Nick's face transformed into fury. 'No need to thank me, Mr Derran. Instead, you may reflect on how neatly I have dodged the need to discuss today's situation with both College and Social Services.'

'I don't need a keeper!' Nick's phone trilled on the counter. He grabbed it without even looking at it. 'Dad, where have you—'

'It's Bill.'

'Oh.' Nick changed the phone to his other ear.

'I saw I had a missed call from you. Is everything OK?'

'Yeah. Yeah, fine now.' A sigh. 'We had a burglary and I couldn't get hold of Dad, but Professor Gosswin is here so it's all fine. Sorry to have bothered you.'

'Shall I come down? Do you need someone to board up a window or anything?'

'No ... I don't think ...' He stared at the broken glass by the back door. 'It's fine. Thanks for calling back.'

Professor Gosswin frowned at him when he put the phone down.

'What's that for?' he snapped.

'Why refuse your godfather's offer of help – and company?'

'He's just being nice. I don't need—'

'It is not always about need,' Professor Gosswin cut in, though her tone was strangely gentle. 'With those you love, it is also about wanting, and being wanted, when you are in distress.'

'Yeah, because what Bill really wants today is to drop all his work and come down to Cambridge to help me clean up the house.'

'Sometimes I wonder why I speak at all when I so rarely seem to be heard.' Professor Gosswin sighed, then pushed herself to her feet. 'I shall speak to the police officers about securing that back window for the night.'

Standing alone in the kitchen, Nick slammed the nearest open cupboard door shut. Then the next, then the one after. When the police asked if they could get at the window, he stomped his way upstairs and spent the next while shoving the clothes the burglars had strewn about the room haphazardly back into his father's drawers, only to take them all out again. His hands shook as he folded them carefully. Suddenly his throat was stinging. He sank on to the bed.

Someone cleared their throat by the door, making him jump. Professor Gosswin used his shoulder to lever herself down to sit beside him, then left her hand there, pressing gently. After a little while, she lowered her hand to reach for his, clasped it, rested their joined hands on his knee.

'I don't want a lodger.' He had to bite the words out around the frustration and helplessness.

'This is one of those cases that is about need, rather than want. But who is to know? Sometimes one can become the other,' she said, but softly. 'You need not to be living alone in this house. And Mr Brethan needs a home. So it is not just about *your* needs. Maybe that will make it easier to accept.'

Nick nodded jerkily, the movement making his neck hurt.

A key scratched into the front door lock.

'Dad.' The words croaked out as his eyes stung afresh.

He tore to the head of the stairs as the door opened. A second too late, he felt his face doing the thing that his father's did whenever he found Nick unexpectedly awake when he got home.

'Oh, hi, Nick,' Bill said, smiling nervously up at him. 'Sorry for crashing in on you mid-afternoon and all, but I figured your plans were blown anyway.'

He tried to lift his chin and grin, tried to make his voice warm enough to wipe away any hint of disappointment. 'You didn't have to come.'

Bill shrugged. 'Just figured I'd drop by in case . . . You know, in case you were still having difficulty getting hold of Mike. I didn't have anything scheduled this afternoon so I thought I'd come early and miss the rush. When I did the morning commute with Mike last time I stayed over, it was so crowded there were people sitting in the luggage spaces. I swear some of them looked like they were considering climbing into the overhead racks. Don't envy your dad that every day.'

Nick made a non-committal noise, felt it catch in his throat.

'Ah, Mr Morrison,' said Professor Gosswin, appearing beside Nick on the stairs. 'It is good to see you.' Something insistent and pointed in the way she said it made Bill turn from hanging up his coat. The Professor nodded at him approvingly. 'Shall we seek out a cup of what passes for tea in this household to celebrate your arrival?'

The police had finished in the kitchen. A corkboard had been nailed to the window-frame.

Bill looked at it with misgiving. 'I'll find someone to come and fix that,' he said, as Nick set about making tea.

'Mr Brethan can take care of those arrangements as his first contribution to the household,' Professor Gosswin said.

'She's making us get a lodger,' Nick explained, grinning when Bill practically blanched at hearing the Professor referred to, in her presence, as 'she'.

'Mike's been pretty resistant to live-in help in the past,' Bill said tentatively. 'I did suggest a nanny – ages ago!' he rushed on, when Nick swung around, spilling milk in an arc across the counter. 'When you first came to live with him, I mean.'

'I didn't need a nanny then, either!'

Bill sighed, took his glasses off to rub at his eyes. 'It didn't seem my place to argue, but it's always been a worry how little . . . How much Mike works. I did talk to him about it,' he said, appealing to Professor Gosswin. 'But it would have been hard to have a third person living in the London flat unless Mike had given up his study. When Nick first moved in, Mike said he'd start looking for a new place once he got everything sorted with the new school but . . . Well, it was all a bit . . . precipitous. I thought he'd figure it out,' he said, flicking a glance at Nick and then looking away, toeing at a wrinkled pea lying forgotten under the kitchen table.

After the tea, Bill set about clearing up the broken glass while Nick sorted out the living room and study, then they sat down to make a list of all the things that were missing. Professor Gosswin installed herself in the study and rang Tim to order him to start packing. Nick snorted at the audible side of the conversation. Somehow knowing that Tim had taken some persuading (or what passed as persuasion with Professor Gosswin) made the idea less uncomfortable.

By the time his father called to say he was on his way back, Nick was resigned enough to dwell with anticipation on how Michael would take the news.

'You've already met, so I won't hear any excuses,' Professor Gosswin insisted calmly in the face of Michael's aghast protestations. 'Mr Brethan is generally easy-going and acceptably clean. His financial situation is straitened – through no fault of his own – so it will be to *everyone's* advantage that he live here. His basic bed and board will be free and, in exchange, he will be a presence in the house as proof against emergencies and times – of which I feel certain there are many – when you, Michael, are detained overnight in London. Mr Brethan will help in the garden with the lawn and also with the general upkeep of the house, including overseeing any workmen who might be needed to make repairs. He will not be expected to cook or do laundry, other than for himself, nor will he provide help with Nick's coursework.'

Nick snorted.

'Be quiet,' she ordered. '*As* I was saying. Mr Brethan will be an adult presence—'

Nick snorted again.

'You are not a piglet, Mr Derran. Please stop grunting like one. As I was saying, while you are more than usually capable of your own care, you are nonetheless under age and, as such, should not be living alone for the better part of the week.'

Michael coughed, fiddling with the tassels on his loafers. When Nick glanced at Bill, he was startled to see that his godfather looked oddly pained.

'This will be good for all concerned,' Professor Gosswin said. 'You do not seem to be in Cambridge enough to be more than minimally inconvenienced by this *ideal* solution, Michael, so I would advise you to accept my help graciously.'

'But—'

'This is how it is going to be, Mr Derran.'

Chapter⁹

(Michaelmas Term × Week 5
[≈ second week of November])

The trailing willow leaves were amber against the blue-green of the frosted grass on the banks, the moss on the trees almost yellow in the early morning light. The water was mirror-grey, slick and oily in the still air, the ripples fat and lazy, rolling away from the boat as they crossed the river to park in front of the boathouse.

They got the boat out of the water and into the racks with minimal fuss and no accidents.

'Well, it's better than last week,' said the coach. 'I might even be able to let you out on your own before you graduate.'

'Hey, we overtook today: that Trinity boat, remember?' protested Brent.

'You overtook them because they rammed the bank,' said the coach.

'It's still better than last week.'

'When *we* rammed the bank, you mean?' Nick said.

'I'm captain, you're cox: we're meant to stand up for our boys.'

The coach shook his head and moved over to talk to the Trinity Hall Men's First VIII, who were huddled within the open boathouse doors looking disdainful.

'Who's for a round of coffee after we wash up? Nick, you with us this time?'

'I didn't even *know* about last time.'

Brent rolled his eyes. 'Don't get in a huff. Most of the stuff we get up to is just spur of the moment: bumping into each other in the JCR or Hall, seeing who's up for the pub or a burger run to one of the Vans. If we called you, it'd be over by the time you got down to College, but today you're here, so … coffee?'

Nick blew out a breath more like a raspberry than a sigh. 'Can't. Have to get home. New lodger arriving today and my dad's conveniently got a work emergency.'

'Next time, then,' said Brent, slapping him on the back.

Yeah, next time, Nick whispered.

Above him, the lead-light windows had steamed up patchily, speaking of damp rather than warmth inside. Usually so smart in its black-and-white College livery, the boathouse seemed as hunched and miserable as he felt to be saying no the first time anyone spontaneously offered to go for coffee instead of a pint so that they could include him. He turned away to head for the Elizabeth Way bridge. When he looked back, the others were sauntering slowly in the other direction.

It started raining before he'd even reached the bridge. By the time he got home, he was soaked to the skin, his socks squelching in his shoes.

He just had time to shower and get the coffee machine on before the doorbell rang. He opened the door holding his 'Liable to bite' mug and his most unpleasant glare.

'Now that's just the sort of welcome I was hoping for,' Tim said cheerfully.

Nick gestured him into the hall. 'If it makes you feel better, you can put it down to Fifth Week Blues. Is the middle of term always so *long*?'

'Yup,' said Tim, stepping inside.

'Where's the rest of your stuff?' Nick asked, peering out of the door but seeing nothing on the path, no car waiting at the kerb.

'My best friend's bringing it later. Just so you're forewarned, Ange is ... interesting. She does a lot of bouncing and she'll almost certainly hug you. Please don't expect me to do anything about it. She's one of those people you feel should only exist in a film, but what you see really is what you get. You'll understand when you meet her.'

'I can't wait,' Nick drawled. 'Do you want a coffee while we talk about all ... this?'

Five minutes later, Nick was turning his mug in slow circles while Tim warmed his hands in the steam from his.

'I don't need a keeper, you know,' Nick said suddenly. 'You

are not here as a babysitter. I don't need anyone to look after me. I never have.'

'Well, that's good to know. I was worried I'd need to provide cuddles and bedtime stories.' Tim slouched back in his chair. 'But, seriously, what *is* your dad expecting from me? Like – and please don't jump down my throat – do you have some sort of curfew he'll want me to enforce?'

Nick looked at him.

'I take it back. Jump down my throat. Just don't do that glaring thing, OK? So how about things like taking you to the doctor or the dentist?'

'Unless I'm delirious, unconscious or bleeding to death, I'll handle it myself, thanks.'

'So, no to mopping fevered brows but yes to calling ambulances in case of imminent demise. Are there any other house rules? You know, set times I'm allowed to watch TV or use the kitchen or . . .'

Nick shrugged. 'Help yourself. We don't have much kitchenware but if there's anything you want, we can get it – within reason. Dad said to tell you that he'll cover basic grocery shopping – list's up on the fridge, just add what you want – but alcohol's up to you.'

'Covering his bases in case I turn out to be a lush?'

Nick flushed. 'No, that's not what I—'

'Joke, Nick.'

'*Failed* joke, Tim.'

Tim grinned, looking about with appreciation. 'Nice. So, care to show me upstairs?' They tramped about the house, one floor to the next. In Nick's room, Tim looked around politely, bent to stare at his grandmother's photo. Nick's eyes went to the bookcase and his mother's picture, safely tucked away between two fat textbooks, the frame dulled accusingly with dust. When he turned back, Tim was reading the postcard above his bed.

> *Grant me the serenity to accept the things I cannot*
> > *change,*
> *The courage to change the things I can,*
> *And the wisdom to know the difference.*

'I didn't know you were religious.'

'I'm not. We're not.' Nick shrugged. 'I saw it in a bookshop and it just ... It's a good thing to remember: to do what you can to make life better, not get stuck looking back. Sometimes, though, I think the wisdom bit is really about knowing *how* to change things, not whether they can be changed.' He flushed then, looking away, and silently led the way back downstairs to the middle level. 'You can take your pick of the guest rooms, but it might be best to have the one at the back, rather than next to Dad. I'll order an extra bookcase.' He leaned against the banister, toeing at the carpet as he waited for Tim to finish looking around.

'You really don't say much unprompted, do you?' Tim said as they returned to the kitchen.

'What did you expect me to say? I figured you could

recognise a sofa and a toilet for yourself. Though do say if you're confused.'

'Is the sarcasm included or do I have to contribute towards it? No, don't consider that a prompt. Why don't you show me the stopcock and fuse box, then I think we're done.'

'The fuse box and the *what*?'

Half an hour later, they were back at the kitchen table with a fresh cup of coffee. 'Look, Nick,' Tim said, 'I think this could work out but if you really don't want me here . . .'

Nick sighed. 'I don't think we've got a lot of choice. Though it didn't seem like you needed much persuading.'

'More like didn't have any other option,' Tim snapped. He closed his mouth on a further retort, pressing his palms flat to the table for a moment. 'I applied well in advance for College accommodation over the summer, so that wasn't a problem,' he said more calmly, 'but I couldn't put my name down early enough for the academic year; I didn't know if I had funding for my PhD until it was too late and if it hadn't come through I'd have been working this year instead to save up. But then I *did* get the funding, only there was nothing decent that I could afford anywhere near College. Gosswin got me a guest room on an emergency basis but now that term's started . . .' He shrugged. 'If it makes you any happier, I think she was as interested to find me a roof over my head as someone to keep an eye on you. It could be worse for both of us. Just tell me if there's stuff that's likely to bug you or your dad and I'll try not to go there.'

Nick looked away. 'We wouldn't be getting a lodger if my

dad were actually living here. He's basically in London. But that doesn't mean I'm in the market for a father figure, OK?'

Tim held up his hands. 'Fine with me. I'm not in the market to be a dad yet or have any of the associated responsibilities.'

Nick nodded once, sharply. 'Then we're clear.' He sat rubbing at a pen mark across the back of his hand. 'When my dad's here he spends almost all his time in the study. He isn't going to care what you do about the house so long as you don't play loud music when he's around. As for me,' he gave a one-shouldered shrug, 'I'm basically pretty boring. I read a lot, go to lectures and study. I don't even watch that much TV. I expect we can both just carry on as normal. I doubt I'll get in your way.'

'And I'll try not to get in yours,' Tim said amiably. 'We'll manage, right?'

'Why wouldn't we? I was managing just fine already.'

Tim rolled his eyes. 'It'd go easier for both of us if you could try not to interpret *everything* I say as an insult. Most people find me pretty easy-going company.'

Nick gave him a look. 'Yeah, everyone says that about me too.'

∞

When the bell rang a few hours later, Tim was poking about with the lawnmower the previous owner had left in their dilapidated shed so Nick reluctantly put down his book and went to answer the door. A tiny purple-haired girl was standing on the front-door mat.

'Oh, hi. You must be Nick. I'm Ange,' she said. 'I am holding Tim's stuff to ransom for hugs.'

'Hi.' It came out more as a squeak than a word.

'Just to get things straight right from the get-go, it *is* OK if I stop by to see Tim and periodically steal a corner of your sofa, right?'

Nick nodded slowly.

Ange grinned. 'Cat got your tongue?'

'You've got ... um ...'

'Beautiful eyes? A knockout figure?'

'Antennae.'

'Oh, these old things?' Ange asked, batting her eyes and then giving a shout of laughter before suddenly freezing. 'Oh, no. You're not one of those people who don't approve of me, are you?' She made a face. 'Please tell me you're not the sort of person who thinks my antennae are sad and stupid. I'll have to not come round so I don't say insulting things if that's the case, then Tim'll be lonely. And of course you'll be missing out too, which would be a pity because, despite the fact that you're kinda freaking me out with the wide-eyed nodding-like-a-bobble-head-doll thing, from what Tim's said you're exactly my sort of crazy ...' She paused for breath, then let it out in a sad sigh. 'Ah. You're one of those people who think crazy's an insult. That is very sad for you, Nick Derran. Can you call Tim to come and get his stuff and I'll just bounce out here on the pathway? I won't even set foot inside. Oh, but you're not talking. Maybe you could take him a note. Do you talk at all? You sort of did a minute ago but then people sometimes go completely mute when I'm around.'

'Mostly because you don't give them a chance to get a word in edgewise,' Tim said, nudging Nick out of the doorway. 'Shall I get rid of her or can you cope?'

'Cope. I can definitely cope,' Nick said.

Ange beamed at him. 'Ha! I knew I liked you.' She frowned. 'But do try to talk instead of just nodding, OK? I mean, it's good when people concede in advance that I'm always right, but still.'

'You're the flower fairy!' Nick said suddenly. 'The flower fairy who was directing traffic when someone pranked the one-way system in Induction Week.'

'I am?' Ange said, frowning for a moment before her face brightened again. 'Oh, yes, I am. I mean, I *was*. I wasn't being a spoilsport, honest. I just didn't think it was very sporting and there was this little girl in one car crying about how she'd never get home again and . . .' She raised her hands in a helpless gesture.

'Your antennae are awesome,' Nick told her.

Ange preened, then shot into the hall to hug his arm.

'Stop playing boa constrictor, Ange,' said Tim.

'Caffeine-ness, Timothy! Produce it this *instant*!' Ange demanded, letting go of Nick long enough to stomp her foot. 'And do not even think about starting with me about my not needing any encouragement to bounce.' Ange pointed a finger at him. 'I am still cross with you. I find it hard to look cross,' she added to Nick, 'but really I am Very Cross Indeed.'

'What did he do?' Nick asked, fascinated.

'He tried to tell *me* off for telling the latest in a long line of romantic conquests to break up with him. But really it was mean of him to go out with her just to get a Christmas invite, let alone try to stop her breaking up with him *just* so *he* could do it *after* the holidays.'

'But it's ages until Christmas!' Nick said.

'Yes, but Christmas turns Timothy into a monster: think werewolf at full moon, only it's hearts he tears out instead of throats. But maybe it will stop being an issue now he has a home. An actually homey home. Has he been good so far?'

Nick pulled a face. 'Awful,' he said. 'He was polite the whole afternoon. I thought the body snatchers had arrived.'

Ange shouted with laughter again and threw her arms around him. 'Oh, I *do* like you! I absolutely like you! Tim never said you were so funny.'

'That wasn't funny. That was mean,' muttered Tim, leading the way through to the kitchen and putting the kettle on.

'You dish it out plenty, Timothy. Time to get a taste of your own medicine.' She darted after him and curled up on a chair, feet tucked up under her. When Tim turned, she stuck her tongue out at him.

Tim reciprocated, to which Ange blew an exceptionally loud raspberry. 'My friends always raise the tone,' Tim told Nick.

'Is that your real hair?' Nick asked Ange, ignoring Tim.

Ange flipped one long purple curl over her shoulder to peer at it. 'Well, it's not the real colour.'

Tim rolled his eyes at Nick. 'I think he meant "Is it a wig?" It's not, by the way. Dyed. She's actually a blonde.'

Ange blew another raspberry, slumping over the table. 'Soooooo boring. Though it is excellent for dyeing all the fun colours. Refreshments!' she said, bouncing in her seat as Tim put a steaming mug in front of her.

'What is this?' Nick asked as Tim passed him a second mug.

Tim opened his mouth to answer just as Ange squealed, leaping to her feet then stopping. She squished her face up and threw herself back into her chair, grabbing her mug to her chest. 'No! No, I'm *not* hugging you. Not even for hot chocolate with marshmallows and sherbet.'

'Do I like hot chocolate with sherbet?' asked Nick, staring dubiously into his cup.

'Of course you do, Nickie.' Ange looked aghast. 'Go on.'

Nick sipped. He tilted his head in consideration. 'Yes,' he said, though he didn't sound entirely sure.

'It's like me. Fizzy and sweet and sharp and weird all at once.'

'I put in extra weird,' Tim said. 'Look, if you're nice to her she'll be here the whole time.'

'Yes, I . . . Oh, no. I won't.' Ange pouted. 'I mean I *will* in the summer, but right now it's boring 'cos I've got a million hours of PhD reading to do this term, and it's mostly UL

West Room periodicals stuff so I'll be practically chained to the UL, and then I've got a job. We're only officially allowed eight paid hours a week, so please don't tell anyone, but Tim'll vouch for the fact that it's just not possible to survive on that, even if you work more than full time in all the vacations.'

'Don't complain. At least your supervisor looks the other way,' Tim said acidly.

'Sorry,' Ange whispered. She sidled up to him and rubbed her head against his shoulder like a cat. 'If I had Dragon Lady Gosswin watching me I wouldn't get away with it either. But my boss at Clowns says you can have as many hours as you want in the vacs. Now, go get your stuff out of my mum's car while I've got time to drop it back to her and still get the last train home. Come on, you,' she said, tugging Tim to his feet.

'Can I help?' Nick asked.

Ange beamed at him and attached herself to his side as Tim led the way out to the car sitting at the kerb. Tim's stuff was mostly boxes of books. It took an uncomfortably short amount of time to pile it up in the hall and the sitting room. Nick shivered as he stared at it.

'It's not that bad,' Tim said, catching his expression. 'I'll have it out of your way in half an hour.'

Nick shook his head. 'Not that. Just ... *déjà vu.*'

'For what?' Ange asked.

'The day Roger threw me out.' The words came out of his mouth instead of ringing in his head as he'd expected them to. 'When I was ten, my mum got sick and my stepfather ...

Well, he wanted to focus on her and it wasn't like he threw me out on to the street, I just moved in with my dad in London, but I didn't have that much stuff to take and it was mostly books like this and . . . I actually didn't mean to say anything. I talk to myself a lot and sometimes I get a bit confused about what I'm actually saying and what I'm not 'cos it's not like it makes any difference when there's no one there to hear,' he said, the words picking up speed, tumbling out faster and faster, 'but it's not like I'm going to be regularly blurting out weird emotional stuff or . . .' He cut himself off, squeezing his eyes shut. 'Can we just pretend all of that happened in my head?' He jumped when he found himself being hugged and opened his eyes to see Ange grinning up at him.

'It happens to me *all* the time,' she said. 'Don't worry about it.'

'That's meant to make him *not* worry?' Tim asked.

Ange scrinched up her nose at him. 'Meanie. I just helped you. Now I'm going and *you* don't get a hug.'

Tim stared at her soulfully.

Ange sighed and threw herself at him. 'You are *horrid* sometimes, Timothy Brethan. I love you anyway, but *please* try not to be awful. Girls are for . . . well, not necessarily for life, but certainly not just for Christmas accommodation. Pretending you're not alone is far more painful than just accepting reality and doing something about it.' She shook her head at him. 'I'm going now. Bye.' She whirled around and flung herself out of the door, slamming it behind her.

'Wow,' said Nick.

'*Is* it OK if she comes over quite a lot? I'm not sure there's much I can do about it if it isn't.'

'She can come over *any* time.'

Tim gave him an interested look.

'Oh, don't start. I can think she's awesome without . . .'

Tim held up his hands. 'Fair enough. And you're right. She *is* awesome.'

'Sort of like a cuddly version of Professor Gosswin.'

'Ange and Professor Gosswin may be equally a law unto themselves, but beyond that it's just too many levels of disturbing to contemplate.'

Chapter 10

Frank was joggling his leg up and down, tapping a rhythm against his thigh, as Dr Davis explained their last week's problem to Susie for the fifth time.

'I just don't understand!' Susie's hands clenched into fists. Taking a deep breath, she smoothed her hair back behind her ears. 'Could you please explain it to me again in a different way?'

Dr Davis cast an appealing look at Frank, who was now picking mud out from behind his nails.

'Can we move on to the next problem, or can Frank and I just go?' Nick asked, trying to make the words friendly rather than snide.

'Frank doesn't understand it any better than I do: he's just too dumb to admit it and get the help he needs,' snapped Susie.

'Why don't we come back to it later,' suggested Dr Davis. 'I think maybe you're just a little . . . frustrated at the moment.'

Frank snorted. 'A bit PMSing you mean.'

Susie swivelled to face him. 'Would you like to repeat that chauvinistic gem?'

'Think that's QED, right, Nick?' Frank sneered.

'You mean proof that you're an inadequate, unpleasant, misogynistic—' Susie turned her back on him. 'I am going to stay very calm.'

'Good luck with that, sweetheart.'

'Now really,' protested Dr Davis, waving his hands in the air as if trying to cool the atmosphere. 'Now, I know that the first term is often very hard. There's so much to learn and adjust to that it feels like the pressure's unbearable, but we all need to stay calm and breathe.'

Susie looked as if she were likely to start breathing fire as she clicked her pen on and off in little machine-gun bursts of fury.

'Let's try another example. Nick, maybe you want to start us off this time?' Dr Davis asked hopefully.

'Quiet for the Chief Swot,' grunted Frank.

'Oh shut up,' said Susie.

'Or maybe we should leave it there for the day,' said Dr Davis.

Frank was out of the door practically before he'd finished speaking.

Nick and Susie packed up in silence. Outside, Nick watched Susie stride off across North Court, then turned away to the p'lodge. It was only five o'clock but fog was starting to swirl across the cobblestones in Senate House Passage. King's Parade was dim and distant, the light from the lamp posts drained and pathetic. Although it wasn't raining, he was wet to the skin by the time he turned the corner into his street. The lights were on in the house, warm and welcoming.

He was halfway across the living room before he realised that Ange was curled up on the corner of the sofa. He turned, expecting to find her sleeping since she wasn't hugging him, but her eyes were open, reflecting the light spilling in from the hallway.

'Hey,' he whispered.

She turned in his direction, her eyes silver and staring. Then she seemed to shiver and uncurled herself. 'Hi, Nick.' The words came out soft and weary.

'Did I wake you?'

She shook her head.

'Are you . . . You're a bit . . . quiet.'

She grinned half-heartedly, shrugged. 'Can't live at a thousand miles per hour twenty-four/seven. My bounce is on standby. I'll be recharged and good to go again in twenty minutes.'

'Where's Tim? I mean, he must have let you in, right? He must know you're still here.'

'Yeah.' She looked away towards the stairs. 'I came over for lunch but now he's sulking. We had a . . . disagreement. If he doesn't come down in a bit, I'll go up to him. We both just need . . .' She made a vague gesture, then yawned hugely, stretching her arms out, a slow uncurl from shoulders to fingertips. 'Tim said you had Formal Swap tonight with your rowing people?'

'Yeah, I'd better get changed.' But he dithered for a moment.

Ange waved a hand at him. 'Don't mind me. I can see how you might think that quiet could indicate that I'm dying, but I promise not to expire anywhere on the premises.'

'Is it just an act?' he found himself asking, without meaning to. 'Sorry. Forget I said anything. You know I do that thing where I think I've said something in my head but I've actually said-said it.'

But Ange just shook her head. 'It's fine, Nickie. And, no, it's not an act. Or not exactly. I spend a lot of the time being the person I want to be. Maybe to begin with it was mostly act, but no one could say it's not a part of me now. No one's just one person. Most people think they should be, but it's just not how it works. As Tim says about me, "what you see is exactly what you get." What he should add is that it's by no means *all* you get. I do everything in extremes, whether I'm happy or sad: there's not much in between.'

'You really are quite like Professor Gosswin, aren't you?'

And for the first time that evening Ange smiled properly. 'That is a truly awesome compliment, Nickie. I'm getting there, but Professor Gosswin's had longer to practise being the ultimate her. Now,' she added, 'off you go and get changed before you're late for your dinner.'

By the time he came down again, the lights were on in the living room and Ange was lying on her front, staring up, wide-eyed, at an anime programme on TV. 'Look, Nickie! Pretty prettiness!'

He grinned and waved, but only got as far as pulling down his coat in the hall before she skipped over to hug him hard around the middle then ran back, giggling, to the TV.

'Tim, you've got a guest! Stop being a prat and come down and talk to her!' he yelled up the stairs before he swept the door closed.

In the hour since he'd walked away from KP (as the crew had instructed him to call King's Parade), the fog had settled over the town centre. As he hurried down Tennis Court Road, modern Cambridge became the London of Jack the Ripper: lamp posts looming out of the opaque grey air. People faded to shadows of themselves. Outlines were softened and distorted. The buildings seemed to ripple, though the pavement shone with thick black light and fleeting glimpses of crimson, like drying blood. The air tasted of iron.

Behind the high railings around Peterhouse, the windows glowed like far-off islands.

The crew were gathered in a dank stone anteroom by the doors to the dining hall, tugging awkwardly at the shoulders of their gowns as they waited for their hosts: the crew of the Peterhouse Men's Second VIII, who'd dined with them at the previous Trinity Hall Formal Hall for their part of the Formal Swap. Nick hadn't dared try his luck by joining them, but the crew were confident that he would slip through the net at Peterhouse, where the staff didn't know his age.

Nick caught the words 'Lents' and 'wooden spoon' as he approached. 'What's this?' he asked when the circle parted to make room for him.

'The Lent bumps.'

'What do spoons have to do with a boat race?' Nick asked, trying to resettle his gown on his shoulders, but the weight of the gathered semicircle of fabric kept pulling it backwards, off his shoulders.

'The idea of the bumps is to, well, bump the boat in front, right?' Brent said, rolling his eyes. 'If you bump, or get bumped, you don't have to "row over" and go the whole length of the course. If you bump on all four days, the whole crew gets blades – inscribed oars. But if you *get* bumped all four days, you get wooden spoons and everyone avoids you like the plague. So we need a plan for who we can definitely bump on at least one of the days.'

A butler in a smart black suit jacket, waistcoat and grey trousers came marching across the passage, shoes clicking on the stone. He pushed open an iron-reinforced door under a stone arch and the gathered crowd slowly filed into the hall.

On either side huge stained-glass windows were faded against the foggy night. Head-high burnished wood panelling with intricate mouldings rose into whitewashed stone and brick below a carved wood ceiling ribbed like the hold of a Tudor galleon. Stencilled decorations outlined the windows and filled in the walls between them. Two long dark wood tables stretched the length of the hall along the windows and down the centre. The wall of the other side was broken by a carved stone fireplace, with a half-length table to either side.

Benches lined the tables, with one grand chair at each end.

At the head of the hall, the panelling was hung with portraits of former College Masters. It reached nearly to the roof, giving way to a minstrels' gallery with a scroll and a fuzzy Latin inscription painted on the back wall. Below, a wooden dais was set a few inches above the rest of the tiled floor so that High Table could sit across the width of the room, as in Trinity Hall. In the daytime, the huge semicircular bay of windows at the end of High Table would spill light across the fellows and their guests. Now it was dewed with fog on the inside and out.

Nick filed down the length of one of the tables with the rest of the crew, staring at the precision-set silverware and crystal, a generosity of forks and spoons ranged about the royal blue tablemats. The bread plates were white with a dark border and the college crest at the centre. There were ornate square-bottomed silver candlesticks and tall, carefully folded linen napkins, and even college-crested salt and pepper shakers.

They'd only just clambered over their bench to sit when a gong sounded and everyone was standing once more, or at least trying to stand. One of the twins nearly tumbled backwards when Brent accidentally trapped the sleeve of his gown against the table. The butler fixed a dark look on them. Brent and the twins bundled the hanging tails of their gowns into their armpits and scrambled to their feet as Nick peered round them to watch the fellows process in to High Table.

The crew moved to sit again, only for the butler to cough as only a butler can cough.

One of the fellows adjusted his glasses and then started to drone his way through a Latin grace. The Peterhouse students echoed the 'Amen' and again the crew moved to sit. The butler coughed at them once more.

'Talk about putting the formal in Formal Hall,' Brent whispered to Nick. 'Thank God TitHall understands the point of Hall and puts the focus where it should be – on the booze.'

Another grace ensued. This time the crew waited to take their cue from their Peterhouse hosts, who promptly sat. The butler gave the Trinity Hall holdouts a haughty sniff and turned away.

'So what do you think of Formal Hall?' asked Brent an hour later as the waiting staff came round with coffee and College mints.

'You mean was having bad food passed over my shoulder, while grumpy old men glared down at us from the walls, everything I always hoped it would be?'

Brent laughed. 'I wonder what they had to eat on High Table. Bet it was better than the rest of us got.' A waiter appeared at his shoulder with the port. 'But this will make it up to me. Pour away!' he commanded, making an uncoordinated gesture a little like the royal wave that nearly knocked the decanter out of the waiter's hands. 'Oops.'

The waiter raised his eyes to the ceiling but poured him half a glass.

'Aw, don't be stingy with me,' Brent whined.

The waiter looked at the butler, then withdrew. Brent blew a raspberry at his back. The butler advanced three paces and Brent quickly turned back to the table.

'Duller than ditchwater. You wait till we can sneak you into a TitHall SuperHall. Now there's a party. Last time, we had call-outs. You know, where someone calls things out and anyone it applies to has to drink.' He giggled into his port for a moment. 'First one was who was going commando and that girl who looks a bit like Jessica Rabbit had to drink.' He giggled some more.

'Sounds like a blast,' Nick said unenthusiastically. 'What are you doing?'

Brent was peering around suspiciously. Seeing that the butler was occupied with the fellows, he grabbed his coffee cup and saucer and slipped the whole thing into an inner pocket of his suit jacket. 'Sh!' he whispered. 'Got a bet on with my mate. See who can get a full set of china from all the Colleges by the time we graduate. Gotta Formal Swap with all of them to make it happen. Like a treasure hunt.'

More like kleptomania, Nick mumbled into his coffee, trying to remind himself that this was fun: that twenty years from now he and the crew would meet up and they'd talk about this as the height of happiness. If only it felt like that now.

Chapter[11]

(Michaelmas Term × Week 8
[≈ end of November])

The neighbours' cat was curled on the fence again, green glare fixed on Nick as he sat at the kitchen table, wading through his last assignment of the term, having already finished writing up his scruffy notes from the last two lectures. He tried not to think about how he would fill the holidays with so much of his work already done.

At least it's better than the school holidays. He'd invariably spent those in the clinical emptiness of his father's law firm offices, sitting in deserted conference rooms, all slick black leather, white walls and abstract grey and blue prints. Working through his homework and coursework and anything extra he could find to keep himself busy was how he'd ended up so far ahead at school. 'Change the things you can,' he'd kept telling himself. Only work seemed to be the one thing he knew how to change.

Where books had been a comfort before at Roger's, at his dad's they had become a necessity, old books best of all: thick heavy tomes with stories that spread and twisted through other worlds, where he could walk like a ghost in the footsteps of other lives. The first holiday after he'd moved in with his dad, he'd fallen headlong into *Nicholas Nickleby*, letting the soft creased pages sweep the office away, replacing the cold chrome and plastic seats with a deep leather armchair beside a fire and, outside, a narrow cobbled street between wood and stone buildings. It had felt safer to ache for the characters' misery than his own. A clean sort of sadness instead of the sticky unpleasantness of self-pity.

'I thought you said you were going to get light bulbs?' Tim snapped, slamming into the kitchen and practically punching the kettle on.

Nick looked up from the mess of papers spread across the table. 'So glad to see you're in a good mood,' he snapped back.

'How many times do we have to have this conversation?' Tim slumped back against the counter, shading his eyes with a hand. 'Either we just agree that I do the shopping all the time or you actually *do* it when it's your turn.'

'I'll do it tomorrow, OK?'

'So I get to work in the dark tonight?'

'Just take a bulb from Dad's study.'

'And what if he decides to stay for the weekend after all, instead of going up first thing tomorrow?'

'When has he done that since you've moved in? Use the bulb from the hall for now.'

'So we can all fall over the mat when we get back later, after Gosswin's Christmas party?'

'Look, I've got to go out in a bit anyway. Dad asked me to pick up a present to take tonight. I'll get the light bulbs then.'

Tim sank into a chair with a sigh. 'Let's just do both on the walk down.' He slowly leaned forwards until he could rest his forehead against the table.

Nick grinned. 'So I guess you're not going to be able to enjoy all the free alcohol tonight.'

Tim turned his face to glare at Nick. 'You wait till you're old enough to drink.' He pushed himself up as the kettle growled to a boil.

'Hey!' Nick said, when Tim took his mug away to the sink.

'Nick, this tea is some hours cold and dead.' He swilled the dregs out and tossed in a fresh teabag. 'And as for tonight, here's a lesson for you: almost all good hangover cures have alcohol in them.'

'Please tell me you're going to get drunk in front of Gosswin.'

'I said I wanted to cure my hangover, not get myself defenestrated, thank you *very* much.' He thumped a fresh tea clumsily down on Nick's coaster then groaned. 'Please tell me you're not going to study every day during the holidays too.'

Nick cradled his tea between his hands, slurping a sip. 'What else would I do? Get a job? Oh, right. I'm *fifteen*. Or I suppose I could get drunk and then sit about all day, moaning.'

Tim, who'd pillowed his head on his arms, lifted one hand to flip him the finger.

'Do you know what I should get Gosswin from Dad? He's never very specific when he wants a present for someone. Usually Secretary Sandy takes care of it. I think he said to get some brandy or Scotch but—'

'You know they're not going to let you buy alcohol, right? If we walk down together instead of you haring off early for an hour in the library, you can pick something out and I'll be the responsible adult. Well, let's not stretch a point. I'll buy: you pay. And in return for my being totally magnanimous and even-tempered in the face of great provocation over the light-bulb situation, you will clear the laundry racks and do some of that ever-growing mountain by the machine. Or do I have to play nanny and start telling you that you're forbidden to do your homework until you've done your chores?'

'Give me a break. It's Dad's laundry.'

'Then tell him to do it. Come to that, why do you have to pick up Gosswin's present anyway? You going to start buying your own next?'

Nick shoved away from the table and poured the rest of his tea down the sink. 'What's wrong with helping out when he's so busy?' He stomped towards the stairs.

Tim dragged himself to his feet and started upstairs as Nick's door slammed above him. 'I am far, far too young to be even partially responsible for a teenager in full strop,' he told his bedroom door, resting his forehead against the wood for a moment while the stamping crescendoed in the attic. 'This was *not* part of the deal.'

Nick was toeing at the doormat when Tim came back down, pulling on his gloves and trying not to wince as his eyeballs protested the descent from one step to the next. Nick's face brightened considerably when he saw Tim's distress.

'You are a cold and unfeeling human being,' Tim told him.

'Why did you get so trashed anyway?' Nick asked.

'Tough week to forget, friend's birthday to celebrate. I would say you know how it is but—'

'Is it worth forgetting for an hour or two when you'll have even more time to remember the day after while you're feeling rough?'

'That,' said Tim, yanking Nick's hat down over his eyes, 'is an astute and grown-up question. Please refrain from wisdom while I am in this fragile state. And stop mocking me: my hangover is not that funny.'

'Says you,' Nick answered, hunkering down into his coat.

The pavement glinted like broken black glass, catching the light in sullen orange and vicious silver-white glints. Nick heaved a sigh of relief as he pushed his way into the warmth of the off-licence. He flinched out of the way as Tim moved him a step to the side so he could get past.

'Chill,' Tim said. 'I'm too cold to chuck you through a window.'

Nick made a sound that was probably meant to be a laugh, ducking away to prowl down the next aisle.

'Give me strength,' Tim whispered to the ceiling. 'And now I'm doing it too. I'm talking to myself, and the furniture and the walls. I bet Gosswin knew this would happen.'

'What are you mumbling about?' Nick asked, popping his head around the corner of the aisle. 'Aren't you always telling me it gets up your nose when I do it?'

'It does.' *Especially since you say all the important stuff under your breath*, Tim added, under his. 'Now, please, for the love of all that is good and decent in this world, Moderate Your Volume as you tell me how much your dad wants to spend.'

Nick shrugged. 'Doesn't matter.'

Well, it's all right for some, Tim muttered.

'Mumbler,' replied Nick.

'Pest!' groused Tim, picking a bottle off the shelf. 'Come on. This'll please her.'

Outside Tim shoved the bottle into Nick's arms. 'Your present, you carry.'

'Why are you *running*?' Nick panted, trotting to keep up. 'And why's it been such a bad week that you needed to blitz yourself? The coffee shop can't be that bad with Ange there, but you said you had a "tough week to forget". I know we're not best mates or anything, but what's the big secret?'

'Broke up with my girlfriend.'

'Oh. Sorry.' Nick frowned up at him for a few paces. 'Um ... I thought you broke up with your girlfriend weeks ago. Isn't that why Ange was cross with you the day you moved in? Or was there someone else and that *other* break-up was the reason for the argument you had that time I found Ange camped out on the sofa while you sulked upstairs?'

'Does my pointed silence not give you the sense that I'd rather not talk about it?'

'Sorry. Forgot we don't actually talk to each other. I'll stick to the snipe-and-banter.'

'I like the snipe-and-banter,' Tim said.

Nick looked up at him solemnly, no humour in his sharp little face. 'Don't you ever get tired of it?' he asked, then shouldered past Tim into the p'lodge before he could answer.

Tim caught up with him at the bottom of the stairs to Gosswin's rooms only for Nick to let go of the heavy wooden door before he was properly through it. At the top of the stairs, he snatched Nick's hat from his head so that his hair stood up in all directions, grinning beatifically at Nick's growl.

'Already torturing each other like feuding siblings, I see,' Professor Gosswin said, handing them each a glass of sherry.

'The very thought causes me physical pain,' groaned Tim.

'Back atcha,' Nick snarled. He held the bottle of brandy out to Professor Gosswin. 'From Dad.'

'And will your troublesome parent be gracing us with his presence?'

'Bill's bringing him ... Or not,' he added as Bill, but only Bill, appeared in the doorway and gave them an apologetic wave.

'Should you be having that?' Bill asked, eyeing the glass in Nick's hand.

Professor Gosswin fixed Bill with a look. 'One very small glass of College sherry is *de rigueur* for all my guests, Mr Morrison. Go and find one for yourself *forthwith*.'

Bill saluted.

'Tim's got a hangover. Make sure you speak loudly to him,' Nick told Gosswin, as he followed his godfather.

'Mr Morrison visits quite regularly, I hope,' Professor Gosswin said, watching Nick and Bill bickering amiably over the drinks table.

'He's been once since I moved in,' Tim said.

'I suppose it is a start. And how are you finding life in the Derran household?'

Tim shrugged. 'Michael's hardly there. Nick and I get on all right, I guess.'

Professor Gosswin's eyes narrowed.

'I mean,' Tim hurried on, 'Nick can be touchy, but we rub along. I know you hoped I'd develop some sort of weird big-brother complex and take him under my wing but I told you I'm not up for that. And it turns out he isn't either. He doesn't ask me for anything, and I don't boss him about. It seems to work. Anyway, Nick's hard to get to know: he says all the important stuff in mumbles.'

'He doesn't mumble with *me*,' Professor Gosswin said. 'Not only do I refuse to tolerate it, I have brought Mr Derran to understand that I want to hear what he has to say.'

'Look, it's complicated. I can't help knowing stuff Nick would rather I didn't. I see how much time he spends alone. I know that even when Michael is around, he scurries into his

137

study at the first available opportunity and barely emerges for meals – and even then he's more focused on his phone than talking to me or Nick. Nick's scarily patient with him: I know it's not how *I*'d be if my dad told me he was coming home for dinner then showed up three days later. I don't think it's that they feel I'm intruding on their family life.' He let the *because there's no family life to intrude on* remain unspoken, though something in Professor Gosswin's eyes told him she understood. 'Nick's . . . He's just so . . . composed. Self-reliant. I figured maybe he'd be a bit freaked out underneath it all about the burglary, though I haven't seen much sign of it. But there's always this tension, like a tight little spring. He's not exactly restful company.'

'He throws himself into his work too much,' Gosswin said softly, the tone bringing Tim up short. 'There needs to be something else in life for a boy that age. He needs a role model who does not spend every waking moment working.'

'You picked well with me.'

Gosswin gave him a pointed look. 'You, Mr Brethan, have a reasonable balance between your academic and social life.' Her eyes travelled past him.

Bill and Nick were laughing. There was colour in Nick's cheeks. He looked like a normal teenager.

'Now, Mr Brethan,' Professor Gosswin said sharply, 'you should go and speak with your former Director of Studies. He is lurking in my kitchen, devouring the olives. I have business with Mr Derran.'

Tim watched the dignified, upright figure stride through

the crowded room to stand next to Nick. They moved away to the window together. Gosswin took hold of Nick's arm to settle herself into an armchair, then he sank on to the footstool beside her.

'Thick as thieves. Would you believe it?' Bill asked, coming to stand next to Tim. 'Seems my godson has found a most unlikely kindred spirit.'

By the time the taxi dropped them back at the house after the party, it was past midnight. As they shed coats and scarves and hats and gloves and shoes in the hall, Tim realised that the house had never felt so much like a home. Watching Bill drape an arm over Nick's shoulders to propel him upstairs, laughing over his hiccups as he started to feel the effects of the second sherry Gosswin had slipped him, Tim had to wonder how often Bill wished he were Nick's father.

∞

'Hey, do you want to get an almost-end-of-term coffee?' Nick asked, as Frank closed the door on their last supervision of Term.

'Busy,' Frank grunted, pushing past.

Susie hitched her bag up, looking weary and frustrated. 'I'm sorry, Nick, but I'm skint. You won't believe how happy I am that it's the end of term. I just did the same as everyone else in Fresher's Week – you know, bops and Cindy's – and I didn't drink any more than they did, but I guess their parents are loaded because I burnt through most of my loan for the term by Week 3. Nearly had to go and ask for hardship money.'

Nick shrugged awkwardly. 'I could get this one.'

Susie smiled, reached out to pat his arm. 'That's sweet of you, Nick, but it wouldn't feel right.'

''Cos letting me buy you a coffee is practically the same as taking candy from a baby, got it,' Nick snapped, turning away.

'Nick . . .' he heard her call, before her voice trailed off into a sigh. 'Have a good Christmas!' she shouted just as the fire door slammed closed behind him.

It was sleeting across Front Court, the wind driving the icy rain under umbrellas. Nick didn't even bother with his. For a while he loitered under the arch by the p'lodge, watching the courtyard turn progressively greyer and dimmer, then hunched into his coat and hurried into the shelter of the corridor between the buttery and the dining hall, before lunging out again to hurtle around the path by Latham Lawn. He clattered through the doors into the library and up the wooden stairs. The cushioned window seats overlooking the river on the third floor were empty. He tossed his backpack and coat aside to drip on to the fuzzy squares of coarse carpet that captured dirt as if it were treasure. Shiny black patches of trodden filth shone under the lights.

An hour later it was time to meet the crew down by the boatsheds, though they kept their outing short, keen to head back to their rooms for a hot shower as soon as they'd packed away.

'See you for the Christmas party later,' Brent said, stretching with a groan.

'Are you sure the porters won't just chuck me out?'

Brent clapped him on the shoulder. 'Trust your captain, kid. I've got it covered.'

'You mean you'll wing it.'

'Well, it worked for the Formal Swap with Peterhouse: got you into *a* Formal Hall that way, didn't we, even if it wasn't at College. Besides, if they try to keep you out tonight, we can just decamp to my room, OK?'

Nick grinned. 'I'll hold you to that.'

But the barkeeper seemed willing enough to let Nick in, though he was presented, without being asked, with a series of lemonades while the others guzzled their way through an astonishing amount of 'College plonk', as Brent called it.

'You OK, Nick?' one of the twins asked, leaning against his shoulder.

'Brilliant,' he lied.

'I'm sad,' the twin confided, sniffing despondently. 'I'm not sure why, but I'm very, very sad.'

Nick tried patting him on the shoulder. This made the twin tear up. 'Be right back,' Nick said, slipping out of his chair.

'You going to the bog? Gonna come too, like girls, always going in pairs.' The twin giggled to himself for a moment before the giggles became hiccupy.

Although Nick locked himself in a cubicle, when he emerged the twin was waiting for him, slumped against the wall, using the hand dryer for support.

'It's all just so . . .' The twin took a shuddering breath. 'It'll all be gone soon. We'll be *old*. Then we'll be *dead*.'

Nick slipped away while the twin had his face hidden in his hands. 'Your brother's in the loos. He's a little . . . morose,' he reported to the other twin, who just shrugged.

'Always happens,' Brent said. 'Be in there for hours. You know, that's going to be a problem,' he added thoughtfully. 'Need to have a slash.' He made a face. 'Last time he was like this, he cornered me against the sinks and told me about every girl who ever turned him down. Hugged me every time I tried to get past him, then threatened to cook himself to death with the hand-dryer if I didn't promise to help him find a date by Valentine's Day. I can't face it again. Can't you get him out?' he appealed to the other twin.

'Nope. Not his keeper.'

'Suppose I could try the girls' loo,' Brent said dismally, then suddenly brightened. 'Always wanted to see what it looked like in there. Yup. Going on an adventure to the girls' loo!' he announced to much cheering from the rest of the crew.

Brent processed proudly down the corridor with the rest following. In front of the door to the ladies', he turned and saluted his men then marched inside. The crew held their breath. A few seconds later, he came back through the door, pursued by two petite girls with worryingly determined looks on their faces.

'Busted,' Brent said. 'But you're welcome to punish me,' he told the girls.

One pushed him on to a barstool. 'You will sit there.'

'Anything for you,' he said soulfully, staring blearily at her left eyebrow.

For a while they clustered around him, digging in their handbags, soon joined by a chattering posse. Five minutes later they stepped back and presented Brent with a mirror.

He squinted at his face. 'I make a *hot* girl. But I'd have gone with the glitter purple not the blue,' he added, poking at the eyeshadow compacts laid out on the bar counter. 'Whatcha say, boys? Who wants a snog with your captain?'

He spent the next five minutes chasing the non-crying twin around the bar, until the barkeeper chucked them out just in time for both to throw up in a Front Court window-box. Nick used the opportunity to slip away.

In Trinity Lane, he turned down towards Clare, wandering to the gates into King's so that he could watch the light moving behind the stone tracery around the Old Schools windows. It didn't look real. The intensity of the colours, the beauty of the shadowy buildings made it seem like something computer-generated: stronger, better, more vivid than the real world ever was. The cobbles were indigo and bronze under the lights, shining with the ground mist that crept up the lawns behind King's Chapel from the river. He watched the windows again as he walked back the way he'd come, then turned away up Senate House Passage.

Every step seemed to turn the world more ordinary, more real, comforting and sad at the same time, like he'd turned his back on the impossible because he didn't have the courage to hold his ground.

He yawned his way into the kitchen a little after midnight to find that Tim had covered the table with paperwork and was sitting, elbows braced against the wood, with his head in his hands. 'Does getting drunk with people make you understand them better?' he asked.

'What?' Tim looked up, shook his head. 'No. Why would it?'

'Everyone had a blast tonight except me. Either there were a bunch of in-jokes going on or I missed what was funny. Or maybe I am the most boring bookworm the world's ever known and I really don't know fun even when it's puking on my shoes.' Nick slumped into a chair, then got up again when he saw a flash of frustration cross Tim's face. 'Oh, don't sulk. I'm not after a midnight heart-to-heart. I'll go up as soon as the kettle boils: you only have to put up with me for the next two minutes.'

'Did I say anything?' Tim asked mildly.

Nick looked away. He kicked lazily at a table leg. 'Just . . . why does anyone bother? By the morning surely you know that you only had a good time because you were drunk. There's no conversation to remember. There's nothing interesting or important or . . . It's just so *pointless*.'

'The boatie scene not all it's cracked up to be?'

Nick shrugged. 'I thought I'd feel happier knowing I had people to go out with. People who didn't just have me there on sufferance. But for that type of stuff aren't people pretty much interchangeable? Can you really build a friendship on the fact that you happened to be one of the people there when

Brent stormed the girls' loo? I just watched. It wouldn't have made any difference if I wasn't there.'

Tim grinned. 'You are not getting me to say that I think you should storm the girls' loos yourself next time.'

But Nick didn't smile like a normal person would have. He just fixed Tim with that strange solemn expression and let the silence grow thick and awkward, as if he were waiting for something while the kettle fizzed to a boil in the background.

Chapter[12]

(Christmas Vacation
[≈ start of December])

With Tim working double shifts at the coffee shop, the house was too quiet. Maybe it was some lingering uneasiness after the burglary, though he knew the chances of a repeat were minimal, but Nick found he'd got used to having another living, breathing presence around: someone to talk to now and then, even if it was just to say 'How about a cup of tea?'

For a while he occupied himself looking up Shakespearean insults to use on the boat club. Neither 'fustilarian maltworm' nor 'flagitious giglet' exactly ran off the tongue, but short of resorting to Latin nothing else seemed quite impressive enough. But there were only so many webpages on esoteric insults with genuinely original material and soon his laughter sounded forced even to his own ears.

Turning on the TV for the sound of another voice only made him feel more alone: talking to himself seemed strange and unnatural after a month where his words weren't just falling on empty air. It had surprised him how much he'd enjoyed sharing his space: how far that went towards making the world seem more real, less distant.

With a sigh, he packed up his work and set off for the library, but detoured at the last moment into Clare to stand on the white stone bridge under the glorious copper beech, beautiful even naked of leaves. On the left, on the far side of the river, King's College meadow was pale primrose in the cold sunlight, the weeping willow blue-white with frost, trailing into an iron river between silver banks. The dried leaves of the beech hedge that edged the Fellows' Garden rattled in the wind. The shadowed flagstones were treacherous with ice, the air sharp as salt.

To the right, he could see Trinity Hall's library jutting out over the river, all raw red brick and tall glass windows. He'd been standing just here, the day of his interview, when he'd decided that he absolutely had to go to Cambridge.

And now here he was. And there *it* was. *My College*, he breathed.

Ten minutes later, he was looking out of one of the windows he'd watched from the bridge. Only he seemed to be just as alone here. No other silent students labouring over their notes. No quiet camaraderie. *If even Cambridge students don't spend their holidays in the library . . .* The words caught awkwardly in the air, seemed to hang there, mocking him. His skin prickled with embarrassment though there was no one to see, no one to hear. Sighing, he scooped his books back into his bag and hurried around Latham Lawn to Dr Gosswin's staircase. Arriving half an hour early for an appointment with the Professor was inviting an argument, but better that than the slippery, shivery emptiness of the library. Yet all she said when he knocked, then popped his head around her door was, 'You're early. Good. You can make me coffee now.'

There was something comforting about being able to move around her gyp room almost without thought. It was nice to know a space that wasn't his so intimately: to know exactly how to make her coffee. Apart from his dad, Tim and Bill, he didn't know how anyone else in the world took their coffee. It seemed somehow like a failure.

'For someone with such poor social graces it is incomprehensible that you should adopt such a relaxed and comfortable demeanour in my presence,' she told him, when he brought the coffee tray in. 'You have yet to attain the elevated position that would afford you the impunity to be irascible that is *my* due.'

'My supervisor's been telling tales, hasn't he?' Nick threw himself back in his chair. 'So I got a little frustrated last week about this extra activity graphing a transformation. I figured out how to get the right answer, but I didn't really *get* it. I'm never going to get a First if I don't understand what I'm doing, and my supervisor wasn't going to explain it because stupid Frank couldn't even do the basic bit of the problem. If teachers can't focus on the difficult stuff at uni because they've always got to focus on the stupid people, when can they?'

Professor Gosswin steepled her fingers. 'Your life would

be easier, Mr Derran, if you didn't categorise the majority of other people as stupid.'

'But they are—'

'They are more stupid than you, yes. Most of the world is more stupid than you. I can sympathise with your frustrations, Mr Derran, without thinking you are doing yourself any favours in the manner in which you choose to tackle these frustrations in front of your peers.'

Nick clenched his hands on the arms of his chair. 'Why am I not allowed to get frustrated? Susie *cried* in our last supervision and she just got a pat on the back. Frank spends half the time swearing and he just gets a laugh. Why is it a problem when *I* show how I feel? Why is it any less important that I'm frustrated just 'cos I'm frustrated at a higher level than they are? I'm not doing it to make them feel bad, so why do I have to be understanding about the fact that they're not being stupid to annoy me?'

'And what did your father say when you talked to him about this?'

'He said I've got as much right to learn as they do.'

'And that "standards have gone down and those who can't keep up should find themselves another university to study at", I dare say.' She shook her head.

Nick looked away to the window and shrugged.

'You will use *words*, Mr Derran, to reply to my questions. You must refrain from this louche and unpleasant habit of raising a shoulder by way of response. It is a most imprecise form of communication.'

Nick scowled at her.

'The glare at least is unambiguous,' she conceded.

'Everyone keeps waiting for me to run up against something I'm not clever enough for. They keep saying it gets harder and if there's already stuff I can't do—'

'If your supervision partners are likely to pass with at least a Third or, at worst, an Ordinary, what are you likely to pass with, Mr Derran?'

'My dad says that a First from Cambridge will open doors for the rest of my life.'

Professor Gosswin sat back in her chair. 'And so it will. But then, Mr Derran, I dare say your intellect will do much the same, to much the same degree – especially if you could learn to be somewhat less of a challenge on a personal level.'

'Some people like a challenge,' Nick grumbled, sitting forward to reset the chessboard for a new game.

'But *most* people like a quiet, easy life, Mr Derran. My life would have been quite different if I had been willing to concede that point.'

Nick looked up at her. 'You're not sorry you didn't.'

Professor Gosswin's eyes brightened. 'Only sometimes.' She cleared her throat, waving her hand at the board. 'Leave this and fetch me another cup of coffee, you inconsiderate boy.'

'Isn't it a bit late for you to have so much caffeine?'

Professor Gosswin rolled her lip up in a sneer that showed her crooked left incisor: a sign of certain danger. 'When I am ready for a nursemaid I shall *not* offer you the job.'

By the time Nick came back with the replenished coffee tray, Professor Gosswin was standing by the window, looking out over Latham Lawn to the roofs of Clare and the spires of King's Chapel. She turned slowly, gesturing at a brown-paper package on the chessboard. 'Something to occupy yourself with over Christmas,' she said dismissively. 'Now pour the coffee.'

Nick did as he was told as she settled back into her chair, then sat turning the book – because it could only be a book – over in his hands.

'It is not a watch, Mr Derran. It does not need to be tossed or wound in order to work. Put it in your bag and stop fussing at it.'

Nick pushed up from his chair then stopped and turned back. 'Thank you,' he told the floor by her right foot. 'You didn't have to.'

'Of course I didn't. Why do you always persist in telling me that I *don't* have to do things, when I am perfectly well aware of that fact?' She shook her head. 'Now, return to your seat so I can trounce you once again.' She turned the board to take the white pieces and advanced a pawn.

Nick picked a pawn at random.

Gosswin slapped his hand away from the board and moved a different piece for him. 'Think, Mr Derran, *think*. You cannot blunder blindly on to the board and expect fate to guide you silently to victory.'

'Well, nothing else is working.'

'Perseverance, Mr Derran. Chess is a game played between

people. And all things between people that are of any worth require perseverance.'

Nick sighed as she slammed a knight down for her turn.

'People sometimes do not learn as fast as they should, nor indeed as fast as they need. But sometimes we have to accept that there are types of learning that cannot be rushed. It's a difficult lesson for those of us who are usually quick on the uptake,' she added wryly. 'There are things I think I am only just starting to learn now, when it is almost too late for them to be useful. On which note, is your godfather joining you for Christmas?'

'Yeah, but how's that related?'

'And Mr Brethan. What are his plans?'

'I haven't asked.'

Professor Gosswin heaved a sigh of great forbearance. 'Then maybe you should,' she said.

∞

The book lay open across his knees, glowing as if even the cover were gilded in the last of the sunlight spilling between the houses opposite. A group of kids raced past, yelling and laughing, piling up the front path of one of the neighbouring houses and through the front door. A group of teenagers sauntered in the opposite direction, pulling faces and looking disdainful.

'Whatcha reading?'

Nick started, nearly dropping his book as he jolted

upright. Tim was slouched in the doorway, looking unshaven and shadow-eyed.

Nick's hands pressed the book protectively to his chest. 'Something Professor Gosswin gave me . . . to read.'

Tim shrugged. 'I didn't think you were going to play tennis with it.'

Nick grinned. 'It's . . . Well, it's a good book, but it's less about the content and more . . . I guess you could say there's another meaning to it.'

'Ah, a mystery. Fair enough then.' Tim let his satchel drop to the floor. 'Coffee?' he called, as he loped through to the kitchen.

'You OK?' Nick asked, coming to lean in the doorway.

Tim shrugged. 'Why?'

'You look,' he made a vague gesture in the air, 'disreputable.'

Tim laughed, though there was something brittle about the sound. 'Sounds about right.'

'I thought you were going to see Ange.'

'I was.'

'She stood you up?'

'Nope.'

'Did she tell you off about a girl?'

Tim gave him an aggrieved look.

'What?' Nick raised his hands. 'You don't tend to upset her in any other way. So what did you do?'

'Just leave it alone, Nick.'

Nick watched him splat a teabag on to the floor then

slosh milk across the counter, cursing as he grabbed a cloth to clean up the mess. 'Anyway, I've been meaning to ask what you're up to for Christmas: when you're going to see your family—'

Tim hunched over the counter. 'When do you want me to go?'

'What do you mean?'

'When do you want me to clear out?' Tim snapped.

'Hey, I was just asking—'

'You tell me the dates I should be gone, and I'll go.'

'I know you said to leave it alone,' Nick snapped back, 'but I thought you meant your fight with Ange, not *all* topics of conversation.'

'It's not . . . Look, just tell me what you want me to do and I'll do it.'

Nick raised his hands in a helpless shrug. 'I don't want you to do *anything*, except not yell at me for nothing. I was just asking about your plans. If you're going to be here it would be good to know. I mean, we don't have anything special planned but I guess if there's something particular you like for Christmas dinner we should order it or find where we can buy it, or,' he wrinkled his nose, 'I *suppose* we could find a recipe.'

Tim's face did something so odd that Nick wondered if perhaps that was how he looked when people said he went blank and remote. 'But you must want some time . . . I mean, family time.'

Nick peered into his mug as if checking it was clean,

rubbed at a mark on the rim. 'Bill will be here, but you like him, right? He's coming on Christmas Eve and going to his sister's on Boxing Day. Some years we go to his but Dad thought it would be fun to do Christmas in Cambridge this year. Not that we do much: play board games, watch films. Well, mostly Bill and I do that and Dad creeps off to work till Bill fetches him back. It's kind of like you'd expect: not terribly jolly but ... I just assumed you'd want to go and see your parents.'

Tim snorted. 'That wouldn't be jolly at all. They ... They died the summer before I came to uni.' He cleared his throat, looking away, but Nick stayed silent, staring at him. 'I thought Gosswin might have said.' He cleared his throat again. 'Anyway, no aunts or uncles, no grandparents. My sister's in America. I'm going out just after Easter for her wedding but no way does my budget stretch to a transatlantic Christmas as well. The plan *was* to go to my girlfriend's and then I thought maybe Ange might invite me but ...' He cut himself off, clenched his jaw for a moment. 'If you're really sure you don't mind me being here, I can stay in my room whenever you want, or go out for a bit ...' He turned only to jump when he found Nick standing next to him, hand raised as if about to touch his arm.

Nick jerked back. Then he glanced up with an oddly shy smile. 'You're more than welcome, Tim. You don't have to go anywhere, even your room, unless you want to. I mean, you'll probably want to but,' a deep breath, 'just so you know you don't have to.'

Tim nodded awkwardly.

Nick turned away to fiddle with the kettle switch, cheeks pink. 'So ... so if you're staying and all, *is* there anything special you want? Like ... um ... Brussels sprouts or ...'

Tim burst out laughing. 'I do *not* want Brussels sprouts.'

'Good. We've never figured out how to cook them properly. They always turn into grey mush. Even the ones that are pre-prepared from those "extra nice, extra expensive" food ranges. We don't, er, really cook, of course. Unless you count nuking leftovers.'

Tim laughed as he was supposed to. 'So how about you? Any aunts or grandparents to visit?'

Nick shook his head, applying himself to making a fresh pot of coffee. 'Nope. My ... my grandmother died before I came to live with Dad, and his parents died before I was born. He's got a brother in the States but we never see him.'

'How about your mum?'

Nick looked away to the window, just as Tim had. 'She's dead too.'

Tim drew in a sharp breath. 'God, no one said: no one told me. I'm *sorry*, Nick. I had no idea.'

Nick shrugged. 'I didn't know about your parents.'

'Why didn't Gosswin ...' He broke off with a sigh.

'I keep asking Dad if we can go and visit the grave,' Nick said quietly. 'Do you do that? Visit, I mean?'

Tim leaned back against the counter, crossing one foot slowly over the other. 'They wanted to be cremated and have their ashes tossed out to sea down where we used to holiday in

156

Cornwall, but I haven't been back since. There doesn't seem much point without anything specific to visit.'

Nick nodded, fixing his eyes on the floor, then they both just stood there, drinking their coffee in silence.

Chapter[13]

(Christmas Day = 25 × December [even in Cambridge])

The windows were fogged up from the inside with air that smelt of spice and burnt sugar. The coffee table was awash with dirty plates. Nick curled himself into the corner of the sofa opposite Tim, smiling lazily at Bill and Michael as they sprawled in the armchairs, sleepy with too much food and brandy.

'Well, this is a nice turn-up for the books,' Bill said, around a yawn. 'None of the food ruined or turned to sludge, and no complaints from Nick about being bored with his academic work. A toast to Cambridge, and the new generation.' He inclined his head to Nick then Tim.

Tim coloured and mumbled something incomprehensible as he set about gathering up the dirty dessert plates.

'I may have to institute a house rule against muttering, since it seems to be infectious,' Michael said with a touch too much cheer.

With a sigh, Nick pushed up from the sofa and grabbed the cream and brandy butter to take through to the kitchen.

'Don't abandon us for Tim just yet,' said Bill, catching his arm and tugging until he sank back down. 'Though I'm glad to see it's working out so well with him living here.'

'It's in his best interest, isn't it, to make nice?' Michael said. 'Not such a high price for free accommodation. *Including* over Christmas.'

Bill frowned at him, noting Nick's wince. 'Given how much of today you've spent with the rest of us, versus on the phone in your study, I really don't see you've got much cause for complaint, Mike.'

'And Tim's done more than his fair share of the cooking and the clearing up,' Nick put in quietly.

Michael grunted.

Bill rolled his eyes. 'Oh, give the hard-done-by act a rest, Mike. Come on. I'll go and give Tim a hand while you and Nick pick out a board game. Derrans versus all challengers.'

'I think Monopoly,' Michael said as Nick took their stack of games out of the cupboard.

'Are you sure we should be giving Nick any ideas about world domination?' Tim asked, settling on to the sofa again.

'Talking of domination, you didn't tell me what you got on your last assignment, Nick,' Michael said, putting the racing car on the first square.

'Give or take an alpha,' Nick muttered, taking the cat for himself.

'What does that mean?'

'A II.1. I couldn't do this graph thing.'

'Have you figured it out now?'

Nick shrugged. 'I think maybe it's something you can either do or not. Susie couldn't do the problem, but she *aced* the graph. She said she could just see it in her head.'

'Ah, an idiot savant.'

'She's not an idiot, Dad,' Nick said quietly. 'She's kind of . . . impressive when she isn't crying.'

'She cries in lectures?'

'Mostly in supervisions. And it's not my fault, before anyone says anything.'

Bill and Tim both held up their hands.

'Why would it be your fault?' Michael asked.

'My supervisor says I'm not very sensitive to the fact that there's a lot of stuff I find easier than the others.'

'Well, you can't help being a genius. And why would you want to?'

Nick sighed. 'I'm *not* a genius, Dad. And actually I don't know that I *do* find it easier. I think I just work harder. Well, harder than Frank anyway. He never seems to do *anything*. Susie's not lazy but I still do at least double what she does so—'

'So why shouldn't you show what hard work *and* brains can achieve?' Michael interrupted.

Nick shrugged again, turning his attention to tidying up the Monopoly bank.

'Well, a II.1's not so bad,' said Michael. 'And at least you've finally got your supervisor to actually give class marks.'

'I tried to get a rough percentage out of him, but he went all sorrowful.'

Michael threw up his hands. '*Sorrowful*? In our day … Well, you've met Gosswin. Cambridge is a place for Gosswins and people like us. People who don't need to be … *cuddled* through life.'

'I think it's "coddled", Mike. Maybe we've done enough damage to the brandy for one day,' put in Bill, swapping Michael's glass for a coffee cup.

'Give that back, Morrison. I said "cuddled" and I meant "cuddled". This is a stage of ridiculousness beyond coddling. When did students get so precious about their feelings? I can't remember anyone caring a hoot for mine – or anyone else's – when we were undergrads. The way I remember it, the fellows had a hearty disdain for the vile little worms interrupting their research and their drinking with a need for lectures and supervisions. Don't you remember when we were up, Bill? People used to keep their lights and music on all night to kid others into thinking they were studying twenty-four/seven, whereas really they were sleeping with earplugs and eye-masks on.'

'Really?' asked Tim, grinning. 'People *did* that?'

'Certain people did,' said Bill pointedly.

Tim tipped Michael an imaginary hat. 'That is clever, sneaky and cruel all in one. I quite like it.'

'Maybe you can find a tutor for this graph stuff, Nick,' Michael said, dealing out the property cards as Bill dithered over the tokens.

'I'll read some more over the holidays. See if I can work it out.'

Michael smiled, clapping him on the back. 'Guess it would be a pity to let First Term work beat you after all those years complaining how bored you were at school.'

'That is quite enough work talk for Christmas Day,' Bill said. 'I suspect I am a Scottie dog rather than a top hat,' he added mournfully. 'How do you classify yourself, Tim?'

'Old boot. I'm surprised you're not a battleship, Nick.'

'Why're you an old boot? Because you're single and stuck with us rather than some girl you didn't like?'

'Who says I didn't like her?'

Nick gave him a look. 'Ange said you were only going out with her for a Christmas invite. This', he made a gesture at the room, 'has to be better than that.'

'You mean you give me a higher-quality hard time than she would've?'

The doorbell rang before Nick could reply. 'I'll get it,' he said, trotting through to the hall. He opened the door expecting carollers only to find Ange on the mat.

'Nickie! Merry Christmas!' she shouted, throwing her arms around him. 'I won't stay and interrupt, really I won't. I just popped over from Mum's – she's in the Shelfords so just up the road – but here.' She rummaged in her bag, frowned, rummaged some more. 'Where . . . Here we are!' She pulled a violently purple scarf out of her handbag and flung it around his neck. 'All the best boys wear purple.'

'If you say so.'

'I do: I very do! And I made it so it's extra-specially purple.'

'I didn't know—'

'That we were doing presents? Of course not, Nickie. That's not the point. Just wear it and stay warm and that will be lovely.'

Nick grinned shyly at her. 'Shall I get Tim?'

'Tim's here.'

Nick turned to see him slouching in the doorway, but he was frowning rather than smiling.

'Merry Christmas,' Ange whispered. 'I brought you a present.'

'Merry Christmas,' Tim echoed, but his tone put an edge on the words.

Ange sighed. 'Don't be like that.' She held up her hand when he opened his mouth. 'This is exactly why it wouldn't have worked. Don't ruin us, Tim. We're good enough as we are. Just be grateful for that.'

Nick hunched into the depths of Ange's scarf, wishing he could dig himself down into the floor.

Tim sighed, then stepped around him. When Nick dared to look up, Ange was standing in Tim's arms, eyes the wrong type of bright. As Nick slipped away, he saw Tim's face turn so he could press a kiss to her hair.

Chapter[14]

(Christmas Vacation
[≈ first week of January])

'I don't suppose you could make your New Year's resolution something to do with giving up the whole torture-by-chess routine?' Nick whined as Professor Gosswin pressed his king's face into the board with unnecessary relish.

'While there are things about the past I would be overjoyed to change, my present life is almost entirely to my satisfaction. Though I suppose it is incumbent upon me to consider the lives of others.' She nodded. 'My resolution is to meddle more frequently and to a greater extent.' She gave Nick a beatific smile. 'So, Mr Derran. What are your goals?'

'A starred First?'

Professor Gosswin glared at him. 'If that is the sum and total of your goals for the year, I shall be disappointed in both your ambition and your imagination.'

Nick rubbed at his forehead. 'The usual, I guess,' he

said, pushing up from his chair and wandering over to the window. 'Friends. To get on better with my dad.' He shrugged. 'I'm not sure how to change those things, but if I work hard enough, I probably *will* get a First. Seems like a good move to focus on the thing that's definitely achievable. I mean, I'm always going to be difficult and prickly and different, but I'm not always going to be young: even if I'm never quite in step with other people age-wise, it won't matter so much once I'm an adult. And if I've used the time to get myself a really good degree from Cambridge, it's not exactly wasted, is it? Even if I do have to just tread water about all the other stuff I want.'

'It's certainly the easy option.'

Nick turned away from the window, frowning. 'What's easy about working hard?'

'Exactly as you said, Mr Derran: there is a clear connection between effort and marks – at least for people with your intelligence. There isn't a formula for achieving the other things you want. Now, I'll grant that you have taken steps to remedy your loneliness, but you do not give it your full attention.'

Nick turned his back on her. 'And what else should I be doing? You can't make other people change. You can't make them like you. And it's not like you can just manufacture family members when you're short of a few.'

'When you do not have a traditional family life, you must either do without or find yourself a non-traditional one.'

'Because that's so easy to do,' Nick sneered. 'There are bits of family lying around everywhere. Or maybe there's a mix you can buy in the supermarket.' He snapped his mouth shut, raised his arms in front of his face, rubbing the heels of his hands against his forehead. 'That's not ... I know you ... It doesn't mean I don't love the book. It's ... It means ... What you said in the inscription ...'

He jumped when he felt a touch on his arm, looked down to see Professor Gosswin's hand on his wrist. She squeezed once and then sat back in her chair, shaking her head at him. 'You can waste your life grieving for the family and friends you wish fate had set before you as a child, or you can focus on the fact that as an adult – or a near-adult in your case – you may choose what to set before yourself. Now,' Professor Gosswin said, her tone businesslike once more, 'tell me about the first Brethan–Derran–Morrison Christmas.'

Nick shrugged, shifting uncomfortably in his chair. 'Tim cooked a lot. He insisted on doing all the washing up. It was a bit weird actually.'

'I imagine he was grateful.'

Nick tilted his head. 'Maybe.' He sighed, fidgeting with a loose thread in his sleeve.

'Yes, Mr Derran? In what way did Mr Brethan seem ungrateful?'

Nick shook his head. 'Not that.' A deep breath. 'I asked my dad if we could visit Mum. Her grave, I mean. He said maybe. But then one day it was too rainy. And one day he was busy ... It's her birthday soon and ... Well, I suppose I could go by myself. I'd have to get a taxi – there's no train station nearby – but Dad would probably be happy enough to pay so long as he didn't have to be there.'

'Which of course is the least important consideration,' Professor Gosswin said. 'If I were you, perish the thought, I would ask Michael outright, while', she continued, talking over Nick's attempt to protest that he'd tried, 'Mr Morrison was present.'

'Oh.' Nick sat back in his chair. 'I'll do that.'

'Of course you will, stupid boy! Why else would I have suggested it?'

Nick grinned.

'And stop that inane smirking. Next minute you'll be trying to kiss my cheek.'

Nick blinked. 'Would you like me to?'

'The thought fills me with equal parts horror and revulsion. Go away *instantly*. What did I do', she asked her ceiling, 'to be saddled with this impertinent creature who refuses to quail or grovel?'

'Mostly you remind me of my grandmother.'

Professor Gosswin turned purple with outrage. 'In what possible way', she bit out, 'do I seem *grandmotherly* to you? I am the wolf who *ate* Grandma.'

'Exactly,' said Nick. 'That's exactly what my grandmother was like. Only I knew what she meant.'

'And what do you believe that I mean?'

Nick coughed, fiddled with his watch strap, eyes on the ground. 'About earlier, I didn't mean it like it sounded. Your gift. The book you gave me ... I ... I think so too. I mean, the inscriptions ...'

Professor Gosswin took a sharp little breath, refusing to meet his eyes. 'You're welcome, Nick,' she said. 'It was time for it to have a new home. Somewhere it could do further good. It has given me everything it can and there is nothing I need the pages for now that my memory can't supply. It is a good place for it to belong.'

Nick swallowed, nodded. 'I ... just ... Thank you. It ... Thank you.'

'Yes, you've said that, Mr Derran. You know how I feel about people repeating themselves.'

Nick grinned, pushing himself to his feet. 'See ya,' he called over his shoulder, as he ducked out into the hall.

'*What* did you say to me?'

Nick hunched his shoulders and sidled back into the room, then darted forward and kissed her cheek.

Her bellow of outrage followed him down the stairs and round the curve of Latham Lawn.

Chapter[15]

(Lent Term × Week 1
[≈ third week of January])

'Winner is TitHall Men's Third,' the guy in charge of the quiz announced into the first true hush of the evening.

Nick flinched as Brent sprang to his feet, bellowing in triumph. He leaned away only to be rocked back into his seat as Brent gripped his shoulders and shook him.

'Bossy and brainy! TitHall *rules*!' he yelled. 'Our cox beats your cox on and off the water!'

The crew struck up a chant of 'Free round, free round' and suddenly Nick found a beer in one hand and a shot glass in the other.

'Why is the St John's Boat Club called Lady Margaret anyway?' Nick shouted over the roar of noise.

'No idea,' Brent said, clapping him on the back. 'Bottoms up—'

'Boat race!' someone from the other team yelled and

suddenly everyone was standing in a line, tipping back their shots like an alcoholic stadium wave. Squeezing his eyes shut, Nick threw the liquid into his mouth. For a moment, everything was fine, then he was doubled over, coughing and hacking, eyes watering. The others were stomping and dancing around him, jeering at the other quiz team, whose battle cry of 'Olly, olly, Lady Maggie' trailed off dismally as they realised they'd already lost.

'Three NOTHING!' came the roar from his teammates.

Sniffing and wiping his eyes on his sleeve, Nick sighed and took a sip of his beer, then another. It soothed the burning in his throat.

'Ha! We are *unstoppable*!' Brent cried, throwing himself on to his stool and nearly off the other side. 'Oops,' he said, steadying himself by casting an arm over Nick's shoulders. 'So, shortstuff, I thought you were a maths genius. Where did all that stuff come from about Shakespeare? *How* do you know about *Jane Austen*?'

Nick shrugged. 'I like to read.' He took another sip of his beer. 'I wanted to do English but they wouldn't let me. Said you need more "life experience" to be able to truly understand literature.'

Brent pulled a face. 'What do they know? You were, like, on fire, my man. Gee-Nee-Oous!'

'I'm not a genius.'

Brent didn't listen. 'Here,' he said, thrusting another shot glass into Nick's hand. 'S'only fair you get to enjoy your share of our winnings from LOSERS, LOSERS, TRIPLE LOSERS,' he yelled at the other team.

Nick squeezed his eyes shut as the shouting started all over again.

'Come on. Knock that back,' said Brent. As Nick put the glass tentatively to his lips, Brent tipped it upright for him, then snatched it away, slamming it down on the table and pounding happily on Nick's back while he coughed and gasped. 'Here you go,' he said, passing Nick's beer back to him.

'I think I've had enough.' He took a sip of the beer then tried to push the glass away, only for Brent to press it into his hands again.

'Aw, don't be a *spoilsport*. Live a little! Come on. Won't do you any harm. I was getting trashed Friday to Sunday like clockwork at your age. We're not in College. No one who cares is here to see. Just enjoy it!'

Nick laughed as Brent chinked glasses with him. He took a deeper swallow of his beer, then clattered the glass awkwardly down on to the table. Brent clapped him on the shoulder.

By the time they piled out of the pub, the floor had started rocking gently, as if they'd put out on the river. Although Nick found he could make out barely two words in five amid the roar of voices, everything everyone said had become extremely funny. Once they were all assembled on the pavement, they turned as a pack and staggered back towards College. The others were singing, or at least loudly slurring, a song Nick couldn't have hoped to recognise. But since none of them seemed all too sure of the words, or the tune either, Nick just recited the bit of 'Kubla Khan' that came to mind and the others seemed content with that as a counterpoint.

'Boaties rule!' Brent shouted at the sky. 'Best days of our lives, lads. Best days.'

'Best *nights*,' someone else called.

'Like you could get it up right now,' said one of the twins, whom the crew had tacitly given up trying to tell apart.

For a moment all progress ceased as they clung to each other, giggling.

'Go on. I dare ya,' Brent said to the other twin.

'Watch this then!' shouted the twin and took off running straight at a lamp post. He launched himself into the air and clung on about two metres up, then pulled his scrabbling feet on to the base of the post. With a grunt, he leapt upwards, clinging briefly a half metre higher before he slid slowly back down, legs folding helplessly so that he ended up sitting on the pavement, arms and legs hugging the post.

The others roared with laughter while the twin righted himself with great dignity. 'Thassh five rounds to you, mate, 'lesh you can get higher.'

'You said you'd climb it!'

'You're too sssshicken to even try. I win 'lesh you try. You're just sssshicken. Sssshickened out in the pub crawl in Freshersh Week. Got no balls. Got a tiny little dick. Afraid everyonesh gonna see.'

'Yeah? You think so? Double or nothing. Starkers from here to Trinity Lane and we'll see who's got the puny eppickwument.' Brent stopped, frowning, then shook his head. 'Ready?'

'Ha!' said the twin. 'Shteady . . .'

The 'race' started with much hopping and stumbling down the street as they tried to run and pull their trousers off at the same time. A passing biker cursed them individually and collectively as he was pelted with jumpers, T-shirts and a pair of belts.

The others stumbled along after, collecting the discarded clothing as they went.

Nick watched the twin shove Brent into a postbox, then get pitched over a bollard in turn.

'Ouch. That *had* to hurt,' someone muttered.

'Feeling no pain,' sang one of the others. 'Hundred proof through my veins and feelin' no pain . . .'

'Captain scores!' came Brent's yell from the corner as they staggered around the curve of the road.

'Freeeessshing my cobblersh off. Wheresssh my kit?' the twin was moaning. 'You're a cheater. Cheating cheat-y cheater.'

'Hey, ladies. Wanna pick which one of us is the winner in the *big* stakes,' Brent yelled, making an unpleasant gesture with his hips as a huddle of girls passed on the far side of the street. 'Come on! Free show! Free . . . Oh bollocks.'

Nick followed Brent's suddenly riveted gaze, swerving sideways to hold on to the wall as the street seemed to tip. When his eyes focused, Brent and the naked twin were frantically hunting through the discarded clothes the others had collected as a pair of uniformed police officers approached.

'Evening, boys.'

'Evening, off'cers!' came the chorus.

'Getting a bit rowdy, aren't we? Anyone else want to drop their keks and let it all hang out and freeze off?'

The crew shook their heads, averting their eyes. The naked twin looked between the clothes in his brother's arms and the police and took off down Trinity Lane, a crumpled T-shirt held protectively to his crotch. Brent groaned and abandoned his jeans to follow in his boxers. 'CO-O-O-OLD!' came the receding wail.

The police turned to the rest of them. 'And which college might you all be from?'

The others fixed their eyes on the ground.

'We're going to be following you back somewhere, lads, so those of you who're still fully clothed might want to be a bit more co-operative and save us the effort. We'll end up having a much less friendly chat with your porters if you make us go for a midnight jog first.'

'Trinity Hall,' the clothed twin said.

'All of you?' asked the second police officer. Nick looked up to find that she was staring at him. 'Aren't you a bit young for a grad? One of these your brother, then?'

Nick shook his head. 'Not a grad. Still an unner ... under ... undergraduate,' he got out, then had to stop to swallow.

One of the others elbowed him, hissing, 'Townies call us *all* grads.'

'And what name should we run by your porters, then?' the policewoman asked.

'Nick.'

'We'll get back to the last name in a minute. Let's try for an age now.'

'Um,' said Nick.

'Um!' said the policewoman. 'Yeah, you look spot on for "um". But I always thought students were a bit older than "um". So let's try that in normal numbers, shall we? Thirteen maybe?'

'I'm fifteen!' retorted Nick indignantly.

'Ah, a fifteen sort of an um. That makes sense. Well, Nick aged um-slash-fifteen, how come you're with this lot?'

'Trinity Hall Men's Third Boat cox,' Nick said proudly. 'I *yell* at them.'

'He really is a student too. They let him in early,' Nick heard one of the others say.

'They let me in early,' parroted Nick, nodding and then wishing he hadn't. He closed his eyes and swallowed hard, then turned and launched himself at the nearest rubbish bin, heaving the evening's pub quiz 'winnings' into the basket.

'Well, at least he's neat,' said the policewoman. 'Let's take you back to your room—'

'Nick lives out,' one of the others piped up helpfully. 'His dad's got digs out by the station.'

'Right. If you lot can be trusted to get back to College without losing any of *your* clothing, we'll leave you to it and catch up with your porters later. Not you,

Nick-who-yells-at-them,' the policewoman said as Nick turned to stagger after the others. 'I think we'll let your parents pick you up from the station instead. Have a little heart-to-heart on the way about peer pressure and hanging out with the wrong sort.'

∞

Nick shivered as the doors to the street opened, not bothering to look up. He'd been sitting in the waiting area at the front of the Parker's Piece police station, under the desk officer's watchful eye, for over an hour, sipping slowly from a cup of lukewarm water. When the police had called the house, they hadn't been impressed to find the only responsible adult present was a lodger who had no legal role in Nick's life. They'd had to get Michael to fax over a note authorising Tim to pick Nick up. Tim had obviously been in no hurry to oblige. The clock above the desk sergeant now read 03.18.

'Nick.'

He squinted into the glare of the strip lights, wincing against the pain in his head as his eyes watered. 'Hi,' he whispered, attempting a smile that Tim did not return.

'Who do I have to talk to?' Tim asked.

Nick gestured towards the reception desk, getting slowly to his feet as Tim marched over. He leaned wearily against the counter as Tim talked with the desk officer, showed his passport, signed a form.

'Come on. We've got a taxi waiting outside.'

Nick cringed, hands over his ears, when Tim slammed the car door.

'Seatbelt,' he ordered tersely.

Five silent minutes later, they were home. Tim paid the driver, then pushed past Nick to open the front door. 'Michael says he'll be home tomorrow afternoon to talk.'

'Oh joy,' Nick mumbled, trailing him into the kitchen.

'Do you want paracetamol?' Tim didn't wait for an answer, slamming the packet and a pint glass of water down on the table.

'I'm sorry to drag you out in the middle of the night,' Nick said, eyes fixed firmly on his shoes.

'This is *not* what Professor Gosswin had in mind when she suggested you needed a housemate in case of emergencies. She meant flood, fire and food poisoning, not drunken run-ins with the police.'

Nick hunched his shoulders miserably.

Tim sighed. 'Drink the water, Nick. I'm tired and I want to go back to sleep while it's still night-time.'

'You don't have to stay up,' Nick said quietly. 'I've finished doing stupid things for the next few hours.'

Tim leaned back against the counter and scrubbed a hand across his face. 'Look, it's nothing I haven't done myself. But I was older and with friends who didn't scarper and leave me in the lurch. I just ... This is proper *in loco parentis* levels of responsibility. I didn't sign up for this.'

Nick slouched down even further, applying himself to the water. He pushed the empty glass back on to the table.

Tim took it and refilled it. 'Drink this in the night and you'll be just about OK in the morning.'

Nick clutched the glass to his chest. 'Thanks for coming to get me.'

'You're welcome,' Tim said stiffly. 'Let's just go to bed, OK?'

He let Tim steer him through the living room, flicking off lights as they went. They clumped wearily upstairs, Nick turning off to the second flight.

'I really am ... sorry,' Nick said. The words were lost as Tim's door snapped closed.

∞

When Michael let himself into the house, Tim was sitting at the kitchen table, head propped on his hand, sipping his way through his third cup of coffee since lunch.

'You look done in,' Michael said, dropping his briefcase in the corner, then helping himself from the cafetiere. 'I'm sorry about last night, Tim. I appreciate you holding the fort. Where's Nick?'

'Upstairs. Shall I call him?'

'Think I'll have my coffee first, then I'll go find him.'

Tim settled back, shuffling his papers awkwardly, as Michael heaved a long-suffering sigh.

'I'm going to have to tell him the Boat Club's out, aren't I? I mean, there's no way he can avoid getting caught up in this type of thing otherwise. I wish it weren't the case but ...

You're still a student, Tim. You know how these things work. It's for the best, right?'

Tim shrugged. 'I suppose if he promised not to drink again—'

'It's never going to work, though, is it?'

'I honestly don't know, but ... Look, I'm really sorry if you were expecting me to keep a better eye on Nick. Maybe we should spell out some ground rules, if there's something you're expecting me to do. Like if there's a curfew or something Nick should be keeping. I mean, I can't be responsible for knowing where he is *all* the time, but maybe he should call the house if he's not back before ten or something.'

Michael nodded. 'That sounds like a very sensible idea. I don't mind if he wants to be out late for a film or something, but you're right: he should let us know where he is.' He rubbed at his temples. 'Nick's just always been so *responsible*. He didn't have anyone to hang out with at school, so he was always home when I got there. I never really had to worry about him getting into trouble.'

'Of course. I didn't mean ...' Tim blew out a sigh, reaching back to rub at his neck. 'I don't want to be here on false pretences: I know it's my role to deal with emergencies, but I'm not sure if I'm comfortable being a pseudo-parent, having day-to-day responsibility for someone—'

'Of course not, Tim,' Michael said, waving further protest away. 'It's not what we said at all: not what I'm expecting. We won't put you in that position again, though I really appreciate you bailing us out – no pun intended.' He shook his head, yawned, took a sip of coffee.

Tim ran a hand through his hair. 'So, um … just to be super clear so I don't let down my end of the bargain, *is* there anything else you want me to help with?'

'Like hanging, drawing and quartering, you mean?' Nick asked from the doorway.

Tim saw resignation flash across Michael's face.

'Could we skip the talk if I promise I won't get drunk again?' Nick asked hopefully. 'It wasn't all that much fun – and certainly not worth the trouble afterwards.'

'The trouble's mostly been Tim's,' Michael said tartly.

Tim winced. 'Let me know what you guys agree and I'll see we keep to the rules,' he told Michael, grabbing his papers and hurrying out of the room without looking back, even though Nick was clearly trying to catch his eye.

Nick sighed as he sank into Tim's chair.

'We're going to have a new system, Nick. If you're not going to be back by ten o'clock, I want you to call the house and leave a message or text Tim. And if you're going to be later than you say, you've got to let him know.'

'Oh, Tim's going to *love* that.'

'It was Tim's idea.'

Nick scowled. 'I doubt he thought it through. He's made it perfectly clear he's not interested in being my keeper.'

Michael cleared his throat, sipped from his coffee mug. 'So, the other thing I wanted to talk about … You're not going to like this, Nick, but I'm afraid you're going to have to quit the Boat Club.' He waited a moment, but Nick didn't say anything. 'I know this isn't what you want to hear, but there's just no way you'll be able to avoid further trouble. It wouldn't be responsible of me to let you continue putting yourself in that position. I mean, if you want to stick with the rowing, I suppose we could talk about that, but I really don't want you involved with the rest of it.'

Nick closed his eyes, absently tracing patterns on the table. 'OK,' he said softly.

Michael frowned in surprise. 'Nick, I don't want you telling me one thing—'

'I said "OK"!' Nick snapped, then sighed. 'I'll quit. I won't cox any more and then it's not an issue. It wasn't as if I really liked the actual rowing. The whole point was the social stuff so if I can't do that ... Not that I enjoyed it all that much anyway – they're not really my sort of people – but at least I tried.' *Only it was just a different sort of loneliness. Maybe that's all there is.* He whispered it to the table, his lips barely forming the words, as his father turned aside to check his phone.

'Why don't you think about what other clubs or societies you could join?' Michael said, sliding his phone back into his pocket. 'There must be something where the social elements don't revolve around alcohol.'

'What, like CICCU?'

'Kick *who*?'

'It stands for ... actually, I don't know exactly what it stands for – Cambridge something something Christian

Union. But who did *you* know at Cambridge outside the God Squad who didn't drink? I tried all the book clubs and they were a wash-out. I'm short and small and not terribly co-ordinated. Exactly what else am I going to be any good at?'

'How about . . . how about pool?'

'I don't play pool. And even if I did, most people play pool in bars and pubs, Dad. And before you ask, yes, I tried the film club too, but everyone basically just sat around after the showing and drank. No one really wanted to discuss the film.'

'I enjoyed fishing as a boy.'

Nick gave him a flat stare. 'I'd rather have the whole College laugh at me for trying out for the rugby team.'

'Well, there's nothing wrong with trying, Nick.'

'Except I hate rugby. I've *always* hated rugby.'

'There's no need to be belligerent. Though it makes me wonder if I should ground you for a few weeks, seeing as how you *did* land yourself in the police station.'

'Like I've got anywhere better to be any more,' hissed Nick.

'Oh for heaven's sake, Nick,' Michael said, getting up to make a fresh pot of coffee. 'I'm only trying to help. I've got a meeting in a few hours, but I've come home to have a chat, so let's not waste the time arguing.' Michael turned only to find the room empty.

Chapter[16]

(Lent Term × Week 2
[≈ end of January])

The light spilling through the windows splashed across the side of Professor Gosswin's face, making her eyes look backlit and feral.

'I gather that Mr Brethan was helpful to you after the unfortunate incident with the "boaties".' She said the word as if it were somehow uncouth.

'Yeah.' Nick shifted in his chair. 'He was pretty cross but he still made me drink all this water before I went to bed so I wouldn't feel too hungover in the morning.'

When he looked up, Professor Gosswin was smiling: a strange, slightly melancholy twist of the lips.

'You look positively mellow right now.'

Professor Gosswin lifted her lip in a sneer. 'I look "mellow", do I, Mr Derran?'

'Not so much now.'

'It is a pity about the rowing but the thing about good ideas is that they often fail to take account of how complex and unpredictable the real world is. Some refinement is clearly needed. Have you thought, perhaps, of offering your services as secretary to a sporting club? Those who run around perspiring and becoming malodorous, not to mention unclean, need someone to be focused on loftier matters.'

'I get enough maths in class,' Nick grumbled. 'And I doubt they'd want to put their accounts in the hands of a fifteen-year-old. It never helps that I look my age.'

Professor Gosswin sighed, suddenly looking tired. 'I don't suppose it does.' She rubbed at her eyes.

'I don't know what's wrong with me, but people ...' He shrugged, turned away to pick at a catch in his thumbnail. 'They just don't seem to want things from me. Some people, everyone wants to be friends with them: wants to talk to them, get to know them, be close to them. And other people ... I do all the right things – at least I try to – but I just feel so ... humiliated.' He hunched his shoulders, crossing his arms over his chest. 'It's all so hard and nothing ever comes of it and I don't know *why*, unless there's just something wrong with me. At least I know how to be clever. If I can't be anything else, that's still good, right?'

'Your worth does not lie only in your academic ability. You surely see that.' She raised her hands, massaged the sharp angle of bone beside her eyes. 'It is always better to accomplish something than nothing, but coming of age is about more than learning who you are inside: it's as much about who you are in relation to others – and who you want to be.' She sighed softly, looking away to the light spilling through the window. 'No matter how hard we try, no one ever sees inside us. It's who we are on the outside that leaves a mark on the world and so, in a way, all we *ever* are is the person we show to the world.' Suddenly she smiled, her voice losing the odd wistful note. 'That being the case, we should all strive to put on a great show.'

'But if you're just pretending—'

'Not pretending, Mr Derran. realising that who you are on the outside may as well be different from who you are on the inside since no one will ever know the difference. We all have a difficult relationship with ourselves. But we can have better relationships with those around us if we choose to act as the person we want to be. And sometimes, over time, who we are on the inside comes to match. Those who suggest it is the other way around don't understand the way humans work.'

'And where does the waxing philosophical come in?' He expected Professor Gosswin to snap at him, but instead she just sighed, shifted stiffly in her chair.

'Impossible boy,' she said, but almost fondly. 'You still think you're here to learn mathematics.'

'And chess. Shall I bring the board over or do you want coffee before you trounce me?'

'You're not listening. Like so many people, you think that the important moments in the story of a life are big and loud, where really they're small and quiet. Someone on the outside would think these moments unworthy of note, but you must recognise the important moments of your own life when they happen, Nicholas. It is very important.'

She sighed again, rubbing at her right temple. 'Now fetch me a coffee and perhaps a paracetamol.'

Chapter[17]

For once, supervision went smoothly. It was his turn to work the problems through with Dr Davis and today Susie and Frank seemed content to sit back and watch. It was almost friendly. Until the end of the supervision, when Frank and Susie rushed off in different directions without even saying goodbye.

It is sad and pathetic that your major goal for term is to get invited to someone's room for tea, Nick was telling himself when he realised that Brent had just stepped out of the p'lodge ahead of him. He dithered instead of turning back into the passage to North Court and then it was too late.

'Oh, look, it's our favourite dropout,' said Brent.

'I said I'm sorry. My dad—'

'Say no more,' said Brent. 'Daddy's little boy always does as he's told, right?'

'Because I had *such* good reason to keep hanging out with

you lot, you mean, seeing as how you all came with me to the police station to make sure I was OK.'

'Poor baby,' cooed Brent. 'Were oo scared?'

'And it was kind of you to call the next morning to check how I was doing. You're such a mate.'

'Why would I call you when you'd already emailed to throw in the towel?'

'That's right,' Nick said, snapping his fingers. 'I only waited one entire day before emailing. Didn't give you, oh, twenty-four entire hours to get there first.'

'Diddums. So how's it going being Mr No-Mates again?' sneered Brent.

Nick felt his face flush. 'Who says I am? Sorry to disappoint, but you're not that important even in *my* life.' He turned away, leaving Brent to shout after him as he hurried through the doors between the buttery and the dining hall, then out the other side by Latham Lawn.

He was still distracted when he let himself in through the heavy door at the bottom of Gosswin's staircase, nearly catching his fingers as it slammed shut at his back. He plodded upstairs, dumping his bag in the open kitchen door and flicking on the kettle before letting himself into the study.

'I know you said I was here to learn more than chess, but could we pretend that's why I'm here today, not hiding out from Brent and the crew?' He stopped, realising that Professor Gosswin hadn't turned from her chair by the window. 'Are you asleep?' He crept forward a step, another.

He winced when the floorboards under the Turkish

carpet moaned a thin, tortured sound. Then he realised how loudly the Professor was snoring – great ugly wheezes and snuffles – and grinned, stepping forward more confidently and bending to peer round into her face to see if her mouth was open, debating whether he could bring himself to take a photo on his phone if she were drooling.

And then the air disappeared from the room.

One of the Professor's eyes was mostly open. The other seemed to have slipped down in her face, leaking fluid on to her sagging cheek as if it had been punctured. Her lips were parted, mouth all twisted to the side, and the snoring wasn't snoring but . . .

He knelt in front of her. Put his face in the line of the open eye, but there was no sign of recognition, no contraction in the pupil as he blocked the light. He slid his hand on to hers on the arm of the chair.

'Professor?'

Her fingers trembled and twitched under his. He drew back.

Found he was standing.

Found himself at the door.

On the stairs, then by the dining hall.

Suddenly pushing through the door into the p'lodge.

The porter at the desk was signing someone into a ledger. Nick watched the ballet of his hands as he tucked the pen away, rolled the pages of the ledger closed, slipped it away under the desk.

'Everything OK, Nick?' the porter asked, frowning at him.

'I think Professor Gosswin's had a stroke,' someone said with his voice.

The porter's frown deepened. 'What? You mean you've just seen her ... Hold tight.' He ducked his head into the back room and Nick heard him order someone to call an ambulance. 'Right. Let's go and see,' the porter said, lifting the flap at the end of the counter and stepping through.

Nick felt his eyes close, found his sight blurred when he opened them, though his cheeks felt hot and dry. He looked up, expecting the porter to be angry and impatient, but he was just smiling the same kind smile. 'There, lad. We'll make sure she's comfortable till the experts get here to see what exactly's the matter.'

Nick had to put his fist to his mouth to stop the funny sound in his throat from coming out. He let the porter turn him to the door and then there they were, in Front Court again.

By the dining hall again.

At the bottom of Professor Gosswin's stairs again.

'I should have run,' Nick heard himself say. 'Why didn't I run to get help? Why ... What if ... What if ... Why didn't I run?'

∞

The sight of his thesis notes spread across the table brought a thrill of horror: one part can't-do-this-it's-too-hard, one part too-tired-for-this, and one part TV-is-more-fun.

Come on, brain. Think. Tim knocked his fist against his forehead. *Think thoughts. Clever thoughts.*

He put his fingers to his laptop keyboard. He took his fingers away. He made himself a fresh cup of tea. Then fetched a biscuit. The kitchen clock read 15.02. He'd been sitting at the table for a full hour.

He reorganised his notes. 15.29.

He put his fingers to his laptop keyboard and took them away, then cursed loudly and foully and finally wrote a sentence. He deleted the sentence. He wrote a new one and tapped the space bar to start a second. His mobile rang.

'Yes?' he snapped.

'Tim?' Nick's voice was only just recognisable.

'What's wrong? Are you OK?'

'Professor Gosswin.' Nick took a wavering breath. 'I went over for tea. After my supervision. She . . . she was just sitting there. Her face was . . .' Nick throttled a sound suspiciously like a sob. 'They're saying she had a stroke. They let me come in the ambulance.'

Tim closed his eyes. 'Are you at Addenbrooke's?'

'Yes. The porters know and they said they'll take care of things but . . . I don't know who to call now. I don't know.'

'I'm sure the porters are handling it, Nick. They'll have all her emergency contact details. Just hold tight, OK? I'll be there soon.'

'You don't have to come. I just . . . I need to know what to do. My dad's in a meeting and—'

'Why don't you call Bill while I'm on my way? I bet he'd want to know too.'

Silence on the other end of the line.

'I think that's a good idea, Nick. Give Bill a ring and I'll see you soon, OK?'

Tim was halfway to the hospital before a near miss as he cut through a red light made him realise he'd forgotten both his helmet and his bike lights. Padlocking the bike to the first railing he found in the parking lot, he called the p'lodge as he jogged inside, following the signs for A & E as the porters filled him in.

It took him a minute to spot Nick sitting absolutely still in a corner of the waiting room, eyes locked blankly on a plastic potted plant that looked as if it had somehow managed to die despite never having lived. He looked small and thin and scared, his face all sharp angles and shadows.

'Nick.'

The boy started, looked up then away. 'Hi.'

Tim exchanged tight-lipped smiles with the weary woman who'd been sitting next to Nick as she moved to the opposite chair to make way for him. He sank slowly on to the wheezing foam, risked putting a hand on Nick's shoulder. 'The porters are on to Gosswin's lawyer: she'll be here later. They said her niece is too far away to come until the weekend, but she'll take care of discussions with the doctors by phone. You don't have to worry. It's all being handled.'

Nick nodded mutely, staring at the ground. He didn't

pull away from Tim's touch, though Tim could feel him struggling to suppress the hitch in his breathing.

'How about we get a cup of *really* grotty coffee?'

Nick shook his head, sighed, shrugged. Tim crossed to the vending machine, returning with two polystyrene cups steaming dispiritedly, as if it were too much to bother.

'Here.' Tim pressed one of the cups into Nick's hand. 'Drink.' Setting his own cup down on the floor, he fished in his pocket and pulled out a chocolate bar, breaking off half and offering it to Nick, who had cupped his hands around the coffee, staring into its grey depths as if hypnotised. 'Eat it, Nick.'

He stared blankly at the chocolate, then shook his head even as he took it and raised it to his mouth.

Tim watched his hand drop. 'Nick.'

He shuddered but took a bite, grimacing as he chewed, then swallowed convulsively as if he'd been fed sand. Tim sighed, guiding the coffee cup to Nick's mouth, relieved when he rallied enough to shake him off with a look of faint irritation.

'Yuck,' Nick reported, wrinkling his nose.

'I think the idea is that since you're already in hospital it doesn't matter if the coffee poisons you.'

Nick made a somewhat pathetic attempt at a smile. 'Thanks for coming,' he whispered, as if he'd lost the ability to speak normally.

'Gosswin's been very kind to me. And hospitals aren't good places to be alone.'

'Like when your parents died?'

Tim took a sip of his own coffee, gave himself a moment to choose his words. 'My sister was there. She's older. Took care of things.'

Nick nodded, fixing his eyes on Tim's for the first time since he'd arrived, but he didn't venture anything further. Grateful not to be pressed, Tim chanced putting his arm about Nick's shoulders, not surprised when he simply sat stiffly, neither leaning into comfort nor pushing him away.

'Her face was all purple,' Nick said suddenly, and Tim could see the liquid in his coffee cup rippling. 'She was sitting in her chair, facing the window, and her face was all purple. One of her eyes was sort of open. I thought ... I thought she'd died but there was this horrible *horrible* rattling sound and I realised ... Her face was all ... melted. Melted.' Tim felt the bones in Nick's back sharpen through his jumper as he went rigid, as if holding his breath. When he raised his head, his face was dry, though there was a feverish flush of colour highlighting each cheekbone.

When Professor Gosswin's lawyer turned up, she waved aside Tim and Nick's explanations with a simple, 'Yes, I know who you both are.' Then she disappeared to talk to the doctors. Afterwards, she sent them off with little information but a promise to call 'when things become clearer'.

Nick let Tim lead him to a taxi. On the way home, Nick called Bill and then his father, leaving a second message on each phone in a hard flat voice. When the taxi pulled up at the house, he followed Tim silently up the front path and inside, slumping bonelessly into a chair as Tim set about heating tinned tomato soup.

The sound of a key in the front door brought Nick's head up.

Tim had to turn away from the look of mingled despair and relief on Nick's face as Bill appeared in the kitchen doorway.

Chapter[18]

(Lent Term × Week 4
[≈ second week of February])

Nick was startled when Susie fell into step beside him after supervision as if it were something they did every week.

'I don't know why I don't get it. I used to get it. I used to get everything.' She adjusted her bag higher on her shoulder. 'I really don't like not being the smartest any more. I want a Cambridge degree but maybe I'd be happier as a big fish in a smaller pond.' She sighed. 'Or maybe I just need to figure out how to fit in more work and less having fun. I know I'm not working hard enough but I just can't seem to . . .' Another sigh. 'I don't know what happened. I know you're meant to "find" yourself at uni, but I didn't realise that meant losing yourself first. I don't seem to know who I am any more. One minute I'm one me and the next minute I'm someone else. I'm not even sure if I know who I *want* to be. Well, I know the bits I want but not how they fit together into an actual whole person. You know what I mean?' She spun suddenly to stand in his path so that he had to step backwards not to walk into her.

'Um?' Nick offered.

Susie rolled her eyes and set off again. 'Just you wait. You've got all of this to look forward to.'

'Did you ever meet Professor Gosswin?' Nick asked.

'The Dragon Lady? Didn't she have a stroke?'

'Yeah,' Nick said, turning his head as if following the flight of the seagull gliding from one side of North Court to the other. 'I would *love* to see you call her that to her face.' It came out cracked and awkward. 'I mean, she'd take it as a compliment. She'd love that people think she's practically mythical.'

'What does the Dragon Lady, mythical or otherwise, have to do with my existential crisis?'

'She's basically an arch villain whose superpowers are snark and disdain, but it's just her being herself to the nth power. Like she's more herself than people usually are.'

'Wish I knew that trick.'

'Sometimes you do.'

Susie gave him a wan smile. 'It's nice of you to say but ...' She ran a hand over her face. 'When I got here I decided I wanted to see if I could be a different person. No one at College saw me spotty and fat at school. They don't know about the time I cried in the loos when Miles Franklyn dumped me in the middle of the Winter Dance. So I thought to myself, what's to stop me being someone who really believes she's sexy ... like a Cambridge version of Rizzo. I keep trying it out and it feels nice: like maybe I do have that in me ... but not consistently. Like I can't hold on to it. And when I *do*, I seem to stop being all the other things I like about myself.' She scraped her hair back. 'Anyway, enough of that. Thanks for the figurative shoulder and all. See you tomorrow.'

She was gone before he had a chance to say anything, even goodbye.

Girls are really, really weird, he muttered as he set off for the p'lodge, trying not to let his thoughts drift to the fact that this time last week he'd been sitting down at Professor Gosswin's chessboard.

He detoured by his pigeonhole, found a leaflet in it advertising the 'TitHall June Event'.

'What's the June Event?' he asked the porter on duty.

'Think a normal bop – you know, Viva night – on steroids. Only with live music and a bit of food. It's ticketed for alcohol so you'd have to ask the Senior Tutor about whether it would be OK to come if you had a parent with you.'

'Yeah, it's going to be loads of fun with my dad there.'

The porter gave him a sympathetic grimace, looking all too glad at the excuse to turn away when a delivery man slid a large box on to the counter.

As if Dad would come with me even if I wanted him to.

Of course that thought led on to one about whether Professor Gosswin could talk to the Senior Tutor for him ... *Only she can't talk to anyone, you idiot*, he muttered at himself.

The lights were off at home when he let himself in, but

there was a rustling of papers from the kitchen and he found himself smiling as he dropped his bag by the sofa. 'Do you want a coffee?' he asked Tim as he flicked on the kettle.

'No thanks.' Tim didn't even look up from the papers covering every inch of the table.

'Biscuit?'

'No.'

Nick took his mug and retreated to the window seat in the living room, trying to settle with his latest assignment, but the house was too quiet and he found himself wandering back to the kitchen for a glass of water he didn't want.

Tim glanced up with a glare, then shifted pointedly and turned his attention back to his papers. Nick loitered in the doorway, taking in the circles under Tim's eyes, the angry stabbing gestures as he moved the pen from one page to the next.

With a sigh, Nick returned to the window seat. The sun was storm-yellow on the pavement, the trees dipping in the wind. A hail of prunus flowers swept the pane then crumpled to the sill like a pile of dead butterflies, all squandered beauty fading to brown.

He picked up Professor Gosswin's book, but had only just parted the pages when he closed it again, pressed it to his chest, hand splayed protectively against the back cover.

Half an hour later, he'd still made no progress on his work. He tossed his notepad aside, padding into the kitchen. 'Do you want to order a pizza tonight? Watch a film?' he asked as he fished in the snack cupboard for crisps.

'What?' Tim looked up blankly, his eyes dazed. 'No ... maybe ... Look, ask me again in an hour, OK?'

Nick sighed and set about making a fresh cup of tea. Tim started when Nick put a steaming cup down by his elbow. 'You look like you need something. Are you sure you don't want a biscuit?'

'No. Thanks for the tea—'

'But please get lost now?'

Tim threw down his pen, running his hands through his hair. 'Just give me an hour, all right? It'd be much better if you didn't try to talk to me until then. Look, I'll go upstairs. Get out of your way.' He started to gather up his papers.

'You don't have to do that, Tim. I just ... Are you OK?' Nick stepped closer to the table, frowning down at the papers. 'Those are bank statements, not your PhD.'

'And you say you're not a genius,' sneered Tim, then shook his head, rubbing the heel of his hand against his forehead.

'Can't I help?'

Tim sighed, slumping back into his chair. 'Thanks, Nick. And thanks for the tea, but seriously. Give me an hour and I'll be good as new. It's not your problem.'

'And I'm not yours, but you'd still help me if you could,' Nick said.

Tim flinched as if stung, giving Nick a chance to pick up one of the pages. Tim gritted his teeth over the first words to come to mind, snatching the paper back.

'Look, Tim, money problems are fixable. I can—'

'No. Just ... no. I'm not going to take money off you, Nick.'

'Why not? If it's fixable, why not fix it? "Change the things you can", like my postcard says. We both know you'll pay me back.'

'And in the meantime your dad would be *so* impressed—'

'It'd be none of his business. I wasn't planning on asking *him* to lend you the money. You're not after a fortune or anything, are you?'

Tim sighed, pressing his knuckles into his eyes.

'Come on. I don't believe you've been betting on the horses and I haven't noticed any brand-new Porsches in front of the house—'

'My sister's getting married.'

'Yeah, you said the other day.'

'In America. In eff-gee-and-aitch-ing Sedona, Arizona. Which seems to be the most expensive place to get to on the planet, and the hotel ...'

'How much could it possibly be?'

'Enough,' growled Tim. 'Enough if you don't have it. I've been saving for a *year* and even without rent I'm going to have to get a maximum overdraft on all my accounts.' He sighed, throwing his pen against the wall and locking his hands behind his head as he turned away. 'I know you're trying to help and I appreciate the thought, Nick, but an audience for my tantrum is not going to improve my mood.'

Nick ignored him, sifting through the papers to pick up Tim's notepad. 'This isn't a lot. No, listen, Tim,' he said, stepping back and raising the pad behind him when Tim moved to grab it. 'I've got an account for birthday money that I *never* use. I can lend you what you need. Actually I can lend you more, then you don't need to have overdraft fees.'

'Nick, please—'

'Why *not*, Tim? Really, why not? Because you're embarrassed to borrow off me? Because you're too proud?'

'I thought I had it under control. I was working up to ask—' Tim cut himself off.

'You were going to ask Professor Gosswin,' Nick said. 'You were working up to ask her for a loan.'

Tim clenched his jaw, the muscles working in his cheek.

'Well, then you can ask me. Or rather you don't even have to ask. I don't need the money right now and you do.'

'I know you think this is a good idea—'

'It's a *brilliant* idea. There's absolutely *nothing* wrong with it apart from your attitude.' Nick's face was flushed with frustration. 'I know we're not close or anything, but I thought we were sort of friends at least. You came to pick me up from the police station.'

Tim blew out a breath. 'That's different, Nick.'

The flush vanished from Nick's face and his lips thinned. 'Your deal with Dad is to be around and help with emergencies. But you didn't have to be nice to me.'

'I was nice, was I?'

'Well, for two in the morning, you were. And you didn't have to come to the hospital when Professor Gosswin ... I know you did it more for her than me, but you still didn't

202

have to. I'm not going to hold the money over you, so just get over yourself, OK? Your angst is not that special.'

And Tim laughed.

'I'll interpret that as a "Yes, Nick. Thank you *so* much, Nick. You're a star among housemates, Nick," even though your expression says "Let's not get carried away." Just leave me a note with the amount you need in order not to be in hock to anyone, and your bank details, and we don't ever have to talk about it again.'

'I won't be able to pay you back for—'

'You've got until I graduate or you move out. That long enough?'

∞

The area of Cambridge around Addenbrooke's was nothing like the University: ordinary, unenchanted. There were lots of old trees, and different textures of hedge, but the houses were unexceptional: faux-stucco plasterwork and flat-roofed one-car garages. It was less than two miles from home, but the taxi journey seemed to take an hour, stop-start stop-start all the way up Hills Road.

Nick let Tim lead the way through the hospital corridors, Michael following behind, eyes on his phone, reinforcing the message that he'd 'need to go soon: can't take the day off on the spur of the moment.'

The nurses of the High Dependency Unit were expecting them, just as Gosswin's lawyer had promised they would be when she'd called to let them know they could visit now. The duty nurse watched them carefully as they took it in turns to cleanse their hands with the stinging gel from the alcohol-rub dispenser, then led them down the ward to the far corner.

'We don't usually have more than two people round a bed at once in HDU, but we'll make an exception,' the nurse said, pulling the curtain closed between Gosswin's bed and the next patient. 'Just remember to use the hand sanitiser again when you leave.'

In the week since the stroke, Professor Gosswin's face had somehow become both swollen and lax: wrinkled, grey and unimpressive.

'She looks like a normal person,' Tim said. 'I feel like she's going to rear up from the bed like something out of a horror film and try to bite my nose off for even *thinking* that.'

Nick didn't say anything, just slid his hand into the curl of the Professor's limp fingers.

The figure in the bed shifted, grunted, opened one watery blue eye. The other stayed at half-mast, the lashes fluttering.

'It's Nick, Professor. Nick and Tim and Michael.'

The Professor slurred a hoarse, unrecognisable word, her other hand lifting up from the bed before settling back on to the covers.

Nick pressed the back of the hand he was holding. 'I know you must be so bored right now, but they're moving you to a recovery home soon and I'll bring your chess set once you're settled there.'

One side of Professor Gosswin's face lifted up into a

leering smile. Tim took a step towards the door, but Nick just smiled back at her.

'I know,' he said. 'But you'll have to wait to insult us, I'm afraid. It'll be good motivation, stocking up all the shouting for later on.'

When Professor Gosswin's eyes slid shut and stayed shut, Nick sighed, placing her hand gently back on the bed. 'I don't suppose she'd want us to stick around and watch her sleep,' he said quietly.

There was a taxi waiting outside the hospital when they left. Michael started to shift about awkwardly, checking his phone, his watch, his phone again, the moment they climbed in.

'Shall we drop you at the station, Dad?' Nick asked.

'Would you mind? It was good to see her, pay my respects after all she's done for us, but, well, life goes on, right?' He raised his hands helplessly.

When they got home, Nick made tea while Tim got down the biscuit tin. They sat, staring into their mugs for an hour before Tim left for a meeting with his supervisor. When he had gone, Nick curled on to the window seat, zipped Professor Gosswin's book into the front of his hoodie and fought his way through the week's supervision problems, trying to ignore the odd way his heart seemed to be punching at his ribs rather than beating: the way his throat burned as if he'd drunk acid, making his vision swim with tears every time he swallowed.

∞

It was a relief to escape the glaring lights of the Cockcroft Lecture Theatre. He cut past the ugly round frontage of the Mond building, the crocodile design on the right-hand side of the door its only redeeming feature. In Free School Lane, he stopped for a minute to look at the quaint little courtyard of St Bene't's, then turned away on to KP.

'Hey, Nick! Nick Derran!'

Nick turned to find a stocky young man in a football uniform calling to him from the cobbled forecourt of King's.

'Sam Barton,' the man said, jogging over. 'From school.'

'It's only been a few months, Sam. You haven't changed *that* much,' Nick said. 'Just wasn't expecting to see you here. I thought you were at York.'

Sam shrugged. 'I am. I'm here for a Varsity match. Look, I've been meaning to say something – apologise – if I ever saw you again.'

'Why would you need to apologise? You were always perfectly nice. There was even that time when the lacrosse team—'

'I'd forgotten about that,' Sam said, making a face. 'Not really my finest hour either. You tried to thank me and I said something charming like "Don't think this makes us best friends or anything."'

Nick toed awkwardly at a loose pebble. 'You were better than the others.'

'That's not a rousing endorsement, you know. But fair,' he added. 'Anyway, the thing is, you said this thing to me once. And I realised later, much later, that I said something really stupid in reply.'

Nick frowned. 'I have no idea what you're talking about. It can't have been a big deal, so don't worry about it.'

'It was the only time in forever you didn't ask what the top mark was after a test. Everyone noticed and started pestering you about what you'd got, only you wouldn't say.'

'Well, everyone was always cross when I *did* ask: they said I was trying to make an excuse to tell everyone I came top, so I thought I'd just not say anything. But then everyone got shirked off about me being secretive. It's not your fault I couldn't win.'

Sam rolled his eyes. 'Not what I was going to say. The point was that big row in the locker room before PE.'

'When I gave in and told everyone what I'd got and they were even more furious 'cos they'd figured I was hiding the fact I'd done badly, only I wasn't?' He shifted his bag to sit more comfortably on his shoulder, letting his eyes drift to a couple pedalling up KP on a tandem bike. 'So what?'

'That was the day Pete Simms stamped on your arm in his football boots during PE.'

'Oh. I remember *that*,' Nick said, finally dragging his eyes away from the tandem as it wobbled out of sight. 'You went up to the San with me. You waited for me afterwards. That was pretty nice of you actually.'

'Do you remember what I said? About not being such a show-off?'

Nick shrugged. 'Not really. I guess I was. I *am*. It's my own fault I never listen.'

'But you said this other thing. You said, "If everyone's

going to hate me, then it might as well be for something good, like being clever.'"

'It sounds like me.'

'And I said,' Sam pressed on as if he hadn't been interrupted, '"They might not hate you for being clever if you didn't shove it down their throats so much." I should have listened.'

'To what?'

'To the fact that you thought people were going to hate you no matter what.'

Nick's face went blank.

'I don't know why, but I just didn't hear that bit of it. All I heard was the bit where you said you weren't going to stop setting people off. Back then I didn't get that you were doing it almost like an attack—'

'I wasn't—'

'Of *course* you were, Nick. Maybe you still don't see it, but sometimes you're kind of aggressive about it. I know you think you're just interested in how you're doing for your own satisfaction, but it's not that simple. Anyway, that's not the important thing; if I'd had half a brain I'd have asked you *why* you thought everyone was going to hate you: why your only choice was to pick the how and why.' He took a deep breath. 'I'm sorry for that, Nick. I should have known better. I should have understood enough not to ignore something like that.'

Nick blinked, swallowed tightly. He raised a shoulder in a shrug. 'It's . . .' He cleared his throat. 'That's a while ago now. Just some stupid comment I made in the school corridor.'

'Was it?' Sam asked. 'Maybe it could have been important if I'd been listening.'

Nick opened his mouth but nothing came out.

'Look, I have to go but ... good luck, OK? It's great you're here, in this place. If anyone should be, it's you. I hope this is the start of something better.'

'It is,' Nick got out.

Sam smiled. 'Good. I always figured you were one of those people who'd get happier and happier as you got older. Not like stupid Pete Simms. The best's already *way* behind *him*.'

Nick laughed, though the sound was odd: thin and strained.

He watched Sam hurry off with a final wave over his shoulder.

Chapter[19]

(Lent Term × Week 5
[≈ third week of February])

Nick stopped under the high ogee arch of the Old Cavendish Laboratory to tug his hood up against the rain.

'Hey, Nick, wait up!' Frank skidded to a halt next to him, shaking his head to stop his hair dripping down his forehead. 'A bunch of us are going down to Clowns, sort of an informal study group thing: wondered if you wanted to tag along. Full disclosure and all, I want to pick your brains about some of this probability stuff.'

'You know this isn't my best course, right? Or have you blanked out our last supervision entirely?'

Frank shrugged. 'You can explain what three standard deviations above the norm means and beyond that I really don't care. There's a coffee in it for your pains.' He held out a hand.

Nick gave him a sceptical look but shook it anyway.

The others were already shedding coats at one of the long tables when Nick and Frank squeezed through the coffee-shop doorway past the largest buggy in the world.

'Bit cramped. You're OK to sit on my lap, right, Susie?' Frank said.

Susie pulled a disgusted face. 'You couldn't just decide that *not* being a pillock might at least get you a smile, whereas this whole schoolboy "If I pull your pigtails, you're bound to fancy me back" routine is practically an invitation to defenestrate you.'

'What if I offered to buy you one of those huge hazelnut white-chocolate things?'

Susie's eyes brightened. 'Oh Frank, you really know what a girl wants.'

He grinned, elbowing Nick in the side.

'An offer to trade a grope for the price of a drink that'll get her fat. Why would I drink that many calories when I could have a nice cup of tea *and* a huge chocolate brownie? Both of which I'll be buying for myself, thanks,' she said, pushing up from the table. 'If I come back and find you in my seat pretending to be a cushion, Frank, your day's going to go from bad to worse.'

'Um . . . couldn't go and get our drinks, could you?' Frank whispered to Nick as Susie marched off. 'Next one's on me, promise, but I think I'd better give her a bit of space.'

'Nick!'

Nick jumped as a small blue blur hurtled deftly between the tables and knocked him backwards into the wall.

'Nick, Nick, Nick! You're here! With peoplings! With human friendy peoplings!'

'Hi, Ange.'

'Why haven't you come in before now to see me? I did say this was my coffee shop, right? Or Tim did? Didn't you miss me? Of *course* you missed me. You're a house full of boys. Do any of you ever hug? Of course not, useless things ... Oh, you're wearing your scarf.' She patted it fondly.

'Hell-o, pretty lady.'

Ange looked up to find Frank grinning at her over Nick's shoulder. 'Oh no. Oh *yuck*. He isn't *yours*, is he, Nick?' she asked.

'Do I look like the type of bloke who fancies little boys?' Frank asked, pouting. 'No offence, mate,' he added to Nick.

Ange surveyed Frank from head to foot. 'You look like a Neanderthal. I don't want to think about what you fancy. And it had better not be me,' she added, brandishing a teaspoon in his face. 'Don't even think about it. You do not want to experience my experimentation with martial arts involving sugar tongs.'

Frank blinked at her. 'Maybe I don't,' he conceded, pulling a face at Nick as he squeezed around to the far side of the table.

'Really, Nick?' Ange asked him, aggrieved.

Nick shrugged. 'He's the one who invited me here.'

Ange heaved a sigh. 'Well, that's a point in his favour, but hopefully next time one of the other ones can do the inviting and you can leave him at the farm with the other things that go oink. Anyway, the rest look like an OK sort of crowd. Nerdy. Weird. Socially inept.'

'It's in the Cambridge admissions rules for Mathmos now, haven't you heard? How come you ever got to like Tim, given he's basically the opposite of all that?'

Ange beamed at him and swooped in for a hug that pinned his arms to his sides. 'Tim Brethan is just as inept as anyone here, only he hides it better than most. He is a bother and a nuisance.'

'And your best friend?'

'Well, yes, and that, of course.'

'Only that?' Nick asked.

Ange rolled her eyes. 'Tim Brethan is a wonderful and amazing best friend, but he is a *horrible* boyfriend. If I went out with him, he would end up hurting me in ways I couldn't bring myself to forgive and then I would hurt him by dumping him and never speaking to him again, and where would that get us? You can't go out with someone in the hope that they'll become their best self, Nick. Remember that, won't you?' she said earnestly, tugging on his scarf. 'You can hope, but you can't count on it. You've got to pick people for who they are *already*. And, yes, people change, but you never know *how* they'll change. If you don't start by thinking a person, as he or she is, is good enough already then ... Well, you'll spend your life looking to be with someone who isn't the person you're with.' Ange set about settling Nick's scarf more comfortably about his neck. 'I've already got everything I want from this version of Tim Brethan. And that's what I told him just before Christmas, when he asked me out mostly to get an invitation to Christmas dinner and only a little because he figured it was time we "gave it a go".'

'Oh,' said Nick. 'Wow. That was a really thorough answer to a question I thought you'd just ignore.'

'Be careful what you ask then, huh? People sometimes tell you the truth.'

Nick grinned at her. 'There aren't other people like you, Ange. Most humans have boundaries instead of bounce.'

Ange wrinkled up her nose. 'Did you really not want me to tell you? Was it a bit TMI?'

Nick shrugged. 'It's good to know why Tim was so cross and you were so sad. I mean, even I know it's not really that easy to be so sensible about love.'

For a moment, all the happiness went out of her face. Then she shook herself, bounced once on the balls of her feet and smiled. 'Well, now you know everything you could possibly need to, so just you sit there and make nice with all these other weird peoplings and I'll go and bring you something yummy. And something less so for the caveman.' With that she skipped away to start crashing about behind the counter.

Although there was no discussion of maths *per se*, there was a lot of gossip about various lecturers, professors and fellow students. Better still, the afternoon produced a general invitation to a film the following evening as they all started the long process of pulling back on their layers of jumpers, coats, scarves, hats and gloves.

'Hey, Nick,' Frank said, as they stepped out on to the

street, 'you *will* be a mate and let me borrow your assignment notes tomorrow night, won't you? I'm really in the sh— the weeds, I mean.'

'You can swear, Frank. I'm not two.'

'Oh, right. Well, you don't mind, do you? I mean, it's not like I'm going to copy stroke for stroke or anything. I just don't know where to start and I could really use the chance to go through someone else's workings: just to see how to do it, yeah?'

Nick shrugged.

Frank beamed, clapping him on the shoulder. 'Knew we'd end up pals. See you tomorrow then!'

'Are you sure you want to do that?' someone whispered by Nick's ear, making him jump.

'I think he means well,' he said as he turned to find Susie standing behind him.

'Do you?' she asked, raising an elegant eyebrow. 'I'd have given you more credit. Nick, I'm not trying to be mean but . . . you *do* know Frank's the sort to latch on for what he can get, right?'

'So?' Nick said diffidently. 'Today's the first time anyone outside the boat club invited me anywhere. If it costs me the loan of some homework, I don't mind. It's not like Dr Davis is going to think I've been copying from Frank. Besides, if Frank doesn't figure it out for himself sooner or later it'll come out in the exams. But then it'll be no fault of mine and I'll have had something of a social life in the meantime.'

Susie laughed, her expression lightening. 'I didn't have you pegged as the super-villain type. Good for you, Nick. Keep it up.'

∞

Nick glared across the table as his father starting replying to the eleventh email since they'd sat down to lunch. Bill promptly developed a convenient fixation with the last of his beans. The silence grew loud with anger.

'So,' said Bill, 'so I was wondering ... There's this village fete near me next Sunday. I thought you might fancy popping down for the day. There're usually a few local authors who do readings, so you'd like that, Nick.'

Nick raised one shoulder in a shrug.

'Sounds great,' Michael said, not looking up.

Nick's hands clenched into fists around his cutlery.

'Come on, Mike. Just give us ten minutes without the phone,' Bill said. 'You know,' he added, turning to Nick with a too broad, too bright smile, 'I think your dad's actually slightly *better* about focusing on the world around him than he used to be.' He held up a hand as if Nick had protested instead of just stabbing a pea around his plate. 'You wouldn't credit the number of times he put his pen in his coffee instead of his pencil holder. And then there was the famous coffee-and-cornflakes incident ... Didn't even bat an eyelid. Just munched away, muttering over his notes.'

'It was during Finals!' said Michael, setting the

phone aside.

Bill rolled his eyes so hard he moved his whole head. Nick would have appreciated the effort if he hadn't been so humiliated that it was necessary.

'And you remember that time you tried to make roast chestnuts only you didn't know to pierce them first and they exploded in the oven?' Bill said, face flushing with laughter. 'And you were *nothing* to Yvette ...'

Nick saw the moment Bill realised his mistake. 'I'm going to visit Mum next week. On her birthday. Whether you come or not,' Nick said into the sudden quiet. 'If you won't take me, I'll get a taxi—'

'Bill's just invited us down to this shindig of his. Why didn't you say—'

'I've been asking you for a *month*.'

Michael sighed, arranged his cutlery on his plate, then beside it again. 'Nick, I'm not sure that visiting the graveyard— It's not like she's, well, *there*.'

'I'm not a toddler, Dad. I just want ... I want to pay my respects. Last year you kept saying maybe on her birthday, or maybe on Mother's Day, but it never happened. I want to go. I want to know I've gone.'

Michael sighed. 'Well, maybe we *will* go on Mother's Day this time, like you suggested. Or we could visit Gosswin in Addenbrooke's again. Wouldn't that be better?'

'I can visit Gosswin by myself, like I have the other four times I've gone, seeing as how she's only two miles away. You don't have to come to see Mum, but it's the second anniversary and I haven't been since the funeral so I'm *going.*'

'But Bill—'

'It's just a stupid local fair, Mike,' Bill interrupted. 'No big deal and there's always next year.'

'Why didn't you just say something earlier, Nick?'

Nick slammed up from his chair and stormed out of the room.

As he started upstairs, he heard his father huff, 'Lord save me from teenage strops … No, don't start clearing up, Bill. Just leave it for now.'

Nick caught the sound of their chairs scratching away from the kitchen table, then footsteps moving closer, from the kitchen into the living room. He hovered at the top of the stairs, torn between going down to apologise and carrying on to his room.

'Why are you glaring at me, Morrison?' Michael demanded from below, sounding aggrieved.

'Just because we've swapped to more comfortable chairs doesn't mean you're off the hook.'

'Nick's the one throwing the hissy fit!'

'I expect he was hoping you'd remember what next weekend was,' came Bill's voice, 'and that he'd already talked to you about it.'

'You and Nick both know I've got a lot on my plate—'

'So much you couldn't remember that next weekend's Yvette's birthday?'

Nick found himself sinking down on to the top step, arms wound around the banister.

'She hadn't been my wife *years* before she died,' his father was protesting below. 'Why do I have to remember her birthday?'

'Because she's your son's mother, Mike! Yvette will always be that, no matter how much you try to ignore the fact that she ever existed. You don't even have a photo of her, at least none that isn't tucked away in some dusty old corner.'

Nick lost Bill's next words as his thoughts turned to the photo frame hidden in his bookcase. He nearly pushed himself up to fetch it out, put it proudly on display, but his fingers froze on the banister post. No one went into his room apart from the cleaner. No one knew where the picture was: no one apart from him, and what would he do if he took it out? Turn it the wrong way round? Endlessly shift it so that the reflection off the glass always obscured her face? Try to avoid ever looking at that part of his room, as if it didn't exist? Might as well treat the picture as if it were a Medusa, ready to turn him to stone if he met her eyes.

Better the shame of leaving the photograph hidden. Some days he didn't even remember it was there.

From below, Bill's voice again, soft but insistent. 'Do you ever talk about her with him?'

'For God's sake, Bill, where would I even *start*?'

A motorbike growled past outside: Nick felt the throb of the engine match the angry beat of his heart.

In the living room he heard Bill sigh. 'Sometimes you can do more harm saying nothing than saying the wrong thing.'

'Have you met my son, Bill? Honestly, what does a person

say about this? "I'm sorry your mother went loony tunes and refused to see or speak to you in the two years before she died. I think it stinks too.'"

For a moment there was nothing, perhaps because they were silent or speaking too quietly to be heard.

'If you and Nick won't feel I'm intruding, I'll go with you on Saturday,' Bill said eventually. 'But if I do this, Mike, you have to *promise* that on the Sunday you'll do something with Nick, just the two of you. Drive to the Norfolk coast. Have some fish and chips. Walk on the beach. Just take yourself away from your desk and turn off your phone. And try not to go endlessly on about Nick's studies. He probably thinks you'd forget about him completely if he didn't have some brilliant new marks to tell you about.'

'Oh, give over, Bill. You know as well as I do that Nick's always been driven to excel with his studies. And, yes, of *course* I've encouraged him, but it came from him. It was his idea to come to Cambridge, not mine. He wanted to do this. And maybe I do talk a lot about his work, but it's the only thing that's simple. He's always doing well. It's something happy we can share—'

'And that would be fine, if there was other stuff you talked about too.'

For a moment, the house went still, as if the building were holding its breath. When his father spoke, it was softly but with a strange intense note in his voice Nick didn't recognise. 'I do try, you know, with Nick. I have these times when I get home at a reasonable hour for a week and then ... I don't know what happens. It just seems so hard suddenly. And then I think, "Well, I'll just have a day off," and suddenly it's like I can't face it any more and then I think, "If I've already failed, why—" I'm so close to finally making named partner, maybe after . . .'

Nick crept down one stair then another, but for a while there was silence below.

'I understand that, Mike, but I worry that in a few years, when you suddenly decide you're ready to have a bigger part in his life, you'll find you've used up all your second chances. He's not going to be a kid forever. Soon he's going to be an adult and then he's going to turn around and say, "You didn't want me when I needed you, so why should I want you now that you need me?" And I don't think you're going to like it, Mike. I don't think you're going to like it at all.'

Nick could only just hear his father's reply over the bass beat of his blood in his ears.

'*Thanks* for that, Bill. What a *happy* thought to end the day on.'

'I'm not trying to make you happy, Mike. I've spent the last five years telling myself it wasn't my business and "what do I know since I'm not a father?" But one day I'm going to be there when you realise what a little bit more time with Nick now would have meant to your relationship and, when you ask me how it happened, I want to be telling the truth when I say I tried to make you listen.'

Nick strained into the silence.

'What if I don't know how?'

'Then you'd better learn, Mike. Somehow you'd better learn.'

Silence again, or if they were speaking it was too softly for Nick to hear.

'Let's have a drink, Mike. Let's just have a long drink. I promise the only topics of conversation will be cricket matches on Fenner's. Getting our University Blues. Old triumphs from when we were young.'

Nick pushed himself to his feet and crept away upstairs as laughter broke out in the living room. He went to the bathroom to brush his teeth, but there was something wrong with the face looking out at him from the mirror: too many shadows, too many angles. His hand fumbled for the light switch. He ended up putting hair gel on his toothbrush the first time round, but it was better in the dark. He didn't have to face himself there.

∞

This is pathetic, he told himself, as he skimmed another review of the film he was seeing later. He wasted a further half-hour watching a series of interviews with the actors.

'It's meant to be a trip to the cinema, not a research project,' Tim said, sniggering, when he realised what Nick was doing.

Nick stuck his tongue out and stomped upstairs to get ready. He spent the walk to the Grafton Centre trying out different ways of sounding clever rather than like he'd studied up. But when the others arrived it turned out they'd already dissected the reviews and specials on the way over from College.

Nick's Plan B – to buy the biggest bucket of popcorn available – was more successful: soon the group were clustered round him as they queued.

'ID,' said the doorman when Nick presented his ticket.

'You've got to be kidding me,' muttered Frank. 'Look, mate, how often do you take a passport to the cinema? Surely a student ID for the Cambridge University Library—'

'If your little brother is eighteen, I will eat that extraordinarily ugly hat you're wearing.'

Frank growled. 'Look, you—'

'I don't have any other ID,' Nick cut in. 'But I *have* got a ticket and my student—'

'You can show me a thousand student cards and I won't believe you're eighteen. Now, there's nothing stopping a person buying a ticket from the machine, but it's an 18 certificate so . . .'

Nick sighed. 'See you on Monday, OK, Frank? *In lectures*,' he added loudly.

The doorman rolled his eyes.

Frank shuffled his feet. 'Sorry, Nick. Before you go, you couldn't give me those . . .'

Shoving the popcorn into Susie's arms, Nick wrestled his notebook out of his bag, trying not to meet anyone's eyes. He pushed the book into Frank's hands then turned away. A chorus of desultory goodbyes echoed after him.

If he'd been a character in a film, he would have screamed at the night skies. At the least he would have turned his face to the clouds and let the rain pour down on him. Instead, he pulled up his hood, dug his hands into his pockets and set off for home.

It was nice to let himself into the house to the sound of music in the sitting room, lively big-band stuff with a happy honking of brass. The stereo was playing at a satisfying volume, though the living room and kitchen were empty, and Nick found himself smiling unexpectedly as he started pawing through the kitchen cupboards, looking for junk food, while his feet moved to the music of their own accord.

'Maybe you should join the ballroom dancing squad.'

Nick whirled at the voice.

'That looked like actual dance steps,' Tim said, an expression of perplexed amusement on his face.

Nick ducked his head. 'My grandmother taught me,' he said.

When Tim came and slouched against the counter next to him so he could help himself to the bag of nachos, Nick sighed.

'I used to go to stay with her in the holidays,' he found himself saying without quite meaning to. 'Even before my parents split up, my mum ... Anyway, I always used to go and stay with my grandmother and she loved this sort of music. She had this huge garden, or it seemed huge to me. Herb beds, lots of old brick walls with climbing roses and honeysuckle. We used to grow seedlings together. Lupin and marigold and hollyhock. We'd plant them in the Easter holidays: by the summer they'd be potted up and ready to go out in the garden when Mum dropped me off. It's funny, I only ever remember it being sunny or storming. Storms were when we'd listen to music and she'd show me how to dance. And then she'd read to me. We used to read together for *hours*. And she *still* found time to cook. This one time she put me on a footstool to mix in the eggs for a cake and I puffed flour in a huge mushroom cloud over the whole table. She just laughed and hugged me so we were both covered in cake mix.' He shook his head, pasted on a more normal, less wistful smile. 'It'd be nice to be able to bake stuff now. Wish I'd paid more attention.'

'You and me both,' said Tim. 'My sister was always the one in the kitchen with Mum when it was time to cook. Not sure if that's 'cos she was the girl or 'cos I liked going to the shed with Dad and she didn't. Thing about spiders.' He grinned. 'I thought you were going to the cinema tonight?'

'Got carded.'

'You don't have much luck with your attempts to socialise, do you?'

'You mean fate's telling me to be a hermit and to spend even more time with my head buried in a book? Maybe this is one of the things I need to be wise enough to accept I can't change.'

'That's clearly what it is,' Tim said, rolling his eyes. 'Anyway, while we're on the subject of somewhat-less-than-happy stuff, is there anything I can get for the weekend? You know, something to cheer you up after ... after you visit the graveyard. I mean, it's been a pretty sucky term. Might as well be sucky with ice cream.'

Nick shrugged. 'Dad and I are going to Norfolk on Sunday.'

Tim blinked in surprise. 'That sounds like a good idea.'

'Yeah,' Nick said. 'It was Bill's.'

Chapter²⁰

**(Lent Term × Week 6
[≈ end of February])**

'That looks fresh,' said Michael, stooping to peer at a poppy wreath at the base of the war memorial. 'I wonder who left it. Is that a card?'

Nick stared down at his father's head as he bent to read the message, then turned away along the path that cut to the left through the garden of graves.

Bill loitered for a moment, then followed. 'Is it your grandmother's plot too?' he asked, matching his pace to Nick's.

'Grandfather's. My grandmother wanted to be cremated. Mum was meant to put her ashes on the roses at her house but she . . . she wasn't well, so I did it.'

'Have you ever gone back to visit?' Bill prompted, when Nick didn't go on.

'Mum said she couldn't keep the house with bits of her

mother floating about everywhere, so ...' Nick snapped his mouth shut with an audible click. 'I don't know who she sold it to. It would be awful if they'd torn up her garden, chopped down the roses.' He closed his eyes. 'I'd rather imagine it's all still there and one day I'll buy the house back and ...'

He opened his eyes, looking on down the path, and there was Roger, standing by one of the graves, a bouquet of lilies – red and gold, her favourites – in his arms. For a moment it was like looking through a camera viewfinder as the focus sharpened painfully then dulled to vagueness and finally resolved to normal. There was a sharp ringing in his ears, like the echoing slow-frame aftermath of a bomb blast in a film.

'Is that Roger?' Bill asked, squinting down the path.

Nick nodded as if his head were badly connected to his neck. He hoped his face was blank rather than stricken, but his skin felt tight, his eyes dry with staring.

'It is, isn't it?' Bill was saying, still squinting ahead into the sunlight. 'Have you seen him at all these last two years? Since the funeral, I mean.'

'We haven't talked since the morning after Mum ... after she got sick. Not that we talked then.' The words came more easily than he'd expected, his voice calm and level. 'I got up and he called Dad. Said I had to be gone by the time he got back from work. And that was it. We didn't talk at the funeral.'

A sound echoed across the graveyard. Roger was staring in their direction. His eyes fixed on Nick with something like rage, or fear, or grief. Suddenly, he crouched to slam his bouquet into the flower-holder at the base of the headstone with a movement like a sword thrust. Then he stalked off down the curve of the path that led around the far side of the church.

Nick let out a sigh that felt equal parts relief and disappointment. For a moment, he looked away past the moss-grown wall to the village beyond. A woman in tweeds and wellies, surrounded by a pack of dogs, squelched past. She touched her hand to her gamekeeper's hat when she saw them looking her way.

'Where on earth has Mike got to?' Bill asked, making a show of looking around for him.

'If he doesn't actually want to come to the grave that's OK. Everyone deals with grief in their own way, right? I don't need to make this hard on him.'

Bill looked down at him, his expression torn. 'Would you rather have a bit of time by yourself?'

Nick shrugged. 'I don't mind. It's good of you to come at all. You didn't have to.' He felt Bill watching him as he set off down the path again, cradling his own bouquet to his chest. Glancing back, he saw Michael, phone pressed to his ear, gesticulating wildly. The woman in the wellies stopped to glare at him. One of her dogs paused to pee on Michael's car.

When he carried on to the grave Bill matched him pace for pace, but then stopped a few steps away as Nick reached the plot and crouched beside the stone, hand hovering in the air over Roger's flowers. Above them, a cherry tree was just coming into leaf. A sudden wind clattered the branches together, making Nick recoil and look up with a start of horror entirely inappropriate to the sight of the grey and blue patched sky, the fast-moving clouds. He swallowed, shook his head as if that would push away the echo of the sound of fins beating against shards of glass.

'Penny for your thoughts?' Bill asked, crouching next to him.

Nick looked away to a cluster of daffodils polishing their budding trumpets against a nearby headstone. 'I wonder whose grave that is,' he whispered. The writing had all but been weathered away, what was left obscured by the shadows of the branches swaying across the pocked grey and yellow surface. 'You can't read the inscription any more, but someone still visits, leaves flowers. Do you think it's just the church wardens or the person's family, even after all this time? Someone who's still grieving.'

The leaves on the cherry tree were shiny and strange: a deep red-orange, like molten copper.

Nick sighed. He put his bouquet carefully down on the grass, then tugged Roger's from the grating.

Bill drew in his breath.

Nick dropped the flowers back into the holder, laid his own bouquet along the bottom of the stone, then climbed abruptly back to his feet.

Bill stood too, reaching over to squeeze his shoulder. 'Do you want ... I mean, do you need ...' Bill stopped, took a deep breath. 'I've noticed Mike doesn't have any photos of your mum in the house. Do you ... do you want me to find you one?'

Nick flinched. 'I've got a picture,' he whispered. 'In my room.'

'Oh. Good. Just thought I should check: you know, in case.'

Nick nodded without lifting his eyes from the gravestone, his throat working. 'Do you think I should stay a bit longer?'

'It's up to you, Nick. What do you *want*?'

Nick laughed, an oddly cheerful sound. 'I want to stop dreaming about the fish dying.' He turned away, let his feet lead him down the path away from the war memorial. 'The fish tank broke. The night she got sick. I tried to gather them up but they were so quick. So desperate. There was this angel fish. It kept flapping about over my toes. I couldn't seem to get hold of it. It kept arching about in the splinters of glass. It was the strangest noise. Like tinkling and clapping together. I scooped it up eventually and got it back in the water, but I guess there wasn't enough left or I hurt it when I grabbed it, or maybe it had shredded itself on the glass, but when I put it back in the water it was dead already.'

There were no words to describe the way it had floated to the surface, belly-up, already beyond hope.

'By the time I caught the next one there was no water left to put it in. It felt so strange in my hands: like a butterfly trapped against a window. And then it wasn't anything.'

Bill waited for him to continue, but they walked on, a full circle around the church and then they were back at the war memorial.

Michael saw them, held up a hand as he turned away to

finish his call. He slipped his phone back into his pocket with a smile. 'Right, shall we go find some lunch?'

∞

There were good bits to the day. The way the car sailed smoothly down the long straight road, field after field after field rushing by. The way the road curved to the left and suddenly the landscape was endless woods, all bracken and fern, yellow and brown with damp. The sudden flash of a lichened silver birch, the darkness of stunted firs. The way the world opened out into a horizon of sea and sky.

They stopped and wandered a stretch of deserted pebble beach, pointing out shells and interesting bits of seaweed while the sky faded to palest yellow, the sun colourless above the hard grey water. Over the roar of the wind and the waves, the gulls screamed relentlessly.

Now the storm outside the house, clawing around the chimneys, sounded little different.

A yelp. Nick spun to see a figure looming in the kitchen doorway.

The light flicked on, momentarily blinding him.

'God, Nick,' said Tim, sounding shaken. 'Gave me a heart attack. Eyes glinting in the dark.'

Nick blinked against the brightness as he watched Tim's gaze move from the glass in his hand to the whisky bottle on the counter. When Tim looked up to his face again, he met his housemate's eyes defiantly, lifting the glass and drinking deeply, jaw tightening as he forced back his reaction to the burn of the alcohol. 'You going to tell my dad?' he croaked as nastily as he could manage over the urge to cough.

Tim crossed the kitchen to lean against the table. 'How many glasses is that?'

'My first. Thought I'd try it. It's what everyone else seems to do when things go wrong. Not sure why, though, so you needn't worry. I'll be done after this.'

Tim sighed. He pushed away from the table to fetch down a second glass, poured his own measure of whisky then put the bottle away.

'Are you going to tell him?' Nick repeated.

'Not if this is just a one-off. I make no promises if it's the start of a habit.' Tim swilled the liquid about the bottom of his own glass. 'You could try talking to me about it, you know. My sister bottled things up after our parents died. Didn't do her any good.'

Nick snorted, taking another deep swallow from his glass.

'I might just understand,' Tim said gently, taken aback when Nick's head snapped up, a sneer twisting his face: an expression far too old for it.

'You don't know how I feel,' he hissed.

'Maybe I don't,' Tim found himself saying before he could stop himself. 'I lost *both* my parents after all. *And* my sister moved halfway across the world.'

Nick pushed himself away from the counter, gulping back the last of his drink with a sound midway between a cough and a bark of laughter. Slamming the glass down on the counter, he glared at Tim with a depth of disdain that made Tim's jaw clench with anger.

'You *don't* know how I feel,' he whispered, voice sharp as broken glass. Then he was gone, flitting out of the kitchen and away up the stairs.

Tim cursed under his breath, resisting the urge to punch a fist into the counter. Instead, he fetched out the bottle again. It took two further glasses to wash away the freshness of the sting of his anger at Nick. At himself.

Chapter[21]

(Lent Term × Week 7
[≈ start of March])

When Nick stepped out of the p'lodge to find the Men's Third VIII standing across the path in Front Court, he turned back on himself and walked away, out of College again.

It would probably have been fine, he muttered angrily at himself as he followed Trinity Lane left into Trinity Street. *This is Cambridge University, not sixth form.* But he didn't feel equal to the possibility that there would prove to be little difference. *They'll have forgotten after the Lents. Better to wait until then. Not like I needed to be in College today. The library can wait.* It would have been different if he could have visited Professor Gosswin, but without being able to seek refuge in her set there was no point pushing his luck.

The sun had disappeared when he turned at Round Church into St John's, the buildings rearing around him like a Tudor castle, cold and forbidding, ready to repel invaders. Even after eight months, he was still surprised by how different all the colleges were: how different courtyards within the *same* college were. The red-brick walls of First Court then Second Court pressed in on him as the clouds boiled angrily above the town. He half expected to find archers leaning out of the arrow slits or over the crenellations tipped in tawny stone, usually the colour of clotted cream, today grey and dull under the darkening sky.

For once the Bridge of Sighs seemed forlorn, as if all the beauty of the stone tracery, the lancet windows opening over the Cam, had been drained away. He walked to the Backs and then along, through the gates into Clare and up the long path to the bridge.

There was a precarious magic to Cambridge: a feeling that time didn't work the same way there. That you could walk through a day stepping in and out of the past, the present, the future, all quite seamlessly, with no one batting an eyelid. The city floated below the fog of modern worries, all its rush and roar one step out of reach. Perhaps that was why the beauty of the willows weeping into the river, the gold of King's chapel, the white of Clare, the wine-red of Trinity Hall, seemed suddenly painful, like something slipping through his fingers.

The walk home seemed to stretch, long and cold, when all he wanted was to be there, now, curled up on his window seat with Professor Gosswin's book under his hands. Instead, there were tourists standing in his path, and mothers with buggies ploughing a furrow through the crowds, and cars splashing up water from potholes.

By the time he stumbled through the front door, tripping on the mail on the doormat, his throat felt raw with frustration and disappointment. He slammed about the kitchen, turning the act of tea-making into one of violence. When the kettle was grumbling on the counter, he slumped into a chair, hands in his hair, torn between laughter at his own ridiculousness and tears.

Upstairs, he found himself staring at the postcard on his wall.

> *Grant me the serenity to accept the things I cannot change*

Serenity seemed too much to hope for, but as always there was one thing he could do something about: one way to turn misery into success.

He splashed his face with water, collected his supervision work, tucked Professor Gosswin's book under the window-seat cushion and forced his mind on to his Analysis I problems.

When the phone rang a while later, he answered without looking at the display, still finishing a line in his equation workings. 'Hullo?'

'Hi, Nick.'

'Bill! Everything OK?'

'Fine. I heard Professor Gosswin's going into a nursing home. Just thought I'd check in.'

Nick laid his pen down carefully, cleared his throat.

'Different people recover at different rates,' he said. 'It doesn't mean she's stuck there forever. It's not an exact science.'

At the other end of the line Bill sighed.

'I'm not expecting a miracle or anything but it's too early to give up. It can be six months before a trajectory really becomes clear.'

'Well, it's good to keep positive so long as you don't expect too much.' They were both silent for a moment. 'Look, Nick, I know your dad's away this weekend so I was wondering if you might like to come down to mine for a day or two: have a change of scenery.'

The face reflecting back from the window beamed.

'Your dad and I had a talk over lunch the other day and we thought—'

We thought ... A stricken look replaced the smile. 'It's exam term. I have work to do.' The words came out sharp and cold.

For a moment there was silence on the other end of the line. When Bill's voice came again, it was full of surprise and hurt. 'A weekend off won't do any harm, surely.'

'You don't have to do that,' Nick said, voice rough with pain. 'You're not my father's keeper, or mine. You don't have to pick up the pieces: it's not your problem.' He'd hung up before he realised what he was doing, pushing the phone away so roughly it clattered off the far side of the table on to the floor.

∞

Tim looked up from his breakfast with a raised eyebrow when Nick let the phone ring and ring. 'Are you *still* dodging Bill? It's been three days. Can't you give the man a break? I don't know what he—'

'Well, since it's none of your bleeding business, that's not a problem, is it?' Nick snapped. The kitchen seemed suddenly dim and small, as if the feeling in his chest had squeezed the walls in. 'I've got a lecture.'

He pulled his coat on, setting a glare on his face as he opened the front door, but the day was unexpectedly bright and sunny, the world big and wide and full of other people with other problems.

Parker's Piece was his and the seagulls', a white sea under a fierce sun. Nick paused in the middle, turning slowly around and around as he stared up at the cloudless sky, feeling tiny and isolated and peaceful.

Frank wasn't at the lecture and Susie hurried off the minute it was over, the rest melting away before he'd had a chance to ask if anyone fancied revising together over a cup of tea. The streets were hectic with tourists, frantic with hurrying irritated students, people on bicycles speeding the wrong way up pedestrianised streets. He headed towards College, planning to work in the library, but at the last moment swerved away and darted through the dreary forbidding entrance to Caius instead.

Emerging into the light, he stepped on to a flagstone path lined with an avenue of peeling silver-barked plane trees. All around, the buildings soared up in blue-grey spires and gothic turrets, like a transplanted French chateau. Wisteria twined around windows and doorways, shimmering with the silver-white of unfurled buds. It always seemed preternaturally quiet here, like a secluded monastery rather than a college, as if he had stepped out of time and space. The trees embraced overhead, elegant and secretive, shading the path. It would be beautiful when they came fully into leaf. Nothing like the over-pruned trees, mutilated into order, that lined his father's street in London.

'*Excuse* me,' said a sneering, nasal voice. 'The *College* is *closed* to visitors.'

Nick turned to find a bald porter in a stiff black suit glaring at him. 'I'm a student,' he said, drawing his library card out of his pocket.

The porter took it with a scornful expression. His eyebrows rose. 'Very well,' he said, making a dismissive gesture. 'You may continue.'

Nick was tempted to pull a face, but the man stayed staring after him as he set off up the path. The inner court held wallflowers and pansies in happy reds and yellows and burnt orange, but he let the path lead him to the right, past the herbaceous border in front of the chapel, where forget-me-not and tulips cowered below a tottering ceanothus.

Look at all that dead wood! With a disconcerting jolt, he almost thought his grandmother's voice was real. *Why aren't the gardeners pruning properly? That'll have to go right back.*

The sudden wish to be there again, in her garden, was like something wild and clawed in his chest, bringing tears to his eyes. For a moment, he nearly dived into the nearest staircase doorway to run up and up the winding steps until somewhere in the damp grey shadows he found a place where he could sit down, bury his face in his knees and let slow silent tears soak his jeans. He could practically hear his own ragged breathing already echoing down the stairwell, but instead he strode out of the gates.

Along the Backs, the shadowed ground under the trees at the back of King's was all bluebells and wild buttercups. He cut the corner along Queens' Green to follow Silver Street, stopped to stare downriver. Under the Mathematical Bridge wood hyacinth nestled among a flood of daffodils.

All his favourite places – all the beauty that usually made the worst days bearable – suddenly seemed flat and unlovely.

Even though his work was on track, the lure of a First seemed dim lately. A minimum requirement, rather than a sufficient condition for happiness. Maybe it had been the less important part of his birthday 'this time next year' wish after all.

He walked back towards College down KP, telling himself the story about the traffic cone a night climber had balanced first on one spire of King's Chapel, then, as soon as they'd half-erected a scaffold to remove it, the opposite one. Then the tale about the Christmas an enterprising team of climbers covered all four corner spires with Santa hats. Anything to take his mind off the pain lodged in his throat, a promise of tears that refused to be swallowed down. Outside Trinity, he tried to smile at the wooden chair leg Henry VIII brandished above the Great Gate.

Finally, sitting with his back against one of the yew trees in the Jesus grounds, damp seeping slowly into his jeans, he opened his notebook, fixed his eyes at the top of the page and read viciously, word after word after word.

∞

Two hours later, he was staring into the toaster while the edges of the bread turned black when the sound of a key crunching into the front-door lock startled him from his daze. He popped the toast out and threw it in the bin. 'Tim? I thought you were upstairs. Do you want a pizza or should we try cooking pasta again?' he called.

'I'm up for pasta.'

Nick whirled round to find Bill standing in the doorway.

'I hope you don't mind that I let myself in with the spare key your dad gave me.'

Nick shook his head.

Bill gave a hesitant smile when Nick continued staring at him. 'Right, then. Saucepan.' He bent and pulled a pot out of the cupboard.

Nick backed up to give him space then stood staring vacantly at the side of Bill's face as he tipped salt into the water in the pan. One teaspoon, a shrug, another.

'My ex-wife always said the key with pasta was to put plenty of salt in the water. Of course, she never said what "plenty" amounts to for the culinary deficient among us.'

When Nick didn't laugh, Bill put a gentle hand on his

shoulder and steered him to a chair. Nick craned his head sideways to watch him, frowning, but though he opened his mouth once, he shut it again without saying anything.

'Now, where does pasta sauce live?'

Nick watched Bill opening cupboard doors, one after the other.

'Am I getting any warmer?'

'On the left,' Nick whispered. He swallowed. 'I'm sorry,' he blurted out. 'I didn't ... I didn't mean to be ungrateful.'

Bill turned with a smile, which quickly became a frown. 'It's not a question of gratitude, Nick.'

Nick looked away with a shrug.

'I didn't mean to upset you when we talked on Tuesday. I just thought it would be nice for you to get away from everything for a little bit.'

Nick pushed hurriedly to his feet and started setting out cutlery. 'It would have been nice,' he whispered over the clatter of the silverware. 'It would have been *lovely* if you weren't just doing it for my dad.'

'Talking to the table again? Gotta keep those forks in order,' Bill called from his place at the stove. 'I couldn't get away before now, but you've been rather pointedly dodging my calls, so I figured I'd better come in person to apologise for whatever I said that made you so upset. I really did mean well, you know.'

Nick let the pepper grinder topple out of his hands. He'd always hoped against hope that Bill didn't see things for how they were with Michael. But he did. Of course he did. And he felt bad about it. Was trying to do the decent thing. But that was all it was. Kindness and pity, not love: that was all it ever was.

'I've got to go,' someone said in a thin, desperate little voice, and then he was out on the street, running, running.

∞

'Is everything all right?' Tim called, peering down from the landing.

Bill let his hand fall from the door latch. 'I can't seem to do anything right with Nick this week. I don't suppose you know where he would run off to?'

Tim frowned, starting down the stairs. 'You could try his mobile.'

'I doubt he'd answer. He's *not* happy with me.'

'If you need to head home again—'

'No, no. If nothing else, maybe I'll get points for sticking around. I imagine Michael does precious little of that when things get difficult.'

Tim grimaced. 'Has Michael always been like this?'

'God, I hope not.' Bill sighed, leading the way back to the kitchen. 'I've never wanted to push things – tread on Mike's toes – but I'm starting to think perhaps I should have ... I don't know. Done more, I guess, even if it *was* interfering.'

Tim busied himself setting a little pan on the hob next to the pot of water and tipped the jar of sauce into it. 'While we're on the subject of failures to communicate with Nick, I managed to say completely the wrong thing the other night because I'm obviously missing something important about what happened to his mum.' He raked a hand through his hair. 'I'm not volunteering for any cosy heart-to-hearts on the subject,' he added quickly, 'but I don't want to be cruel out of ignorance.'

Bill pushed his fingers up under his glasses to rub at his eyes. 'Yvette ... Yvette was always very ... fragile. When she and Mike split up, I didn't really see Nick much for a while. Then one day Mike gets this call. Yvette has had some sort of breakdown – bad enough that they institutionalised her on the spot – and Roger point-blank refuses to look after Nick for another day. It's a bolt from the blue, so Mike's trying to find out what's going on, whether Nick's there to live with him permanently, and it's the middle of term so we're scrambling about, trying to get Nick into a new school ...'

Leaning back against the counter, he stared blankly into the floor. 'Yvette wouldn't take calls from Mike or Nick, wouldn't let either of them visit. Eventually she got out of the hospital, but she ended up back in another one about a month later. Then another ... It was pills in the end: she hoarded them, then did a bunk from the hospital. A dog-walker found her on the beach a few days later.' He sighed, looking away, not wanting to see Tim's reaction. 'Look, Tim, I know this is a bit awkward, but you're the one who's reliably *here*. If ... if I gave you my number, do you think you could call me if ... if ...'

'If Nick needs help?' Tim shrugged, pulling a face. 'I'll do what I can, but I'm not going to snitch on him about every little thing. And you know I'm away for a week at the start of term for my sister's wedding—'

The front door snicked shut. A moment later, Nick appeared in the doorway. He started at seeing them both, then ducked his head.

'Think we're about ready to eat,' said Bill gently. 'How about you finish setting the table?'

Nick's head came up. After a moment, he gave a tentative smile. Bill nodded, smiling back, and busied himself with straining the pasta.

'Just going to run upstairs,' Tim said, leaving them to it.

'I thought you'd have gone.' Nick directed the words past Bill's left shoulder.

'I wasn't going to go before we'd talked, Nick. Not when I'd upset you so much. You know that was the last thing I meant to do – at least I hope you know that.'

Nick nodded, turning away to fetch drinks.

'I'm sorry, Nick. For whatever I said that hurt you so much.'

Nick flinched, raising a shoulder as if to ward off a blow.

'I really was just trying to help. Because I *do* want to help. If I can. You know you can always call me, whenever you want. For *any* reason. If you need someone to talk to or . . . or somewhere to get away to . . .'

Nick turned then, stared up at him with those steady, unblinking blue eyes. Bill tried not to wriggle under the intensity of that gaze, knowing he was being weighed, but a spatter of sauce from the boiling pot distracted him and the opportunity was gone.

'Thank you,' Nick said politely. 'I appreciate that, Bill.'

Bill felt his neck flame with a mix of anger and frustration, wondering how he'd managed to set himself a dozen paces back with Nick all in one disastrous day. It had been years since Nick had been so coolly distant.

'Right, are we ready to eat?' Tim called as he trotted back into the kitchen.

It was only when they sat down that they realised Nick had put the knives and forks on the wrong sides of the plates, had set out drinks but no glasses. He wouldn't meet Bill's eyes during the meal, or as they cleared up, washed the dishes, put everything away.

'I'm sorry I have to go,' Bill said, trying to catch Nick's gaze as Nick helped him into his coat an hour later.

'It was really nice of you to come all this way to check up on me. Thanks for dinner,' Nick said blandly. 'Have a safe journey home.'

Chapter 22

(Easter Vacation
[≈ start of April])

The library was cool and furiously hushed, full of anxious finalists carrying enormous piles of books to the reading desks, flicking through one then another and then another, putting off any actual work for as long as possible before subsiding to scribble frantic notes that would make no sense even to them by the end of the day.

The light moved the shadows from one side of the shelves to the other. The wide padded window seat on the third floor had become a familiar haunt over the past fortnight. With Tim using every waking moment of the holidays to boost his finances ahead of his trip to America, the house had become empty. Even in the comfort of the front bay window at home, clear bright sunlight making the carpet warm under his feet, Nick suddenly felt strange and out of place. He'd taken to wandering the town, where at least the act of walking helped against the strange churning in his stomach, as if disaster were stalking him, just visible at the edges of his vision.

During term-time, the Jerwood library had always been a place he could be alone without feeling lonely, with the Cam below and Clare and King's stretching out at his feet, books and fellow students all around. Only it hadn't been like that recently, and especially today.

Nothing was what he'd hoped for from Cambridge. The work was usually interesting, rarely too hard. He was developing basic friendships with Susie, Frank and some of the others in their Thursday study group. Then there was Tim. And Ange, dropping by to brighten the house with hugs and laughter.

But for a while there had been the boat club: people he belonged with, even if he didn't particularly like them.

Most of all, there had been Professor Gosswin. College felt empty without her: without the possibility of dropping into her set when it felt like the world was closing in, dark and grey.

It had all become somehow precarious, like he was still waiting for life to start: waiting for happiness to catch up with him, though he'd thought for a while that it was finally on the horizon. Maybe if time could just stop for a while, he'd be able to figure it out, but it kept grinding on, rushing him forwards without anything changing for the better.

He'd started dreaming of the fish tank almost every night: it felt like a warning, though with his work on track – tasks ticked off daily on the revision timetable he'd drawn up for the eight weeks until the exams – he couldn't think what trouble could lie ahead that he wouldn't be able to avert. He was changing what he could in his life, doing everything possible to ensure his First, and as for the rest – the friendships he'd hoped to make – wisdom said that if he'd tried and failed, maybe it was time to accept that it couldn't be changed. At least not for now.

Sighing, he tucked his notes into his pocket, fetched his new bike from North Court and headed off to HM Prison UL.

For a while he browsed the latest exhibits in the chilly underground exhibition centre. Then he walked the central hall, staring up at the criss-cross plasterwork of the vaulted ceiling. In the stacks, he played with the timer dials on the ends of the bookcases that turned on stretches of dim lighting, buzzing a countdown until they clicked off, plunging the narrow passages between the shelves into darkness again.

When the closing bell rang at seven to signal the quarter-hour warning, he trailed out into a bitter evening wind after the last harried students. Shivering, he wheeled his bike into Burrell's Walk then pedalled slowly down to the crossing. Riding down Garret Hostel Lane was like sailing along a raised causeway with ditchwater glinting coldly on either side. The wrought-iron lamp posts threw round patches of yellow light on to the railings and illuminated the odd clump of bulrushes on the dark banks. He dismounted at the bridge, too tired to pedal up the steep hump, then continued into

Trinity Lane, following it round to the left and then crossing Trinity Street into Rose Crescent.

As he locked his bike to a lamp post, a homeless man who looked little older than Tim was asking a passer-by for change.

When Nick crossed out of Gardies with an extra packet of fries, the relief on the man's face as Nick offered the paper bag made his throat ache. 'It's just chips,' he said, 'but at least it's hot.'

''S kind of you. Appreciate it,' croaked the man. His lip cracked as he forced a smile, a drop of blood welling vivid against his skin. 'First person who's stopped in an hour.'

Nick gave him a tentative smile, left him sinking a chip slowly between his lips, his tongue curling around it, licking away the salt as if he were tasting champagne.

The pavement was already slick with dew as he wheeled his bike back to College, left it in the North Court racks, then trotted down to the river. Perched cross-legged on the wall, the toes of his trainers sticking out over the eight-foot drop to the water, he huddled into his jacket and forced the food down, though his throat felt like it had closed. As if he had been crying.

When he finished, he tossed the bag into the bin and turned to go, only for his feet to return to the wall. It was quiet and still in the dark. The cold pushed the swirl of thoughts from his head as if he'd moved through a storm to the calm beyond.

Eventually, he checked his watch, slipped his phone out of

his pocket and dialled home. The answering machine picked up. 'Hey, Tim. Just reporting in. I should be home in half an hour so don't send out the search party. I've already eaten.'

Pedalling up KP ten minutes later, his face stinging in the wind, he thought he saw someone waving to him outside St Catz. Before he had a chance to raise his hand, a girl darted in front of his bike to join her friends.

The water in Hobson's Conduit looked thick and oily as the bike juddered over the cobbles on to Trumpington Street. The Fitzwilliam Museum loomed white and immense to his right. The Botanic Gardens sailed past on his left, mist creeping stealthily out of the dyke to garland the bushes by the fence. The rains had raised the level of the ditchwater so that the surface caught the light in odd flashes past the railings curtaining it from the path along the road.

Something slammed into his right arm just above the elbow.

The bike spun ninety degrees to face the path, throwing him over the handlebars so that he hit the raised pavement with his shoulder, tumbling helplessly head over heels.

The world wheeled around him.

Blinding pain as his arm impacted against one of the railing posts.

As he curled over, the ground dropped away and he fell.

The cold of the water hit him like a blow, forcing his mouth open in a gasp.

Filthy, silted liquid rushed over his teeth, around his tongue, down his throat.

Thrashing, still disoriented, with no idea which way was up or down, the world rolled dark and icy over and around him.

Striking out, his hand sank into thick, heavy mud and he pushed off. His face broke the surface. Flailing wildly, he managed to get his knees under him. Bent over, waist deep in freezing water, he hacked and choked and gasped as his lungs seized against the pain of silt in his breath. His eyes streamed as brackish water rose up his throat and into his mouth, slick with mud and mucus. For a while there was nothing but the need to breathe.

Gradually the coughing jags subsided.

When he finally lifted his head, he realised he was kneeling in the ditch. Wiping the back of his hand across his mouth, he pushed up, staggering as the mud reached out a thousand hands to hold him down. Grabbing a handful of grass on the bank, he hauled himself upwards, heard his feet suck loose from the bed of the ditch. He slithered up the bank on his belly then crawled under the bottom rung of the railings and let himself collapse on to the path, panting.

The cold forced him back to his feet. He staggered against the railing, clinging as he fought for balance, then slid down into a huddle, knees drawn up to his chest. Pressing his face against the sodden fabric of his jeans, he raised a shaking hand to feel at his arm. The skin above his elbow felt tight and hot.

Cars passed steadily on the street but there was no one on the pavement in either direction. Looking to the side, through the curtain of his dripping hair, he saw his bike, chain trailing, front wheel dented, lying in a heap. One of the lights had come off and shattered. Pieces of red glass littered the path like fresh blood.

Trying to draw a deep breath, he winced as his chest protested, clenching painfully. One fist pressed to his breastbone, he clawed his way up the railing to his feet, then reluctantly bent to grab a handlebar and pull the bike upright. Reaching clumsily into his pocket, he realised that his phone was gone, presumably lost in the mud at the bottom of the ditch.

As the shivers took hold, thrumming through his muscles like electricity, he turned the bike and, using it to support his weight, started wearily up the street again.

It's just a mile, he told himself. *Fifteen hundred metres. Three thousand steps.*

As he turned into Brooklands Avenue, the trees blocked the worst of the wind, but by the time he reached Hills Road and cut across to Warren Close his teeth were chattering so badly he had to lock his jaw to stop it burning with pain.

Across Station Road into Tenison.

The shivers became convulsive, shuddering up from his stomach so that he stumbled against the bike, driving it into a lamp post, a garden wall, a road sign. His fingers stopped burning with pain, grew numb, though his trainers continued to squelch nastily, rubbing blisters into his ankles and toes. His jeans had grown so stiff and heavy he wondered if they'd started to freeze solid.

The thought surprised a bark of laughter from his mouth. Someone crossed to the opposite pavement away from him.

'Hot shower,' he whispered to a cat eyeing him disdainfully from a fence post. 'Not far.'

The shivers were so bad now he felt as if he were on the brink of retching.

The world narrowed to the next fifty metres. The next twenty. The next ten.

He'd been cold, cold, cold forever.

When he reached the house, he could barely bend his fingers to work the latch on the garden gate. He let the bike topple sideways on to the hydrangea bush and staggered to the house. Leaning against the door, he managed to work his key out of his pocket but couldn't hold it still enough to get it into the lock. Finally, he forced it in, wrenched it to the left and stumbled inside. The hall was dark and he immediately fell over the mat.

'Nick, is that you?' Tim's voice, calling from the kitchen. 'Where the *hell* have you been? You said "half an hour" in your message.'

Nick staggered to his feet, grabbing hold of the post at the bottom of the stairs and pressing his forehead against the smooth paint. The warmth of the house was making his head spin.

'I was getting ready to call your dad – Oh, for . . .'

Nick knew Tim was standing in the living-room doorway, but he was having too much trouble keeping his feet under him to spare the energy to look up.

'How the hell did you get this pissed?'

The hall was suddenly flooded with light. Nick shrank away, turning his face to the wall.

'Are you *wet*? What did you do? Jump in the river? You know what, I don't want to know.'

'Not drunk,' Nick gasped. 'Car knocked me off my bike. Fell ...' He had to stop to cough. 'Fell in the ditch by the Botanic Gardens.' He flinched as Tim reached for his arm. ''M OK. Just,' cough, 'cold. *Very cold*.'

'God, are you hurt? Did you hit your head? Do you need an ambulance?'

'No. 'M fine. Just need to warm up.'

'Nick ...'

He managed to tilt his head to squint up into Tim's eyes. 'Just cold. Be fine.'

Tim looked anything but convinced. 'We'll see,' he said dubiously.

Suddenly Tim's arm was about his waist and he was being dragged up the stairs. They staggered into the first-floor bathroom, Tim yanking at the light cord as they passed so that the bobbin on the end bounced about, smacking against the tiles.

'Just perch there for a sec,' Tim said, lowering Nick to the edge of the tub. 'Keep hold of me, OK? Don't fall back.'

Nick's fingers were too cold to work the buttons on his jacket.

Tim pushed his hands away with a sigh. 'I've got it. Just hold on to me, Nick. I don't want you slipping and cracking your head against the wall.'

'But it'd be the,' cough, 'perfect end to the … evening,' Nick croaked, but he fisted his hands into Tim's shirt anyway.

'OK, right arm. *This* one, Nick. Let go of me a sec that side.' Tim ripped the coat off his arm, making Nick hiss. 'Sorry. *Ouch*. That looks … Maybe we *should* go down to Addenbrooke's.'

Nick forced his head up. ''S not broken.'

Tim didn't look convinced.

''S not. Please, Tim. I'm just cold. Don't want to go anywhere.'

Tim's forehead furrowed, his eyes reading uncertainty as he pursed his lips and took a breath through his teeth. 'Let's get you warmed up then we can see. Left arm now.'

Nick listed left as Tim tugged the coat free.

'Hold *on* to me, Nick. Right, time to stand up. You think you can pop your fly for me: get those jeans off?'

Nick nodded, flushing when Tim had to pull the stiff fabric down his legs, then cursed when he realised they should have taken off his trainers and socks first. Nick sighed, letting his head drift forwards to rest against Tim's shoulder as Tim fumbled with his laces.

He felt Tim lean sideways, heard the rattle of the plug chain, the splutter of the taps as the water came on. 'I think for both our sakes we'll just leave the boxers for now.'

Nick gulped a sound that had been intended as a laugh.

'In you get.'

Head reeling as he fought to keep his balance, he stepped

over the edge of the tub, letting Tim guide him down the wall to sit hunched into a ball in the corner of the bath.

He jerked back as the water reached his toes. 'Too hot!'

'Sorry.' Tim adjusted the taps, put his hand under the stream of water to check the temperature. 'Close your eyes a minute. I want to wash some of that muck out of your hair.'

The plughole glugged as Tim opened it to wash the grit down the drain.

'Good enough,' he said eventually, replacing the plug and turning the water back to the faucet. 'Let's see if we can get that a bit hotter now.'

Nick winced as his fingers and toes began to burn. But the shivers were subsiding and, with a sigh, he uncurled, letting his legs drift straight as he slumped against the side of the bath.

'No sleeping in the tub, Nick. House rules,' Tim said, flicking a finger against his cheek. 'Eyes open. *Open*, Nick.'

'Bully,' whispered Nick, squinting wearily up at him as Tim smoothed the hair out of his face.

'Warming up?'

'Yeah,' Nick sighed. 'The water feels … soft.'

'Well, let's get you out and into bed.'

Nick groaned but sat up, let Tim help him to his feet and balance him as he stepped over the rim of the tub. Tim threw a towel over his shoulders then steered him up the stairs to the attic, a hand against his shoulder blade to give him momentum when he nearly tumbled backwards.

'So, here's what we'll do. *I* am going downstairs to make

you a hot drink and *you* are going to change your boxers without toppling over and giving yourself a concussion: deal? No falling, remember!' Tim called as he thumped away downstairs.

Nick waited till the sound of Tim's footsteps had faded before dropping the towel and his underwear, kicking it into a sodden pile in the corner. He crawled into bed to pull on fresh boxers, wriggled into his pyjamas, then pulled the quilt from underneath his body, cocooning himself in it and almost instantly drifting into sleep.

A clatter on the stairs jolted him awake.

He pushed himself up reluctantly and yawned until his breath caught, forcing him to draw at the air in jerky little bursts and let it out in a series of shallow sighs. He slumped limply against the wall as Tim passed him a steaming mug. When his arm trembled stupidly under the weight, he cradled the cup to his chest, tucking his head forwards to sip at it. 'Thanks,' he whispered.

'You can thank me by continuing to pink up so you look less like you've been in the freezer overnight.'

Nick snorted, winced as it turned into a barking cough. He pressed the mug to his chest, massaging it around his breastbone. 'Don't drink the Cam,' he croaked.

'It's not generally recommended. You have heard of Cam Fever, right?' Tim said, putting the tray down by the door and settling on the edge of Nick's bed with his own mug. 'Why didn't you call me? You *do* know this counts as an emergency, right?'

'Lost my phone when I fell in.'

'Ah,' said Tim. 'Payphone?'

Nick shrugged. 'Where? Didn't have any change anyway. Suppose I could have hailed a taxi. Maybe.'

'The person who hit you didn't stop?'

Nick shook his head, slurping blissfully at the froth on top of the hot chocolate.

'Wonder if he was drunk. We'd better call the police—'

'What for? Didn't see the car, the licence plate or the guy driving.' Nick shrugged, wincing as every joint protested.

'Let's have another look at that arm.'

Turning to lift up the sleeve of his pyjama top, Nick realised the heel of his hand was grazed and oozing. 'Pass me a tissue?'

Tim peered closer as Nick dabbed at the cuts. 'Yuck. Let's get some antiseptic on that. Back in a sec.' He clattered away again, returning with the first aid kit he'd insisted they buy after finding there wasn't even a plaster in the house. 'Put the mug down and have a look at your knees and elbows. Think we might need to do some work there too.'

'I can do that,' Nick protested as Tim started dabbing at the graze on his elbow.

'Humour me, all right?'

Tim's weight was warm against his hip, his hands gentle as he held Nick's arm steady to clean the dirt out of his palm. Nick let his head fall back against the wall with a sigh. Suddenly, his eyes were stinging, his throat hot and tight. He couldn't remember the last time either of his parents had cleaned him up after an accident. Probably no one had since his grandmother had died.

Drawing in a sharp breath, he looked away to the window.

'Sorry,' said Tim.

Nick shook his head. ''S OK. Doesn't hurt.'

Tim cast him a sceptical look. 'OK, tough guy.'

Nick curled the nails of his free hand into his palm, forcing the tears away.

'You OK?' Tim asked gently, though he kept his gaze on Nick's hand.

'Yeah,' he managed hoarsely. 'Just really … tired. Bit … off. I'm sorry to ruin your evening. It must be …' Glancing over to the bedside table, he realised the clock was reading two in the morning. 'How did it get so late? You've got work in a few hours—'

'Not a problem, Nick. You didn't *choose* to get hit by a car.'

Nick blinked at him, realising only now that Tim's clothes were patched with wet and smears of mud. 'You must be cold—'

'I am absolutely fine, Nick. Now, do you think you could go to sleep?'

Nick yawned in response.

Tim laughed. He tucked the covers up to Nick's shoulders. 'I'll keep my door open and you will call me – you *will*, Nick – if you feel funny in the night. I mean it. I will not be a happy person if I wake up to find you passed out in a corner somewhere.'

'No passing out in corners,' Nick mumbled between yawns.

'Promise?'

'Mm.'

'I'll translate that as a yes. Sleep well.'

Nick made an effort to say thank you as Tim patted his shoulder, but he was already falling asleep and the words drifted away into the dark.

∞

'Sit,' Tim ordered, as Nick appeared in the kitchen doorway the next morning, hair sticking up in spikes, eyes barely open. 'You get caffeine *after* we've checked out that arm.'

Nick mumbled something incomprehensible, wincing as he twisted his arm to look at the scarlet and purple bruise above his elbow. He prodded it, rotated the arm experimentally, felt gingerly along the bone. 'Not broken.'

'Got X-ray fingers, have you?'

'It's not broken,' Nick repeated. 'It's just a bone bruise. It'll de-swell in a few days.'

'"De-swell"?'

Nick grunted. 'You know what I mean. Now *give me tea.*'

'Your humble servant lives but to serve.' Tim dipped a curtsey in his direction. 'What's the scar from?'

Nick snatched his fingers from tracing the white scrollwork of scarring along his lower arm. 'Mixture of things. Jerk at school stamping on me in football boots. Then the fish tank got broken, the night my mum . . .'

'When she had the breakdown?'

262

'Yeah.' He pulled his sleeve down again. 'I was trying to save the fish but . . .' He shrugged, then sneezed. '*Please* tell me I am not about to get a cold.'

'Ah, but didn't they let you into Cambridge early precisely because you pick things up fast?'

Nick groaned, bending forward to rest his forehead against the table. 'I thought you had work?'

'I traded with Ange for tomorrow. I had to tell her why though, so expect to be hugged to within an inch of your life shortly after closing time at Clowns. Actually, she told me to hug you in the meantime, but maybe we could just pretend that happened?'

'Our little secret,' Nick promised.

Chapter[23]

(Easter Term × Week 0
[≈ second week of April])

The nursing home was less than a mile from a tiny village station twenty minutes outside Cambridge, but it felt like the middle of nowhere: a splay of buildings in a little housing estate of bungalows and tiny two-storey semi-detached properties abutting on endless flat fields.

Tim skirted around a dispirited stand of yucca plants and a rotting palm tree to the front doors. They were locked, but a buzz at the doorbell produced a click and, when he pulled, the door opened.

A rotund little man was waiting for him in the hall, rocking happily backwards and forwards on his heels. 'Could you just sign in here?' he asked, gesturing to a visitors' book on a table by the front office.

'I'm here for Professor Gosswin. Nick's probably with her already—'

'Yes, yes. Every Thursday, and most Tuesdays. We *do* try to chase him away before it gets dark but ... Well, it's hard to *insist* when he's being so devoted. I wish all our patients had people who visited half as regularly. I *did* try to tell him the other day, you know, that he didn't have to stay so long: should get out in the fresh air and have some fun, but you know what he said? He said how nice it was that everyone here's always so happy to see him. Isn't that a nice thing for a boy his age to say? I'm so glad he'll have someone to travel home with tonight, especially with that nasty cold he's got. Now then, if you'll just come along here.'

The little man trotted off down the hall, past a set of floor-to-ceiling windows looking out over a tiny duck pond where an extremely indignant goose hissed viciously at them through the glass. The volume steadily increased as they walked, TVs blaring at appalling decibels from some rooms, shouts coming from others. An old woman, pacing back and forth in front of her door, spat a string of curses so vile and creative at them that Tim's eyes widened. The stench of disinfectant made the air prickle in his throat, though it couldn't eradicate the sweet foul odours beneath. The corridor ended in an open-plan room filled with coffee tables and low armchairs. A set of French windows overlooked a badly mown lawn.

The little man's beeper went off, making him jump. 'Must run, but it's just that far door on the left,' he called as he hurried away.

Tim threaded his way through the tables to where a door stood ajar.

' ... took me the whole morning yesterday to do one question from last year's exam paper. And I'm pretty sure I got it wrong. I don't even know where to start with the problems for supervision. I'm trying, I swear I am. I just don't know what's wrong with me. Yesterday, every time I sat down to work I had to get right back up again because I couldn't, I don't know, I just couldn't stomach it. I can't seem to think straight, like my head is full of this ... ringing. Like I'm trying to think through treacle. And of course the exams are all my dad talks about.'

Through the half-open door Tim saw Professor Gosswin raise a shaking hand. 'Thu ... nnnn thu ... thu,' she croaked, her voice wavering and slurred.

Nick leaned forward to take her hand as it fluttered in the air. 'I know,' he said. 'I'm even worse at chess than you remember. Can't even beat myself. How about this?' Holding Professor Gosswin's hand, he nudged a bishop across the board. 'What do you think?'

Gosswin subsided, gumming at her lip.

'Pretty pathetic, right? Think that sums me up right now. I had a fight with Bill the other week. It was so stupid. He was just trying to be nice but ... And Tim. He made this effort after we went down to visit Mum's grave, offered to talk about his parents, and I just ... I appreciate that they're trying to be kind, I *do*, but it's only because they feel sorry for me and I *hate* that. I don't want people to be kind because they're sorry for me. I want them to—'

Professor Gosswin made a garbled noise, reaching out to the board, then across it, taking Nick's hand.

Nick sighed, curling his fingers around hers. 'I wish ...' He stopped. 'I reread your book, you know. All the time. Sometimes I just wish ...' Another sigh. 'I can't decide if I hope you're OK in there or that you don't understand any of this. You'd hate it. I know you would.'

There was a definite quiver in the slow breath Nick drew as he leaned over the board to move a pawn forwards.

'I know I'm being stupid: that I shouldn't expect anyone to want me to be their problem when my dad doesn't any more than Mum did. I think she must have got pregnant with me by accident.' The next breath hitched painfully. 'I think my grandmother was the only one who really wanted me. I mean, at least Roger *noticed* me enough to hate me. Sometimes I wish Dad cared enough to hate having me around. He just can't be bothered. He doesn't hate me and he doesn't love me and he just doesn't really care. I went down to visit Mum once, you know, after the breakdown, while she was in hospital. She wouldn't even see me. Made them turn me away. Dad didn't even know I was gone.' A sigh like a sob. 'Sometimes I wish he'd died instead of my grandmother. Sometimes I really wish he'd died instead.'

The tears were silent, a trail of light curving down the side of Nick's face. But despite the occasional hitch of breath, a

267

long shaky exhalation, his voice continued, quiet and fierce and desperately, furiously contained.

'I'm going to do so badly in the exams. It was all *fine*, all under control, but suddenly I just can't ... can't anything. Can't think. Can't focus. You're going to be so disappointed with my results.' A sigh then, even quieter, 'You're going to be so disappointed in me. I don't even know what Dad will say. It's always been the thing I could change. I can't change my dad. And I can't seem to change not having proper friends, even here, but I've always been able to *prove* I was clever. Not just think it but show myself that I am good at something. Good for something.' A sniff, then something that could have been an attempt to laugh.

Tim backed slowly, silently away till he was out of sight of the door, then hurried back to the entrance hall. Bending over the visitors' book, he quickly scribbled his name out, then rapped smartly on the office door. The little man looked up with a smile.

'Sorry to disturb you, but do you think you could not say anything to Nick about my being here today?'

The man blinked at him, nonplussed. He raised his hands in silent question.

'I, er ... Nick was talking to Professor Gosswin. He seemed ... upset. I don't think he'd like to know he was ... overheard.'

'Ah,' said the little man, face softening. 'Yes, I *do* see.'

'You won't say anything?'

'Oh, no,' said the little man.

Tim set a swift march to the station, not wanting to take the chance of ending up on the same train as Nick. In the carriage, he pulled out his phone, finger hovering over Bill's name on his contacts list.

The landscape passed in a blur of blue outlines of trees, a white flash of low neat cottages, a dim grey field, his own troubled reflection in the glass.

Chapter[24]

(Easter Term × Week 1
[≈ third week of April])

The St John's crypts were echoing and dank, smelling of mould and decay, the vaulted ceiling of the New Court colonnade dispiriting and clammy. The golden stone of the building opposite was breached by gorgeous ogee arches filled with lead-light windows, but Nick turned his back on it all, breaking into a run down the steps and on to the path around the lawn. He ignored the aptly nicknamed 'Wedding Cake' frontage of New Court as he cut to the right and then around towards the wooded stretch by the back gates.

Whatever it was that had always made it so easy to focus on his studies, push his worries away and lose himself in the work, had disappeared. Suddenly his revision seemed to have multiplied a thousandfold and the time until the exams seemed both too long and too short. He couldn't even hope to scratch the surface of his revision timetable in the weeks left, though he never seemed to do anything but pore over his notes, pen in hand.

The days had started to merge, endless and fleeting, filled with sick anxiety stretching forwards, stretching back. Even with Professor Gosswin's book resting on his knees, the cover familiar and comforting under his hands, everything felt wrong: subtly, intangibly wrong.

When he woke in the mornings, he wanted to roll over and start the night all over again: just sleep until it was over and he wouldn't have to watch the days slip past, knowing that he was moving closer and closer to disaster because, out of the blue, he just couldn't do it any more.

Couldn't figure out the problems.

Couldn't see through the fog in his head, as if everything had become blunted and blurred.

Wild anemones glowed around the lush green of bluebell stems slowly creeping out of the ivy. Primroses tinted the banks. Under the trees along Queensway, following the little clay path along the Backs, crocuses dusted the ground like a purple carpet. He ran up the long drive to Trinity, stopping short of the bridge, then walked the avenue in reverse, trying to focus on the daffodils in the long grasses, the magenta and pink of cyclamen ringing the trees, the heart-aching tenderness of silver-green tulip stems spearing up from the ground.

He ended up outside King's Chapel without consciously making the decision to head there, though he'd been meaning to go to Evensong since the start of the year. He stepped tentatively through the side door, expecting to be asked for ID, but no one questioned him as he followed a group of students up the aisle only for his steps to falter as he looked up and up and up; fluted white columns blossomed into an immense fan-vaulted ceiling so detailed it looked as if it were made of lace turned to stone. Stained-glass windows glowed like gemstones, rising from floor to ceiling, caught in the most delicate stone tracery he had ever seen. If the chapel was beautiful from the outside, it was like nothing on earth inside, making something deep in his chest hum half with pain and half with joy, his eyes stinging as if he might cry.

A jostling crowd caught him up and carried him through the arch in the centre of the intricate wooden rood screen into the top end of the chapel. Parting around a lectern, the students filed into the dark pews to either side of the aisle, facing inwards. Against the walls the panelling stretched up the height of two men, each seat divided from the next by a thin pillar of carved wood.

He was staring up at the ceiling when the choir arrived so that one moment he was only dimly aware of people moving around the chapel and the next the music had started. The boy sopranos soared above the organ, echoing into the highest reaches of the ceiling, and for a little while everything else faded away and the world became suddenly bigger and brighter, where for weeks it had been growing dimmer and smaller.

At first it had happened slowly, quietly, so that he was barely aware of it, but some time in the last fortnight it had all started spinning out of control, spiralling inwards into a tight curl of misery. At night he dreamed of standing amid the shattered glass of the fish tank, scooping the tiny desperate bodies into the water only for it to keep draining away, slipping through his fingers: an ending he should somehow have been able to change. It wasn't the wisdom to know that the past couldn't be changed that was the problem. It was finding the courage to change the present when there was nothing left to hold on to.

∞

Doubled over, coughing his way through his first revision supervision, Nick found he didn't have the faintest idea where to start with the problem in front of him.

'Oh, dear,' said Dr Davis, trying to sound sympathetic, though the moue of distaste and the way he shifted away told a different story. 'There. Take a deep breath now . . .'

Nick gritted his teeth to stop himself from snarling that he was having trouble enough taking *any* sort of breath. He pressed his fist against his breastbone, choking back another round of hacking coughs.

Susie made a sympathetic face, while Frank rolled his eyes to the ceiling.

'OK, Nick. Let's try again. What principles might help, do you think?' Dr Davis asked.

'I don't know,' Nick gritted out, rubbing at his forehead. 'I just don't know.'

Dr Davis sighed. 'I know you're full of cold, but try to stay calm, Nick, and tell me what's confusing you.'

'Everything.'

Frank snorted. 'Lo, how the mighty have fallen,' he teased, though with a shade too much satisfaction for it to be friendly. 'Even *I* could do that question.'

'Well, good for you. There had to be once this year you could do something I couldn't, especially as *I've got the flu.*'

'Now, gentlemen,' said Dr Davis, flapping his hands between them. 'Now, now, that *isn't* the way to get along. Since this is a revision supervision, and Nick's clearly sub-par, why don't you get us started, Frank?'

Frank flashed Nick a look of triumph that turned into grimace. 'Oh come on, Nick. Don't *cry* about it, OK?'

'I'm not! Don't your eyes water when you choke?' Nick gasped, hunching his shoulders over the pain in his chest, trying to swallow the urge to keep coughing. He lost the battle, curling over the tearing rattle of his breath. Although the sun was out, the air was cold, burning his lungs as if it were water. By the time he managed to draw breath, there was sweat on his forehead and his hands were shaking. He turned away to spit something foul into a tissue.

When he turned back, Frank was pulling a disgusted face. 'Not to be unsympathetic, but didn't your mother ever tell you to stay home when you're making like Typhoid Mary?'

Nick shot to his feet, then tottered, closing his eyes as the room swooped around him. His ears rang.

A hand on his arm brought him back to the present. 'Just

shut up, OK?' Susie was saying to Frank. 'It's not funny. No one's laughing. I'm going to get Nick a taxi home. Back in a sec.' She bent to gather his stuff into his bag and slung it over her shoulder before he had a chance to protest. 'Come on,' she said, tugging at his arm. 'You need to be in bed. Actually, you need to get some antibiotics, 'cos if that's not a chest infection then I don't know what is, but let's start with getting you *home*.'

His legs felt strange as they made their way downstairs. He blinked in the sunlight as his eyes watered again. His skin itched with heat as if he had a fever, but he knew he didn't because his stomach was full of shivers and there seemed to be an icicle lodged between his ribs.

When Susie guided him to one of the window seats in the p'lodge, he slumped gratefully down, pressing his burning forehead against the cool of the wood and wrapping his arms about his body.

'Nick?'

He looked up to find Susie leaning over him, one hand on his knee. 'Do you think you're OK to walk to the end of KP by yourself? The taxi should be there by the time you are.'

Nick blinked at her, nodded. 'Thanks,' he rasped.

She gave him a tight little smile. 'If I weren't making such a muck of this year, I'd come with you, but I *really* need the extra supervision time.' She sighed. 'Feel better, OK?' she said, hooking his bag over his shoulder. 'And make sure your dad takes you to the doctor. Forget about revision for now. You'll get a First in your sleep.' She patted his arm then hurried back into College.

Sighing, then regretting it when he had to fight not to start coughing again, Nick stumbled out of the p'lodge and started wearily up Senate House Passage. He had to push his way through a crowd of tourists who seemed determined to stand across the whole street while they examined a piece of gutter with loud astonishment and a red-carpet-worthy barrage of photo-flashes. Hoping fervently that the tour guide was spinning them some dreadful fib, Nick shoved his way through and practically fell out the other side, turning into KP with relief until the wind forced him to stop and hunch over the catch in his throat as the urge to cough needled the inside of his chest.

The taxi driver glared as he opened the door and tossed his bag inside. 'Derran?' he demanded.

'Yeah.' Nick managed to croak out the address, then curled sideways into the seat, debating whether he could bother to tell the driver to turn down the radio before his head exploded.

Outside the house, he fumbled a note out of his wallet, told the driver to keep the change, and let himself in, dropping his bag in the hall and practically toppling on to the sofa. The house felt strange with Tim still away in America at his sister's wedding. Michael had made it home most nights, but usually not until the last train: at best they spoke for ten minutes in the kitchen before going to bed, and another ten in the morning before Michael hurried back to the station.

'But it's not like I have to get used to there never being anyone home, like after each time Gerry stayed over while Dad was away,' he mumbled to the sofa cushions, turning his back on the room, on the empty house. 'Tim'll be back this evening. Have to pull yourself together before then. Gotta stop being such a baby. You fell in the drink and got too cold. Picked up a dose of Cam Fever, 'cos if you can get it from the river, you can get it from the ditch. People get Cam Flu all the time. 'S not like you're dying.'

But it didn't feel like any cold he'd had before. He couldn't have described exactly what was wrong, only that the world had become narrow and grey, and the desperation he'd felt building during his failed attempts to revise was now despair. He couldn't seem to push himself like he always had before. There didn't seem to be anything left. It was all just too much: one thing after another, always a fresh catastrophe around the corner. And it looked like the next one was going to be failing his exams.

Closing his eyes, he rubbed at the coldness in his chest and willed the world away.

The sound of the front door racketing into the wall woke him. Rolling over on to his back, he blinked blindly up at the ceiling. Light flooded the room, making him squeeze his eyes shut.

'Nick! I assumed no one was home.'

'Dad?' Sitting up, rubbing sleep from his eyes, Nick heard the stereo come on – a CD of Chopin nocturnes – as he accidentally pressed the remote, lost somewhere under the sofa cushions. He winced as he watched Michael catch his foot on the strap of his discarded bag and stumble. 'Sorry.'

'Why the hell did you leave it in such a stupid place?'

'What are you doing home? I thought you were off to the States later today?'

'I *am*, only I had to make this brilliantly timed detour when I got a call from College saying you'd had some sort of meltdown in your supervision.'

Nick groaned, running his hands through his hair. 'It wasn't a meltdown. I was just sick, struggling to focus.' He had to stop to curl over the burning in his chest, hissing air through his teeth as he tried to suppress the urge to cough.

'Apparently your supervisor was concerned about your mental state. Said that you were unusually upset to be having difficulty with your revision work.'

'The guy's an idiot,' Nick snapped. 'They're all just waiting for me to get frustrated so that they can throw up their hands and say I'm too immature. It's nothing that Frank and Susie haven't done half a dozen times each. I didn't yell.' A flutter of breath. 'Didn't cry.' He grunted, pressing the heel of his hand to the centre of his chest.

'Well you must have done something inappropriate. And apparently you hadn't done your supervision work—'

'Wasn't there a *week* during college you had the flu and didn't manage to get your work done?'

'It's not the same, Nick! You know that. You, of all people, can't just refuse to do something because you're under the weather. *Especially* with exams coming up.'

Nick stared wordlessly up at him.

Michael threw his hands in the air. 'I don't have *time* for this, Nick. I'm meant to be on the way to the airport!'

'Well, *go* then!'

Michael huffed out an angry sigh. 'I thought I'd come home and we'd have a reasonable conversation, but you are clearly in the middle of some tantrum. When you stop feeling sorry for yourself, we'll talk on the phone and I'll figure out something to say to your supervisor.'

'Whatever,' Nick mumbled, rubbing at the pain in his forehead.

'If you're going to be like that, there's no point my wasting any more time here. I'll call when I land. Just … take some paracetamol and some Lemsip and go to bed.'

'You can't have paracetamol and Lemsip together: Lemsip's paracetamol-based too. Or do you *want* me to overdose myself?'

The words were out before he'd realised what he was saying.

Chopin's final nocturne grew frantic, pleading, in the background.

'That was uncalled for. I'll talk to you when you're prepared to be reasonable, not vicious.'

The door slammed.

Stumbling to his feet, wishing the floor would stop feeling like it was rocking, Nick felt his way along the furniture to the kitchen and guzzled a glass of water only to spit half of it out over his jeans as he doubled over coughing, feeling like his lungs were shredding.

Snatches of words whirled through his mind. Who had called from College? What had they said? It was like the walls were whispering, hissing to him about all the things he didn't want to think about: the way he couldn't work, couldn't understand any of it any more; the way the one thing he'd always been able to count on was suddenly slipping through his fingers. Because he wasn't going to get a First at all. He was going to fail his exams: fail them absolutely, irredeemably. And if he didn't have that, then what was there?

He was halfway down the street before he realised he'd left the house. It was only when he reached the station that he understood that he desperately wanted Professor Gosswin. He skirted past the guards and stepped straight on to the train at the platform, letting it whisk him away from Cambridge into a world of vast flat fields, broken by oceans of waving marsh grass and reeds. Water glinted yellow as little footbridges fled from his carriage window.

Leaning his forehead against the blissful, blissful coolness of the glass, he stared out at the passing world. The train was freezing and he drew his legs up, wrapping his arms around himself as his stomach cramped with cold.

The walk to the nursing home had never seemed so long, bent over the awful ache in his chest, trying to fight back the shivers that seemed to come from deep inside.

The staff waved absently at him as they buzzed him in, letting him find his own way to Professor Gosswin's room.

Her face was turned to the door, as if she'd been waiting for him. There was something like a smile on her face, though perhaps it was just the way the stroke had distorted her features. But he needed it to be a smile: needed her to be glad to see him. He sank to the floor at her feet, pressed his forehead against her bony shin, and raised his fist to his mouth to hold back a sound of pain as he fought not to cough. Something in his chest made a sharp crackling sound like the slick plastic foil cut flowers come in.

Professor Gosswin's thin fingers fluttered, shaking, on to the crown on his head, wound themselves into his hair.

He closed his eyes, letting the tears spill down his cheeks.

∞

'Nick dear, what on earth are you still doing here?'

Startled, Nick looked up to find one of the nurses bending over him.

'You look like you've been fast asleep,' she said. 'I'd offer you a lift back to town if I wasn't just on shift ten minutes ago, but there's a train coming in about,' she checked her watch, 'fifteen minutes. You go on down to the station now. You don't want to miss that one too.'

The room slid to the left, like it was rising up a steep wave, as he struggled to his feet. The edges of his vision darkened.

The nurse laughed as he staggered into the wall. 'Better rub some life back into those legs before the pins and needles attack.'

She turned away, shaking her head as she lined up a series of pill pots on Professor Gosswin's side-table. The Professor reached out a shaking hand.

'Oh no you don't,' said the nurse, moving the pills out

of reach. 'I'm on to you. No more tiddlywinks with your medication.'

Looking back from the door, Nick saw Professor Gosswin turn in his direction with that maybe-smile on her face. Nick smiled back, then started down the corridor.

Outside, the evening air felt wonderful. The nursing home was always hot and stuffy but today it had been stifling. It was growing dark now, a bleak sort of sunset, the sky turning from threatening orange-grey to dirty blue-brown. For some reason, the walk to the station seemed to take half an hour, but he arrived with ten minutes to spare. It must have been a mistake with the clock because the train seemed to pull up instantly, hissing to a stop then percolating unpleasantly as it idled at the platform. Somewhere metal shrieked along metal, making everyone in the carriage cower.

The journey fled past as if he'd stumbled on to some special fast train. Yet when he walked out of Cambridge station it was already dark: dark and still, as if it were very late.

The air was pleasantly cool against his skin, the night soft and gentle around him. Being free of the shivers was wonderful, though it was odd that the night was so much warmer than the day had been.

The hall and living-room lights were on when he let himself in. Someone was moving about the kitchen. He padded through the living room and peered around the door.

Tim was standing at the counter, glaring down at the

floor tiles, looking exhausted and rumpled from his flight. Inexplicably the kitchen clock was set to 23.55.

'Hi.'

Tim's head jerked up. 'Nick!' Relief flooded his face in a way that made Nick smile. 'Are you all right? Where have you been?'

'I went to see Professor Gosswin.' He had to stop to breathe. The urge to cough was gone, but somehow the idea of a deep breath felt wrong. He fluttered in a few shallow ones instead. 'It's not really,' breath, swallow, 'midnight, is it? I thought,' breath, swallow, 'it was only about six o'clock. How ... How was the wedding?'

Tim wasn't listening, shaking his head as he pulled his phone out of his pocket and flicked through his contacts list. 'Bill must have just missed you. I'll give him a ring so he can stop worrying.'

The kettle came to the boil as he turned away so Nick crossed to take down the mugs. As he lifted his arm, coughing overtook him.

He saw his knuckles turn grey as he clung to the counter.

Whiteness exploded behind his eyes.

When his vision came back, the world was scarlet, as if he were looking through a blood-red window-pane. The floor slid to the side, kept sliding, his stomach swooping as if he were about to be sick.

Suddenly he wasn't sure which way was down and he had to know: he had to lie down before he fell.

'Tim ...' Not even a thread of a whisper.

The world went black. He couldn't see, though he knew his eyes were open. The room was turning around him, tilting up: up so that the floor was becoming the ceiling.

It was almost a relief to be falling. For the world to be simply going away. Just going away, like he'd wished for days that it would, fading away into nothing.

∞

The hospital clock read 03.48.

Bill sighed, rubbing wearily at his eyes. 'You know, until now I thought it was impossible to have another day as utterly God-awful as when my wife left me. I should have known it was going to be bad when Mike insisted on interrupting my afternoon meeting to tell me about his argument with Nick and topped it off with the news that he was on the way to the airport for a three-week trip to the States.'

Tim looked up blearily.

'Do you know what he said? "I'm sure it's just a tantrum but with his exams coming up I'd really appreciate it if you could give him a quick ring later: try to talk some sense into him." And of course the main thing he was worried about was this thing at the supervision: how it would affect Nick's exams.'

Tim rolled his shoulders stiffly, reaching back to rub at a sore muscle. 'When I left for the States, Michael was being all martyred about how much effort he'd gone to, arranging to be home at night; how he wasn't flying out until I was on the way back . . .'

Bill scrubbed at his face again. 'There might have been the start of a rant about that. I, er, hung up at a certain point.'

Tim quirked an eyebrow. 'That's going to set the tone beautifully for when you call tomorrow to fill him in on all this.' He made a vague gesture at the waiting room.

Bill groaned. 'The one saving grace is that it is – was – Friday and I could afford to pack it all in early. Thank God I don't have to rearrange anything until Monday. You're not back at work right away, are you?'

Tim shook his head. 'That would have been lovely, fresh off a transatlantic red-eye. But, no, it's officially term-time so no extra hours at the coffee shop. For once, it's a blessing to be under-employed. I've had quite enough excitement to welcome me home.' That afternoon, he'd trudged from the station to the house, lugging his suitcase, only to find Bill just pulling up at the kerb. The house was dark and empty, no messages on the answerphone. It had been Tim's suggestion to try the nursing home.

'I can't believe I missed Nick at Gosswin's by less than five minutes. I was so relieved, when you called, to know he'd be home when I got back. Should have known better than to think the day was on the up.'

The last thing he'd expected, as he let himself in through the front door, was a frantic shout. He'd found Tim kneeling on the kitchen floor with Nick lying bonelessly in his arms, lips blue and face bloodless.

He was dialling an ambulance even before he'd knelt to check Nick's pulse, trying to ignore how hot and dry his skin felt, the crackling of his breathing, like his lungs were full of tissue paper, the elderly wheeze at the end of each shallow breath.

It was only when the paramedic asked 'Dad' to step back that he'd remembered Michael. He'd sent Tim to try Michael's mobile, knowing already that it would be switched off because where would Mike be while his son was lying unconscious on the kitchen floor but midway across the Atlantic?

'I've never been so glad that Nick's still under sixteen. I don't know what I would have done if they hadn't let me come in the ambulance. You know, you didn't have to follow on, Tim. If you were any more exhausted, you'd be asleep on your feet. You could have stayed home. Nick wouldn't have known.'

Tim gave him a half-hearted glare. 'Like I said, there's no way I *wasn't* going to come. Thanks for the taxi money, though.' He yawned again. 'Do you think they'll tell us something soon?'

They stared morosely up at the clock only to flinch when a nurse stopped suddenly in front of them.

'Still here, I see,' she said wryly. 'I can tell that throwing you out is only going to see you sleeping in the lobby, so I'm going to give you ten minutes to look in on him to set your minds at rest. Then I'll be packing you off home until morning visiting hours. You *only* get those ten minutes,' she said, as they pushed themselves hurriedly, if stiffly, to their feet, 'if we're completely clear on the fact that your boy's asleep and I'll not have you waking him: he needs the rest more than the reassurance you're here. Are we in agreement?'

'Yes, ma'am,' Tim said, giving her his most winning smile.

'You're looking rather too much the worse for wear yourself for that to have the effect you're intending,' the nurse told him. 'Now, like the doctor said earlier, with teenage cases of pneumonia we often find a huge improvement in just the first twelve hours of getting them on a good strong dose of IV antibiotics. Your son's X-rays weren't too bad so we may only need to keep him twenty-four hours for the IV. I'll be surprised if it's more than forty-eight. He's young and otherwise healthy, if a bit thin. He'll be fine recovering at home on some oral antibiotics. I know he was a bit blue about the gills when the ambulance brought him in but that was shock as much as anything. His oxygen saturation is already back up, so don't you worry. Now, one last signature and I'll give you those ten minutes,' she said, passing Bill a clipboard.

Having avoided telling anyone that he wasn't Nick's father without actively lying – no one seemed to have noticed that their last names were different – Bill made sure his signature was more than usually vague, but the nurse didn't even look at what he'd written. She just tucked the clipboard under her arm and led them to a little cubicle at the end of the ward.

'We've got him on his own until those labs come back. Just a precaution till we're absolutely certain there's nothing else lurking in his system that might be bad for the other kids on the ward,' the nurse explained. 'Remember, now: no waking my patient!'

Bill stood for a moment, staring down at Nick in silence, while Tim threw himself into one of the plastic chairs, braced his elbows against his knees and dropped his head into his hands.

Bill rubbed the back of his neck as every part of him protested at the fact that it was nearly four in the morning after a long day and horrifying night. He still felt cold and shaky from the shock, the fear of the endless fifteen minutes in the ambulance on the way to the hospital.

'It's my fault.'

Bill sank into the second chair, reached over to pat Tim's shoulder. 'Of course it's not, Tim. You weren't even here—'

'Nick had an accident. About two weeks ago. Some idiot driver caught him with his wing mirror and he came off his bike, fell in the ditch by the Botanic Gardens.' Tim's face was dull red as he hunched forward over his knees, staring at the linoleum. 'He was a bit bruised, but I put him in the bath to warm up and he seemed fine. I tried to get him to go to Addenbrooke's the next morning just to be sure, but he didn't want to and there didn't seem to be anything specific to worry about and I kept a close eye all week. I mean, I knew he had a cold but I *swear* it was just a cold when I left for the States.' His bloodshot eyes lifted to Bill's. 'I swear it was only a cold.'

'Of course it was, Tim. Look, these things happen. It was *Michael* here when that cold turned into something nasty, not you.'

Tim shook his head, looking away. His hands, hanging between his knees, wound into a ball. 'I should have called you. I said I'd call you. I knew things weren't going well. I knew Nick was struggling. There was this night – the night you went down to visit his mum – I found him drinking Michael's whisky. I should have told you that time we chatted but ... he'd only had a bit and it was just the once so I figured, well, it's nothing I didn't do – to extremes – when my parents died.' He swallowed uncomfortably. 'I nearly did call, you know, right before I left. I went down to visit Gosswin one day and Nick was there and I overheard some stuff, but I knew he'd never forgive me if he realised I'd heard, let alone told anyone ... and I didn't want to get in the middle of it.' He sighed. 'You see, Bill? You shouldn't have trusted me with something so important.' He rubbed a hand across his mouth, his face a mask of self-disgust under the over-bright hospital strip lighting.

Bill squeezed his shoulder. 'Tim, out of all the people involved, you are the *least* to blame. This was never meant to be part of your role in the household. It's Mike's job: Nick's *his* responsibility, not yours.'

'Nick's not really anyone's responsibility. That's basically what he told Gosswin – that no one gave enough of a damn to make him their problem,' Tim whispered to the floor.

'Mike never did manage to get things together after Nick came to live with him. He expected Yvette to take care of Nick and after her breakdown—'

'Not to insult the dead, but some of the stuff Nick said to Gosswin ... I don't think she did a very good job either, even before the breakdown.'

'Probably not,' Bill said. 'Probably not.' Looking across at Tim, Bill found him staring vacantly at the ground once more, the marks under his eyes standing out like bruises. Everything about his posture said that he wanted nothing more than to find somewhere flat to lie down and fall asleep. 'I'm going to tell Michael to stay in Washington,' Bill heard himself say.

Tim stared at him for a moment, his mouth coming open, but then he closed it. Nodded. 'Isn't he going to want to come home?'

'I won't lie to him, but I don't think it'll be hard to persuade him to stay away. If I thought Mike would use this as an opportunity to be a real father I wouldn't steal it from him, but I don't honestly believe he'd bring himself to do it. And what a terrible waste that would be. I know I'm not Nick's first choice, but maybe I'll be enough. Love is love, right?' he said lightly, as if it were a joke.

'I don't think Nick's the type to turn his nose up at being cared for – so long as he really believes that's what it is, not pity.'

Bill gave him an odd, arrested look. 'So that's what I did wrong last month.' He shook his head. 'I've been so worried about looking greedy to be a father rather than just his godfather that I've made Nick think it's all about Mike.' He sighed. 'There's my closest friend leaving this gaping hole in his son's life and here I am, trying not to step into it. It always felt too much like temptation to be the right thing. I just wish I'd been keeping a close enough eye to . . . Well,' he said, sitting up straight, 'I'll start now. I'll call the College tomorrow, see if the Senior Tutor will agree an aegrotat, or are they calling it a DDH now? The University still has a Deemed to Deserve Honours allowance, right, for students who're seriously ill during exams?'

Tim nodded.

'I'll get them to request one in case Nick isn't well enough to sit the exams. Sounds like he will be, but maybe knowing it doesn't matter will take the pressure off enough for him to relax and focus on getting better.'

The nurse reappeared by the door. 'Your ten minutes are up.'

Bill and Tim exchanged a look, but got to their feet without argument.

Half an hour later, Bill was standing in the Derrans' kitchen, listening to Tim stumble up to bed. Leaning against the counter he poured himself a generous measure of Michael's best single malt. 'I'm in sore need of courage,' he told the bottle, 'and beggars can't be choosers.'

∞

Nick looked up with a smile as Bill rapped a smart tattoo on the doorframe the next morning.

'You're certainly looking better today,' Bill said as he stepped up to the bed. 'How're you feeling?'

Nick shrugged, raising a hand to rub absently at his chest. 'OK.' A thread of sound, following by a rattling, crackling cough and a grimace. 'OK,' he repeated, slightly louder.

'Well, you sound like a one-person percussion section,' Tim said, leaning in the doorway. 'In other words, *gross!*'

Nick's smile broadened, bringing a faint flush of colour to his cheeks. 'Hey,' he croaked. 'How was the wedding?'

'The trip was as expected: exhausting, mostly vomit-inducing and frequently exasperating. The coming home was where all the excitement was at. I mean, I would commend you on your swan-dive technique but since the whole thing involved you *spectacularly* and *thoroughly* breaking that promise you made me about not passing out in corners, I'm thinking I'll go with stern and disapproving,' he said, perching one hip on the edge of the bed.

'Sorry,' Nick whispered, grinning, though the smile left his face as he looked down at the blankets. He shuddered in a breath, let it out as a hitching, careful sigh. 'What . . .' He swallowed. 'What did the doctors say about the exams?'

'They said you'll probably be fine, but I've already talked to College,' Bill said, draping his coat over the back of the chair beside the bed. 'You've got a DDH if you need it, but let's cross that bridge if we come to it. The important thing is that it doesn't matter: all your supervisors are happy to sign off on the fact that your work this year has been exemplary. That's all Part I exams are about anyway: they don't count towards anything. So don't even think about it for now. Just focus on getting better. I talked to your doctor this morning and he said he'll probably let you come home tomorrow, so you're only stuck here for a day. We just need to have a little chat about ... well, about who's going to be there when you get home.'

'Maybe they'll let me stay an extra day.'

Bill frowned as he settled himself into the chair. 'I know you must have had quite a scare too, Nick, but surely you don't *want* to stay in hospital?'

'No, I just ... I might be a bit rocky tomorrow, but the day after I'm sure I'll be fine, or at least I'll *manage*. I always do,' he said quietly, not looking at either of them.

'Nick, the issue isn't that you'll have to manage *alone*. There's no question of you staying in hospital if you don't need to.' But Nick's face was tightening into the careful expression of polite disinterestedness that Bill had always hated.

'Bill's going to be staying for the next two weeks,' Tim interrupted. 'And I'm around, whether you want me or not. The thing is your dad being in Washington.' He shot Bill a meaningful look when Nick ducked his head.

'I talked to Mike, Nick, and of *course* he wants to be here but ... you might be very annoyed with me for this but *I* said he should stay in the States. I know that things have been ... tense lately, and I know how Mike gets. You should be feeling better by the time he gets back and then you can have a proper talk. I probably shouldn't have made that decision for you, but I just thought—'

'It's fine, Bill,' Nick said. 'But you don't have to muck up your life to be here while my dad's away.'

'Nick, that part of the issue is *not* up for debate. Even if Mike *hadn't* been away, you'd have had me camped out in your guest room. We're family so there's no question that I want to be here, Michael or no Michael.'

Nick gave an odd little shiver.

'Anyway, I've got a key so you can't keep me out. You'll just have to like it or lump it.'

Nick's eyes were fixed on the bedclothes, his face impassive, but his shoulders, swamped by the hospital gown, grew rigid.

'Of course, if you want I'll go and call Mike right now. Tell him to come home. What do you think, Nick? It's up to you.'

Nick closed his eyes.

'Geez, Nick,' said Tim, 'get all excited, why don't you, about the prospect of our company?'

Nick snorted half-heartedly. 'Nah.'

'We made a deal, Nick. Remember what you told me when you persuaded me to let you loan me the money for my trip?' Tim ignored the look of surprise Bill shot him. 'You said that we were friends so it wasn't a big deal. So stop making a big deal out of this. Besides, you've forgotten Ange. Do you seriously think she's not going to be round every day, plumping your pillows and trying to spoon-feed you soup? I won't have to do anything but sit back and watch you squirm.'

'Bully,' Nick whispered, though he was biting his lip to stop himself from grinning.

'Right, well I'll consider that settled then,' said Bill. 'Now,

Tim and I need some coffee so why don't you have a kip and we'll see you in a bit?'

'You don't have to—'

'Oh but we're looking forward to watching the nurses torment you,' Tim cut in. 'I am going to store up *so* many embarrassing stories. Like the outfit. I was thinking I could get one of those disposable cameras from the gift shop and . . . click-click.' Tim mimed taking a picture.

'Pick on me while I'm lying in a hospital bed, why don't you?'

'Well, now that I have permission . . .'

Nick moved to kick him but Tim had fled to the door by the time he got his legs untangled from the blankets.

'Think now is the perfect time for that coffee, Bill. See you down there.'

'Your bedside manner sucks!' Nick called after him, prompting a fresh round of coughing.

Bill stepped forward to rub his back, wincing at the way Nick's shoulder blades shuddered beneath his hand. 'Enough talking for you,' he said fondly. 'Lie back now.' He drew the covers up as Nick settled against the pillows. 'See you in a bit.'

'Bill,' Nick said, as he reached the door. 'Thanks.'

Chapter[25]

**(Easter Term × Week 2
[≈ end of April])**

'So since my X-rays were good, can I stay up to watch the film?' Nick coaxed as they climbed into Bill's car in the hospital car park.

Bill smiled as he started the engine. 'They were and I'm very glad about it, but your bedtime is still going to be ten o'clock sharp for at least another week, just like I said.'

Nick pulled a face. 'I can't remember a time in my life when I had a *bedtime*.'

'Even with your mum?' Bill asked, trying to keep his tone nonchalant.

Nick looked away out of the window. 'She wasn't all that different from Dad, really,' he said softly.

'Nick, one of the things I want to do when you're feeling better is talk about your mum.'

Nick glanced his way, then down at his hands, picking at a broken nail. 'That's going to be a fun conversation.'

'That's your father speaking.'

Nick turned in his seat to look at Bill, frowning but tilting his head as if trying to work something out.

'I've always assumed that the two of you had some sort of conversation about Yvette and then it was just too painful to keep raking it all over, but am I wrong about that, Nick? *Did* you ever have that conversation?' From out of the corner of his eye, he could tell Nick was leaning towards him, still and intent. 'Don't get me wrong: I don't have any answers. No one has ever really understood what went wrong: why she got ill the way she did.'

The car ahead swerved suddenly away from the kerb and Bill's attention went to the road. He slowed but the other car seemed fine again.

'I mean,' he said, eyes on the other driver, 'I mean, we all did our best to figure it out after her first breakdown – your grandmother and your dad took her to all the best doctors ...' The other car slowed, indicated left, then right, then left again. 'They really did all they could.'

The driver ahead flicked the windscreen wash on, the spray arcing back so that Bill had to put on his own wipers.

'But everyone was nonplussed that it didn't happen *before* Finals, but *after* she got her First—'

Next to him, Nick jerked suddenly, a full-body shock of motion.

'You *did* know she'd had a breakdown just after we

did our Cambridge Finals?' But he knew the answer even as the words crossed his lips: knew that instead of 'gently broaching the subject' his distraction had landed him in the deep end in the stupidest place possible for this conversation. He clicked on the indicator, pulled into a bus layby.

Nick's face was as open as he had ever seen it: full of questions and fear and hope.

Bill turned to face him, bracing an arm on the steering wheel against the pull of his seatbelt. 'I'm sorry, Nick. I never meant to get into it now . . . And it's not like I have a lot I can tell you. All I really wanted to say is that, whatever went wrong for your mum, you can't read anything into what she did afterwards. I know it must have been . . . awful when you couldn't see her or even talk to her on the phone.'

Nick's face went blank, his eyes empty.

Bill clicked off his seatbelt to face him properly. 'I mean, maybe she thought it was *better* if you didn't see her while she was so sick. Or maybe there's nothing *to* understand about why she did what she did. Maybe there isn't any explanation, however hard that is to accept. But whatever the case – no matter how it feels – you have to know that what she did was about her. It wasn't about you.'

Nick turned away to the window, looking out at a beautiful house half-hidden behind a screen of trees and hedges. It bowed out into two storeys of bay windows, ending in a flat roof standing as a balcony for the third-storey rooms.

A smart guard rail of crenellations, tipped with burgundy tiles, made the house look like it should have been part of a castle.

'Nick, listen to me. Yvette was sick before you were even born. Whatever the reason for the second breakdown, it was *not* because of you.'

'You don't know that!' Nick whispered, refusing to look around. 'You can't *know* that.'

Bill hunched awkwardly over the gearshift, but Nick shrugged away from his touch. 'I *do* know that, Nick.'

Nick shook his head, took an unsteady breath. 'You don't *understand*. You weren't *there*. It was my fault the fish tank broke. Roger and I were fighting and it broke and she just kept *screaming*. Screaming and screaming and screaming . . .' He flinched away when Bill reached out to grasp his shoulder. 'Don't! Please, Bill, just *don't*.'

'Nick. Nick, look at me.' He tried to get an arm about Nick's shoulders, but he shuddered violently away, pressing himself into the corner of the seat against the doorframe. 'Whatever happened with this blasted fish tank was not what made your mum ill. If something that small could trigger it, then the breakdown was inevitable. It would have happened sooner or later—'

Nick shook his head. 'You don't *understand*,' he choked out, curling his forearm in front of his face as he took a shuddering breath.

'Then explain it to me, Nick. Explain it to me. Or if you can't talk to me, maybe you could talk to someone who doesn't know you, doesn't know Mike or Yvette: a professional who can—'

Nick's head snapped round, his eyes filled with horror. 'I'm *not* like her. I'm not *crazy*!'

'I know you're not,' Bill said, gripping Nick's shoulder. 'That's not what I meant—'

'I got sick because of that car knocking me into the Cam. I'm not going crazy. I don't need to see a shrink. I'm *not* going to live in one of those *places*!' he gasped, face feverish with despair.

'I never said anything of the *sort*, Nick. It's absolutely the *furthest* thing from my mind. The way you've handled everything that's happened, there's not a chance you're like Yvette. Not a *chance*. I just meant that maybe I'm not who you want to talk to, but it might help to talk to *someone*. Even normal people need a good listener now and then. Someone to help them get things straight in their own head—'

A shattering horn blast sounded behind them, making them both jump. Bill craned round to see a bus indicating to get into the layby. When he turned back to Nick, he found him slumped limply in his seat, staring dazedly through the windscreen, pale and wrung out.

'Nick . . .'

'Please, Bill,' Nick whispered. 'Not here. Not now.'

The bus beeped its horn again, then a third time. With a growl, Bill slammed his hand down on the button for the hazard lights. 'I know this isn't the best place for this conversation, but maybe now is as good a time as any. I don't know what part of this I'm not understanding, Nick, so I need you to tell me. I can't help if you don't tell me how.'

But Nick just shook his head, rocking it back and forth against the headrest, eyes squeezed shut.

His forehead was hot when Bill reached out to push the damp hair out of his eyes. This time, Nick didn't pull away, just sighed: a little sob of breath.

'Nick, I promise you there is *nothing* you can tell me that will make me think what happened to your mum was your fault.'

Nick gasped a breath as he looked up at him, searching his face. He opened his mouth to speak, then doubled over as a coughing fit overtook him.

With a long blast of the horn, the bus swerved around them.

When Bill turned back to Nick, he was rubbing wearily at his chest, expression shuttered. 'Can we go home now?' he croaked. 'Please, Bill, can we just go home?'

Bill let his head drop for a moment, let his breath out in a sigh. 'When you're ready, I promise I will help you fix whatever it is that's wrong. I *promise*.'

Chapter²⁶

(Easter Term × Week 3
[≈ start of May])

'So ... I have the best, most amazing plan for how you can spend your summer,' Tim said as he and Nick sprawled in the deckchairs on the back lawn, listening to the distant sounds of Bill and Michael clearing up lunch in the kitchen.

Nick squinted across at Tim. 'Did I do something horrid to you in a previous life?'

Tim growled. 'You're horrid to me in *this* life. Here I am, being *such* a good housemate, like the world has never seen before,' a snort from Nick, 'and you ... you *mock* me! I should just refuse to tell you.'

'My luck this year says you're unlikely to remain silent.'

Tim threw up his hands, but lazily, as if it were too much effort with the sun soothing them both into a sleepy daze. '*Here*, you ungrateful wretch,' he said, reaching under his chair to extract a glossy brochure. He tossed it on to Nick's stomach.

'Year 12 Summer School,' Nick read. He sucked in a sharp breath. 'You think I need to go on a summer-school course in case I flunk my exams.' He bit the words out carefully, as if chewing ice.

Tim sat up with a groan. '*Seriously*, Nick? The thing you take from the brochure is that I expect you to fail your exams?'

'Why else would you think I need to go to a summer school?'

'Why am *I* going to a summer school?'

'You're not going: you're teaching.'

'*And* . . . Oh for God's sake, Nick. Put the pieces together.'

Tim almost laughed at the expression on Nick's face as his head shot round, his expression stunned but pleased and . . . There it was: the disappointment. The blinds coming down.

'And we can skip the bit where you start up with the old "You don't have to involve me just 'cos you feel sorry for me" spiel. Truth is we're a helper down. Plus, as low man on the totem pole, we'll be able to get you to do *all* the scut work, so don't think you'll get to spend the whole time panting after pretty girls or pretty boys or both, as you fancy. Anyway, while this might be a good opportunity to find out, mostly there'll be a load of prep with the miserable bunch of miscreants I call my friends and—'

'Is Ange going?'

Tim rolled his eyes. 'Yup. It doesn't pay much—'

'We get *paid*?'

'Well, I imagine you'll get paid even less than we do, but yeah: we get paid, even though the courses are free to the students. It's for people from state schools who're the first in their family to look at university or who're in care or ... You know, people who might not even have the opportunity to come and *see* Cambridge otherwise. I had a word and they could really do with an extra pair of hands on the Physics course, the Maths one and the STEP maths-entrance-exam-thingie one: they always have a current Maths student for that and they haven't found anyone yet, so they're being ... receptive to your age. Anyway, it's a bit of prep and then three sets of four days. None of the courses overlap so you won't be overworked and since it kicks off in July, it won't interfere with your exams. So what do you think?'

'OK.'

'Just *OK*? Just *OK* to my sheer brilliance?'

'Everyone has their moments.'

'When you are least expecting it,' said Tim, 'I will *get* you for that snerk.'

'Snerk is not a word.'

'Of course it is! You knew exactly what I meant by it.'

'It's still not a word. It's certainly not a *noun*.'

'No, it's usually a verb. I snerk, you snerk, he/she/it snerketh.'

∞

'Of course it's not going to be simple,' Tim found himself muttering at the coffee machine an hour later. 'It involves Derrans: why would I think it'd be simple?'

'It is *very* kind of you, Tim,' Michael was saying. 'And I've got nothing against the idea in *principle* but ... Well, it doesn't seem quite fair that you should have to spend so much of your summer keeping an eye on Nick when you're working—'

'I wouldn't have suggested it if I didn't think it would be fun for *everyone*,' Tim said, trying to keep his tone calm and even. 'Ask Nick. He'll tell you my best friend already likes him more than me: Ange treats him like her favourite stuffed toy whenever she's here.'

'That's kindly put, Tim—'

Nick turned away to start loading the dishwasher.

'I'm getting to know Tim quite well, Mike,' Bill cut in, 'and mostly he says what he means.'

Michael sighed, throwing up his hands. 'Well, I can see I'm being outmanoeuvred. But this thing about Nick getting paid—'

'We *all* get paid,' Tim interrupted, trying to keep his voice level.

'Well of course *you* do, Tim.' Michael heaved a sigh. 'I suppose I could always make a donation to the programme to even things out.'

'Great,' Tim hissed at Bill, letting the spluttering of the coffee machine cover the sound of his voice. 'Now Nick'll think I've invited him to get the money or that it's basically a way for me to babysit him. That'll do *wonders* for his self-esteem.'

'What's that?' called Michael, turning from the sink.

'Tim, I know Nick's muttering bug is contagious, but try to hold firm against it.'

'Bill and I are just plotting.'

'What are you plotting?' Nick asked. '*Why* are you plotting *together*?'

'That's for us to know and you to find out,' Tim said, reaching out to flick his nose. Nick slapped his hand away with a growl. He gave Bill a suspicious look.

His godfather smiled. 'Tim and I are united in our plans to keep you out of trouble. We were just saying maybe your dad's donation should be contingent on you coming up with a really good idea for how to use the money. Then you can get some extra CV points *and* feel you've actually done something to bring that money in for the programme.'

'Ah, Bill,' moaned Tim. 'You're such a spoilsport. I could have strung the reveal out for *days*.'

'Lovely as this series of in-jokes to which I'm not party is, I don't see why I'm playing odd man out in my own home,' Michael said testily. 'Have it your way, Bill, and on your head be it. I give my blessing if Nick promises,' he added, raising a hand in warning, 'that when he tags along with Tim, he won't be any trouble.'

'You can't make him promise that,' Tim said, casting an infuriated look in Bill's direction. 'I might start to feel unloved if Nick wasn't tormenting me.'

Chapter[27]

**(Easter Term × Week 8
[≈ second week of June])**

Senate House Lawn was awash with students sitting in loose clusters, all waiting for their exam results. The sun was out, the grass lush and cool, but there was nothing relaxed about the atmosphere. No one sprawled, sunbathing. Instead, they sat or reclined awkwardly on their elbows, pulling at the grass and snapping at each other, searching for things to talk about to distract themselves from the wait.

'So two weeks from now, while I'm here fetching coffee and photocopying my backside off like all the other good little unpaid interns trying to make their CVs decent, you're going to be lazing on the deck of a yacht and getting drunk? You're such a waste of space, Frank,' Susie said, wrinkling her nose in disgust.

'Didn't you want to work in London for the summer?' Nick asked around a yawn.

'That would have been great … apart from the fact that none of the internships covered travel expenses. Bad enough to have to work for six weeks and not get paid a penny, let alone spend over thirty quid a day on travel.' She lifted her arms above her head in a languorous stretch. 'We should go punting one day.'

'Count me in for punting,' Frank said, raising his hand.

'I was talking to Nick. You won't be here.'

'I can arrange to be here for anything that might involve you in hotpants and a bikini top.'

'How do you lurch between fancying me and just being incredibly vile and sexist in half a heartbeat?' She flopped back on to the grass, draping an arm across her eyes. 'I can't believe the exams are over. I keep having nightmares about them. God, that Analysis I paper.' She shuddered.

'At least you were in the Corn Exchange with everyone else, rather than in our supervision room in College,' Nick grumbled. 'So many shades of weird and disconcerting.'

Frank laughed. 'Seriously? That'll teach you to get pneumonia instead of revising. Were they just keeping an eye to make sure you didn't expire or is it 'cos of your age?'

'In case of death,' Nick said, while Susie extended her foot to kick Frank in the thigh.

'Nice sympathy, Frank,' she said.

'Can't you stop kicking me and go down to the Faculty Office for an update on our results?' Frank asked. 'You're our Year Rep—'

'Which is why I've already been down twice today, and

why I went twice yesterday, and twice the day before,' Susie snapped. 'Just sit there and brood in life-threatening boredom like everyone else.'

'Couldn't we flirt to pass the time? Then you could wound me to the soul with a cutting put-down when the results arrive.'

'I could do that *now*,' she said, 'only I'm too stressed out to bother. Just shut up, Frank, and— Hang on. Who's that?'

Across Senate House Lawn, clusters of heads turned as a harassed-looking man stopped to talk to one of the smart-suited custodians by the wrought-iron gates. The two came hurrying around the flagstone path.

'Is this it? Oh God, this is it,' someone was mumbling in the next group over. 'Please, *please* let it not be a Third. Please, please, *please.*'

A crowd of students converged on the men as they halted by one of the glass-fronted message boards along the lower walls of Senate House. The custodian took out a key and swung open the front of one of the screens used to post exam results.

'Board 8. It's us! Maths!' someone shouted.

The crowd swarmed forwards as the official pinned two flimsy A4 pages up inside the shallow box then strode off. There was a breathless hush as the custodian calmly locked the screen again. He turned as if on parade and marched through the parting crowd. As soon as he was gone, the students surged forwards in a scrum of pushing, frantic bodies.

Nick hung back where the others had left their bags.

A whoop, a shout of joy. Two boys pushed through the left-hand side of the crowd, high-fiving as they raced off towards the gates.

More happy calls. A chorus of groans.

A group of six pushed out of the crowd, two members elated, three looking pleased and one crestfallen. Nick watched a girl who was beaming so hard her cheeks must have hurt put her arm about the girl who looked like she was going to cry. Slowly the crowd around the boards thinned.

'Nick! What are you doing? Don't you want to know?' Frank asked, swaggering over.

'Didn't you look for me?'

'That'd be telling,' he called over his shoulder, tapping his nose.

Taking a deep breath, Nick walked slowly over to Board 8. The remains of the crowd frayed around him, students spilling away, chattering happily or slinking miserably with eyes averted.

When he reached the board, there was almost no one in the way. He stepped up to the glass, felt someone clap him on the back and thought for a second that he was going to throw up. Acid rose into his throat. He braced a hand against the wooden frame around the glass and focused his eyes on the pieces of paper pinned up inside.

It took him a moment to figure out how everything was organised. He'd known that results were called class lists, but he hadn't realised this meant they were divided into actual lists of who'd achieved which class mark. 'Mathematics Tripos, Part 1A' read the title across the top of the first page. Underneath it simply said 'Class I'. Below that were three shallow columns of names, followed by italicised initials for each student's college. The Class II.1 students were below, stretching down the rest of the page. He started there.

D . . . Da . . . De . . . No Derran.

He took a shuddering breath, let his eyes move across to the second sheet and the equally long list of II.2s.

D . . . De . . . No Derran.

A Third? He swallowed. Let his eyes drop to the bottom of the page and the shallow columns there.

No Derran.

He let his eyes close. He couldn't have got an unclassed pass: an *Ordinary*. He'd struggled less than he'd expected in the exam, more than he'd hoped, but it couldn't have been *that* bad.

He let his eyes drift back to the II.1s. Surely his name *had* to be there, unless . . . He looked up to the Firsts.

And there it was.

Derran, N. *TH*

He heard himself make a noise that sounded more like pain suddenly relieved than joy, halfway between a sob and a whimper.

'Boo!' whispered a voice in his ear.

He started with a yelp. Susie was standing behind him, grinning. 'I'm starting to realise you're all noise and hot air, you know,' he snapped at her, rubbing at his ear.

'Oh, *please*. I'm all *character* and *style*. Frank's the noise and hot air. I only got a II.1, but next year I'm getting a First, and then I am *so* going to give you a run for your money for Senior Wrangler in our final year.'

'What's a Wrangler?'

Susie held up a hand. 'Stop. Right. There. Do not say another word. How can you not know this?' She shook her head. '*Wranglers* are the students who get Firsts in their final year. Whoever gets the highest mark is Senior Wrangler, then it's Second Wrangler, Third Wrangler . . . I don't honestly know how many Wrangler places there are. I guess all the way through the Firsts. The worst mark of the whole year used to be called – and, apparently, *given* – a wooden spoon. But just so you know, the Senior Wrangler spot is *mine*, mini-genius or not.'

'We've *had* this conversation, Susie. I'm not actually a genius.'

'Yeah, yeah. Pot-ay-to, pot-ah-to. At a certain point, minus the loony-tunes *Beautiful Mind*-style geniuses, we're all somewhere out there beyond the third standard deviation. So unless you're going to say that there are categories of genius and you're upset you're not at the very top of the pile, just admit that there are a whole bunch of us here who are, give or take, as near as geniuses compared with everyone else.' She shrugged. 'Who's going to argue? *You're* not, are you?'

'With you in this mood?'

Susie grinned at him. 'Come on. Time to celebrate. I guess

I should feel sorry about the fact that half my friends are sulking or crying, but they *mocked* me when I had a meltdown in First Term so I'm finding myself all out of sympathy. We all got what we deserved and you can't say fairer than that. It's their own fault for being daft thespy types too busy mucking around backstage at the ADC theatre or prancing around pretending they're the new comedy stars of Footlights to do any studying until ten minutes before the exams.' She shrugged, then grinned. '*I* worked my socks off after the world's worst start to a Cambridge career so now I deserve to eat ice cream with happy people, even if they do include Frank,' she sighed as he came jogging over to join them.

They bickered their way down the pavement to the ice-cream trolley, then wandered down to King's, passing Brent on the cobbles outside the Great Gate. Brent flipped them the finger, practically snarling as his eyes met Nick's.

Frank craned back over his shoulder to watch him stalk away. 'Was that aimed at me?' he asked. 'Because I'm not sure I even know who that is.'

'It was for me,' Nick mumbled just loud enough to be heard.

'Really?' said Susie with interest. '*Tell.*'

Nick hunched his shoulders. 'He's captain of the Men's Third boat: I was their cox for a few months, only there was an incident and ... Anyway, I quit. I heard they had a bad time at the bumps, so I guess they sort of blame me.'

'Rowed over, did they?' asked Frank, nodding knowledgeably.

'Wooden-spooned it,' Nick said.

Susie snorted. 'People take that stuff seriously?'

'People take a lot sillier Cambridge things far more seriously than that,' Nick said testily.

'Well, that's true enough,' she conceded. 'Let's go through here,' she said, gesturing to the little gate on the right of King's bridge, leading the way down into the thick cool grass in its shadow. On the river, groups of tourists punted by guides in waistcoats and straw boaters glided serenely past, while smaller punts, propelled by the tourists themselves, collided with the bank, other punts, the bridge. A group of Japanese tourists in smart suits were sculling furiously with a single oar to where their punt pole was stuck upstream in the mud. On the far side, a woman wheeled a bike with a wicker basket along the raw orange clay of the riverside path.

Susie flopped back into the grass with a sigh. 'So, you going to any of the May Balls, Nick?' she asked around a yawn.

'Not allowed.'

'Why— Oh, all the free booze,' Frank said. 'That sucks.'

'I bet they'll be open to being talked round in our last year and by then you can save up enough to go to every ball you can get into,' Susie said.

'Hey, we could do a May Ball Crawl. One ball a night,' Frank suggested. 'Anyway, that's two years away. The big question is "What are we doing for Suicide Sunday?"'

'You leave me and Nick out of it,' Susie snapped at him. 'Just ignore him,' she said, seeing the sick look on Nick's face. 'It's just moronic back-to-front Cambridge-speak, like the fact that May Week is actually two weeks in June. Suicide Sunday is seventy-two hours or something where people just drink solidly without sleeping or sobering up. The dimmest of them – Frank will probably be one – get carted off in ambulances to have their alcohol poisoning dealt with at Addenbrooke's. It's pathetic: a bunch of people who don't know how to have fun thinking that getting drunk enough must count for something. On that delightful note, I'm off to Cherry Hinton to report in to my family about my results before they send a search party down to College and make me rethink the wisdom of going to Uni in my home town.'

Nick's new phone chirped as they climbed back up to the path. He hung back to answer, waving them on ahead.

'So have they been posted yet?' Tim asked.

'Yeah, hang on a sec! Bye!' he yelled after the others.

'You with friends? I can bother you later—'

'No, they're heading off.'

'So . . .'

'So . . .' Nick echoed.

'You really want to play that game? Well, in that case, I guess you don't want this treat I got to celebrate with.'

'What treat?' Someone tapped him on the shoulder. Nick whirled to find Tim grinning down at him.

'And . . .'

'I got a First.'

'Duh, of *course* you got a First.' Tim wrapped an arm around Nick's shoulders, steering him away from King's and down KP towards Senate House Passage. 'Who said you were going to get a First? *Me.* Who *insisted* on it? *Me.* You know, when you get a First again next year you get book tokens and a chance to autograph the College book of scholars. It is entirely overrated, but kind of nice all the same. In any case, you can now officially call yourself a Cambridge Scholar.'

It brought Nick up short for a moment, frowning. Then he laughed.

'What was that about?'

'Just something Professor Gosswin wrote. In the book she gave me. A prediction, I guess.' He shook his head. 'So what's the treat you bought for *this* year?'

Tim rolled his eyes to the sky. 'You see what I have to put up with, here? I have no idea what you've done to deserve me.'

Nick sighed. 'I must have been *awful*.'

Tim cuffed the back of his head as they slammed through the p'lodge doors into College, then ran across Front Court and through the double doors into the corridor between the buttery and dining hall, bursting out the other side.

'Right,' Tim said, as they settled on the wall over the river. He set his bag down between them and produced two plastic champagne flutes with a flourish, then a mini-bottle of *spumante*. He popped the cork to a cheer from a passing punt. 'Here we go. A toast to Mr Derran's first First.'

Nick grinned as the glasses came together with a dull crunching noise.

'Maybe less with the toasting and more with the drinking before these things split,' Tim said. He nudged Nick's shoulder. 'Proud of you.'

Nick nudged him back. 'You were waiting for me, weren't you?'

Tim shrugged. 'I went to find out if the results were posted after I finished at Clowns, then I looked around for you a bit. No big deal. Hey, what did your dad say?'

Nick stared at him. 'I forgot to call him,' he whispered, shock and wonder warring on his face. 'I just forgot.' He blinked blankly for a moment. 'I was too busy being happy.'

Tim grinned. 'Fair enough.' He put his hand over Nick's when he drew his phone from his pocket. 'Call Bill first, OK? He deserves it more. Plus, he's sent me three texts already today asking if you were OK and if you'd heard, so it might be best if we didn't keep him waiting any longer than we have to.'

Nick brought up Bill's contact details but let his finger hover over the call button for a moment. 'I wonder if Dad has even remembered.'

'He'll still be pleased, Nick. And, hey, maybe he's just trying not to crowd you since they're never very reliable about when they'll post the results.'

'Yeah, maybe,' Nick said, but he sounded wistful rather than angry. 'Bill really texted you all those times?'

'You just got a First, Nick. Don't go joining the slow learners' club now.'

Nick shook his head, smiling as he looked away over the river. 'After a year of dreaming about today, I thought the big moment would be finding out my results.'

Chapter[28]

(End of Academic Year
[≈ third week of June])

The Blue Lagoon Lounge at Charlie Chan's Restaurant on Regent Street lived up to its name: all blue and chrome and grey, with potted palms and mirrored walls and artful downlighting.

'Swanky,' Tim said, sniggering as they sank into their seats. 'I feel like we're somewhere in Vegas.'

Nick grinned. 'Casino chic?'

'You're the one who booked it.'

'It's nice and clean and has chairs rather than benches, so I, for one, am not complaining,' said Bill. 'How about some starters and champagne while we wait for Mike?'

'By all means, bring on the champagne,' said Tim. 'In which case, here.' He passed Nick an orange envelope.

Nick ripped into it. '"Good one, Genius",' he read, grinning as he opened the card. '"You didn't screw up your exams after all! Told you so."'

'Now there's a touching sentiment.' Bill rolled his eyes as he produced his own card. 'I'm afraid I've gone the traditional boring route.'

Nick opened the card, grinning, but his eyes stayed on the message. He slid his thumb across the writing as if wiping away a speck of lint or trying to touch the words. 'Thanks.'

Bill frowned at the oddly shy smile on Nick's face as he set the cards in the centre of the table. Nick's phone beeped at almost the same time as his own. Bill glanced at the message then rubbed wearily at his forehead. 'Your father is giving me a migraine.'

The arrival of the starters, a protracted argument over the relative merits of straw mushrooms versus shitake, and the subsequent arrival and demolishing of the main courses saw them through four further iterations of Michael's insistence that he'd 'be there soon'.

'This is the longest "soon" I've ever seen,' Tim said as Nick wound his way across the packed restaurant towards the sign for the loos. 'How the hell can Michael be missing this?'

Bill tossed his napkin aside. 'I knew I should have come down today, instead of last night, just so I could go by the office and drag him away on time.'

'At least you're here, not busy being "stopped for an hour at Tottenham Hale".'

Bill topped up their glasses with the last of the wine. 'I have to hope it's the truth. I seem to have as much trouble giving up on Mike as Nick does, even though friendship's a choice while family …' He trailed off with a sigh. 'Well, maybe that's a choice too.'

'At least you're choosing in Nick's favour,' Tim said. 'Sorry if I'm being rude about Michael.'

Bill raised a hand. 'You're entitled. Especially since you're stuck here, helping pick up the pieces when I know it's not a responsibility you ever wanted. Pretty high price for your rent.'

Tim blushed. 'Yeah, I remember saying something like that a few months ago. I've changed my mind, you know,' he said, flicking a quick sideways look at Bill.

Bill smiled softly. 'Yes, I know.'

'All good for your celebration?' asked the waiter, starting to clear the plates. 'You must be very proud of your son,' he said, nodding at the congratulations cards.

'Mm,' said Bill, forcing an awkward smile. 'We're all very proud of Nick.'

'You haven't finished the wine too!' Bill and Tim turned in their seats to see Michael hurrying over.

'Dad!' called Nick, darting joyfully through the tables. He stopped a foot away, made an awkward movement just as Michael did the same. With an embarrassed laugh, they tried a rough, shoulder-slapping hug then quickly stepped back.

'You OK, Bill?' Michael asked.

'What? Oh yes, fine.'

Tim watched Bill push himself to his feet and head over to the front desk, suddenly moving as if he were in pain.

'What's he— Oh, he's not going to pay, silly blighter,'

Michael said, already hurrying after him. 'Oi, Morrison. Hands off your wallet!'

Nick and Tim grinned at each other as they followed, leaving Bill and Michael to it when the friendly squabble became rather pointed on Bill's side.

'Do you think Bill's OK?' Nick asked, as they stepped out into the softness of the hot evening air.

'He's just ticked off with himself for not making sure your dad was here earlier.'

'Why's that *his* fault?' Nick shook his head. 'Let's leave them to catch up.'

'Make up, more like,' Tim said with a snort. 'By the way, probably should have mentioned this – oh, an hour ago – but you've got a soy-sauce splatter on your nose.'

Nick stopped dead in the middle of the pavement, a look of outrage crossing his face before he dived at Tim, who raced off down the street with a bark of laughter. When they reached Parker's Piece, Tim slowed to a walk, watching Nick pelt on into the low-slanting sunlight.

Chapter[29]

(Long Vacation
[≈ second week of July])

The Kingston Arms was dim in the fading light, the windows cloudy with condensation from the fug of the fire glowing behind the soot-caked grate. The low ceilings and shiny new wood gave the pub a cramped but cosy feel. The bartender knew them by name after a month of weekly pub quizzes and often let them hide away in one of the corner booths, nursing one drink apiece through an hour at a time.

'Ange, please stop using my head for leverage. Why are you *climbing* on me?' Tim whined as Ange pressed a knee into his thigh, craning over the back of the booth to peer at the far corner of the pub.

'I'm checking that Nick's really gone to the loo. Right. Start talking,' she commanded, curling back into her seat. 'What is *up* with him today? What did his horrid father do now? Or was it you, 'cos if it was you—'

'Hey. Hey!' Tim fended off one finger, then another. 'What is with the poking? It wasn't *me*. Actually, it wasn't even Mike. It's ... a girl. You know he turned up the other day with that big bunch of flowers?'

'Wasn't that for visiting Gosswin after work?' asked Ange, wide-eyed.

'It was for Sarah.'

'Sarah ... Oh, the one with the beautiful yellowy-greeny eyes and the cornrows,' Ange said.

'Didn't you notice them smiling then looking away from each other all through Induction? Anyway, I persuaded him to offer her and a few friends a tour of the town during lunch hour. You should have seen him when he came home. This great big smile that shouted "I like someone and she likes me back". He went so red when I asked about it, it's just as well you weren't there or we'd still be hearing about how adorable it was next century.'

'Ah bless,' said Ange, going rather pink.

'Well, Day Two Nick joins them for lunch then suggests a group of them go to one of the "Shakespeare in the Gardens" plays in the Scholars' Garden at John's. Hence Day Three, the flowers and a walk by the river at sunset. And, hey presto, Day Four they agree to go out to dinner, only Nick—'

' ... goes completely overboard and books somewhere *über* fancy and does the too-many-compliments-in-a-row, no-holding-back thing and just totally, utterly freaks her out,' Ange interrupted glumly.

'How do you know that if you didn't even know they were going out?'

Ange pulled a face. 'Duh. What else would Nick do? Don't you know him at *all*?' She poked Tim viciously in the arm. '*That*,' she said as he opened his mouth to protest, 'is for not explaining things properly to him.'

'How is this *my* fault? Look, you try talking to Nick about relationships without humiliating him if you think it's so easy. At least he got a first kiss ... and a four-day girlfriend is better than no girlfriend at all. Though it'd be better if she hadn't dumped him by text.'

'Oh poor Nickie. Who *does* that?'

'Well, it's not like they were *engaged*.'

'It's his first time going out with someone. Of course he's upset. He's not an unfeeling swine like you are when it comes to girls.'

'Who said I was being vile to anyone, at least lately?' Tim asked, raising his hands.

'Exactly *why* were you cosying up to whatshername from Fitz during last week's pre-Induction meeting?' Ange demanded. 'It's a long time until Christmas.'

'Maybe I was just after sex, not a holiday invitation.'

Ange gave him a sceptical look. 'I know what you look like when you're on the prowl and that wasn't it. That was your "this may have invitation mileage" look.'

'Why can't you just take me home with you as your *best friend*, if you won't have me any other way? You could see it as protective custody for all the girls of Cambridge.' He'd meant it to come out joking, but somehow the words turned hard and bitter on his lips.

Ange blew out a sigh like a raspberry, scrunching up her face. 'I'm giving you some tough love so that you grow up a bit.' She curled her arms around Tim's nearest shoulder and rested her head against his collarbone. 'You can't just borrow someone's family to pretend you're not lonely then dump them when you don't feel the need to pretend any more. Love's a two-way thing, Tim: it's not just about what you get from people but how you respond.'

Tim's mouth flattened to a tight line. He tried to shrug her off, but she just wound her arms even tighter around him.

'Why so glum?' Nick asked, sliding back into his seat.

'Talking about Christmas,' Tim said. His voice came out flat and toneless. 'Enough to depress anyone.'

'I figured you'd be gossiping about me.'

'Busted,' Tim said, nudging Ange. 'Her fault not mine.'

'I'm sorry about your girlfriend being so mean, Nickie,' Ange said, scooting around the table to cuddle up to his side. 'It happens, you know?'

Nick blushed, hunching his shoulders. 'We weren't even officially going out but …' He sighed. 'At least I've got crushing Tim at the quiz tomorrow night to look forward to.'

'Who says you're not going to be on my team? You're *my* housemate.'

'Boys, boys,' Ange said. 'Nick is on *my* team and that's how it's going to be. And on that note, I'm out of here. Bye, Nick!'

She cupped his face between her hands, planting a kiss on his forehead. 'Don't let it get you down.'

Tim and Nick watched her skip to the door, then followed at a normal pace.

'What the hell?' Tim snapped suddenly.

Nick turned to see Ange standing very close to an extremely good-looking man. The man smiled adoringly down at her, raising a hand to tuck a piece of hair behind her ear.

'Since when does Ange have a boyfriend?' Nick asked, eyes wide.

'She doesn't,' Tim growled. 'They've only had dinner twice.'

Ange started bouncing on the spot. The man lifted his hands to gently press down on her shoulders, stilling her. Something made him look over her shoulder at them. He frowned and bent to say something to Ange. She looked back and her face was suddenly bleak instead of sunny and open. The wind whipped her hair in front of her face, then away again, seeming to take the sadness with it. She lifted a hand to wave at them, then tucked her arm through her companion's and led him off down the street. He looked back once, but Ange reached up and tugged on his collar until he was focused on her again.

'So it's all right for her, is it?' Tim snapped, turning on his heel and marching away in the opposite direction, 'but it's not all right for me, oh no ... She can date whoever she wants, whenever she wants—'

'When's the last time Ange had *any* boyfriend? She hasn't since I've known her.' Nick grabbed hold of the back of Tim's coat, dragging him to a stop. 'Wow,' he said, when Tim practically snarled at him. 'Who knew you did such a star turn in jealous tantrums?'

Tim raised a finger to object and then sighed, deflating on to a low wall. 'I bet that girl from Selwyn would go out with me. I bet I could arrange for Ange to see us snogging each other's brains out.'

'And *I* bet Ange would just think you were getting even more immature,' Nick said, rolling his eyes. 'You really think that's the way to change Ange's mind about your prospects as a boyfriend?'

Tim groaned, dropping his head into his hands. 'I am taking romantic advice from a fifteen-year-old.'

'The fact you *need* advice from a fifteen-year-old is what you should be worried about. Look, instead of showing off to Ange about how many pretty girls you can date and dump, maybe you could think about just not dating *anyone* for a while. Maybe you could even go out for a coffee with her and her ... date,' he said, '*without* bringing a girl to show off the fact that you don't have to be single if you don't want to.'

Tim sighed, playing with the sparkly tassels on his violently pink scarf: a Christmas present from Ange. 'But what if I do all that and she still ... I don't want her to say no and mean it. Do you think ...' He trailed off. 'Never mind.'

'Do I think you've got a chance? Yeah,' Nick said softly. 'If you stop screwing around with ten different girls a month and concentrate on showing Ange you'd actually like a relationship with her, I think you've got a pretty good chance.' He grinned at the expression on Tim's face, caught somewhere between hopeful and shy and uncertain.

'It's usually only six girls a month,' Tim said, but half-heartedly.

Nick rolled his eyes. 'Come on,' he said, blowing on his hands. 'I can't believe it's this cold here in *July*.'

'What can I tell you? Welcome to summer in Arctic Cambridge. Smell that bracing wind direct from the Urals of Siberia.'

'My breath's misting.'

'Tomorrow we're going to go out and buy you a better coat.'

'Hold up a sec,' Nick panted, stopping to cough, rubbing at his chest.

'You are *not* to catch pneumonia again,' Tim ordered. 'Come on. Let's get you home.' He wrapped an arm about Nick's shoulders and turned them towards the station. 'I swear, if you get so much as a sniffle, I am going to chain your ankle to the radiator until it goes. God, I can hear your teeth chattering. Here.' He pulled his own hat from his pocket and tugged it on to Nick's head.

'Aren't you cold?'

'I will be fine as long as I don't need to do a reprise of the whole catching-you-while-you-swoon act.'

'I did not *swoon*,' mumbled Nick, as Tim tugged the hat lower down his forehead.

'Were you conscious to know one way or the other? No.'

'I still didn't swoon.'

'Why, 'cos you're not a girl?'

''Cos I'm not in a Regency romance. I'm not in *any* sort of romance.'

'Oh woe! Woe is young Nick, bereft and heartbroken, and not in the least little bit sorry for himself—'

'Your sympathy overwhelms me. Don't think I'm above dishing it out about Ange if you push me.'

'More walking, less wheezing.'

Nick's retort was lost in the roar of a passing motorbike as they rounded the corner into their road.

'Did you leave the lights on, Nick? Hello?' Tim called as he unlocked the door. 'Bill?'

'Nick?' came Michael's voice.

Kicking off his boots, Nick exchanged a surprised shrug with Tim and hurried into the kitchen. 'I didn't know you were coming home tonight.'

'I left a message on your voicemail but I guess you didn't hear it,' Michael said.

'We were in the pub—'

'I thought we agreed you weren't going to drink!'

'He wasn't,' Tim cut in. 'He was just with me and Ange. *We* had a beer each. *He* had a lemonade.'

'I'm not sure I'm happy about you taking my son to pubs—'

'It's *one* pub, Dad: one local pub where everyone knows me. There is absolutely zero chance of me getting in trouble there. The only danger is that I might actually have a bit of fun!'

Michael rubbed wearily at his forehead. 'Please don't shout, Nick. I've had a headache since three o'clock. It's perfectly reasonable for me to be concerned—'

'I guess there's a first time for everything,' Nick snapped.

'The last thing I need tonight is that sort of attitude. I thought it would be a nice idea to come home early, have dinner together and—'

'When exactly did you tell me this? I don't know why you're cross with me for not being here when I didn't know you wanted me. *You're* the one who keeps telling me to get a social life.'

'But *why* does it have to be in a pub?'

'Do you know how good I am at pub quizzes?'

'What on *earth* does that have to do with the price of beans?'

'It means I'm good at something that involves a team and people having fun together and me being an equal!' Nick closed his eyes, took a step back. 'I'm going to bed.'

'Nick . . .' Michael sighed as Nick stalked off, then jumped as if he'd forgotten that Tim was there too, silently making tea.

'Sorry. Didn't mean to be underfoot,' Tim mumbled, keeping his eyes averted.

Michael shook his head, slumping back against the counter. 'Talk about the day from hell.'

'I'm sorry to hear that,' Tim said coolly, gathering up the mugs. 'I'm going up now. Night.'

Ignoring the fact that the stairs to the attic were dark, Tim padded up, pausing at the top to let his eyes adjust. Nick was sitting on his bed, leaning against the window-frame and looking out into the night.

'Hey,' Tim said, sitting down at the foot of the bed and holding out a mug. 'Sorry the day went from bad to worse. Look, your dad just had a rotten afternoon and then he was disappointed not to find you home—'

'Home and waiting just in case he had time for me.'

Tim wriggled on to the bed so that his back was to the wall and he could draw his knees up to mimic Nick's pose.

'I really liked Sarah,' Nick whispered.

Reaching out, Tim patted his foot. 'I know.' In the dim light, he could just make out the vague lines of Nick's face, the unhappy set of his mouth, the brightness of his eyes in the dark.

'It was nice to have someone to be close to. Not sex, I mean.'

Tim could hear the blush in his voice.

'We weren't ... We didn't ... Just ... Not even the kissing. Just being close.'

Sighing, Tim set his mug aside on the bookcase and shifted over, putting his arm around Nick's shoulders. 'Hey, I know we're manly macho guys and everything,' Nick gave a hiccup of laughter, 'but I don't mind if you need a hug once in a while. I kind of need hugs as well sometimes. We could have a rota or something.'

Nick gave a soft laugh. After a moment, he relaxed sideways against Tim's body. 'Thanks,' he whispered.

Tim squeezed his shoulder, grateful for the darkness. Somehow it seemed to make it easier to offer comfort. For Nick to accept it. He'd have to remember that.

He rested his head back against the wall with a sigh, thinking that Ange would approve, and suddenly he was smiling into the dark. *It's not just what you get from people but how you respond.*

Chapter 30

(Long Vacation
[≈ last week of July])

The day had gone as well as could be expected. Bill had turned up the previous evening, announcing just a shade too nonchalantly that he was staying over. He'd taken Nick to visit Professor Gosswin in the morning, then out to Audley End House for lunch. Tim and Ange were waiting for them with a feast of cookies and cake when they arrived back.

Before Ange left, she fetched a brightly wrapped package from her coat. 'It's a bobble hat 'cos Tim said you needed one and it's got a happy face on it because today is sucky but other days won't be.'

Nick was smiling when he came back from letting her out, and then the phone rang. Tim reached to pick it up but Nick shook his head. 'It'll be Dad. Let it go on the machine.'

Bill turned away as the speakerphone clicked on.

'Hi, Nick. Just Dad. I'm sorry I'm not there for your mum's ... anniversary, but I'm thinking of you. Bill said he might pop down, so hope you're having a nice time together. Guess I'll try you later if I can get away. Bye.'

'Well, that was awkward,' Tim said into the stinging silence.

Nick made an attempt to laugh. 'Shall we order a curry? Figure it's the least Dad owes me for bunking off out of the country just so he wouldn't have to be here today.'

'Hey, the man gets points for the quality of the bunk. Australia. Literally the other side of the world.'

'Oh, and the world's most pathetic explanation. "You don't really mind about the day itself, do you, since it's not like it's something to celebrate?"' Nick said.

'Well at least you're looking on the funny side,' Bill said, regretting the words the moment they were out of his mouth.

Behind Nick's back, Tim made a gesture like putting a gun to his head and pulling the trigger.

The rest of the afternoon passed in near silence. A heated debate about what to order for dinner was a welcome interlude, but when the food came Nick fixed his eyes on his plate, stirring patterns in the rice rather than eating it. When Bill sighed for what had to be the tenth time in as many minutes, Tim had to consciously resist the urge to echo him.

'How about some dessert?' asked Bill with so much false cheer Tim felt embarrassed for him. 'I bought chocolate cheesecake.'

Nick set his cutlery neatly down on his plate. 'Thanks, Bill, but I don't think I'm up for it right now. Maybe later?'

Tim collected up the dirty plates, poking Nick in the stomach as he passed, receiving an indignant 'Hey! What was that for?'

'Because I can,' Tim replied, grinning, though the honest answer would have been 'Because that's the first time you've shown any life all day.'

'Going to put salt in your coffee,' Nick muttered darkly.

'Heard that. You try it, I'll put vinegar in yours.'

'Bully,' Nick muttered sulkily, though the expression on his face said otherwise. 'Bill?' He shot his godfather a significant look, then flicked his eyes in Tim's direction before disappearing into the next room.

Tim raised his eyes to the ceiling. 'Nick's subtlety overwhelms me. What do we need to discuss?'

'Just plans for Christmas,' said Bill as he set to with the washing up. 'Nick's got a bee in his bonnet about it this year. Said he wanted me to ask you nice and early.'

Tim groaned. 'It's not Nick. It's Ange. She's put some stupid idea in Nick's head—'

'Actually, I think he's got his own ideas. Something about "taking Professor Gosswin's advice", though he wasn't very specific on what that advice involved. Anyway, it's my year to host so—'

'No worries. I'll watch the house,' Tim said, grateful that the fridge door hid the expression on his face as he pushed the leftovers on to an empty shelf.

'Actually, I was hoping you'd come with us. Nick has this whole series of plans worked out: walks in the woods, films to watch, things to attempt to cook.'

'That's really kind of you, Bill—'

'Lord, Tim. Please don't make this one of *those* conversations. I have enough of them with Nick. Could we just bypass "you don't have to" and "it's really not necessary" and skip to the part where you accept gracefully?'

'Nick shouldn't have bothered you,' Tim said stiffly, annoyance warring with affection in his tone.

'Nick wants to spend Christmas with his family. Now, as far as I can see, that consists of you, me on a good day, Professor Gosswin – not that she's coming, of course – and Michael, when he turns up. Unless you've got a better offer, I'd really appreciate it if you could come along. I can't promise excitement but my sister's doing half the cooking so you won't get poisoned and Nick'll be good company. You don't seem to mind me turning up practically every other day, so I figure—'

'Well, are you coming?' Nick asked, leaning in the doorway.

Looking down into his hopeful, upturned face, Tim smiled. He gave Bill a small nod. 'Yeah. Thanks, Bill. That would be great.'

'Does it ever snow? If it snows can we get a sledge? There's that big hill behind your house, that would be *awesome*—'

'Let's not pin too many hopes on the British weather, Nick,' said Bill. 'Why don't we cut up the cheesecake and see if we get tempted?'

As Tim passed to fetch the plates, he met Bill's eyes with a shy smile and inclined his head very slightly.

Bill smiled back. 'So what's on the box?'

'Not TV,' Nick groaned. 'Trivial Pursuit?'

'If we have to,' Tim said. 'Lead on—'

'You know the line's actually "lay on", right, in *Macbeth*?'

'Can you at least wait till we start playing for the torrent of useless facts?'

'They're not useless. They're *perfect* for driving you up the wall.'

'Maybe I'll just umpire,' groaned Bill, sinking into an armchair. 'Have you thought about trying out for *University Challenge* next year, Nick?'

Nick stared at him. 'No. But I am now.' He fixed his eyes on Tim.

'No,' Tim said.

'How about a bet?' Nick asked, grinning. 'Unless you beat me at least twenty-five per cent of the time, you have to try out too.'

'No,' said Tim.

'Ange'll make you,' said Nick.

The game – and rematch and re-rematch – passed the time. Neither Tim nor Bill commented on the fact that Nick's eyes kept drifting to the clock, or the way he looked almost relieved when the minute hand crept up to ten.

'Hope you don't mind if I go to bed a bit early,' Nick said rather too brightly.

Bill sighed as Nick carried his uneaten cake into the

kitchen, clingfilmed the plate and slid it into the fridge, then hurried upstairs with a soft 'Night' tossed over his shoulder.

Tim watched Bill head up after him, looking older and wearier than he'd ever seen him. He listened to them moving about, waited for the click of Bill's door, waited a further ten minutes, then crept upstairs to sit at the bottom of the steps to Nick's level. Five minutes later, a soft glow illuminated the staircase from above.

Nick started when Tim padded into his room. In a moment his face went from strained and hollow-eyed to blank. 'What's up?' he asked, filling the words with icy politeness.

Tim shrugged. 'Just thought I'd come and sit with you for a while, since you're still awake.' He leaned forward and clicked off the bedside light. 'Stop reading for a bit, Nick. I know Gosswin's book is your favourite, but you've read it a million times. Just take a minute and look at the sky. You've got such a great view from here. Pity to ignore it.'

He fixed his eyes on stars and waited as Nick's glare practically wrote the words 'Go away' in the air between them.

Finally Nick turned his own gaze to the window with a soft sigh. 'What do you do, Tim, on the anniversary of your parents' . . . on the anniversary?'

He sounded young, Tim thought. Young and unwilling, or unable, to stop himself from asking. Tim sighed. 'The first year was the worst. My sister had a scholarship to Yale, so we sold the house and then she went off to America and

I came here.' He tried not to think about that last night, curled up together in sleeping bags on the living-room floor, the remains of their previous life boxed up around them. 'She dropped me at College and went straight to the airport, while *I* went and bought myself a bottle of something cheap and nasty and gave myself the worst hangover of my life.' He shook his head. 'Stupid, isn't it, how one day's so important? They're not any less dead every other day of the year.'

'But you don't let yourself think about them the other days,' Nick said.

'Don't let myself wallow and be pathetically sorry for myself, you mean?' The words came out sharper than he'd intended: full of self-loathing. 'Anyway, now I spend the day with Ange, then have a few drinks once I'm alone. I love Ange but she always tries to get me to *talk* and I just want ...' He broke off with a sigh.

'Someone to watch the sky with,' Nick finished for him. 'What day is it? Your anniversary?'

Tim felt his hands curling into fists at his sides. He had to grit his teeth not to snap that just because he was trying to offer a little sympathy, it didn't mean he wanted Nick intruding on the very worst day in his year.

'Fifteenth of August,' he heard himself say, hoping his tone made it quite clear that the last thing he would want on that day was Nick's company.

'OK,' said Nick. 'Maybe if it's warm we can sit in the garden.'

As the moon emerged into a clear patch of sky, Tim could

make out a smile on Nick's face before the room faded into darkness again.

And he thought of Ange and what she'd said about love being a two-way street. Maybe it would be OK if Nick kept him company on the fifteenth after all.

'Did you like living with your mum?' Tim asked before the moment could pass.

A rustle in the darkness as Nick shifted. 'I wanted to. At the beginning. I didn't really know my dad. I mean, he's always been like this: working like there's no tomorrow.'

'It must have been weird going to the wedding when she remarried,' Tim said clumsily. 'You never mention him – your stepfather. What was he like?' It felt like a mistake, the moment he heard the words in the air. He found his fingers crossing reflexively by his leg, as if hoping against hope that he hadn't just ruined the chance that Nick would talk to him. And all because he'd decided that he could do a better job than Bill: get further before Nick shut him out. 'Hey, you still awake?'

'He hated me.' Nick's eyes glittered fitfully in the darkness as the light brightened, dimmed, brightened.

'It must have been tough with your mum being ill, but I'm sure he didn't *hate* you, Nick.'

Nick made an indecipherable noise.

'Your mum can't have thought that.'

'My mother didn't want to think,' Nick bit out. 'Not about things that didn't suit her. And of course no one was allowed to do anything to upset *her*,' he said, the words

coming out fast and loud. 'It was pathetic really, he only—'
He cut himself off with a hiss of breath, crossing his arms
over his chest. Tim felt as much as saw him shake his head.
'I'm not having this conversation. It's none of your business
anyway.'

Tim let his head drop back against the wall as Nick
pushed himself up from the bed and hurried across the room
only to stop, outlined at the top of the stairwell.

'What the *fuck* are you doing there?'

'I heard a noise,' came Bill's voice from below.

'So you decided to come and eavesdrop? I bet it was your
idea in the first place for Tim to come and talk to me. My
dad's palmed enough trouble off on him already—'

'Hey, I'm no one's errand boy,' protested Tim, standing up.
'I was worried about you.'

'Of *course* you were,' Nick sneered.

'That's uncalled for,' Bill said firmly, coming up the steps
so that Nick had to back away across the room. 'Now let's just
take a deep breath and we can talk—'

'I don't want to hear it, Bill!' Nick turned away from the
stairs, slapping the flat of his hand once, hard, against the
slope of the ceiling, then letting it rest there, his forehead
braced against his wrist. 'I don't want to hear anything you've
got to say. I just want you both to leave me alone.'

'Nick, you know that you and Roger not getting along is
not what made your mother ill, don't you?' Bill asked, coming
up the last few steps into the room.

'Just go away!' Nick shouted, stalking into the corner,

his back to them. 'Just leave me alone! Today's bad enough without you trying to … to …'

'We need to finish that conversation we had in the car, Nick. You can't grieve in silence.'

'Because I'm bound to feel *so* much better if I tell you how awful it was not to get to say goodbye?' Nick's tone was hard, mocking.

'Wasn't it, Nick? Wasn't it awful and unfair and unnecessary?'

Nick shrugged carelessly. 'And the way she treated me for the rest of her life wasn't? At least now there's a good reason I don't get to see or talk to her, right? At least now she's not choosing to have nothing to do with me.'

'Nick—'

'"It is what it is": isn't that what they say?'

'Then why do you talk about this fish tank instead of her?'

Nick stiffened, turning away again, his back rigid.

'Why that, out of everything?'

Nick pressed his fingers into his eyes, then smoothed his hands down his cheeks. 'I don't know why I dream about the fish instead of her. I didn't even *like* the fish.' He made a noise like a laugh, heard it turn into something else. 'It's just … small enough to think about. It's the only part of it that is. But that makes it all sound like some big mystery and the only reason it's important is that it was the last time I saw her.' He looked away to the window, took an uneven breath. 'Roger and I were fighting. We were fighting and Mum came in and …' He closed his eyes, stuttered in a breath. 'It was an accident when he hit her. It was just an accident. He didn't even realise she was there. I grabbed for her arm, only I caught the lamp and it fell and the fish tank broke and she started screaming. Screaming and screaming and screaming—'

He stopped, bracing a shaking hand against the low slanting ceiling.

'It was pathetic really,' he spat, voice low and vicious, before Tim or Bill could step forward. 'It was all just an accident. She wasn't hurt and the fish ... they were just *fish*. But she kept screaming. She screamed and screamed and screamed until he managed to get some of her pills down her throat. Then he took her straight to the hospital and I ... I cleared up the fish. I cleared up the fish and it never even occurred to me that that was it. That was the last thing between us. And I was so angry with her. So *angry* with her for only being upset when it affected *her*. I'd wished for there to be a row. A great big row so she'd have to do something. Have to see that I ...' He stopped on a gasp, trying to swallow down the sob in his voice.

Bill stepped forwards to curl his fingers gently about Nick's arm, trying to turn him away from the wall. 'Nick, when you said that Roger hated you—'

'I didn't *care* about that,' Nick near-shouted, pushing Bill's hand off his arm. 'Why would I care about *that*? I hated him back. He wasn't *anything* to me and I wasn't anything to him. He wished I'd never been born and I wished she'd never met him. But I didn't *care*. It didn't *matter* that he hated me. It mattered that my *mum* didn't care that he did. It mattered that she didn't care about me at all.' His voice broke on the words.

He wrenched away from Bill's hands when he reached out again.

'No, don't touch me!' he shouted, raising an arm to ward him off. 'You shouldn't touch me,' he gasped, voice hoarse with fury. 'You don't *understand*. I *wanted* them to fight. I *wanted* her to be upset. When he hit her, part of me was glad!' The shout dissolved into an ugly gulp. 'You see? *That's* why Roger hated me. He knew what I was inside, what an awful person I was …' He hissed out a breath, sobbed in another. 'But at least he hated me for it.'

His eyes were liquid with tears when he looked up. 'You know when they say that the opposite of love is indifference, not hate … well, they're *right*. She didn't even care enough to hate me. But I hate *her*. And you can't grieve someone you hate, Bill. Even if you should,' he whispered. 'So I don't need to talk. I don't need to come to terms with it. I just need it to be different.' He closed his eyes, letting the tears standing in them spill over. 'And I know that's stupid and pointless because no one can turn back time or change the past. I *know* it. But I can't seem to *feel* it because I need it to be different. I need *her* to have been different.'

For a moment they stood silently in the darkness, then Bill sighed. 'I know it sometimes doesn't seem like it, Nick, but Mike *does* care about you. He just doesn't know what to do.'

'And you do? Tim does?' Nick asked, gesturing roughly

at Tim, standing silent in the corner. 'You still *try*. You still do *something*. You're here, Bill. You're *here*,' he said softly, as much wonder as pain in his voice. 'You don't have to be, but you are and . . . I want that to be enough,' his voice quavered on the word, 'but I'm not sure what to *do*. I don't know how being a family *works*.'

'Ah, Nick.' Bill drew him gently into his arms, smiled wanly over his head as Tim stepped forward to put a hand on Nick's back.

Chapter[31]

(Long Vacation
[≈ first week of August])

'What are you doing here?' Ange asked, when Nick opened the front door. 'And don't say you live here. I thought today was your dad's big day and you had that fancy do at his law firm in London to go to? Or is it tomorrow?'

'No. It's today.' Nick turned away, leaving her to close the door. 'I want him to see how it feels when I say I'll be there but never turn up. Are you going to tell me to rise above?'

'Hey,' Ange said, reaching out to catch at his hand, 'I'm on your side, Nickie. If it's the right thing for you that's all I care about.'

'Oh.'

She smiled, patting his cheek, then cuddled into his side as she tugged him into the sitting room and through to the kitchen, where Tim was putting on the kettle. 'Good boy,' she said, leaning over to kiss Tim's cheek. 'Or maybe not so much.

I see you've made lots of lovely washing up for me to do,' she added as she peered into the sink.

'Have I ever asked you to do our washing up?'

'Of *course* you haven't asked! But you know I love you both, so *naturally* I'm going to find it impossible to leave you living in squalor.' With a sigh she tossed her bag on to a chair and rolled up her sleeves. 'How *old* is this sponge? It is un*utterably* disgusting. Do you *want* to give yourself botulism poisoning?'

'I don't think you get spontaneous botulism,' Nick said, looking dubiously at the sponge.

'This is not spontaneous,' said Ange, brandishing it. 'This is a work of many weeks of slovenly … slovenliness. You are both *revolting*. Now find me chocolate. Fetch! Think of it as tribute, laid at the feet of a superior being – no, not literally! Not on *this* floor!' she wailed when Tim made to put a packet of chocolate fingers by her toes.

'She is *never* to be allowed minions,' Tim whispered to Nick.

'And what, exactly, are you?' Ange asked.

'Friends?'

Ange opened her mouth, finger upraised, then stopped. 'Oh. True. Can't you be both? Sometimes you manage both.'

That's mostly because you have a tendency to walk all over us, Tim muttered.

'You're mumbling!' shouted Nick above the roar of the kettle as he set out their favourite mugs.

'It's practically a rule in this household. I was fine until I met you.'

'Oh, what an out-and-out fib,' said Ange. 'Now— Oh, Nickie, what is it?' she asked, as Nick turned away from the kettle suddenly, looking pained.

'I've got to go to London.'

Ange beamed and threw her arms around him. 'Of course you do. Now where's your wallet? Is your suit ready?' She put a finger to his lips before he could speak. 'Just smile and nod. Well, or shake your head if your shirt isn't ironed and you need a hand because, trust me, this is a Once in a Lifetime ironing offer.'

Tim groaned. 'Give me the shirt. You do *not* want to let her near an iron.'

'Just because— OK, fair enough. Tim will iron your shirt and I will ... Um, Tim can tie your tie and I can ...' She made a complex gesture in the air. The boys stared at her. 'I'll just be the cheering section, shall I?'

'Just go and change, Nick,' said Tim.

Ten minutes later, Ange was patting down Nick's pockets, much to his mortification, as she checked to see that he had his phone and wallet and keys.

'Stop fishing in his pockets like Gollum looking for the One Ring. Ange, he's not big enough for you to climb on him like that,' Tim said, tugging her back and wrapping his arms around her.

'I'm helping!' she squealed, bouncing on the spot.

Tim pressed his cheek to her hair. 'You're endearing in a

scary sort of way, but helping … not so much. Say "Happy Making Named Partner Day" to your dad from me,' he told Nick. 'I won't let her go until you're safely out the door.'

Nick lifted his hand to the latch, then let it drop again. 'I'm such an idiot. I know it won't really make that big a difference to him whether or not I go, but I'd rather have what I can get than nothing at all. Change the things you can, right? You probably think that's stupid but—'

'No, Nick. We don't think that's stupid at all,' Tim said gently. 'Go on now. The two of us will feel horribly abandoned, but what can you do when you're in demand?'

Tim blew out a sigh when the door crunched shut. 'At least he won't spend the rest of the evening pacing. Or sighing. I swear, a hundred times this afternoon. God, I hope it was the right thing to do, to encourage him to go.'

Ange turned to frown up at him. 'Why wouldn't it be? It's an important day for Michael. Of course he has to be there.'

Tim shook his head. 'You don't see it, Ange, but Nick gets so excited every time Michael comes home two nights in a row. He does this thing, you know, when we've been out and we're coming home: just as we turn the corner into our road, his shoulders come up and he peers round the bend. At first I thought he was worried about finding the house had been burgled again. Took me ages to realise he was looking to see if the lights were on 'cos Michael's home. It's like he can't stop himself from hoping, even though he knows better.'

'Well maybe one time his dad *will* get it together and

350

it really will be the start of something better,' Ange said, following Tim back to the kitchen.

'Nick's been living with Michael since he was eleven. If it hasn't changed by now—'

'You're not jealous, are you?'

'Why would I be jealous? I may not have parents any more, but at least mine wanted me— Forget I said that,' Tim said, squeezing his eyes shut. 'I never said that.'

'I didn't mean like *that*. I meant that if Michael were around a bit more, then Nick wouldn't be.'

'Oh, thanks, Ange. That's really nice. Like I'd prefer Nick to be unhappy just so he's available at my convenience. Thanks for the charming compliment.' He lurched to his feet and stalked out of the room, drowning whatever she called after him in the noise of his footsteps on the stairs.

In the bathroom, he let the cold water run over his hands, splashed some on his cheeks, across his forehead. In the mirror, his face looked flushed and hurt and guilty.

Chapter[32]

(15 × August
[Long Vacation])

Nick didn't say anything when Tim put the vodka down on the patio. When he lifted the bottle for the first long, deep swallow, Nick turned to watch him, but by the time he lowered it again, Nick was looking up at the stars.

The bite and burn were a pain he could grasp: tangible, specific. Something to distract him from the other pain that just *was*. As if it were too huge for him to feel.

When he lowered the bottle for the fifth time, Nick held out his hand. Wiping his sleeve across his mouth, Tim passed it over, watching as Nick sipped, grimaced, then sipped again before handing it back.

'It's nicer with orange,' Nick said.

'I'm not drinking it for the taste.' His voice came out sharp and unpleasant.

Nick shrugged. 'Doesn't mean it can't taste nice too.'

Tim sighed, glared down at the bottle. 'Maybe next year. Perhaps it'll make me a nicer drunk.' He took another swallow then set the bottle clumsily aside, letting his hands drop between his knees as he craned back to look up at the sky. 'Stupid light pollution. Saw a picture of the stars above Lake Titicaca in Peru once. Like looking through a telescope and we've got ...' He made an uncoordinated gesture.

'Yeah, but Cambridge isn't about the sky, it's about the ground. The buildings, the gardens ... It's as beautiful as anything man-made anywhere on *Earth* and we get to go pretty much wherever we want, whenever we want.'

'Not in the mood to count my blessings,' Tim growled. 'I'll feel lucky and privileged tomorrow.'

Nick flicked a glance over at him but didn't comment. Tim watched him lean back on his hands, swinging his feet over the edge of the drop-off to the lower half of the garden. For once he looked perfectly at ease, as if he were quite happy to sit there and watch the dull grey and orange sky until morning.

Tim took a fast, burning pull from the bottle, hunching over to stare down at the grass below his bare feet.

'My sister called,' he said, though he hadn't intended to voice the thought. 'Made everything worse. She sounded so happy. I want to be happy for her. Just not today.' He didn't want to hear about how she was starting to build a new family so she could forget about the one she'd lost and left behind in England. 'I knew when she went over there that she wasn't coming back but at the wedding ... The way she stood there with her in-laws, glowing as she looked up at them … She only misses us now when she has to.'

He sighed, mumbling a curse when he heard his breath hitch. From a surly drunk to a weepy one: what a gamut of fun. A bark of laughter escaped, startling him. And his breath hitched again.

Nick had gone very still next to him.

Something touched his sleeve tentatively.

'I know we're both manly macho guys,' a nervous intake of breath, 'but I don't mind, you know, if you need a hug once in a while.'

His own words, but in Nick's voice, little more than a whisper, hesitant and shy.

He wanted to laugh, wanted to say, 'My night on the rota?' and carry it off as a joke, maybe accept the briefest of mutual back-slapping embraces, but the laugh came out wrong and the words didn't come out at all.

He had turned before he knew it, hands clenched in the back of Nick's T-shirt, pressing his face into Nick's shoulder.

For just a second, Nick froze. Then he relaxed and his hands came up to grasp Tim's shirt in return.

Nick must have felt the sob, even though Tim gritted his teeth over it, choked the sound back down his throat.

Nick's fingers flexed ever so slightly against his back. Then, with a soft sigh he rested his head against Tim's shoulder in return, tightened his grip.

The pain burned in his throat, behind his eyes, in his chest, for what could have been an hour or a handful of minutes.

When he finally pulled away, Nick matched him movement for movement until they were sitting side by side once more. For a span of heartbeats, Tim felt Nick tense on the verge of speaking, then he sat back and turned his attention to the sky once more.

A plane blinked mournfully from one horizon to the other.

An hour later, Nick stretched with a huge yawn. 'How about some hot chocolate?'

Looking up into his face, Tim saw nothing but an easy smile: no comments, no questions.

He nodded.

In the morning, Tim made himself two extra cups of coffee. He didn't thank Nick and Nick didn't ask him if he was all right.

Chapter[33]

(28 × August
[Long Vacation])

In the morning they visited Professor Gosswin. Although it was Nick's birthday, he took her flowers: a bunch of imperial purple sweet peas. The Professor's mouth lifted on one side as he put them down on the table by her chair.

'Sut,' she slurred, gesturing at the chair opposite. 'Play. 'N' 'im.' She inclined her head in Tim's direction. 'Two ugainst one. Beat,' a breath, 'you birth,' she promised.

And promptly did.

When Nick bent to kiss her cheek, she slapped gently at his shoulder then reached up a shaking hand, patted gently at his face. 'Frst class,' she said. 'Always frst class.' A snort. 'Nut with chess.'

'Not with chess,' Nick agreed, ladling books out of his backpack on to her bed. When he looked up, she was smiling at him. He watched her eyes move to Tim and then back.

'Yeah,' he said. 'I've been reading your book. I think maybe I get it now.'

'Sluw,' she said.

Nick huffed a laugh. 'We'll see you soon.'

When Tim turned back in the doorway to raise his hand in a wave more like a salute, he didn't recognise the expression on her face.

'Learnin',' she said. 'Cle-ver boys. Learnin'.'

Though clouds loured over the village as they walked back to the station, the rain held off and by the time they were back in Cambridge, turning down Garret Hostel Lane, the sun had come out.

Ange and Susie were reclining together at the back of one of the College punts, directing Frank's efforts to load an extraordinarily large wicker hamper.

'Nick! Tim!' Ange squealed, springing to her feet and rocking the punt so badly Frank nearly pitched overboard.

'I've got a bone to pick with you, Nick!' called Susie.

'Um, happy birthday and all that?' Tim suggested.

'What does this look like?' Susie asked, gesturing at the hamper.

'Frank trying to butter you up?' Nick asked.

'Yeah, well, I'm sharing the bounty,' Susie said. 'Though I don't see why I should, since "Do you fancy punting up to Granchester tomorrow?" does not in any way convey that this is a birthday party. Especially one that involves *Frank*, given that he's meant to be on a yacht or at the very least the other side of London.' She pointed an elegant finger at Nick. 'You—'

'Oooo, pretty, pretty sparklies!' Ange cried, seizing Susie's hand to examine her nails.

'All accounted for?' Tim asked as he reached over to unlock the padlock that chained the punt to an iron ring on the College's lower wall.

'Cast off, good sir!' cried Ange. 'Onwards! Onwards! To victory and ... well, not so much "glory of the realm", but Granchester's not so bad.'

With the faintest bump against the wall, the punt sailed into open water. A deft thrust saw Tim turn them upriver.

'Near-perfect technique,' Susie said. 'I don't know you yet, but I like you.'

Tim grinned, doffing an imaginary cap to her, then returning Frank's glare with a grin. 'Going to have to work on your punting skills, old chap. But first, to the order of the day: a certain birthday—'

'Hey, how about a celebratory bridge hop, birthday boy?' Frank asked. 'Go on, I dare you.'

'No!' said Tim. 'No way. We've already done a hit-and-run and pneumonia this year. We're not doing head-injury-by-bridge or drowning.'

'What's bridge hopping?' Nick asked.

'It doesn't matter because you're not—'

'It's when you climb on to a bridge as the punt passes underneath, run across the top, then jump down into the punt as it passes on the other side,' Frank said with a wicked grin at Tim.

'That sounds—'

'No. No. No. No and *completely not*!' Tim sighed as Nick's face closed up. He squeezed his eyes shut. 'On your eighteenth birthday, when doing stupid things is your prerogative and entirely your own responsibility because you're officially and legally a grown-up, we will do a bridge-hopping trip up the Granta. This is my only offer.'

He expected Nick to look happy, not equal parts wistful and surprised. 'My eighteenth?' he said softly.

'Provided you don't die agreeing to Frank's more idiotic ideas in the meantime,' Tim said, searching Nick's face for an explanation for that odd look. 'You know perfectly well that Bill is going to ask me what we did today and I do *not* want to have to tell him a *humungous* fib about why I've delivered you home half-dead instead of in the same state of health as you woke up in.'

'Champagne!' Ange crowed as she delved into the hamper.

'Apparently even you have your moments, Frank,' Susie said as he popped the cork.

He handed the bottle to Ange, lolling back in his seat as she passed him a glass. 'I could get used to this,' he said, trailing his free hand through the water. 'Champagne in the sunshine and double the usual eye candy.'

'Aw, Frank. Didn't realise you'd noticed,' said Tim, giving him a wink. 'Back atcha, cutie.'

'To the birthday boy!' cried Ange, squirming to her knees so she could reach over to chink glasses with Nick. She started a rousing chorus of 'For He's a Jolly Good Fellow', which was promptly taken up in six-part harmony by a passing punt.

'And many more!' they roared, Ange and Susie craning round to toast their fellow singers.

'I *love* Cambridge,' breathed Susie. 'I am *never* leaving.'

'Why would you *leave?*' asked Ange, wide-eyed. 'Why would *anyone* ever leave?'

∞

Bill was there when they got home. Michael was running late.

In the end, by the time they'd laughed and fought their way through a chaotic attempt to cook Nick's grandmother's lemon cake, dealt with the enormous mess that was the kitchen, then taken entirely necessary showers to clean up, it was past nine-thirty and none of them fancied dinner anyway.

'Dad says he'll be home in half an hour, so let's just wait. Then we can all have cake together,' said Nick.

'Who knew cooking was such good exercise?' groaned Tim, resting his head on the table. 'Hope you've got your wish all sorted, 'cos I tell you, if you're not swift with the candle-extinguishing and cake-cutting I may just fall asleep in my chair and nose-dive into the icing.'

'You know what I've always hated about maths?'

'What? Who?' Tim lifted his head, blinking blearily at Nick. 'I hope that was not *a propros* of your birthday wish, 'cos if it was—'

'It's ... related,' Nick said, flushing. 'Anyway, the thing I hate about maths is that so much of it is just about trying different things and seeing what works. I always thought when you got to a certain level it would be about logic and knowing what to do, but it's not like that. It just keeps on being about trial and error. You just have to keep taking your best guess and having a go and seeing what happens until you figure it out.'

'You've lost me,' Tim said, smothering a yawn. 'Pretend I'm listening and understanding.'

Nick rolled his eyes.

'Oh, come on. How is this related to your wish?'

'I just realised that maybe that's what it's like with people too. With relationships. Maybe even if you think other people just know all this stuff you don't, *they* don't either: maybe they've just been lucky with how things worked out or someone showed them what to do . . . or maybe they just tried different things until they figured it out.'

'Ah, so this is about *girls*. I'm liking the direction of this wish.'

Nick shook his head. 'You've just got girls on the brain 'cos you haven't been out with anyone for three entire weeks. It's a record, right?'

'Something like that,' Tim grumbled.

Nick shot him a suddenly intent look. 'I wonder what you might get for New Year if you can tell Ange you've been at Bill's for the holidays and you haven't broken *any* hearts for five entire months.'

'You— No, I can't say that on your birthday. Don't be a smart-arse. At least don't be a smart-arse out loud.'

Nick propped his elbows on the table and rested his chin

on the heels of his hands so he could grin across the table at Tim.

'Stop,' said Tim warningly. 'Desist. Don't even *think* it.'

Nick blinked innocently. 'Who, me? I'm just sitting here—'

'Being a smart-arse. I know exactly which strange little person you learned that move from.'

Nick laughed and sat back in his chair, swinging his foot.

'So what's your wish, then?' Tim asked.

'I'm not going to ruin it by telling you! I will say that it's ... similar to last year's wish. Which came true,' he said, looking startled. 'Huh. I hadn't realised.'

'What was last year's wish then?' Tim asked.

'To get a First and make some friends. Only ...' He stopped, bit his lip. 'My new wish is about the stuff I got this year that I didn't even realise I *could* have.'

'Anything interesting happen while I was rinsing the cake batter out of my hair?' Bill asked, strolling back into the kitchen.

'Nick's been tormenting me,' Tim said pitifully.

'Good, good. Don't let me interrupt,' Bill said, opening the cabinet to take down a set of wine glasses.

'The night's just got interesting,' said Tim, brightening.

The sound of a key in the front door echoed from the hall.

'Of course Michael turns up in time for the alcohol,' said Bill, rolling his eyes. 'Off you go, Nick. Say hi to your dad, then stay in the sitting room for a few minutes while we put

362

the candles in the cake as if it's a surprise. We'll give you a yell when we're ready.'

'Happy birthday!' Michael said, stepping forwards when Nick went to greet him but stopping just the wrong distance away for a comfortable hug.

'Mike! Mike, get in here and help!' Bill called.

Michael rolled his eyes, but hurried through to the kitchen. 'What are you bellowing about now, Morrison?'

Smiling, Nick curled up on the window seat with Professor Gosswin's book, letting his hands warm the leather for a minute. The pages were soft with age and wear. The spine creaked when Nick opened the cover, as if the book were trying to speak.

To a true scholar: a rare treasure.
From your proud father
Matriculation Day, 2nd October 1958

And now to Nicholas Michael Derran, Scholar.
A worthy heir to the spirit in which this book was first given
because the family we find is as truly family
as the one we are born into.
Midwinter Day 2015

A Matter of Facts

Cambridge University and Trinity Hall are real institutions. The physical descriptions of the Colleges, Faculties and the town are accurate, as well as details about courses, the admissions process, formal halls, etc. (at least at the time of writing). Although exam results are also posted via the online CamSIS system nowadays, not only does this sometimes go very much awry, collecting results from Senate House remains a popular tradition. I've gone with the old-school version for the sake of tradition – and drama. All the characters who people the Cambridge of *House of Windows* are entirely fictional and their actions should not be taken as characteristic of different Colleges, Faculties and so forth. I'm just trying to tell a good story in a real place.

Although Cambridge University does, occasionally, accept very young students, all of the details relating to how the University, and Trinity Hall in particular, deal with Nick's age are my own creation. As far as I am aware, Trinity Hall has never accepted a student of Nick's age. My aim was to make the University and College's actions logical and believable, while serving the development of the plot. In the real world, from what I've read about very young students at Cambridge, there is a great deal of care and oversight. The Cambridge in these pages belongs to the World of the Book, not the real world. Even I'm not confused about that, so no one else should be.

Acknowledgements

Many thanks and very big hugs to Andy Shepherd from whom I have nicked (with permission) The Amazing Pointy Dance™. Thanks for all the thoughts about things to include, especially in terms of pranks. Who'd've thought it of you? You were the first person I met at College who made me feel 'Yes, I'm going to be all right here. This is going to be a place I can belong.' I'll always be grateful for that. And for the super-super cool presents! Big thanks to all my wonderful Cambridge friends. Especial thanks to Naz, who didn't make me get down on one knee to propose we had College Kids together. James Wildman, adopted 'College Grandfather'. Neil Rickards, who invited me to my first Formal Swap – among other things. Jens Turowski, a true genius. And all the people I met through Rev, including Guy Brandon, fellow Cambridge writer. And Lizl! You are a wonderful, wonderful friend – thank you for being wonderful to *me*. Hugs to Ian and Phil and Michael Phillips and Ian and Alex and Andrew and all the Gang, especially those there for The Great Bridge Hopping Expedition. And of course Riki, but there's another book where I'll thank you properly.

I owe a debt of gratitude to David Good: you taught me so much more than how to write a dissertation – no little gift in itself. Thank you for backing me to study what I was passionate about, whatever Departments or Faculties that took me to. And to Bobbie Wells, Senior Tutor of Clare Hall, for all the support over the years. Massive thanks to the Trinity Hall porters, who are just brilliant. Thanks to Sam and her colleagues at the English Department for providing reading lists and ancillary information. Also Victoria Mills at Trinity Hall, and many Cambridge staff and porters (especially at King's and Clare) who let me take millions of photos for research, and a very kind lady whose name I forgot to ask at the Old Halls Reception Desk. Thanks to Adrian May of Essex University for thoughts on the first few pages of a much earlier telling of this story. Big thanks to Graham Howes, my Director of Studies at Trinity Hall, and Dr Arno, my Tutor. A special thank you always goes to Jill Shields who made a huge difference. Also to Jem Rashbas for welcoming me into CARET and giving me one of the most amazing opportunities of my life.

Love and thanks to my father (originator of the Zylonation Test for People Suspected of Talking Bollocks) and the Anglo-Italian hordes, my blood family. And to Riki, Fran, Katja and Alexia; Tony and Aoife; Clare and Jenny; and 'surrogate grandparents' Katie and Peter Gray: chosen family of the highest order. And to Krysia, for being the most lovely sister-friend, with whom time and distance are immaterial. And Zedie, who is a treasure. And Janet and David Watson, who are wonderful. To Fauzia and Stuart for all the laugher. And to Chris and Carmel for sending lovely cards when I'm down. To my extended 'theatre family' at the Adelphi, Aldwych and Dominion (extra big thanks and hugs to Fiona, Conia, David, Liz and Caroline), who've read and commented and been so lovely: it is very, *very* much appreciated. And to Simon and Sue, and Sharonjit, for between them arranging one of the most magical nights of my life and generally being extraordinarily kind *and* clever: what a combination!

Claire Wilson is a fantastic human being, a superb editor and the most marvellous agent ever – a fact which any and every member of the Coven will attest to. One of these days I'll find some words that come close to expressing how incredibly grateful I am that you picked me to work with. Big thanks to Lexie Hamblin for contract shepherding – boy, do they go astray! Margaret Halton for being absolutely brilliant: thank you for pushing me and asking All the Hard Questions before I'd cemented anything silly in my head or on the page. It would have been far slower and harder without you. Big hugs to all Claire's Coven for their friendship and support: how lovely to be surrounded by such fantastic writers in a profession that is famously lonely. Particular hugs to the Coven Members I have had such fun with during the writing of *HoW*: Alice, Cat, Giancarlo, Helen, Jon, Kate,

Kiera, Pearl, Ross, Sally, Sara, Tanya and Tom. Special thanks to Gary Meehan for Maths input and sharing my love of snark, Lauren for listening, and Cerrie for being a darling. And Mel, wonderful Mel, for being absolutely fabulous: I'm so lucky that you're my friend.

Enormous thanks to Team Faber for all their support and input and for my stunning cover, which I couldn't love more. Thanks to the hugely talented Helen Crawford-White for her amazing work on both of my books: you made them things of beauty. My editor, Rebecca Lewis-Oakes, bought this book with only a synopsis and a few chapters that were very far from being satisfactory, all on the basis of the promise 'It's not right yet, but it's going to be good, honest!' Massive thanks to Hannah Love for getting the word out – and all the support and fun at so many events. Big thanks to Lizzie Bishop, Emma Cheshire, Emma Eldridge, Paddy Fox, Grace Gleave, Susan Holmes, Alice Swan, Leah Thaxton, Dave Woodhouse and Clare Yates. And especially to Eleanor Rees: I cannot imagine that there is a better copy-editor out there. Endless thanks for working with me again: it's been a pleasure and an honour.

Last but by no means least, a massive thank you to the wonderful people who make up the UKYA community. It has been a tremendous joy to meet you on Twitter and in real life – not least at YALC, where we came out in force. Special thanks to Michelle for all the incredible support for *The Bone Dragon*: I am so grateful. And of course to my bookish 'little sis', Luna. And to Sophie for my first physical letter about the Dragon – and for help with slang. And Rhian, who shows me and so many others how it should be done: with excitement, generosity and kindness. And Kelley, for all the talk about cake, books and cats. Jim for all the #QuizYA fun and Lucy for all the #UKYAchats. And the teams at Edinburgh Book Festival and YALC: among the highlights of my life. A special mention here to Tim Bowler: stunningly talented writer and stellar human being. And to fellow Dream-Teamers, Holly Bourne and CJ Daugherty: thank you for all the laughs, support and margaritas. And Sarah, Lucy, Tash, Pip, James, Sally and all the other lovely LCW folks. And Sarah and Marieke for Book Hunting adventures. And Louisa Reid, who made one of those out-of-the-blue and entirely out-of-the-goodness-of-her-heart offers of help that make the hardest writing dilemmas suddenly seem solvable. I am so lucky to have been invited to belong among such brilliant people, who understand the importance of books, tea, chocolate, cake and, most of all, kindness.

Epigraph taken from *Time to Be In Earnest* © PD James, 2010 and reproduced by permission of Greene & Heaton Ltd.

Ask the author

How would you say *House of Windows* is different to *The Bone Dragon*?

With *The Bone Dragon*, we are inside Evie's head: her thoughts and feelings form the core of the book. Places are imbued with interest through being filtered through her eyes and, often, imagination: nothing is 'fact' – it is all Evie's version of the truth. In *House of Windows*, I couldn't be inside Nick's head to tell the story because, unlike Evie, he isn't emotionally articulate: I could make his inner world clearer to the reader from the outside. Using the third person also let me show how different characters bring their own 'truth' to a situation that, viewed objectively by the reader, isn't quite what any of them think it is.

The Bone Dragon is challenging and demands a lot of readers. *House of Windows* is a gentler book in many ways. It's a book where hope and happiness are sometimes simple and heart-warming: in *The Bone Dragon* everything is tinged with ifs and buts. I love both types of book as a reader and as a writer: different situations call for different books, as do different issues. There are so many stories in my head and I just want to tell them, whether they're YA contemporary or adult historical or fantasy or . . .

Your writing relies on subtext, leaving a lot to the reader's imagination. Why?

It's really important to me not to take control of the reader's imagination, especially regarding moral issues and what the characters look like. When writers dictate to readers, they rob them of the chance to make a book their own by reading creatively. I know that's not to everyone's taste, but it's very much to mine as a reader *and* writer. Readers bring a lot to the table: I want to leave room for them to do so.

I believe passionately that books should capture the diversity of real people in the real world. In a film, what you see and hear is fixed: if diversity is not built in, the viewer cannot add it. In a book, this is not the case: unless the author specifies that all the characters are white or straight or physically healthy (or makes this evident through implication) then it is up to the reader. I would rather urge readers to make their own inner worlds as diverse as the outer one than dictate how they should people their imagination.

You studied at Cambridge – was the book based on your experiences? Did you play any pranks?

Nick's story isn't mine, but his feelings about Cambridge mirror my own, especially in terms of how beautiful it is and how that is always a source of happiness – though not always sufficient *for* happiness. Cambridge is beautiful in the way that all the best fairytales are: full of wonder, magic, and cruelty. As for pranks... that would be telling – but I have bridge-hopped!